About the

Taryn Leigh Taylor likes dinosaurs, bridges and space, both personal and of the final-frontier variety. She shamelessly indulges in cliches, most notably her Starbucks addiction, her shoe hoard and her penchant for falling in lust with fictional men with great abs. She also really loves books, which is what sent her down the crazy path of writing one in the first place. For more on Taryn, check out tarynleightaylor.com, Facebook tarynltaylor1 and X @tarynltaylor

Abby Green spent her teens reading Mills & Boon romances. She then spent many years working in the Film and TV industry as an assistant director. One day while standing outside an actor's trailer in the rain, she thought: *there has to be more than this*. So she sent off a partial to Mills & Boon. After many rewrites, they accepted her first book and an author was born. She lives in Dublin, Ireland and you can find out more here: abby-green.com

Jackie Ashenden writes dark, emotional stories with alpha heroes who've just got the world to their liking only to have it blown wide apart by their kick-ass heroines. She lives in Auckland, New Zealand, with her husband the inimitable Dr Jax and two kids. When she's not torturing alpha males, she can be found drinking chocolate martinis, reading anything she can lay her hands on, wasting time on social media, or being forced to go mountain biking with her husband.

A Dark Romance Series

June 2025
Veil of Deception

August 2025
Surrendered to Him

July 2025
Thorns of Revenge

September 2025
Bound by Vows

THORNS OF REVENGE:

A Dark Romance Series

TARYN LEIGH TAYLOR

ABBY GREEN

JACKIE ASHENDEN

MILLS & BOON

All rights reserved including the right of reproduction in whole or in part in any form. This edition is published by arrangement with Harlequin Enterprises ULC.

This is a work of fiction. Names, characters, places, locations and incidents are purely fictional and bear no relationship to any real life individuals, living or dead, or to any actual places, business establishments, locations, events or incidents. Any resemblance is entirely coincidental.

Without limiting the author's and publisher's exclusive rights, any unauthorised use of this publication to train generative artificial intelligence (AI) technologies is expressly prohibited. HarperCollins also exercise their rights under Article 4(3) of the Digital Single Market Directive 2019/790 and expressly reserve this publication from the text and data mining exception.

® and ™ are trademarks owned and used by the trademark owner and/or its licensee. Trademarks marked with ® are registered with the United Kingdom Patent Office and/or the Office for Harmonisation in the Internal Market and in other countries.

First Published in Great Britain 2025
by Mills & Boon, an imprint of HarperCollins*Publishers* Ltd
1 London Bridge Street, London, SE1 9GF

www.harpercollins.co.uk

HarperCollins*Publishers*
Macken House, 39/40 Mayor Street Upper,
Dublin 1, D01 C9W8, Ireland

Thorns of Revenge: A Dark Romance Series © 2025 Harlequin Enterprises ULC.

Secret Pleasure © 2018 Taryn Leigh Taylor
Awakened by the Scarred Italian © 2019 Abby Green
The Spaniard's Wedding Revenge © 2020 Jackie Ashenden

ISBN: 978-0-263-41745-6

MIX
Paper | Supporting responsible forestry
FSC
www.fsc.org
FSC™ C007454

This book contains FSC™ certified paper and other controlled sources to ensure responsible forest management.

For more information visit: www.harpercollins.co.uk/green

Printed and Bound in the UK using 100% Renewable Electricity
at CPI Group (UK) Ltd, Croydon, CR0 4YY

SECRET PLEASURE

TARYN LEIGH TAYLOR

For Tina – this book would not be without you.
Thank you from the bottom of my heart.

And for Crystal – alpha consultant, proof-reader, sanity-restorer, best friend. I don't know how you do it all, but I sure am glad you do. I hope this one lives up to pineapple-shorted expectations.

CHAPTER ONE

"Ladies and gentlemen, put your hands together for the one and only Lola Mariposa!"

The rush of that moment, the split second before anything happened, hit like a freight train. Nervousness, excitement, fear, anticipation, all toppling over one another, crowding her chest, grappling for dominance.

The curtains whooshed open. The spotlight beat down. She could feel their gazes on her.

It thrilled her to her core.

The music started, the old song sounding a little tinny and scratchy in the top-of-the-line speakers, and just like that, Kaylee Whitfield disappeared completely into her braver, sassier, sultrier alter ego.

The blond wig, blue contacts, and stage makeup helped, of course, but there was something magical that happened when she was out on the stage. Anonymous. Free.

She sat at the prop vanity set, her back to the club, pretending to brush her hair and apply blush. Then the incomparable Ella Fitzgerald launched into the first verse of *"Bei Mir Bist du Schön"* and Kaylee threw a coy glance over her shoulder, careful to keep her sight line just over their heads as she placed her index finger between her ruby-red lips. In a practiced move, she tugged her black satin glove off with her teeth before twirling it over her head and tossing it aside.

She never made eye contact while she was onstage. Because her performances weren't for the crowd.

No, this moment in the spotlight was all about her.

She let the silk dressing gown slip off one shoulder before pulling it back up. Someone in the back gave a catcall, and Kaylee's sultry grin grew more so.

Being onstage was a physical expression for the rebelliousness she'd been swallowing down since she was old enough to realize her mother's terse rebukes of *"You're embarrassing yourself"* actually meant Kaylee was embarrassing her mother, her family, and the esteemed Whitfield name, and that some Draconian punishment awaited her when they arrived home. As a result, Kaylee had learned early on how to blend in, to not cause a scene. She was a master at dousing her wants and desires under an impenetrable veneer of propriety and good manners.

But once a week, burlesque saved her, set her free.

She loved its costumes and pageantry.

She loved its tongue-in-cheek showmanship.

And most of all she loved how in control it made her feel.

There was power in the art of the tease, in bringing people to the brink before retreating, only to do it again. She drew power from leaving them wanting more.

She tugged off the other glove in the same fashion

before pretending to do a final check of her makeup in the vanity mirror and standing up.

As planned, she twirled one end of the sash holding the dressing gown closed and did her slinkiest walk toward the front of the stage. What was completely unplanned, though, was when her coquettish sweep of the crowd—carefully aimed just above their heads, of course—collided with a pair of green eyes that stopped her dead.

Not that she could see their color from the stage. But despite the distance and the dim light of the club, she knew they were rich jade, darker around the edges, and unlike any eyes she'd seen before...or since. That they squinted when he concentrated. That they sparkled when he teased. That they cut when he was angry.

Aidan.

It had been ten years since she'd last seen him. Five since he and her brother had unceremoniously ended all contact. Still, she'd know Aidan Beckett anywhere.

Something suspiciously like desire bloomed in her abdomen, reminding her of hormone-addled summers spent pretending to read books by the pool so she could furtively admire Aidan's sun-kissed chest and the way rivulets of water clung to his back muscles as he and her brother, Max, showed off for the omnipresent bevy of interchangeable, age-appropriate, bikini-clad girls giggling and preening nearby.

If he'd been sitting like everyone else watching the show, she never would have seen him. But instead, he was leaning against the wooden pillar at the edge of the seating area, with a bottle of beer in his hand, looking bigger and broader and more delicious than he had when he'd visited during college breaks. Manlier. Like he knew what he was doing.

In fact, he was so devastatingly gorgeous in jeans, a black T-shirt, and a black motorcycle jacket that she couldn't look away.

With a deep breath and a swivel of her hips, she reminded herself that in addition to being a decade older, she was wearing a damn good disguise. And even if she weren't, there was no way he'd ever associate the sexy, sensual Lola Mariposa with the awkward teenage incarnation of Kaylee Whitfield.

Then Aidan shifted and his tongue darted out to moisten his lips, the way it had all those years ago, right before he'd leaned in and kissed Natasha Campbell, unaware that a young, puberty-addled Kaylee had been jealously spying on the two of them from behind her mother's prized rosebushes.

And just like that, lust and vindication shoved fear of discovery out of the way.

Because if he'd recognized the woman onstage as Max's shy little sister for even a second, there was no way he'd be staring at her with such undisguised hunger.

And Kaylee intended to do everything in her power to make sure he stayed hungry.

She shed the dressing gown with no fanfare, catching her routine up to the beats of music she'd let slip by, reveling in Aidan's undivided interest.

His attention crackled across her skin like an electrical current. A rash of goose bumps followed the same path as she expertly controlled his gaze—rolled a bare shoulder, swept her fingers along the sweetheart neckline of her black satin-and-lace corset, cocked a hip before tracing the edge of her matching panties. She shot him a mischievous smile before bending at the waist as she ran her hands the length of the leg closest to him, from the top of her garter belt down her black thigh-high it held in place. She paused at the bottom so she could undo the strap of one three-inch metallic-edged black T-strap heel, and then the other one.

Free of her shoes, she settled into the rest of her routine, letting her body dip and sway with the music, daring him not to want her.

Even her favorite part of the routine, when she put all the hours of ballet class her mother had forced on her to taboo use and used her perfect *développé* as an opportunity to unhook her garter belt before perching her toes on the stool and tugging the seamed stocking down and all the way off, was dedicated to Aidan tonight.

She spun so she was sitting on the stool and extended the other leg so she could remove that stocking, too, being sure to aim her flirtatious looks in his direction.

Her routine was all vintage bump and grind, from the music to the victory rolls in her faux blond hair, but there was nothing old-fashioned about the way her body was responding to having his eyes on her. She loved being onstage, but it had never turned her on like this before.

Kaylee put her back to the audience so they could watch her loosen the laces of her corset, every cell in her body acutely attuned to Aidan.

When she turned to face front, her body subconsciously angled toward him as she began undoing the hook-and-eye closures that ran the length of the bustier. After unfastening all of them under his careful watch, she held the stiff garment to her body, drawing out the big reveal, and her nipples tightened almost painfully as she imagined how differently her evening might have ended if, instead of a club full of people, this had been a private show for Aidan. Heat pooled at the apex of her thighs, and she bit her lip against the erotic thought of their bodies pressed together.

When her corset hit the floor, Kaylee was clad in nothing but sequined pasties and ruffled panties, but in all her performances, she'd never once felt so deliciously naked or so desperately wanted. She barely heard the applause and whistles. There was only her and Aidan and his stark look of desire as she executed an impressive shoulder shimmy and struck her final pose as the music ended.

She was breathing faster than normal, not from exertion but from the sensual thrill of stripping for the beautiful boy she'd wanted with her whole heart back then and the sexy man she wanted with her whole body now.

He lifted his chin and raised his beer bottle in tribute, and the intimacy of the moment in a club full of people stole her breath altogether.

Then the curtain rushed closed and swallowed him from sight.

CHAPTER TWO

Jee-zus.

Aidan Beckett took a long swallow of his beer.

He didn't know how the fuck it had happened, but he was half-hard for the leggy blonde with the tiny butterfly tattooed on her ribs who'd just seduced him in a room full of people.

He'd never seen a burlesque show before. It was different from strippers. The women had a spark to them. No dead eyes and rote movements. There was joy on the stage. Cheekiness. Playfulness that made you feel like you and the performer were sharing some sort of inside joke, even if you couldn't quite figure out what it was.

He'd been scanning the bar, half cursing his PI for sending him here on a wild-goose chase, half following the dance moves of some redhead in sparkly lingerie shimmying around and mugging prettily about diamonds being a girl's best friend.

Then the audience had erupted in appreciative cheers, and he'd glanced at his watch as the emcee of the evening introduced the next performer.

That's when *she'd* appeared.

Lola Mariposa.

There'd been something…electric about her, something that transcended the mile-long legs. The way she danced. Hell, the way she'd looked at him. Before they'd made eye contact, he would have sworn she didn't even care that she had an audience. She looked like she had a secret she wasn't about to share.

She might be dancing, like the performers before her. She might be saucily removing most of her clothes, like the performers before her. But unlike like the performers before her, there was something aloof about her, a definite "you should be so lucky" vibe, and he'd liked it.

But then, Aidan had *always* liked a challenge.

When their eyes had locked, something had pulsed between them.

Attraction.

Desire.

She'd ensnared him and she knew it. Reveled in it. It was one of the sexiest damn things he'd ever seen.

The kick of lust had caught him off guard. He'd been in a dark place lately. Too dark a place to put the effort into seducing someone. So he'd been making do, tiring himself out at the gym and in the boxing ring, and rubbing one out when the need arose. But for the first time in a long time, his hand seemed like a poor substitution for a down-and-dirty fuck.

The burlesque dancer had made him realize how much he'd missed sex—the give and take, the heat and friction, that release. She'd unwrapped her body and his libido at the same time.

He pushed away from the rough beam at his back

and set his half-empty beer bottle on the tray of a passing waitress.

If it was any other night, he might have sought Lola out. Explored that pulse of want that had crackled between them. But tonight, he had business to attend to.

He'd come to the club looking for someone, but the minute he'd pulled his bike into the parking lot, he'd known the intel was shit.

Little Kaylee Jayne Whitfield, apple of her mother's watchful eye, wouldn't set foot in a burlesque club on the edge of downtown LA. But the PI he'd hired to track her down was the best, and he said he'd seen her car here on Friday nights for the last month.

No silver Audis had graced the parking lot when Aidan had arrived tonight. But his curiosity had him walking inside for Booze and Burlesque Friday anyway. He'd dropped Kaylee's name, and a fifty-dollar bill, but the bartender hadn't heard of her. A quick survey of the patronage hadn't panned out any better.

He needed to have a word with his intel guy.

Aidan pulled his phone out of his leather jacket and headed for the side door of the club. Ignoring the Emergency Exit Only warning stuck to the door in peeling red letters, he pushed through into the parking lot, wedging one of his riding gloves between the door and the jamb. He'd go back in and do a final sweep of the club before he called it a night.

"What's up, Aidan?"

"That's what I want to know. You're sure this is where you saw the car? Because it's not the kind of place a Whitfield would normally frequent."

He remembered a young Kaylee, her dark, shiny hair twisted in a bun, her mother forever dragging her to ballet class or violin lessons. This place was *definitely* not her style. Too seedy for matriarch Sylvia, not fucking seedy enough for patriarch Charles. There'd been a time when he could have talked Max out of his country-club ways and into a night of debauched fun at a place like this—but that felt like a lifetime ago.

Aidan shook off the inconvenient memory and focused on the phone call.

"I told you predictive stuff wasn't a hundred percent. But yeah, it was her car. She's been showing up at that address on Friday nights like clockwork."

Aidan raked his fingers through his shaggy hair, shoving it back from his forehead. "I'll do one more lap, but if I can't find her, we're going to need a plan B."

"Well, she's pretty consistent with her time at the gym, but I'm leaning toward the coffee shop. Her regular haunt starts construction on Monday, and with a coffee habit like hers, I think she'll find a new place for her caffeine fix. I'm running numbers on her most likely deviation now."

Damn. This was getting too complicated.

That's exactly why plan A was for him to "accidentally" run into Kaylee tonight, play the "old friends" card, and hope his ongoing feud with her brother wouldn't deter her from accepting his offer to take her to dinner tomorrow. From there, installing the malware on her phone and downloading a copy of the app should be easy. According to his sources, she was one of five people that Max had trusted to test the prototype version of SecurePay, the digital cryptocurrency app that was poised to take Whitfield Industries to the next level.

Actually, plan A had been to buy the damn SecurePay app legally and have his guys pull it apart to find the string of code he needed to prove Max had violated the exclusivity clause in his contract with John Beckett. Unfortunately, thanks to a security breach, the launch of Whitfield Industries' flagship tech had been scrapped at the last minute. So now if Aidan wanted to gain the rights to his father's legacy, he'd have to improvise.

"Let me know what you come up with."

"Will do."

He hung up and glanced over at his bike, pulling a hand down his face.

Jesus, he hated this covert bullshit.

You have a problem with someone, you tell them to their fucking face.

Like you're doing right now? his conscience asked.

Aidan frowned.

He had no choice. *Right now* was when the stars had aligned.

Charles Whitfield had been indicted for blackmailing a key member of the SecurePay team, Emma something-or-other, and Aidan was damn sure it wasn't the first time. Because five years ago, the same day he'd died, Aidan's dad had signed away all rights to the code that represented the pinnacle of his life's work, a move so out of character that coercion was the only explanation that made any sense.

No way in hell was he going to let Max rule from on high, poised to make billions by commandeering tech that existed only because of John Beckett's genius. Besides, he thought darkly, there was a certain poetic justice to using the only Whitfield who meant anything to Max—the shy, studious girl who'd stared at Aidan with hearts in her eyes, the intense, focused woman who currently served as her brother's PR consigliere—to take him down.

Yes. Kaylee was the nuclear option—the quickest, most brutal way to ruin Whitfield Industries the way Whitfield Industries had ruined his father.

And Aidan wasn't in the mood to wait.

"Damn it."

Kaylee pulled her hand from her bag to find it covered in liquid foundation. Her jeans were coated in beige, her white T-shirt splotched with it. So much for a fast getaway. She'd been hoping to change and sneak out as quickly as possible. Fooling Aidan from a distance was one thing, but she didn't want to tempt fate by running into him again.

She laughed at herself as she flipped the light switch in the tiny backstage bathroom with her elbow. As if Aidan would be looking for her at all. Unlike her, he'd spent the majority of their youth completely unaware of her status as a member of the opposite sex. She stuck her makeupy hands beneath the tap, washing the mess from her skin.

She remembered the first time she'd seen him. He'd stolen her breath, throwing her long-held beliefs that boys were gross and cooties were a fate worse than death right out the proverbial window. A golden boy with shaggy hair and a leather jacket. He'd been fifteen to her eleven, and she'd thought he was the coolest guy she'd ever met. So different than Max's other friends. There was something rough about him, more dangerous than the country-club jerks she'd grown up with. But the best thing about Aidan was that he never ignored her. And sometimes, when Max was busy doing something for their parents, Aidan would talk to her, tell her stories full of adventure—races he'd won, fights he'd started, the trips he planned to take.

Her crush had only intensified with puberty, and by the time she was fourteen, she was counting down the days until Max and Aidan came home from university on break. By then, his boyish promise had been realized, and Aidan had grown into his cocky swagger. He didn't just have the attitude anymore but a muscled body that could back it up. Kaylee had been mesmerized.

By that point, Max was a cool, distant stranger, but Aidan still made time to greet her, tell her a story, flirt a little. At least she'd thought it was flirting, until one fateful evening when she'd come home from studying at the library to find Max was having a get-together. Kaylee had witnessed firsthand what real flirting was like when she'd covertly watched Aidan and their neighbor Natasha wrapped in each other's arms, indulging in the kind of kissing that Kaylee had only seen in movies. She'd fled from the passionate scene with a heavy heart, made heavier when she'd heard that Aidan had gone on to seduce the pretty blonde right out of her bikini. Or at least that was the story as Natasha had told it later that summer.

Her hero worship of her brother's best friend had taken a big hit after that, and to punish Aidan for the transgression of not waiting for her, Kaylee had done her teenage best to treat him with polite disdain. Trouble was, he hadn't even noticed.

And she'd realized for the first time that her crush had been one-sided. It had broken her infatuated little heart.

By the time she was sixteen, they were nothing more than polite acquaintances, discussing things no deeper than how school was going and summer plans. But he was still the most beautiful man she'd ever seen.

Tonight, though. Tonight, Aidan had looked at her like he'd looked at Natasha all those years ago. With heat. With lust.

And it had felt incredibly good to inspire something other than pleasantness in him. Even if he had no idea she was the one doing it. *She* knew it, and she would let the rush of it wash over her for a long time.

After shutting off the taps, she dried her hands with some paper towels and headed back to the dressing area. One of the other girls loaned her a simple black jersey skirt, and she donned it before stuffing herself back into her corset.

She'd sneak out the side door and wait outside until her Uber arrived to take her home. Of all the nights not to drive herself. But last Friday, one of the other performers had let her know some creep had been checking out her Audi, and Kaylee had decided it might be safer to get a ride this week. A woman couldn't be too careful.

She skirted along the billiards area, glad that most of the attention remained on the stage, and Ginger Merlot's performance, where it belonged.

She was almost at the side door, almost all the way to freedom, but she couldn't resist a final backward glance at the man who'd made tonight one to remember. The pillar would probably block most of him, but she tried to discern the sleeve of his jacket from the post anyway. The creaky metal door to her right swung open and the sound stole her attention a split second before she slammed into someone. Someone big and solid. Someone wearing a leather jacket. Someone whose strong hands steadied her, warm against her arms.

She recognized the scent of him on a primal level.

His proximity did funny things to her pulse.

She couldn't look away.

Neither of them said anything.

It took her a moment to realize he was still holding her, that she should pull back. But as she looked up at the man who'd starred in many of her girlish fantasies, she couldn't quite bring herself to do it. Because the rush of hormones and lust, the thrill of being so close to him and having him looking at her that way—like he felt some of the maelstrom of desire churning in her belly—was heady…like a wet dream come true.

And suddenly she wanted that dream. Wanted it desperately.

The seductive siren song of rebellion wound its way through her bloodstream.

What would it hurt?

He obviously hadn't connected her alter ego with her real self. And there was no reason he should.

It was a great wig. She had her contacts in.

Why shouldn't they both have what they wanted?

And he wanted her. She could feel it in the flex of his hands on her skin the second before he let go of her. Could see it in the flare of his eyes, the tightening of his jaw.

And she definitely wanted him. Always had. But there was nothing girlish about it anymore. It was a triple-X, adult-content-warning kind of want.

Kaylee was high on the rush of a live performance, of their public flirtation, so why shouldn't it be Aidan instead of her detachable showerhead that made her come tonight?

She licked her lips, and his eyes dropped to her mouth.

Slowly, he dragged them back up her face. And the wicked, dangerous gleam she saw there made her wet. She didn't want propriety or duty or sweetness from him.

She wanted passion.

She wanted him to want her.

The air grew thick and heavy between them. She could feel her pulse everywhere, as though her skin was beating with it. She didn't see him reach for her hand, didn't remember reaching for his, but suddenly there was skin to skin contact as their palms slid together, and the warm roughness of his hand around hers sent an arrow of lust right through her core. The next thing she knew, he'd turned and was tugging her along in his wake. She had to run to keep up with his long strides. Aidan spared a quick look around the bar before he pushed through a door marked Employees Only, and she followed him inside.

Because in that moment, Kaylee would have followed him anywhere.

CHAPTER THREE

The storage room was dark and smelled faintly of chemicals. After a moment, Aidan found a light switch, and a single yellow bulb buzzed to life, revealing a small room filled with cleaning supplies and paper products lined up on four shelving units.

Kaylee didn't have time to notice anything else, though, because Aidan grabbed her hips and pushed her back against the door, and then finally, he was kissing her. His lips crashed down on hers, his tongue driving into her mouth with a hungry urgency that shocked and delighted her. He tasted a little bit like beer and a lot like sex, and she couldn't help a groan of satisfied pleasure at the culmination of her longest-held fantasy. Kissing Aidan Beckett.

Take that, Natasha Campbell.

Kaylee buried her fingers in his thick hair, raking her nails over his scalp, running her fingertips along his neck and across his shoulders before she pushed his jacket down his arms and he let go of her long enough for it to fall to the floor with a satisfying thump.

Then his hands were back on her hips, and he'd spun

around, walking her backward until she collided with a shelving unit.

He stared down at her, and Kaylee shivered at his hungry look. He shifted closer, cradling her jaw as he lifted her face to resume their kiss. His fingers flirted with the edge of her hair, and some part of her recognized the danger even as his mouth tried to drag her into an abyss of pleasure.

Kaylee had to distract him, keep him away from the wig. She covered his hands with hers, pulled them down her neck and over her collarbone to the top of her corset. Aidan pulled back, but the moment of worry that he'd figured out this wasn't her hair dissipated as he stared down at her, ran a finger over the swell of her cleavage, the look on his face almost reverent. Kaylee watched as he set about unhooking the closures of her bustier, his long, blunt fingers surprisingly deft on the tiny fasteners. She was mesmerized by the look of concentration on his face as he worked diligently on his task. Just him and her, and an understanding born of heavy breathing and no words.

Her corset joined his jacket on the concrete floor, and she bit her lip to keep from mewling with frustrated pleasure as he cupped her breast, running his thumb across the sparkly black pasty that kept her nipple from basking in the attention it craved.

He was so goddamn gorgeous. The years had been kind to him, darkening his golden hair, turning his features more rugged, widening his shoulders and sculpting his body. He was all man now, and proving her younger self wrong, for teenage Kaylee hadn't believed there was a way to improve on the perfection of him.

And now he was hers to kiss, to touch, and she didn't want to miss anything.

She reached for the hem of his T-shirt, pushed it up his chest. Aidan was quick on the uptake, pulling it the rest of the way off. Kaylee couldn't help her sigh. His chest was a masterpiece, all ridges and planes, a smattering of hair across well-defined pecs, and abs that deserved to be immortalized on the cover of a fitness magazine. And then, just for good measure, there was a six-inch scar along his ribs to mar all that perfection and make him look even sexier. Even more dangerous.

She couldn't remember wanting anyone so badly.

Leaning forward, she kissed her way along the ridges of his stomach as she tugged her ruffled panties down her thighs. They fell to the ground, and she licked her way back up to his clavicle.

The rough sound of his voice as he swore raised goose bumps across her chest.

She reached for the button on his jeans, undid it, and then gave his zipper a firm tug, reveling in the inadvertent brushes of her fingers against the evidence of his desire.

At some point he'd retrieved a condom from somewhere, and she tugged her borrowed skirt up her legs in preparation as he pulled himself free of his underwear. Jesus, he was beautiful. Long and thick. Kaylee watched in fascination as he fisted his cock, stroking the length of it twice before rolling on the condom with his other hand.

She was so turned on, desperate for him to ease the ache he'd built inside her. Everything went still for a moment, and then they were all over each other, and he was hoisting her up, the edge of the cold metal shelf pressing into her bare ass. Kaylee grabbed the shelf above her head as an anchor.

The thrill of wanting to touch him but not being able to heightened her pleasure as he buried his lips against her neck and pushed deep inside her. She was so wet, so primed for this, the culmination of this incredible night, and the hot, sweet friction didn't disappoint. He growled with pleasure, nipping the sensitive skin of her neck before laving it with his tongue.

Oh God. This illicit tryst made her feel so damn sexy, like being onstage but more potent. More visceral. To be lusted after by this man she'd wanted for so long was everything. She locked her ankles together at the small of his back, glorying in his panting thrusts, loving everything about the moment. The clean, spicy smell of him, the rasp of his beard abrading her skin, the sound of his ragged breathing.

Aidan was fucking her in a dive-bar supply closet.

Aidan was fucking her like he meant it.

Aidan.

It was too much. Too much sensation. Too many feelings.

The tingling in her abdomen said she was close, even though it was way too soon.

Desperate to touch him, she let go of the shelf above her head and grabbed his face. His beard prickled the palms of her hands as she buried her fingers in his hair and dragged his lips to hers, gasping against his mouth as she came.

The orgasm hit her like a tidal wave, gathering force as it rolled through her before crashing in a burst of pleasure that put everything she'd ever accomplished with her showerhead to shame.

This was not what she was used to—staid, missionary sex with a long-term partner.

This was passion unleashed. Elemental.

This was a decade of wanting made real.

When he'd grabbed her hand and tugged her into a supply closet, Aidan had been expecting a quick, utilitarian fuck against the wall. He sure as hell hadn't expected her to melt all over him after a couple of strokes, but she'd definitely come, gasping against his mouth before she'd kissed him into oblivion.

Sexy as fuck.

And yeah, it had been a while for him, sure, but that didn't explain the way she was blowing his mind right now. There was something about this woman, something different that he didn't understand at all.

He slid his hands up her torso until his thumbs made contact with the soft, sweat-slick undersides of her breasts, and he wondered what shade of pink her nipples might be under the sparkly pasties. Not knowing just made him want her more. He flexed the fingers of his left hand on her rib cage as though he might be able to feel the butterfly etched into her skin.

He was so goddamn close, but he wasn't ready to lose this mindless pleasure quite yet, wasn't ready for this to be over. And then, to his surprise, she tightened her legs around his waist and started undulating her hips. The way she was grinding and twisting herself against him and the sudden restlessness of her body, the soft noises she made in her throat, signaled she was going for round two.

Jesus. She was going to come again, and the realization made him so hot that it took everything in him to hold off the heat and desperation that was building in his balls, the unstoppable rocking of his hips.

He focused on the bite of her nails on his skin, doing his best to read the rhythm of her movements, granting her wordless requests as she brought herself to the brink again, falling over the edge with a sweet cry, and this time, he couldn't help but follow.

His thighs shook as he twisted his hips as high inside her as he could get before he gave in to the inevitable, riding the contractions of her muscles to a climax that rocked through him with such force he had to grab the shelving unit to steady himself.

She was kissing him as she unlocked her ankles and slid down his body, a decadent, satiated kiss that felt like *thank you* and *you're welcome* at the same time. When Aidan had recovered enough to open his eyes, it was to find her staring up at him, sexy and triumphant.

Which he understood. He felt like a fucking conqueror just then.

Aidan leaned down and kissed her again, lingering over her mouth before he pulled away. She smiled to herself as she tugged the skirt back down her thighs and reached for her discarded clothing. Aidan took care of the condom and zipped himself back into place before donning his T-shirt.

On a whim, he grabbed his leather jacket from the ground, pulling his phone and gloves from the pocket before he draped it over her bare shoulders. Startled, she looked up from fastening her corset, and something… familiar flashed through his chest, but he couldn't quite place it. There'd been a flash of vulnerability, a glimpse of the woman behind the vixen, but he couldn't get the pieces to fit.

"Take the jacket," he told her, his voice sounding gruff, even to his own ears. It was too big on her, obviously, and there was no reason he should like seeing her in it, but he did. The realization made him uneasy.

He didn't like the sudden shift in his chest. Meaning being assigned to what was nothing more than some great fucking in a supply closet. A momentary and mutual escape into pleasure. It was just a jacket, he assured himself as he turned away from her and pulled the door open a crack to check if the coast was clear.

It was, and he let her duck under his arm and slip through, awareness prickling all over his skin as she pressed into him more than necessary on her way out. Those electric-blue eyes snagged with his for a split second, a final farewell, and then she was gone.

Aidan closed the door behind her and wrestled his body, so recently sated, back under control before he, too, ducked out of the supply closet. He didn't look for her again, just pushed out the side door, revved up his motorcycle, and took the long way home.

CHAPTER FOUR

Aidan wondered if Lola performed on Saturday nights.

Which was a pretty fucked up thing to wonder.

Unfortunately, there wasn't much else to distract him from thoughts of her as he sat alone in a booth in a shitty pub, waiting for a smug prick. Classic rock and the crack of pool being played in the back corner had nothing on his X-rated memories. He tried to blame his single-mindedness on the fact that he'd broken his sex fast, reminded himself how good it could be and that this...*infatuation* was just the result of being horny.

Except he wasn't just looking for a willing partner, because if he had been, any number of the flirtatious glances he'd received when he'd walked in would have enticed him.

He wasn't thinking about sex.

He was thinking about sex with her.

His abs knotted at the memory, drawing tight beneath his T-shirt. Sure, some of it could be chalked up to newness, to the risk of being caught, but that wasn't the part that still had him by the balls. There was something deeper, something so…trusting about the way she'd looked at him, taken his hand, followed him.

It was almost as though—

"Christ. Remind me not to let you pick future meeting locations. This place isn't 'under the radar.' It's 'waiting to be condemned.'"

Aidan's head shot up at the verbal attack. Liam Kearney, Cybercore's CEO, had managed to surprise him. And that wasn't good. He couldn't afford to be distracted by a hot body and a butterfly tattoo right now. He stood and shook the man's hand once, quick and hard, and if he'd gripped too tightly, it was only because his adversary had done the same.

Kearney ran an assessing gaze down Aidan's brown leather jacket and jeans. "So nice of you to dress up for the occasion."

The two of them slid into the booth across from one another.

"Yeah, *I'm* the one who looks like a fucking moron here." Aidan rested an arm along the top of the beat-up pleather bench. Like he was going to take shit from some prick who wore a three-piece suit to a dive bar. He pulled an envelope containing their agreed-upon price out of his pocket and tossed it onto the table in front of Kearney. "Funny how your distaste for my clothes never keeps you from taking my money."

Liam bared his teeth. It wasn't quite a smile. "Of course I'll take your money. You think Tom Ford suits come cheap? Besides, one of us should look good."

Aidan caught the waitress's eye, and with a tip of his chin she started toward them.

By the time he turned back to Kearney, the envelope was tucked away. Discreet. The prick had style; that was for damn sure. "You want a drink?"

Liam glanced at their surroundings and gave a disdainful shake of his head. "I've got a date with a supermodel in a couple of hours, so it's in my best interest to avoid contracting hantavirus between now and then."

Their server sidled up to the table. "What can I get you, hot stuff?"

"Scotch. Neat."

"And for your handsome friend?"

"He's not my friend. And he's not staying."

She sent Kearney a flirty once-over. "Too bad."

The man placed a hand over his pocket square, which he probably wore to remind himself where his heart would be if he had one. "Sadly, I have a previous engagement."

"Sucks to be me." She cocked her hip, bracing the edge of her tray on the curve of her waist. "So, if you're not friends and this one's got 'brooding bad boy' on lock," she said, thumbing in Aidan's direction, "what's that make you? His flashy, high-paid lawyer?"

Liam reached into his suit jacket and extracted his wallet. "If you're asking if I think I can get you off, the answer is *yes*."

She giggled as he tugged a couple of bills free and held them up between his fingers.

"Why don't you bring my client here a double in a clean glass? And keep the change."

She plucked the money from his hand with a wink. "You got it, counselor."

When she was gone, Liam exchanged his wallet for a shiny silver cell phone, which he slid across the scarred wood of the table.

"This is a prototype version, but we've had good success in the first round of testing. You'll have complete control of the target's phone—location, microphone, camera, texts, whatever you want. Just open the program and get within a foot of your target's phone to install it. Once you're in, download at will. You can remove it remotely."

Aidan whistled long and low. "You've outdone yourself, Kearney."

"What can I say? As the enemy of my enemy, you're practically my friend. That's why I took the liberty of preloading this bad boy with all your stuff. Contacts, photos, apps. It's all there."

Son of a bitch.

"Is this where I thank you for hacking my phone?"

Liam's smile was smug. "This is where you thank me for using my powers for good. I left your passwords the same."

"Nobody likes a show-off."

Which was precisely why Aidan was keeping it to himself that during a recent trip to Asia, he'd acquired a knockoff version of The Shield, Cybercore's upcoming entry into the digital-cryptocurrency ring. At least until he proved both SecurePay and The Shield were based on his father's code. He doubted Liam Kearney would be quite so arrogant when Aidan shut down both products with one fell swoop. But for now, Kearney was still useful to him.

As if on cue, the waitress sent a flirty little finger wave in their direction while she waited for the bartender to pour Aidan's scotch. Kearney returned it. "Funny. That hasn't been my experience."

Aidan squelched the urge to roll his eyes. "Don't you have somewhere to be?"

Liam nodded but made no move to leave. "I don't suppose I need to make clear to you that this tech is not intended for tracking private citizens without their knowledge. Cybercore cannot condone such usage. And if said activity is discovered by law-enforcement agencies, the company will disavow any knowledge of top-secret tech under development for government use being employed in such a manner. We will then prosecute any perpetrator thereof for the theft and misuse of our intellectual property to the fullest extent of the law."

Aidan pointed to his chest and raised his eyebrows in a *Who, me?* gesture. "Don't see any reason that you'd need to."

"I didn't think so." Liam got to his feet. "Pleasure doing business with you, Aidan. We appreciate you choosing Cybercore for all your tech-related needs."

Aidan waited until Kearney had left the bar before he hit the button on the side of the phone and watched the starting graphics flash across the high-res screen.

Although he didn't know precisely what had Cybercore and Whitfield Industries at loggerheads—the feud seemed deeper and more personal than your typical business rivalry—using Max Whitfield's biggest competitor for this scheme was a surprisingly satisfying *fuck you* to the man he'd once considered his closest friend. The man he'd trusted. The man who'd let him down.

Once again, Aidan was pulled out of a recollection, this time by the thunk of a glass on the table in front of him. He needed to pull his head out of his ass and pay attention.

"So how about you, hot stuff?"

He ran a hand over his close-cropped beard as he shifted his attention to the waitress.

She smiled invitingly. "You got plans?"

Aidan lifted his drink in response. "Just a quiet night with my date here."

She shot him a practiced pout. "Well, if you change your mind, you know where I am."

Aidan took a swallow of subpar scotch and watched her walk away.

He'd known something was off with his dad. John Beckett loved technology—tinkering, solving problems, cracking code. A high-paying tech job with Whitfield Industries should have been a dream come true for his father, but instead, with each passing year, John had seemed less excited to go to work. Their phone calls and visits had become punctuated with disillusionment, references to how John felt trapped. Words like *coercion* and *blackmail* started to pepper rants about how his genius wasn't appreciated, and in the next moment, John was stoic, resigned, saying it was no more than he deserved.

At first, the episodes were few and far between. By the end, his father had grown moodier, more taciturn.

Like he'd been after Aidan's mother had died…right before he'd started drinking heavily.

Aidan had known it was getting worse, but instead of flying home from his latest adventure and taking care of things himself, he'd called Max. The one person in the world he'd trusted. The guy who'd always had his back. He'd told his friend all his suspicions, that Charles Whitfield had blackmailed his father somehow, that something was wrong.

Max had assured him he'd take care of things.

Two weeks later, Charles had taken early retirement, Max was the new CEO of Whitfield Industries, and John Beckett was dead.

Aidan had been in Spain when he got the news.

Single car accident. Driving under the influence. Dead on impact.

He hadn't even known his father was back on the bottle.

He should have known. Should have cut his time in Pamplona short. A good son would have.

Regaining control of his father's code and keeping it out of the hands of the family who'd ruined John's life was the least he could do. Too little too late, maybe, but an apology to his father all the same.

Aidan finished his drink in two long swallows and wiped his mouth with the back of his hand. It was time to get to the bottom of what had happened to his father.

He set down the glass and picked up the phone, tucking it away in his pocket as he got to his feet.

CHAPTER FIVE

Kaylee tapped the toe of her Louboutin on the tiled floor. Her usual coffee shop was under renovation this week—a fact she'd forgotten until she'd seen the sign on the door directing her to this location and thanking her for her understanding.

Judging by the length of this line, she wasn't the only displaced coffee patron looking for a fix. She pulled her phone from her purse to check the time. She had about twelve more minutes to spare before she needed to be in her car and on the road. Otherwise she'd be late for work. Max might be an ocean away, but knowing him, he'd tasked his executive assistant, Sherri, with sending him daily reports about the office. Kaylee considered it a matter of pride not to give her exacting older brother anything to call her out for when he got back. The world didn't stop turning because he was gone, and Whitfield Industries wouldn't stop, either. She might have quit before he left, but it was her name on the building, too.

The memory stung. She'd let her emotions get the better of her that day. Last week, out of the blue, Max had announced a security breach, scrapped Whitfield's project, turned their father in to the Feds, and then told her he was flying to Dubrovnik, leaving Kaylee to pick up all the pieces as PR director, daughter, and interim CEO. Something inside her had snapped, shocked that he would just dump all of that on her with no warning, and she'd given him her two weeks' notice in a fit of pride. Truthfully, she was hurt that Max didn't respect her enough to keep her apprised of the life-altering decisions he'd made.

But now that things were somewhat under control again, she was regretting her resignation. The six days since Max had taken off had reminded her exactly what she loved about PR—the challenge and the rush of making people think and do what she wanted them to. It was something she'd never really pulled off in her personal life, but she excelled at it in her professional life. Despite everything, she was damn good at her job, and that was because deep down, family drama aside, she loved it.

As if she'd conjured him, the phone in her hand buzzed, flashing Max's photo and number across her screen. With a frown, she declined his call. Again. She was too busy and too pissed off to talk to him yet.

But underneath the skin-deep layer of mad, there was concern she just couldn't quite purge. It was there in her bones. No matter how much her family infuriated her, she couldn't help but care about them. And the entire situation was just so unlike Max.

No. No emotions.

Being good at PR meant being calm and collected, and if there was one thing that Kaylee excelled at, it was swallowing her feelings. She supposed she could thank her mother's lifelong obsession with perfection for that.

"A lady remains poised and calm no matter the situation at hand."

Besides, screw him, she decided with a certain measure of detached equanimity. She was an adult with a caffeine addiction, and she'd get to work when she got to work, whether he had his assistant tattling on her or not. Max didn't deserve this loyal streak she couldn't quite banish. He hadn't thought twice about walking out on her in the middle of the biggest PR crisis to hit the company since she'd started working there.

She glanced at her phone again. Seven minutes until she should hit the road.

But caffeine wasn't optional today. She hadn't slept well all weekend, haunted by hot, furtive dreams of Aidan's hands on her, of him thrusting deep and driving her out of her mind.

God. She hadn't known sex could be like that. She wasn't sure if it was the naughtiness of semipublic sex, the danger of being caught, or Aidan himself. Maybe it was the magical combination of all three.

The memories brought a secret smile to her lips, even in the midst of the busy coffee shop. Made her square her shoulders. Made her stomach muscles clench with a shot of hot lust. Sex was good for the soul. And good sex, well, that was even better. She seemed to be oozing sensual satisfaction. She'd been hit on three times in the last two days.

"Well, well, well…"

Make that four times in three days, she thought at

the sound of the deep voice close behind her. She prepared to deal firmly and disinterestedly with the ever-classy *What do we have here?* and its accompanying leer, but when she turned, her mind short-circuited and her mouth refused to open.

Which was okay because the man behind her didn't even say, *What do we have here?*

Nope. He said, "If it isn't little Kaylee Jayne Whitfield all grown up," and she had no firm-but-disinterested answer to that, especially not when he was smiling that rebel smile at her—at *her*—the sexy one that flipped up the right side of his sinful mouth.

"Aidan!" She took an awkward step back on her high heel, bobbled on the slick tile. And he reached out to steady her, like he had Friday night when they'd bumped into each other, but not before her phone crashed to the floor.

The sickening clatter left no doubt that it hadn't survived its run-in with the tiles, but she could barely bring herself to care—not when Aidan had his hands on her again. God he was beautiful.

Get it together, Kaylee.

She pulled free, crouching to retrieve her phone at the same time he did. He beat her to it by virtue of his longer arms.

His handsome face grew serious—almost annoyed—as he picked up the phone and looked at it.

"Bad news," he told her, turning it so she could see the shattered screen. "I'm sorry for your loss."

"Ouch." She did her best to smile as he handed her the useless phone, but his fingers brushed hers, and her skin tingled to life. Which was really inconvenient. She didn't need all her nerve endings sparking up an electrical storm right now. She needed to focus on acting like a grown-ass woman instead of a gangly teenager with braces and heart eyes for her older brother's adventurous best friend.

She stood quickly, needing space and cursing the cruel irony that would see all of her mysterious sex-goddess vibes destroyed by the man who'd gifted her with them in the first place. She dipped her head, let her hair shield her face, felt herself getting smaller, trying to escape notice. She couldn't have him ruining her incredible secret night by recognizing her as the woman from the supply closet. She wished she had the darkness of the club at her disposal now. Or at the very least, the magic, confidence-giving power of her sparkly pasties.

Then he stood, still close enough that she could smell him—man and fresh air and leather and motorbike, all warmed by his bronzed skin.

"Stand up straight, KJ," he teased, his voice soft and low as he quoted her mother, tacking on the nickname that only he had ever called her. It reminded her of their past, when he'd sometimes felt like her only ally. A tiny smile curved her lips despite herself as she lifted her face to make eye contact.

But the chaste sweetness of the moment morphed into heat as she looked up at him.

He might not recognize her from the club, but her body recognized every inch of his big frame. Her nipples beaded instantly, and she was glad she was wearing a padded bra beneath her ivory blouse.

Her childish crush on him had been based on nothing but his kindness and her journey into puberty. But what was happening now was built on torrid, sexy memories that raced along her skin. Her belly pulsed back and forth like the shoulder blades of a jungle cat preparing to pounce. And she wanted to pounce. Her whole body purred at the idea of being in his arms again.

Could he feel the sizzle that had taken up residence beneath her skin, or was the heat only flowing one way?

He leaned close so she could feel the warmth of his breath on her cheek, and her heart stuttered an SOS, even as her chin notched up involuntarily to bring their lips into alignment. "Line's moving."

She released the exhalation stuck in her chest in a disappointed sigh as she stepped up to the counter. "I'll have a vanilla latte, please."

"Can I get a name for the cup?"

"Kaylee," she started to say, but before she got to the second syllable, Aidan stepped close behind her, and the dazzled barista stared distractedly over Kaylee's shoulder.

"You can add a black coffee to that."

Aidan handed her a couple of bills before Kaylee managed to retrieve her wallet.

"Oh! You don't have to pay." Kaylee dug into her purse. "I can..."

Aidan's fingertips brushed her wrist to still her hand, and her voice trailed off. Her pulse fluttered madly beneath her skin. "Your money's no good here, right..." He spared a glance at the smitten barista's name tag before adding, "Tanis?"

The girl nodded dreamily. Kaylee was pretty sure Aidan could have said, *This is a stickup—empty the till into this bag or I'll kill everyone in here*, and still gotten the same reaction. Seeing it reminded her that she wasn't a teenager anymore and went a long way toward making her feel more like herself. She tucked a wayward strand of dark hair behind her ear. "Thanks."

"Least I can do. It's been a while."

Two frustratingly horny days, her body reminded her. "Um, almost ten years, I guess?"

It wasn't a guess. She knew. Aside from Lola Mariposa, in the storage room, with Aidan's candlestick, she'd been seventeen the last time she saw him, freshly graduated and all packed and on her way to study at Oxford. Her crush on him had cooled by that point—no sense in pining over someone who would never see you as anything more than a kid sister—but that hadn't kept her from reveling in the goodbye they'd shared.

"You got this, KJ," he'd said in a way that made her believe him. And then Aidan had hugged her. The only hug she'd received. Max hadn't. Her mom and dad hadn't. And for a scared seventeen-year-old leaving her home for the first time, that hug had buoyed her courage, as though being wrapped in his arms had transferred some of his strength to her, some of his wanderlust.

It was a moment that had meant the world.

It was nice thinking someone believed in her.

"So what have you been up to?" he asked.

"University, grown-up job, the usual stuff," she averred. She didn't want to bring up anything that might ruin their easy camaraderie. Besides, she wasn't exactly sure how Aidan and her brother had turned into mortal enemies. It was safer to steer the conversation away from her PR position at the company named after her family and run by her brother.

Aidan shot her a look that said he had other ideas. "Nope. Not buying it, Ms. Public Relations. This is a no-spin zone, so stop being modest and tell me about how you're putting that fancy Oxford education to use nowadays."

The realization that he remembered her major and her alma mater combined with the interest on his handsome face edged the lust in her belly with a sweetness she hadn't expected. Maybe that was why she still didn't mention Whitfield Industries by name, just left it hanging like a guillotine blade, hoping it wouldn't sever this thread of...*something* that was pulsing between them.

"Mostly I write media releases and deal with questions from the press. And every now and then a scandal breaks out and things get interesting." The words fell out of her mouth without her meaning them to, and the sharp pain of the current situation knifed through her gut. That Max had worn a wire, turned their father in for blackmailing Emma Mathison, the head of R and D for SecurePay. That Charles was currently wearing an ankle bracelet, under house arrest after ponying up the five-million-dollars bail. That she'd been completely in the dark about her own father until it had all gone down...

"How about you? What have you been doing with yourself for the last decade?"

He grinned, and her heart stuttered at the flash of

straight, white teeth. "Before or after I got gored running with the bulls in Spain?"

She couldn't help but smile back. She'd always loved Aidan's stories. He was the reason she'd begged her mother to let her study abroad. Actually, getting as far away from Sylvia Whitfield's nitpicking as possible was the reason she'd done that, but Aidan's stories had given her the courage to persevere, to board the plane when her mother had unexpectedly relented and let her go. "Liar."

Her mouth went dry as he reached down and lifted the hem of his T-shirt up his side, revealing that jagged scar across his rib cage. The one her fingers had traced during their time in the storage closet. The one her fingers wanted to touch now. Oh God. It must have hurt and everything, but *damn*. Like the man needed to be any sexier.

The two ladies chattering at a nearby table stopped to take in the deliciously masculine sight of Aidan showing off his wound.

Oblivious, he dropped the white cotton. "Twenty stitches."

"I have a vanilla latte for Karly and a coffee for Hot Guy," called the barista, and Aidan quirked a conspiratorial eyebrow, startling a smile from her. It might not be the heat that had sparked between him and Lola, but it was nice to see him as herself, too.

They grabbed their coffees from the counter. The grande cup looked small in his hand.

"Got time to sit with me for a bit?"

She wanted to. Wanted to indulge the desire simmering in her belly. But she had a meeting that she couldn't blow off, and the prudent part of her—the part that knew the longer she tempted fate, the more likely it was that Aidan might connect her with her alter ego—warned her to get out immediately, before her secret came back to bite her.

With an apologetic smile at the handsomest man to ever flash her at a Starbucks, Kaylee put herself out of her misery. "I'm sorry, Aidan. I really need to get to work, but it was great seeing you."

She reached into her purse to grab her keys. Despite her very smart decision to leave, her whole body shivered when he reached out and touched her hand to stop her. She swallowed against the resurgence of lust as she looked at him. "Then see me again."

"What?"

"Lounge 360. Nine o'clock. I'll buy you a drink."

She really shouldn't. Max would hate that. Her *mother* would hate that.

"I'll be there."

Shit.

He shouldn't have talked to her. Liam's tech was good enough to install without making contact. That had been the goddamn plan.

She'd been completely oblivious to him when he'd taken his place in line behind her, but he hadn't been able to keep his mouth shut.

In his head, she was this gangly, shy teenage girl with braces who stared at him like he'd hung the moon when she thought he wasn't watching. At four years his junior, she'd been mostly off his radar when Max would invite him over.

When she was on his radar, it was just because she'd always seemed so…lonely. He'd felt sorry for her. Sylvia Whitfield had been on her constantly and about everything—*Kaylee, stand up straight; Kaylee, your hair is a mess; Kaylee, stop being so noisy.*

And Max had been weird about his little sister, keeping a very conscious distance, though he'd never explained his reasons.

But she wasn't an awkward girl anymore. And some perverse part of Aidan had been too curious to content himself with the brief glimpse of her profile he'd gotten in the parking lot while he'd waited to see if she'd show up like his intel guy had predicted.

He'd wanted to see the woman she'd become, and so he'd broken his own damn rule and talked to her.

Stunning. That had been his first thought when she'd turned to face him. Then her hazel eyes had flared with surprise and recognition as they scanned his face, and her skin had flushed in a way that made the hair on the back of his neck stand up. Her full lips, slicked shiny with gloss, had popped open in an unconsciously provocative O that had hooked him in the gut right before she stepped back in surprise. He hadn't expected the jolt of familiarity, hell, of *attraction*, that had arced up his arm as he'd steadied her.

He spared a brief moment to wonder if she'd felt it, too, or if it was just the surprise of seeing him again after so many years that had sent her phone tumbling to the ground, smashing both the screen and his plan to install the spyware and get the hell out.

That's what he got for thinking with his dick, which obviously didn't care that she was part of the enemy camp. Though to be fair, neither did his brain, judging by his offer to take her out for drinks tonight. Fucking *drinks* with Kaylee Whitfield.

Now all he could do was hope that she'd replace her phone before they met up again, or this whole day would be a complete waste.

CHAPTER SIX

KAYLEE ARRIVED AT the office eleven hours and forty-six minutes before she was going to meet Aidan for drinks. Which was fourteen minutes late for the daily briefing with Soteria Security, where she was playing the role of Max's factotum.

"I'm sorry to keep you both waiting. Slight issue with my phone." Not exactly a lie, she decided, setting it shattered-screen up on the boardroom table. She placed her coffee beside it and took a seat.

"Damn." Jesse Hastings winced. "I hate to see good tech suffer."

Kaylee had no doubt that, as a certified tech geek and one half of the crack cybersecurity team Whitfield Industries kept on retainer, Jesse felt her pain.

"Me, too, but not as much as I hate having to sacrifice my lunch hour to replace good tech."

"Here. Take this one."

Kaylee did a double take as Wes Brennan, the quieter, more serious half of Soteria Security, pulled a top-of-the-line phone out of his suit pocket and held it up.

"Seriously, Wes?"

"Yeah, seriously, Wes?" Jesse shook his head and turned to Kaylee. "I just gave him that phone this morning. After spending hours configuring the safety features to his exacting standards."

"My old phone is fine. I did some upgrades to it last week that I wanted to test anyway, so I haven't even activated this one." Wes gave his patented low-key shrug and pointed at her broken phone. "Hand it over. I'll change out your SIM card."

Kaylee passed it across the table.

"You ever feel massively underappreciated by your boss?" Jesse asked with a sigh.

Her brother's stern face flashed through her mind. "You have no idea," Kaylee assured him, and they shared a knowing eye roll.

"I saw that," Wes said drily, making quick work of the phone. The second he turned it on, the calls, texts, and emails rolled in with a cacophony of buzzes and dings. With a raised eyebrow, Wes switched the phone to Silent and handed it back across the table.

Kaylee glanced at it warily and set it facedown. "Okay, what do you have for me, gentlemen?"

After the security briefing—Wes and Jesse were still no closer to figuring out who had installed the malware on Emma Mathison's computer that had led to the postponement of SecurePay and the domino of scandals that had followed—she'd spent the rest of the day plowing through the quotidian concerns of running a multimillion-dollar business.

She'd known Max worked hard, but she hadn't quite realized that every day for him was as busy as being in the middle of a PR crisis was for her. It was eye-opening to see firsthand the difference between how her father had run the business—an unapproachable figurehead who doled out more blame than praise—and the more interactive style her older brother had adopted. He was available without micromanaging, and as a result, there was a level of respect for him among his employees that was quite a revelation to Kaylee. She hadn't realized how much she'd let their frigid relationship as siblings color her view of Max as a boss.

His long work hours made infinitely more sense to her now. She'd had to force herself to leave the office at eight o'clock, giving up food just so she could steal half an hour to change and freshen up before meeting Aidan.

The bar he'd suggested was classier and more upscale than she'd been expecting, with chandeliers, gleaming wood, and dim lighting. Floor-to-ceiling windows gave the circular room a three-hundred-and-sixty-degree view of the city.

It was a sexy, grown-up place to have a drink.

She pressed her hand to her abdomen to quiet the sudden zigzag of nerves.

When she'd been getting ready, some annoying flare of feminine pride had reared its jealous head at the memory of the polite nothingness she'd seen in his eyes at the coffee shop. It bugged her that while she'd been drowning in lust, he'd been completely oblivious to her status as a female of the species. Little Kaylee Jayne. Completely beneath his notice.

As a result, she'd applied her makeup with a little more flair—slightly winged liner, faux lashes, and she'd painted her lips with the same red lipstick she wore onstage. Then she'd donned the sexiest dress she owned. Well, not including her Lola costumes, but she never included those. They belonged to her blonde, blue-eyed alter ego. It was the sexiest Kaylee dress she owned. A black shift that skimmed her curves without clinging anywhere, but she hoped it was reminiscent enough of the black skirt she'd been wearing that night to give him a little déjà vu—déjà screw?

It was madness. Her goal at the coffee shop had been to escape recognition, and tonight she was doing everything in her power to jog his memory.

What if he noticed? What if he didn't?

Honestly, Kaylee. Stop fidgeting.

Her mother's voice was loud in her head. Not even a decade of living on her own, it seemed, could banish Sylvia Whitfield's scolding. And it was always loudest when Kaylee was nervous.

"Can I get a shot of tequila, please?"

Partly for some liquid courage, partly to remind her mom's ghostly nagging that it had no dominion here.

Drinks with Aidan Beckett.

Well, sort of.

It wasn't like this was a *date* or anything. Still, it was as close as she'd ever get.

The bartender obliged her, and she let the liquid courage burn a path down her throat. The warmth in her stomach centered her back in her body, got her out of her head.

I can do this, she told herself. *We're just two people catching up. And sure, he doesn't know we manhandled each other against a shelf full of cleaning products, but that's no reason to think things will be weird between us. He didn't recognize me this morning. Not even a little bit. Not even a glimmer. I was the only one drowning in a bunch of sexy endorphins. He was cool and above it all. Like always. The golden boy. Supremely unaffected while women swooned around him.*

Kaylee set the shot glass on the bar with more force than necessary.

"Actually, I'll take another one."

With a smile, the bartender grabbed the Cuervo and gave her a refill.

"Make it two."

The deep voice startled her from her inner monologue, and she blinked at the man in front of her.

He was handsome, in the smooth, generic way of a manufactured pop star. Brown hair, toothpaste-commercial grin, killer suit. Kaylee made herself return his smile.

Warm-up flirting. Something, along with the tequila, to calm her nerves.

"I'm Rick."

"Kaylee."

He raised his shot glass. "To sharing a drink with a beautiful woman."

It was a sweet toast, she reminded herself when the compliment elicited absolutely nothing from her. She clinked her glass to his before downing the contents.

"Starting without me?"

Electricity prickled through her, straightening her spine.

Even his voice was sexy as sin. And in that moment, Kaylee understood why none of her previous relationships had worked out. She needed this, the illicit zing that came from flouting the rules. She got off on hidden pleasures, on keeping secrets. And her schoolgirl crush on Aidan had been her first secret thrill. It was disconcerting, she realized as she turned to face him, that it was still going strong a decade later.

Aidan was dressed in a cream-colored Henley and another black leather jacket—this one was slim fit with quilted sleeves and a mandarin collar—which he'd paired with black jeans and boots.

He didn't look blandly handsome; he looked dangerously sexy. She salivated a little at the sight of him. "Hey."

He tipped his chin in greeting but barely spared her a glance before stepping past her. "We'll take another round." His gaze flicked from the bartender to Kaylee and back to the bartender, making it clear which *we* he was referring to.

The barkeep refilled Kaylee's shot glass before grabbing a clean one for his new customer. Aidan waited until he started pouring before he added, "And another one for my friend here."

Rick shook his head. "Nah, it's cool, man."

"I insist. Consider it my way of thanking you for keeping my girl company until I got here."

Kaylee's fifteen-year-old self went into full-squee mode at the idea of Aidan considering her his *anything*, but her adult self squashed the flare of giddy hope. Male posturing did not a declaration make.

Rick's testosterone obviously rose to the implied challenge, and without breaking eye contact, he rapped his shot glass on the bar so the bartender could fill it.

Aidan raised his tequila. "To new friends," he said, before the three of them drank.

To awkwardness probably would have been a better toast, Kaylee figured, setting her empty glass on the dark wood beside Aidan's and wiping her mouth.

He turned to look at her, and she was almost certain her pulse spiked in direct correlation with the quirk of his brow. "What are you drinking?"

"Uh…" Caught slightly off guard by the abrupt shift in the air that came from Aidan's possessive display, she turned her attention to the man behind the bar. "I'll try the house red."

"I'll take a Macallan 18. Neat." Aidan pulled his wallet from his back pocket and threw two hundred-dollar bills on the dark wood. The bartender delivered their drinks in record time, obviously hoping that if he impressed Aidan with his efficiency, he wouldn't have to make any change. His gamble paid off. Aidan grabbed his drink and handed Kaylee hers.

Both the bartender and Aidan turned expectantly to the other member of this little tableau.

"Sorry, man. I didn't catch your name." The taunt had the other man straightening to his full height, about four inches short of Aidan's six foot two.

"It's Rick."

Aidan reached for her, his hand coming to rest on the small of her back, and her wine sloshed perilously close to the rim of her glass as Kaylee's knees grew woozy at the unexpected familiarity of the touch.

"Well, if you'll excuse us, Rick, our table is ready."

And with that, Aidan escorted her past her would-be suitor and to a prime spot, closest to the window.

Game, set, and match.

Not that she could imagine Aidan playing anything as civilized as tennis, but she had no idea what cavemen used to say when they bonked each other over the head and declared victory.

Kaylee savored the drama of the exit, and even though she was mostly sure he only held out her chair for Rick's benefit, it was still something to have Aidan Beckett being so chivalrous to her.

She sipped her wine and watched as he took the seat across from her. God, the man could sit in a chair. When she was young, she was so in awe of that—his confidence, the way he wasn't afraid to take up space in the world. She admired it because all she'd wanted back then was to shrink, to hide from her mother's judgmental gaze.

Polite society dictated she say something innocuously charming now. Compliment him on his choice of venue. Ignore the thing that she most wanted to know in favor of something bland and acceptable.

The rebellious streak that was the bane of her mother's existence reared up, as it usually did, and instead of opening with polite small talk, Kaylee got straight to the point.

"So, what was with the Mr. Macho routine back there?"

Aidan shook his head, doing a credible job of looking like he had no idea what she was talking about.

"I was in the middle of a nice conversation. That could have been a love connection," Kaylee lied.

"What, that guy?" Aidan scoffed. "He's not your type."

Right as he may be, his certainty pricked the edge of her temper, but she watered it down with self-deprecation. *A lady never feels too much in public.* "Oh really? And what put him out of my grasp? Was he too handsome? Too charming? Or maybe he was too—"

"Boring."

Kaylee tipped her head and raised an eyebrow at that pronouncement, watching as he brought his glass to his lips. The muscles in his throat worked as he swallowed, and just like that, the visceral want that plagued her when he was near tingled along her nerve endings.

When she was a teenager, it had been a vague restlessness—the hollow ache of not quite understanding what her body was asking for. Now she knew precisely what she wanted from him, exactly how Aidan's touch could make her burn.

She looked at her wine. "Well, we can't all run with the bulls, Mr. Pamplona."

"Hey." He shifted forward in his seat, bracing his elbows on the edge of the table and hunching forward over his drink. He ran his thumb hypnotically up and down the tumbler. He had sexy hands. Big. Strong. Capable. A couple of scars and some calluses to keep them from being too perfect. The flaws only made them more appealing.

She could still feel them running over her body if she really concentrated. Which she had. In the shower before she'd gotten ready for tonight. She'd thought it would be a good idea to take the edge off. Instead, it had her feeling primed for action. She shifted in her chair. A bit of a backfire on that plan.

Aidan tapped her knee with his under the table, and with a sigh, she relented. When she flicked her gaze from his hands to his face, he was closer than she expected, and his earnest expression did weird things to her pulse.

"He didn't make a single move when I stole you out from under his nose. And you deserve better than that."

To combat the heat spilling through her chest at the sentiment, she let out a desperate-sounding laugh. "I'm pretty sure not wanting to get his ass handed to him by the big, intimidating guy in the biker jacket just proves that he's also really smart."

Aidan leaned back in his chair at that, a smug grin lifting the corner of his sinful lips.

"What?"

He shook his head. "Nothing." He let a beat slip by, eyes lit with a wicked gleam. "And thank you."

Kaylee took a sip of her merlot and tried not to rise to the bait, but she couldn't help herself. "For what?"

"For your confidence that I could take him."

Not that it was much of a contest. Aidan could probably take any guy in here.

"But you're wrong about him being smart. If he was, he'd be sitting here instead of me."

The compliment warmed places inside of Kaylee

that were already overheating, and she reached for her wine. The sip she took did nothing to cool her, so she took another.

"Well, on the upside for him, it looks like his night turned out okay without me." She lifted her chin in the direction of Rick, who was laughing with a pretty blonde in a green dress.

Aidan hooked his arm over the back of his chair and turned to follow her sight line. After a moment of observation, he turned back to her, shaking his head. "What's happening over there is a lie staged completely for your benefit."

She shot him a skeptical frown. "How could you possibly know that?"

"Because he keeps glancing over here to see if you're watching. He took the path of least resistance and now he knows he made a mistake. That's what happens when you don't fight for what you want. The what-ifs haunt you."

Kaylee swirled the wine in her glass and idly wondered if he was still talking about Rick. "Do you have what-ifs that haunt you, Aidan?"

The question stilled him, furrowed his brow. She leaned forward, bracing an elbow on the table. "Things you want?" she pressed, her voice husky, knowing she was pushing her luck but unable to stop herself.

His eyes snapped to hers, something dangerous in their depths. Something hot. She squeezed her thighs together at the flare of heat that had sparked between them.

"Things you're willing to fight for?"

He wouldn't have to fight too hard for her right

now—that was for sure. If the table wasn't in her way, she'd already be straddling his lap.

Almost as though he heard the dirty direction her thoughts had taken, he shut it down. Two blinks and he was back to the usual unaffected neutrality with which he'd always looked at her. She was Max's little sister again.

"I'm not talking about me. I'm talking about you shooting drinks with guys who don't deserve you."

She forced a smile through the disappointment. "So the moral of your story is 'Don't trust guys in suits.'"

His expression turned serious as their gazes locked. "The moral of my story is Don't Trust Anyone."

"Except for you," she teased, hoping to lighten the mood a little. Restore some of the friendly intimacy they'd shared tonight.

Aidan took a swig of his drink, shaking his head as he set the tumbler back on the table. "Not even me. People are inherently selfish, KJ. When it comes down to it, they'll pick themselves over you every time. You need to look out for yourself."

His voice sounded almost…bleak.

"That sounds like a lonely way to live."

"You think I'm lonely?" he asked, cocking an eyebrow and leaning back in his chair.

As if to reinforce his implication, she could see at least a half-dozen women eyeing him up like they would be happy to relieve him of that particular condition.

"Having anonymous sex with strangers in back rooms doesn't mean you're not lonely."

Aidan stiffened, and Kaylee winced at the blunder.

Shit. She set her wine back on the table. Why had she said that? She was entering dangerous territory. Okay, maybe her pride was a little hurt that he hadn't put it together, but wasn't that what she wanted? To keep her secret? That was what made their rendezvous so hot. That it was clandestine. And it was better to keep it that way, she reminded herself.

Despite that, she remembered the stage, the power of performing, the want in Aidan's eyes, the feel of his body driving deep into hers. And with a deep breath, she set it aside.

She'd gotten her fantasy night. Now they were back to normal.

Well, not quite.

"You've changed," she noted. The charming boy she remembered had been quick to smile, quick to flirt. This Aidan was harder. Still easy with his movements, but stingier with them, too. It seemed to Kaylee that he only moved, only spoke, economically.

He didn't deny it. Just stared contemplatively at her in that way that made her want to roll her shoulders to alleviate the resulting buzz under her skin. She needed a distraction.

"Tell me about Pamplona."

His lips quirked with a hint of a surprised smile. "You don't want to hear about that."

The teasing words were a ghost from the past, part of the little game they played.

"I want to hear everything," she recited back, and she could tell by his hesitation that he was recalling the same memories.

He loosened up as he told her about his adventures, and a familiar ease had settled over the two of them when he got to the part about the Spanish emergency room and the beautiful nurse—Aidan's stories always had a beautiful villain for her to seethe with jealousy over. By the time she was seventeen, she'd begun to think he oversold whatever leading lady featured in his adventurous tale just to see her frown.

The storytelling he was doing now was automatic, the verbal equivalent of changing into sweatpants. As natural to him as breathing. Light. It used to be enough, but it wasn't anymore.

No matter how much she tried to talk herself out of it, she wanted the heat. Now that she knew what it was like to have Aidan want her, to be the focus of his attention, to see those jade green eyes darken with need, she craved it.

To think she'd spent the entire morning worried he'd figure out who she was, and now, two hours into this farce of a "date," she was offended he hadn't connected her with their kinda-public tryst. It was stupid, but she was jealous of herself. Of the hard truth that Aidan couldn't even fathom that Kaylee Jayne Whitfield had the power to bring him to his knees.

Asshole.

She finished her wine with an unladylike swig that would have scandalized her mother.

A gorgeous, gorgeous asshole with a killer smile and some serious prowess in the bedroom. Well, the supply closet anyway.

Man, she felt good all of a sudden. Loose. Like she

was floating a little. "I'm going to powder my nose," she lied, needing to pee so badly that she didn't even grab her purse to perpetuate the fabrication women had been using for decades to excuse themselves. "Don't go anywhere."

CHAPTER SEVEN

AIDAN KEPT AN eye on her retreating form as he dug into her sparkly purse with quick efficiency. Since the tables were close, he took no chances, setting their phones side by side so that they touched when he hit the button that would load the malware. Kearney wasn't kidding about the easy install. When it was complete, he tucked her phone away, leaving everything as he'd found it.

He drowned the flare of guilt with the final sip of premium whiskey in his glass. He shouldn't have told her about Pamplona. That had been...purely sentimental, and he wasn't that anymore. He'd known it was completely ridiculous when he'd morphed the proficient, elderly woman who'd taken care of him into a nubile Spanish goddess just to make Kaylee frown at him in that cute way she used to. She hadn't disappointed.

The first time he'd mentioned a pretty girl in one of his stories, she'd been real, and Aidan had realized it was an easy way to keep Kaylee's crush on him in check. The way she used to look at him sometimes, like he was all good things, had vacillated between humbling and fucking uncomfortable. She'd cast him as a hero, and everything in him rejected the mantle and the expectations that came with it. He hadn't deserved her devotion back then, and he sure as hell didn't deserve it now.

He caught sight of Rick across the bar, still flirting with some other woman who didn't hold a candle to Kaylee, and his right hand fisted with the urge to throw a punch. Expelling a deep breath, he forced his muscles to unclench. It bothered him that he cared.

What had happened at the bar earlier was no big deal. He's been protecting a friend from a creep. It meant nothing.

His conscience chose that moment to remember the heat that had arced between them when her hazel eyes had grown stormy and her voice had turned husky, asking him about things he wanted. Igniting a lust in his veins that made him want to shove the table aside and haul her into his arms.

Christ.

He was all turned around. Being back in LA had him on edge. He couldn't wait to conclude his *business* and get the hell out of here, to wherever caught his fancy next.

Aidan wasn't prepared for the nostalgia Kaylee brought out in him. It made him realize that he'd been alone for a long time. It made him wonder what he'd been missing out on.

And that was a dangerous path. One that had him thinking dangerous things. About Kaylee.

Who had been like a sister to him. The Whitfields

were like family. Well, they used to be. Now they were the enemy, and he'd do well not to forget that again.

When Kaylee came back she stumbled, bracing herself with a hand on his shoulder. He had the distinct impression of warmth in that moment of contact, a warmth that didn't fade as much as it should have when she let go.

"Sorry." She giggled, dropping into the chair with less grace than she had the first time she'd sat.

He noticed the flush in her cheeks.

The glassiness in her eyes.

A quick mental tally told him she'd had two shots and a glass of red since he'd arrived an hour and a half ago. Not wasted, he decided, but depending on when she'd last eaten, definitely feeling no pain. He should have taken her to dinner instead. Shit.

He had the disquieting thought that Max would be pissed if he knew Aidan had gotten Kaylee drunk, and then chastised himself for thinking it. Max was none of his concern.

Kaylee, on the other hand...

"You okay there, kiddo?"

"I feel so amazing," she told him expansively, "that I am going to let that *kiddo* slide."

He had to bite back a smile at that. "In that case, I think it's time I took you home."

Her pretty face lit up. "I've never been on a motorcycle before."

Aidan got to his feet, and Kaylee followed suit, though more slowly and more deliberately.

"Well, you're not going on one tonight, either."

She gave him her best puppy-dog eyes.

"I'm not scraping you off the pavement," he told her, reaching over to grab her forgotten purse from the table and pushing it into her hands. "Max and I have enough problems already."

"Max wouldn't care." Bitterness crept into the words, dulling her inebriated dreaminess from the moment before. "Well, I mean, it might be inconvenient for him because then he'd have to hire another PR director. But I guess he has to anyway now that I quit. I only did it so he'd ask me to stay, but he didn't. He didn't even care."

Aidan stared at her as they made their way out of the bar and into the elevator. Was that really what she thought? That she meant nothing to her brother? Defense of his former friend welled up on his tongue, but Aidan squelched it with a sudden frown.

Fuck Max. His life and the people in it were none of Aidan's concern. Let the bastard fend for himself.

Aidan jammed the lobby button with more force than necessary.

"And if there's one thing Max hates," Kaylee rambled on, blissfully unaware of Aidan's mental strife, "it's to be inconvenienced." She laughed in the way people did when they'd said too much. "My death would definitely annoy him."

Kaylee went silent for a moment, and he felt her glancing uncertainly at him, though he kept his gaze stubbornly forward.

"You wouldn't understand because Max likes you." A cute little frown crumpled her forehead. "Well, not anymore," she said bluntly. "But he used to. What happened with you two anyway?"

This was not the time or the place to discuss it. And she definitely wasn't the person. You didn't explain the battle plan to the grenade. Especially when you still had no idea how much she knew.

Thankfully, the doors slid open, and he grabbed her elbow, partly to steady her and partly to hurry her through the lobby and outside. The evening air was warm but stagnant. Tonight, it reeked of big city—concrete and exhaust and a hint of urine. "Which way is your car?"

She stepped away from him, turning in a slow half circle as she oriented herself.

Two guys walking past took a good long look at her, and Aidan frowned, mostly at them but partially at the sudden protective streak that had him stripping off his jacket and holding it out to her. "Put this on."

Her dress was the kind of sexy that snuck up on you. The classy kind that left something to a man's imagination instead of showing him exactly what he was in for. And though he had no problem with being shown what he was in for—his Friday night with Lola had been epic—there was definitely something in the tease of filling in the blanks. Despite his earlier resolve not to, he liked it a little too much.

Her dreamy smile hit him right in the gut.

Yeah, right. *Protective.* Such a load of bullshit, but he clung to it because the alternative was... There was no acceptable alternative.

"You're not gonna have any jackets left," she mumbled nonsensically, pulling it on and snuggling into it.

Aidan set his jaw against the charming scene. "You got keys somewhere, KJ?"

She shoved the sparkly purse at his chest and he took it as they headed toward the silver Audi she'd left in a nearby pay lot.

Once he had her loaded into the passenger seat and buckled in, he joined her inside the car, though he had to shove her seat back as far as it would go and change every mirror setting.

"You drive stick?"

"Is that an invitation?" She ruined the sultry question with a hiccup, but Aidan's body didn't seem to care.

"Please tell me you remember where you live?" he asked gruffly, trying to resurrect the polite distance he'd managed for most of the night.

She guided him to her fancy building, and the key fob gained them entry to the underground garage. He cut the engine, and silence descended upon them. He looked over to find her eyes closed, her long lashes casting shadows on her cheeks, her mouth curved provocatively at the corner, like she was in the middle of a very good dream.

Self-preservation had him unbuckling his seat belt and getting out of the Audi. He slammed the driver's door with more force than necessary, with every intention of waking her up, because he didn't trust himself to touch her right now, not even to shake her awake.

He circled the back of the car and pulled open the passenger-side door.

"Okay. Let's get you upstairs."

"I'm too tired. I'll just sleep here," she countered, snuggling into the black leather seat.

"What kind of gentleman would I be if I left you sleeping in your car?" he asked sardonically. With an aggrieved frown, she shoved her hand toward him, and against his better judgment, he accepted it.

"You've spent your whole life telling me you're not a gentleman at all," she countered when she was finally standing in front of him. She was tall, he realized, and her high heels made her even more so.

He'd barely have to dip his head to kiss her right now, to bring their mouths into perfect alignment. He leaned forward.

"Aidan?" His name sounded breathy on her lips, and lust coiled deep in his belly.

"Yeah?"

"I think I forgot my purse."

He exhaled at the near miss as she spun away from him.

Aidan didn't mean to stare at that round, pert ass as she dived back into the car, bracing a knee on the seat so she could retrieve her clutch. His mouth went dry. No panty lines.

"Got it!" Her voice was triumphant as she backed out of the Audi, tugging her dress down her shapely thighs as she fixed him with a victorious smile. "Man. We should have shared some appetizers at the bar. I'm starving," she announced, pushing past him. Her unsteady footsteps echoed in the concrete cavern as she headed toward the elevator.

He swallowed as he shut the door and locked her car

with the press of a button, taking a moment to readjust himself before he followed along in her wake.

Nope. He was definitely not a gentleman.

CHAPTER EIGHT

THEY MANAGED THE trip to the elevator pretty seamlessly, though in her inebriated state, Kaylee kept misjudging how much space she was taking up. Every time she brushed against him, which was often, his libido and his brain went to war. Any relief he felt when they finally stepped onto her floor was ruined by his inability to concentrate on anything but the sway of her hips as he followed her to her place. She leaned heavily on the wall as he unlocked the door.

He stepped back. "After you."

With some effort, she disassociated herself from the wall, haphazardly shedding her shoes and his jacket as she meandered into the space.

Aidan followed her in. It was a nice place. Of course. Ritzy, subdued furniture that bespoke old money. Tidy, elegant, no hint as to what lay beneath the surface.

So very much like its owner.

Aidan stepped into the high-end kitchen. "Where are the glasses?"

His question stalled Kaylee's forward progress, and she wandered back to join him, pointing at the cupboard to his right. He grabbed the tallest one he could find and shoved it under the tap before holding it out to her. "Drink this."

"I'm not thirsty."

"Drink it anyway," he suggested, doing his best to ignore the danger of her proximity. All this time, she'd been stuck in his memory as a winsome teen who used to beg him for stories when she worked up the nerve to speak to him. So much time had passed between then and now. So many things had changed.

Kaylee took the glass, placating him with a half-hearted swallow before she set it beside the sink.

She'd changed, too. But he'd do well not to notice that. "You'll thank me tomorrow."

Something dangerous lit in her eyes. His body braced for the impact, all his muscles drawing tight.

"I'd rather thank you tonight."

Aidan gave a silent curse. Damned if he didn't want to let her.

Had since she'd turned around in the bar, looking fresh and beautiful and so goddamned sexy that he couldn't think straight. The buzz between them was unlike anything Aidan had ever experienced, as hazardous as a downed power line.

"Want to know a secret?"

He wanted to know all her secrets. What made her moan. What turned her on.

Goddamn it. He'd been so horny since he'd broken his unintentional sexual fast and lapsed into hedonism with that burlesque dancer. But he was not going to slake his reignited libido with Kaylee Whitfield.

"I've always had a crush on you."

The sweetness of her confession gave him a moment to get ahold of himself, subdue his raging hormones. "That's not a secret, KJ."

But the feeling had never been mutual.

At least not until tonight.

"That's not what you're supposed to say!" Her affronted frown was cute as hell.

He relaxed a little as they fell into old roles, him cajoling, her exasperated. "What was I supposed to say?"

"Something gallant. Or something sweet. Basically, anything but that."

"Duly noted. Now, let's get you to bed." He instantly regretted his choice of words as something dark and sexy supercharged the air between them, turning his innocent words into a lascivious proposition.

"You're a fast learner. That was better already."

She stepped closer, dragged her fingers down his chest. He caught her wrist, stilling her hand. Her gaze dropped to his lips, and he could feel her pulse kick up.

That thrum between them filled his head.

"Do you want me?" she asked.

His eyebrows snapped together. This was definitely not the Kaylee he remembered. "What?"

This time when she lowered her gaze, she didn't stop until she got to his zipper. "Do I make you hard?"

His body responded against his will, and she smiled the kind of smile that could drop a guy to his knees. "Because I want you."

"You're drunk." He tried to shut her down. "You don't know what you're asking for."

"You wanna bet on that?" She caught her bottom lip between her teeth and gave him a look that was all liquid sex and mysterious woman. "I know *exactly* what I'm asking for."

Something about the way she said it made him believe her. Made him want to give it to her, too.

"And you know what else I bet? I bet you fuck like a stallion."

"Jesus, Kaylee." He dropped her hand, took a step back. She was more potent than he'd thought. More dangerous than he'd given her credit for.

"What? I can say *fuck* if I want to. I'm an adult woman."

"You're not acting like it." It was a feeble defense, but Aidan committed, injecting his tone with acid as he tried to get his brain out of his pants and back where it belonged.

She wasn't embarrassed as much as put out, if her pout was any indication. "You sound like my mother."

That startled a laugh from him. Par for the course tonight, he figured. Past and present had collided in the most disorienting way. He pulled a hand over his face, down his beard. "Christ, I really do."

Her answering smile was wobbly. He was objectively struck in that moment by how beautiful she was. The promise had been there in her teens, but the result was like a kick to the chest.

"How is Sylvia these days?"

"The Dragon Lady still rules with an iron fist. Wait." She shook her head, and the force made her sway. She braced a steadying hand on the counter. "Why are we talking about my mother right now? You're not getting out of this that easily."

Beautiful and stubborn as fuck.

He was trying to avenge his father, to tear down the family that had ruined his. She was the enemy, he reminded himself. Max's baby sister. He wasn't supposed to want her. And he sure as shit wasn't supposed to like her.

She zeroed in on his face, searching for what he didn't know.

"Max's kid sister."

His head snapped up. "What?"

"That's all you see, isn't it?"

She looked...disappointed in him, but for the life of him, he couldn't figure out why. Something about the way she'd phrased the question didn't sit right in his chest.

"That's all you are to me."

She stepped close, this time leaving no space between them. Testing the statement. Testing his resolve.

More seductive than anyone who'd been onstage Friday night. The vulnerability of it.

Nothing coy. Nothing but Kaylee looking up at him like she thought he was something special. It was fucking terrifying.

"Prove it." Her hands snaked up his chest, over his shoulders, brushed the nape of his neck. "Kiss me."

She felt good pressed against him. Too good. Like they fit together.

It took everything he had to pull her arms down.

"Not tonight." *Not ever*, his conscience reminded him.

The hurt in her eyes was too much for him to take, but her troubled expression cleared a moment later. "I'm going to change your mind, Aidan."

"No, you're not. Now, come on." He slipped his arm under her knees and picked her up, even though she was perfectly capable of walking. She snuggled into his chest, and just for a moment, Aidan let himself enjoy the feel of her in his arms.

He carried her out of the kitchen and into her bedroom. It took him too long to set her down, and it took her too long to step out of his arms.

The room was girly—a chandelier hung over her bed, which had a curvy upholstered headboard and way too many pillows, but the mattress was big. Probably a king. And he really needed to not concentrate on the bed right now.

Unfortunately, turning his attention back to her did nothing to alleviate thoughts of her bed, only now, he was imagining her naked, licking her lips exactly the way she was doing right now...

He was relieved when she turned away from him, but she ruined it quickly enough with a glance over her shoulder.

"Can you help me?" She caught her dark hair in her hand and twisted it up to reveal the graceful line of her neck. "With my dress?"

Shit.

Aidan swallowed as he reached for her zipper.

This couldn't happen while she was drunk.

The thought stopped him short. *What the actual hell?*

This couldn't happen while she was sober, either.

This couldn't happen at all.

But even knowing that, his cock wouldn't obey his brain, responding instead to the soft rasp of the zipper as he tugged it down and the slow reveal as the material gaped, baring the soft skin of her back inch by glorious inch. He wanted to run his fingertips along the delicate ridge of her spine. Unhook her lacy purple bra. Push the dress off her shoulders.

Lay her down on the bed and fuck her until they were both too weak to move.

Christ, he needed to get out of there.

"I'm going to get your water while you get changed." His voice was rough with desire, and he hated himself for it as he turned and left the bedroom.

But his conscience wasn't done with him yet. The far wall of her living room, he noticed, was dominated by a massive set of shelves packed with books.

When she was a teenager, Kaylee's nose had been constantly in a novel. The reminder of the quiet, studious girl she'd been unleashed a torrent of guilt in his belly. He was here to ruin her brother for his cowardice, and she was destined to be collateral damage at best and the reason for Max's downfall at worst. Aidan swore under his breath. Just because he'd had a soft spot for her back in the day didn't mean he was going to let it derail his plans. The eagerness on her face when she managed to get him alone for a few minutes, begging him to tell her about his latest adventure. He'd always indulged her, trying to make up for Max's intentional coldness.

Aidan used to wonder how Kaylee had grown up to

be so sweet and curious when her mother spent most of her time beating her down, harping on everything from her clothes to her posture to her book obsession.

It always broke his heart a little, watching her desperation to please Max, who never betrayed for an instant how much he loved and respected his little sister.

At the time, Aidan had thought it ludicrous, but it hadn't taken long to see that Max knew what he was talking about. Charles Whitfield aimed his verbal abuse at Max, and while he didn't exactly dote on his daughter, he treated Kaylee with a superficial affection that she lapped up—next to the way Sylvia Whitfield treated her, it must have felt like unconditional love.

He'd always respected that about Max. The way he'd done what needed doing to protect his family.

If Aidan had known it was going to come back and bite him in the ass, he might not have. He'd confided in Max about his concerns over his dad, but when push came to shove, Max had been a Whitfield through and through. He'd sold John Beckett out to his own father. A man Max didn't respect—hell, a man he barely even liked—and in doing so, he'd shattered what was left of Aidan's family. And Aidan intended to return the favor.

As he grabbed Kaylee's water, his conscience reared up, but he pushed it down. There was no room for sentiment and definitely no room for lust. The two of them couldn't be together. She was simply an in to Max's world. Nothing more.

When he returned, Kaylee was slung out on her stomach, one knee drawn up toward her chest, spectacular ass on display in a sexy little purple thong, snuffling drunkenly and fast asleep.

Thank Christ.

Aidan set the glass on her bedside table, beside the stack of books piled on it. But when he turned to leave, he caught sight of a mark on her skin, just beneath the lacy band of her bra, and everything in him went still.

It took a second for his mind to piece together where he'd last seen the tiny, graceful lines that made up the delicate butterfly perched on her rib cage.

In a starkly lit storage room.

In a midrange bar.

On a woman who'd made him crazy, driven him to unparalleled sexual heights.

Well, *fuck*.

CHAPTER NINE

The jackhammering in her head let Kaylee know she was in trouble even before she opened her eyes. There were a couple of other clues, of course. Her mouth tasted like death, throwing up sounded like a viable way to spend her morning, and her mind was replaying an embarrassing highlight reel of her night with Aidan. She whimpered, cradling her head.

She'd practically thrown herself at him, and he hadn't even been tempted. She stumbled out of bed and headed straight for the en suite to brush her teeth and down a couple of aspirin.

She caught sight of the makeup sliding down her face. *Ugh.*

She was a mess.

Kaylee did her best to clean the smudged eye makeup while she replayed her time with Aidan. It would figure that she finally got her chance with him, her chance to be herself—have him see her as the woman she was now, not the girl she'd been then—and she'd ended up acting like a fifteen-year-old at a house party, doing nothing to dispel her kid-sister mantle.

It was mortifying.

With an inner groan, Kaylee made her way to the kitchen. She was at the counter and reaching to grab a mug from the cupboard by the time her muddled brain noticed the coffee was already brewed, which made no sense.

"We need to talk."

Kaylee whirled around, hand to her chest. "Jesus, Aidan. You scared me."

Her heart thundered in her ears, and she forced herself to take a couple of deep breaths. She didn't know where he'd appeared from, but he was wearing the same clothes, including the jacket he'd loaned her. And unlike her, he looked just as amazing as he had last night.

The realization made her self-conscious in her bra-and-sweatpants combo, and she wished desperately she'd taken a moment to brush her hair before she'd begun her migration to the kitchen.

"You stayed here all night?" She turned her back on him, using the moment to calm her racing heart as she poured herself a mugful of coffee.

Her pulse was hammering in her skull, but she couldn't tell if that was because of the hangover or because of Aidan. What was he still doing here? Surely getting her home safely marked the end of any duty he felt to keep her from doing something stupid. Like driving drunk. Or going home with Rick.

What did it mean that he'd stayed? The question sent a frisson down her spine. As Aidan approached, the air got thicker, making it tough to breathe.

She took a sip of caffeine to steady her nerves, but

her hand was trembling so hard that she set it back on the counter before she turned to face him.

Her breasts were heavy, aching at his nearness. God he was beautiful. Big. Starkly male. Imposing. And given the sharp edge in his eyes, angry.

"Did you have something you wanted to tell me?"

He stepped closer, cutting the distance between them to a couple of feet. It should be intimidating, but the leashed danger of him sparked something primal in her, and it made her want to reach out and touch the flames, not quite convinced such beauty could be a threat.

As if sensing her fascination, he stepped closer again, crowding her, and belatedly she realized that the danger was real. Logic told her to step back and maintain some semblance of safety. Something else urged her to step forward and take her chances in the storm.

"I don't know what you're talking about."

He frowned. "Don't you?"

The accusatory tone put her on edge as she racked her brain for what possible grievance he might have already tried and convicted her for. He stepped closer still, and her muddled thoughts got even more so. Against her will, she inhaled more deeply the heady scent of coffee and angry male.

"I'm sorry about last night. If the pounding in my head is anything to go by, I'm way too old to be getting drunk on a weeknight. That tequila hit harder than I expected."

"I don't give a shit about the tequila." His words were edged with steel.

"You don't?" Her forehead crinkled with confusion. "Then what—"

"This," he bit out as he pulled her to him. Her breasts brushed his chest, and he ran a palm up the left side of her torso, igniting the lust that had begun simmering deep in her belly the moment she'd realized he was still in her apartment.

Did he feel it too? The pull of attraction? The realization that he hadn't made a move while she was drunk but that he'd stayed all night anyway made her heart beat faster. The blood rushing in her ears had nothing to do with her overindulgence and everything to do with the man in front of her. The man she'd wanted for so long. The man who finally wanted her back.

She stood frozen, waiting for whatever came next—for him to press his mouth against hers, or sweep his hand up to cradle her breast, or pin her against the counter with his hips. But he didn't do any of those things.

He just stood there looking down at her, their bodies close but not close enough. Their breathing had synced, and nothing moved except for the slight pressure of his hand along the side of her rib cage. The pressure increased steadily, growing slightly uncomfortable before she realized his thumb was digging into her skin, right below the lacy edge of her bra, right where her...

Oh shit.

Her eyes widened with realization. The goddamn butterfly tattoo throbbed beneath his thumb, and she cursed her stupidity.

Aidan's frown deepened at her confession, the one she knew was written all over her face. But the pressure on her tattoo eased, and when he spoke his voice sounded more off balance than enraged. "What the fuck, Kaylee?"

Can you help me with my dress?

The memory made her woozy. It had seemed a brilliantly flirtatious play last night, inhibitions dampened by tequila and Aidan and desire.

Now she saw it for what it was. A huge mistake.

She'd never thought for a second something so tiny would give her away, never considered that he'd noticed the show of teenage rebellion. Ironic, considering she'd been scrupulous about hiding it when she was a kid lest her mother see it and ground her for life.

Hell, Sylvia Whitfield *still* didn't know about it.

She didn't answer, but she didn't need to. He knew.

He knew what she'd done, and he wasn't happy. The accusation in his gaze cut deep.

"It was you."

It took her a moment to realize he was stroking the pad of his thumb back and forth across the winged talisman inked on her skin, shooting tiny sparks along her nerve endings and erasing the pain he'd inflicted a moment ago.

The sweetness of the gesture had lulled her into complacency, and his next swing made her stagger because she hadn't braced for it.

"Did Max put you up to this? Is he trying to figure out why I'm back?"

She'd never been punched before, but she imagined the lurching disorientation his words inspired must be what it was like to be coldcocked.

She was never going to be free of her brother. Aidan was never going to be free of her brother. The two men hadn't spoken in five years, yet they couldn't have been more linked.

"Why would Max have anything to do with my sex life?" Her voice was flat. Cold. An attempt to extricate herself from the box she occupied in Aidan's mind, the few times he bothered to think of her at all. The blunt question seemed to shake Aidan, and he stepped back, jerking his hand away as though he'd finally realized he was touching her.

As expected, talk of Max had leeched all the gray out of their tête-à-tête, and Aidan's hard gaze told her that he was firmly back in the land of black and white.

"It should never have happened."

The dismissal of their liaison, of the hottest experience of her life, piqued her anger.

"You wanted it as much as I did."

He raked a hand through his hair. The look on his face, like a wild animal trapped in a cage, was humiliating. "I had no idea who you were!"

The truth slashed at her.

"Maybe not, but you felt it, too. I know it's never been like that for you with anyone else. I could feel it in the way you touched me."

Aidan crossed his arms, trying to keep her out. "It was anonymous sex. It didn't mean anything."

Kaylee knew this was it, her one shot to take what she wanted. "It wasn't supposed to mean anything, but now that you know it was me, you know the truth. And it scares the shit out of you."

"If I'd known, if I'd even suspected it was you in that club, it never would have happened."

"But it did happen. Because I wanted you. I still want you." Something flared in his eyes, and Kaylee pressed her advantage. "And you want me. All you have to do is give in."

"You think you're a seductress now? Because we fucked in a supply closet? This doesn't end well, Kaylee. That's why it should never have started. You're messing with things you don't understand."

"Maybe I understand better than you think."

"If you did, you would never have resurrected whatever feelings you think you have for me. I don't return them. I never have."

"You didn't then. You couldn't. I was just a kid. But I'm not a kid anymore, Aidan. There's nothing stopping this now."

"Oh no? Then why didn't you tell me it was you?"

"I just…"

"You knew I would have sent you on your way. So you kept your mouth shut. Because you're a liar. Just like Max. Just like Charles. You're a Whitfield through and through. You take what you want when you want it, the rest of the world be damned."

It hurt. Of course it hurt. But the precision of the attack was so out of character from a man who'd always been so kind. He was angry, but she suspected it was more with himself than with her, so she kept pushing.

"Is that what I did? You weren't into what was happening? I thought it was just going to be sex. That you'd never find out. But then the way you looked at me when you put your jacket around my shoulders?"

He stiffened, like she'd accused him of something heinous.

"You looked at me like you saw me, like you knew something was different, and I…"

"You what? Thought if you tricked me into screwing you in a supply closet we'd fall in love and live happily ever after? Grow the fuck up."

And with that he stalked out of her apartment, out of her life, slamming the door behind him.

Kaylee watched him go. His words burning into her chest, even as her fury had her breathing hard. Asshole. He could deny it all he wanted, try to pretend nothing momentous had happened when their bodies touched, but she knew the truth. He'd wanted her in that supply closet. And he wanted her now, even knowing who she was.

CHAPTER TEN

S*he's a fucking liar.*

Aidan landed a one-two combination on the heavy bag he'd installed when he'd renovated his dad's old workshop into a living space.

The words had lost most of their heat days ago, but he made himself turn them over and over in his brain anyway. It was like a shield, something to remind himself that she was a Whitfield, that he should hate her.

The sound of Kaylee's laughter filled the room, mocking him, and he glanced over at his phone. He should turn it off. He'd already accessed the SecurePay prototype and sent it off to his tech guy so it could be analyzed against Cybercore's competing product.

But damn, she had a great laugh. Rich and throaty. And though he had no idea who this Jesse guy was, Aidan definitely didn't think he was as funny as Kaylee was giving him credit for. He was listening in on her daily briefing with Soteria Security, but judging by his erection, you'd think he'd called a goddamn phone-sex line.

For the past three days, he'd been listening to Kaylee

run Whitfield Industries in her brother's absence. And doing a hell of a job of it. She was decisive but fair, supportive but exacting. Nothing like the girl he remembered who used to shrink whenever anyone so much as glanced at her. No, at work Kaylee was in charge. In control. Like she had been on that stage.

Jesus.

He was still having a tough time accepting that the sexy siren in the supply closet and little Kaylee Jayne Whitfield were one and the same.

And the fact that he hadn't put that together on his own made him want to punch things. A person. A wall. He wasn't choosy. Luckily, he was old enough to know better, so he kept his fists directed at the heavy bag.

But no matter how many punches he threw, he couldn't shake the way she'd looked in her kitchen that morning—hungover and beautiful and so effortlessly sexy. The sweetness of her had been in direct contrast to all the dirty things he craved from her as she stood there in her purple bra, staring up at him as his thumb stroked her ribs.

Kaylee.

He tried to name the toxicity oozing through his chest and was surprised to find it resembled betrayal.

But not the kind where he despised her for duping him as much as the kind where he resented her because he'd missed out. He'd had Kaylee in the supply closet, but he hadn't enjoyed it the way he should have because he'd thought she was someone else.

Even knowing, it was hard to believe she was the hot, sexy woman who'd melted all over him at the burlesque club. Hell, maybe she was right to keep her identity from him. Maybe Max's little sister was all he'd ever see her as.

He knew it was a lie the second he thought it.

Because she'd gotten him plenty hard with her clumsy, drunken kitchen seduction, and he'd known exactly who he was dealing with then. He was hard right now reliving the details of that night in the storage room, imagining it over and over without the blond wig and blue contacts.

Jab, jab, cross.

His boxing gloves made satisfying thuds against the sand-filled leather.

It should never have happened. But after realizing how attracted he was to Kaylee at the coffee shop, at the lounge, he wasn't so sure anymore that, had she revealed her identity in the supply closet, he would have stopped.

A bead of sweat dripped along his temple, and he pulled off one of his gloves and grabbed the hem of his white tank to wipe it away.

He'd been a world-class asshole to her and stormed out of her kitchen. She didn't deserve to be dragged into the middle of his issues with Max. But that's what he'd done. Used her. Put her between them.

He listened as Kaylee wrapped up the meeting, but as she and Jesse and the other guy—Wes, maybe?—were discussing what time they would meet on Monday, Aidan lost the signal and static crackled through the phone speaker. It had happened a couple of times before. When the signal was strong, Kearney's tech was the real deal. There were moments that the sound was so crisp he could hear the whisper of Kaylee's sigh, and in the next second it would cut out completely or hum with white noise. Obviously the self-proclaimed tech god still had some bugs to work out.

And he was going to relish letting Kearney know his spyware wasn't all that, Aidan thought with a grim smile. He pulled off his other glove and walked over to the phone so he could stop the app. He dropped his boxing gloves on the end table and unwound his hand wraps with a disgusted sigh.

Usually, hitting the heavy bag cleared his head. But where Kaylee was concerned, not even boxing was doing the trick anymore.

Aidan dragged a hand through his sweaty hair.

Neither were cold showers, he thought wryly, reaching down to readjust himself.

He'd had a perma-erection for the last four days, despite having jacked off so much that he was giving his puberty record a run for it its money.

He pulled off his tank top and headed for the shower. His dick slapped his stomach when he shed his sweatpants and boxer briefs. With a disgusted sigh, he stepped under the warm spray of the shower and tried to remember the last time a woman had affected him so viscerally. He was no closer to finding an answer by the time he'd finished washing his hair.

Aidan grabbed the soap, lathering it between his palms. She'd gotten into his blood, he realized, running sudsy palms across his chest, trying his damnedest not to let thoughts of Kaylee pull his hands south. But as he followed the sluice of water down to his abs, all the while remembering the bite of her nails over his back, the rasp of her breath on his neck, how it felt to be buried so deep inside her that coming became more vital than oxygen, Aidan realized he was going to lose that battle.

She was impossible to forget.

Or at least that was his excuse when he gave in and wrapped his hand around his aching cock.

His knees softened at the contact, and Aidan braced his free hand on the slate-colored shower tiles, tipping his head back and closing his eyes. He stood statue still, letting the rain-head shower wash over him as he stroked himself. And it was good, fuck yeah it was good, but he realized in that moment that his hand wasn't going to give him what he needed, what he craved.

Because right now, he was experiencing Schrödinger's Supply Closet. He'd both fucked Kaylee and not fucked Kaylee, and the paradox was killing him. Because whether he had or he hadn't, she'd come twice with the sweetest cries he'd ever heard.

His hand stilled even as the memory made him harder.

There was only one way he was getting free of sexual purgatory, and it wasn't courtesy of his goddamn hand.

Aidan shut off the shower and toweled dry. Naked, he headed for his room, grabbing his phone on the way past the table. He opened Kearney's spy app and tossed the device on his bed so he could tug on a pair of jeans.

The app beeped as the tracker came to life, and he glanced at the screen. Kaylee was on the move. He froze as she arrived at her destination. He didn't need to look up the address. He remembered all too well—hence all the masturbatory records he'd set over the past week.

Pulling on a T-shirt, Aidan grabbed the keys to his bike and his leather jacket—the one Kaylee had worn home from drinks—and headed for the club.

CHAPTER ELEVEN

Kaylee felt him.

It didn't matter that the club was particularly packed tonight or that he stood off to the side doing a credible job of blending into the shadows despite his size. The electrifying jolt of his attention was undeniable, just like it had been a week ago. Kaylee reciprocated by making her bumps bumpier and her grinds grindier. Because this time there were no secrets between them. This time he knew it was her.

There was only one reason for him to show up here tonight, and she wasn't going to waste it.

After her performance, Kaylee didn't bother with her street clothes. Instead of returning the black jersey skirt she'd borrowed last Friday, as had been her intention, she tugged it on. Then she laced herself back into her corset as quickly as she could.

As expected, he was waiting near the battered exit door. There was an extended moment of staring at one another, a reenactment of that moment before he'd tugged her into the supply closet, but this time with no subterfuge. Aidan's pupils were large in the dim light, ringed with jade, and Kaylee felt their focus so intensely it made her shiver. A slight frown marred his forehead as his eyes searched her face. Like he was looking beyond the blond wig, past the blue contacts, behind the red lipstick.

Looking for Kaylee.

He squinted, and she met his gaze, giving him time to catalog her face, to reconcile her features with Lola's, a glimpse behind the curtain so he could figure out how he'd been fooled last time. How time and makeup and expectation had conspired to keep him from seeing the truth.

And after he'd put all the pieces together, there was a flare of heat in those unforgettable eyes of his and their reenactment of the night that changed everything for her continued as he grabbed her hand. His palm was warm and wide and calloused, just as it had been before, but it felt different this time. Because this time, Aidan was holding *her* hand, not the hand of some nameless burlesque dancer he'd picked up in a club.

And this time, instead of dragging her off for a quick fuck in the supply closet, he pushed through the exit door and into the parking lot.

His bike gleamed under the streetlight, two helmets propped on the leather seat. Wordlessly, he handed her one. She put it on, and even with the wig it was too large. Then, as was becoming their custom, he pulled off his jacket and draped it over her shoulders.

She shoved her arms through the too-long sleeves, watching his white T-shirt pull taut over his muscles as he donned the other helmet.

It was a distinct pleasure watching Aidan. The way his body moved. She'd spent so much of her time back in the day slung out in a lounge chair, pretending to read as she covertly dissected his every move. But there was something luxurious in being able to watch him openly, to dedicate her full attention to the sinuous slide of muscle beneath cotton without worrying about getting caught.

The sight of him as he mounted the bike with a deft grace only heightened the tough, manly picture he made as the motorcycle roared to life.

A thrill shot through her as he turned his head in invitation. With distinctly less grace than he'd shown, she crawled behind him and onto the growling black-and-silver beast.

Aidan revved the engine and Kaylee let the vibrations tingle through her. She fixed the moment in her mind as she wrapped her arms around him and they took off.

It was her dirtiest dreams come true, Aidan between her legs, his jeans abrading her bare thighs in a way that drove her mad. She pressed her breasts against his back, sighing at the delicious pressure as she tightened her hold, speed measured by the wind on her skin.

The ridges of his abs were evident through the soft white cotton of his T-shirt, and Kaylee ran her nails over them, loving how they tightened beneath her fingers and how he punched the speed of the bike in response.

She'd been waiting for this her whole life. For Aidan to want her.

And despite what he might think, this wasn't about fairy tales or girlish wishes.

Aidan made her feel alive. And she craved him for it.

She wasn't looking for forever. She was looking for right now. That wicked thrill she got from misbehaving. From knowing her family wouldn't approve. It was her catnip. She couldn't resist the excitement of it.

Aidan took a hard right, and Kaylee looked around, curious about the unfamiliar neighborhood that was a fascinating blend of commercial and residential. Older warehouses and a lot of auto-body shops and parts stores randomly butted up against old single-story, flat-roofed houses with a distinctly '70s vibe. After a few more turns, Aidan slowed the bike and approached a two-story structure that, judging by the faded paint and two big garage doors on the front, used to be some sort of repair shop.

The garage door on the left began its ascent, and Aidan drove inside and cut the engine. The motorized hum of the door closing behind them accompanied Kaylee's dismount from the bike, her body still vibrating from the ride as she removed the helmet and drank in the odd building.

This side was definitely a garage, with massive silver tool chests lining the wall to her left and another motorcycle—vintage looking, from the '50s or '60s maybe—tucked off to the side. But to the right there was a living room, with an area rug on the concrete floor.

There was a heavy bag hanging from the ceiling, as well as a weight bench and a couple of other pieces that functioned as a gym area.

The back half of the bottom floor housed a kitchen full of stainless steel and exposed brick, and a room with a large window. When this place had been a functioning auto shop that room must have been the office. Beside that was a set of stairs that led to whatever occupied the second level.

It was kind of a loft, kind of a work space, very industrial and, in a weird way, seemed to embody the man beside her, straddling the line between rough and civilized.

Aidan grabbed the helmet from her and set it beside his on the seat of the bike.

With a speculative smile, she wandered out of the workshop area toward the living room setup to their right. She felt more than heard Aidan follow her as she dropped her bag on the couch and stopped in front of the coffee table.

There was a large steel sculpture on it, fire morphing into a herd of running horses. The detail was incredible, the flames blending seamlessly into the manes of the fleeing animals. She reached out to touch the fire, so intricately wrought she half expected it to burn her, but instead the smooth, cold surface leeched heat from the pad of her finger.

Max had something like it on his desk—less intricate, but similar—a horse with a mane of flames.

She glanced over her shoulder, intending to ask about it, but rather than standing on the edge of the area rug where she'd expected him to be, Aidan had taken a seat in the armchair, knees wide apart. His left hand was on his thigh, his right elbow on the armrest as he ran a hand over his beard, watching her with a look of such contemplation that it sucked the breath from her lungs.

Kaylee turned fully to face him. With shaking hands, she ran her fingers up the zippered edges of the front of his jacket before dropping it from her shoulders. She paused for a moment, working the art of the tease, enjoying the tingles that ran along her nerve endings as Aidan's eyes raked over her body. It was…thrilling, the taut, hungry look on his face, knowing that *she'd* put it there. Take that, Lola.

She let gravity and the weight of the leather drag the jacket the rest of the way down her arms before pulling it off and tossing it onto the couch.

Her breath came faster as she watched him look at her, trace her body with his gaze. He flexed the hand on his thigh, and the realization that he was imagining touching her made her wet. Just like that. Ready for him.

She'd thought that night in the supply closet had been potent, but it was nothing compared to this.

They hadn't spoken in days, but Aidan knew exactly how to break their word fast with deadly, sensual precision.

"Take it off." His voice was low, gruff, but it exploded in the silence, ricocheted through her chest.

Kaylee reached for the hooks of her corset.

"Not that."

She looked up.

"The wig."

The words stopped her heart.

Heat washed through her body. With shaking hands,

she tugged off the blond wig and her wig cap together. Aidan's jaw flexed as her dark hair uncoiled, stoking the performer in her. She tossed the wig onto the couch and shook her head a few times so that her hair spilled over her shoulders.

He shifted in the chair, and power prickled across her skin. He might be giving the orders, but he was as much under her spell as she was under his, and she loved it.

She raised her hands to the top hook and paused, quirking an eyebrow in question.

Aidan swallowed, the muscles in his throat working even as his tongue darted out to moisten his lips. He was so intensely masculine, and having his total focus on her was heady in the extreme.

He gave a curt nod of permission, and Kaylee's body turned liquid and wanting as she began the familiar process of unhooking the corset. But if the action was familiar, the desire was not.

In the club during one of her shows, there was an anonymity to the sexy striptease, a coyness and irreverence that gave her near nudity a bawdy sense of fun. Now every move was purposeful and serious and dizzyingly sexy.

As the last hook came loose, excitement rippled over her skin. There was something so intense about the momentous step of taking her clothes off for this man. Of him knowing her identity, of them having sex as themselves.

A shyness she wasn't used to reared up as she gripped the sides of the corset and prepared to remove it.

This was him.

This was her.

Without her Lola persona, she was suddenly and uncomfortably aware of her body.

"Kaylee." His voice was a pleading growl that infused her with courage.

That first night in the club, she'd thought she'd wanted to dance for him, a private striptease to seduce him, show him how different she was from his memories of her as a shy, awkward teenager. But now that the moment was upon them, she found it wasn't what she craved at all.

She wanted Aidan to want her tonight. Just her. Not the stage show.

He'd pulled her out of the club.

He'd told her to take off the wig.

Those facts gave her the courage, and just like that, she dropped the corset. No showmanship, just honesty.

And sparkly pasties.

His breath came out as a curse, ratcheting up her excitement.

Aidan shifted in the chair, leaning forward. "Come here."

Kaylee obeyed, walking toward him in her heels. The jersey skirt rode up her thighs with each step.

She wanted to touch every inch of him before this night was over, but she forced herself to draw out the anticipation, stopping in front of him and waiting until he managed to pull his attention up her body to meet her eyes.

"Well?" She laced the question with challenge. "You got me here. Now what are you going to do with me?"

His face darkened with leashed passion and he dragged rough fingers down her belly with such gentleness that her heart clenched. When he encountered the waistband of her skirt, he began inching the black jersey down her hips, his fingertips skating down her thighs until he reached her knees and gravity took care of the rest.

Then Aidan flattened his hands on her skin, releasing an electrical storm as he ran his palms up the backs of her legs, over the curve of her ass, to her lower back. His thumbs stroked the sides of her torso just below her waist, and through it all, he didn't break eye contact.

It was perfect. Soft. Dreamy. A sweet moment of restraint before the wave of lust crested and swallowed them both.

Aidan's hands tightened, his fingers digging into her flesh, and she felt him fight it, trying to hold on to that calm, peaceful moment before the storm of desire swept them both away. He pulled her closer, just a step, so her shins were touching the rough fabric of the chair between his spread legs and his forehead rested against her abdomen.

She pushed her fingers into his hair, cradling his head there.

His breath raced across her skin, leaving a trail of goose bumps that disappeared under the shocking heat of his tongue before reemerging with a vengeance.

He pressed his lips to her skin, dragging them up her stomach before kissing a path between her breasts. Kaylee braced her hands on his shoulders as he wrapped his arms around her, pulling her onto the chair with him as he leaned back.

Bracing a knee on either side of his hips, she straddled him and slid her hands up his neck to cup his jaw, to hold him still as she lowered her head and captured his mouth.

She'd told him that he fucked like a stallion, but he kissed like a damn poet, perfect rhythm, every stroke of his tongue and nip of his teeth wringing so much feeling from her that he could probably bring her to orgasm just from making out. Tonight, though, she wasn't patient enough to test that hypothesis.

She lowered her hips, pressing herself more fully against his erection.

He broke the kiss with a curse, but she had only a second to lament the loss of his hands on her body before he reached over his shoulder, grabbing a fistful of white cotton and tugging his T-shirt up and off, revealing acres of warm, golden skin.

"Aidan," she breathed, needing to say his name just to prove to herself that this was happening, that it wasn't a dream. Her fingers ached to touch him, to restore order to his shirt-mussed hair, to trace the dips and swells of his chest.

But there would be time for that later. First, she needed to get herself naked so she could feel him everywhere.

She cupped her breast with her left hand, the action immediately capturing Aidan's attention even before she tugged the skin taut with her thumb. He leaned back in the chair to watch, and his hips lifted, grinding against hers as she wedged her fingernail beneath the edge of the pasty and peeled it from her skin.

She watched the rise and fall of his chest as she repeated the same steps with the other pasty.

He ran his calloused palms up her back, pulling her toward him, and Kaylee braced her hand on the chair as he captured her nipple with his mouth, nipping and sucking until she was writhing against him.

"Do you need these?" He hooked a thumb between her hip and her panties, tugging the lace away from her skin.

"What?"

"Are they important for your act?"

"Not really. I—"

He ripped one side with surprising adeptness, then the other.

"I'll buy you new ones," he promised darkly, tugging the ruined lace from beneath her and tossing it on the floor.

Aidan wrapped his arms around her and pulled her hips flush with his, and she gasped at the rough friction of his jeans against her clit.

Oh *gawd*. And she'd thought she'd been keyed up that night in the bar. This was a hundred times more potent, though, because this time when he looked at her, he wasn't seeing Lola.

Aidan stood up, taking her with him. She wrapped her legs around him and braced herself for the ride.

CHAPTER TWELVE

She was driving him fucking crazy.

He needed to get her up to his room so he could have her the way he wanted to, laid out like a feast on his bed. But she kept distracting him, slowing his progress toward the stairs.

Her hands were busy, reaching between them, unbuckling his belt, unbuttoning his jeans.

Then her eager fingers breached the elastic of his boxer briefs and came in contact with his pulsing cock. Almost stumbling with the mind-numbing pleasure of it, he shoved against the nearest pillar so he could pull himself together.

Both of them groaned at the increase in pressure.

"Here's good. Please. I need you inside me."

He wanted to relent, to sink into her over and over until the desire raging through him was sated. It took everything in him to shake his head, to still the mindless rocking of his hips. "No," he ground out, though if she didn't stop stroking his cock like that, they weren't going to make it to the bedroom like he'd intended.

He dragged a ragged breath into his lungs and pushed

her legs down from around his waist. When her feet touched the floor, he stilled her hand with his.

He braced his other palm on the pillar beside her head, trying to make his brain work, trying to make her understand before he fucked this up. Already her mouth had gone slack, and her muscles tensed, preparing to withdraw. He'd do anything to erase the hurt and confusion seeping into the dreamy, hazy lust of a moment before. "I missed out on you the first time, KJ. I'm not rushing this. Not again."

Her eyes widened, and swirling in their depths was relief and desire and something else he couldn't name that almost knocked him to his knees. And for the first time in the history of ever, a woman letting go of his cock got him even harder. He grabbed her hand, and once again the heat of anticipation built between them while he tugged her up the metal staircase that led to his bedroom. Only this time, he knew exactly who was behind him.

He needed to get his fucking jeans off so badly that she was almost running to keep up with him by the time they'd made it up the stairs and crossed the threshold to his bedroom. He toed his boots off, pushing jeans, underwear, and socks off in one move. Then he stood there, naked, torn between savoring the view of her crawling onto his bed and grabbing a condom from the end table.

Condom first.

He ripped the package open, stifling his groan at the contact and pressure as he rolled it on. He was so fucking hard for her, so desperate it hurt. And now she was on her knees on his bed and he wasn't sure he was going to be able to make it last like he wanted.

"Aidan?"

She bit her bottom lip as he joined her on the mattress, on his knees, stopping scant inches from her, not quite trusting himself to touch her and listen to her question at the same time. "Yeah?"

That mouth was going to be his downfall, no doubt about it. "We've got all night to do this as many ways as you want, so please put us both out of our misery and fuck me now. No one's ever literally ripped my panties off before, and I'm so hot for you I can't stand it. We can go slow next time."

His arm was around her waist before she finished talking, and he hauled her up against his body, the warm, wet heat of her aligned with his throbbing cock.

Her whimper undid him as she undulated her hips, working her clit up and down his erection, taking her pleasure as she wrapped her arms around him and her nails bit into his back. He wished to fuck he hadn't put the condom on yet because the sweet slide of her pussy along his length was so damn good and he didn't want to think he was missing even a fraction of it.

He buried his free hand in her hair and pulled her head to the side so he could lick her neck, mark her with his teeth.

"Come for me this way. Grinding on my cock."

She shook her head, even though her hips continued to rock. Her fingers dug into his skin. "I need you inside me."

"After," he insisted. "I want to watch you get yourself off first."

Kaylee gave in to his demand with a moan he felt under his skin. She sped her rhythm, and he lifted his hips to meet hers on each downward slide, increasing the force of the friction until she was biting her lip, clutching his shoulders.

Then she cried out and came apart for him, and it was frantic and messy and goddamn perfect.

"Jesus, KJ. I want to fuck you so bad," he growled, biting her bottom lip as she reached between them, grabbing his dick, positioning herself over him.

"Do it," she whispered, and then he was sliding home, and it was so much better than he remembered from the storage room. Hotter. Sweeter.

Time slowed, and what he'd expected to be a frenzied mating of mouths and tongues and bodies turned way more profound. He wanted to kiss her, but he couldn't stop staring at her, watching her.

Her face was so expressive, her desire so raw. He was on edge just bearing witness to her passion.

He laid her on the bed, her ankles hooked over his shoulders, and the sexy little catch in her breath increased his pace.

This should have felt wrong, but it didn't. It felt so fucking right that he thought his heart might pound all the way out of his chest. She was gorgeous, pink lips parted, dazed with pleasure, and he wished she wasn't wearing those damn blue contacts, because he didn't want any part of her hidden from him right now.

She reached up, put her palm on the back of his neck, fisted her hand in his hair.

Pleasure crackled over his skin like a gathering electrical storm, but something darker and more profound was building low in his gut, and the dual sensations drove his hips forward with more purpose. And still, with so much sensation set to break over him, he clamped his jaw tight. He wasn't going under without her, so he took his cues from her soft sighs of pleasure, the way her orthodontist-perfected teeth caught her bottom lip.

And then, despite the fake blue of her contacts, she met his gaze with a look so real, so full of wonderment as she gave in to the friction, her body tightening under his, clenching his cock. She was fucking beautiful, his KJ, and he tried to hold out, to still the rock of his hips, to let her have this moment all to herself, but then her orgasm hit full force, and the sound of his name on her lips as she came pulled him into the vortex with her, leaving him helpless to do anything but follow her into oblivion.

CHAPTER THIRTEEN

THERE WERE FEW things better than lying in bed next to a naked, drowsy woman.

"I don't even know what you do for a living. That's kind of weird, right?"

Check that. A naked, *curious* woman.

But her question made him pause.

It reminded him that despite knowing each other for so long, they were virtual strangers. In a lot of ways, he didn't know her at all, and that was a bit disconcerting.

"I invest in good ideas."

"Sorry, what?"

"People in the tech industry come to me when they have big ideas and no seed money. I help them fund their projects."

She pushed up on an elbow so she could look down at him. "*You're* an angel investor?"

"That so hard to believe?"

She glanced pointedly at him, and he watched her expressive eyes—God, he hated those fucking contacts—as she took stock of him.

"Let's see…rock-star hair, hard-muscled body, and

a devilishly wicked grin." She shook her head. "You don't look much like any investor I've ever seen. And the *angel* part seems highly unlikely," she teased, leaning over for a slow, deep kiss.

He'd barely recovered from his earlier orgasm, and still the taste of her lips and cleverness of her tongue stoked the need in his belly.

He shifted on the mattress, hooking a hand beneath his head to stare at her. Sated from good sex and with a gorgeous woman stoking his ego, he grinned with pure male satisfaction. "I consider both of those compliments."

Her lips curved in a smile that made him want to kiss her again. "That's how I meant them." Kaylee traced a finger along his chest. "So how did you get into that?"

"I like watching people innovate."

She nodded, and her dark hair whispered across the sensitized skin of his chest. "Because of your dad?"

"Yeah, I guess so. He was never happier than when he was building something, whether it was a computer or a string of code. That statue downstairs? The horses with the flaming manes? He built his own 3-D printer and made that out of a drawing I did in high school."

"That's amazing. Max always spoke very highly of your dad."

Aidan nodded. Max and John Beckett had always shared a connection. They both loved to take things apart, figure out how they worked. Aidan had learned a long time ago that it didn't much matter how things worked, as long as they did. He'd stopped looking too closely at things after his mother's diagnosis. Knowing the particulars didn't change the outcome.

"Yeah. He was a good guy, my dad." Aidan ignored the guilt that accompanied thoughts of his father. Especially here, where his legacy loomed large. He forced his muscles to relax when Kaylee shot him a questioning glance. "Mostly," he added. That made his earlier statement less of a lie, he decided. Five years after his father's death and covering for the man was still like breathing to Aidan.

"Hey, you okay?"

The concern on her face humbled him. Apparently, he'd lost some of his skills at hiding his true feelings. "I'm good. It's my first time back here since he died. I thought the renos would make it feel different. But my old man's still here."

Kaylee glanced around the room. "What is this place?"

"It was my dad's first workshop. It was just a garage back then. Full of ripped-apart computers. He used to let me come hang out here when I was little. Before my mom got sick."

She angled her head on his shoulder so she could look at him, ran her palm soothingly along the planes of his chest.

He skated his fingers down the length of her arm, pulling her closer.

"After she got sick, this is where he came to drink."

Her hand stilled. "What was she like?"

Shit.

Things were too fucking deep for this soon after an orgasm.

"She was a cardiothoracic surgeon."

"Wow."

"Yeah. Pretty cool job. But it meant she wasn't home much. My dad and I spent a lot of time together. And I guess things were relatively normal. Until she was diagnosed when I was twelve. She was dead before my thirteenth birthday. By the time I turned fourteen, my father was a full-blown alcoholic. He'd pretty much given up on everything by then."

Aidan shoved down the bitterness that still surfaced whenever he remembered taking care of his father as though they'd undergone some sort of role reversal during their grief.

"My mom's dying wish was that no matter what, I got the best education, and she made me and my dad promise the money she left us would fund my education. And he did his best to make that happen, enrolled me in the fanciest school he could find."

And still, here he was, naked and spilling his guts.

She smiled at that, and Aidan was glad he was masking the underlying anger in the memory. Finding out that, between booze and gambling, his dad had blown through a lot of the education fund his mother had set up for him.

"I didn't bring anyone here, because my dad was hitting the bottle pretty hard back then. But Max wanted to see the place, so we snuck in once when I thought my dad was at work, and he and your brother really hit it off, geeking out on tech stuff. After that we came here a lot."

"You didn't geek out with them?"

"I didn't feel left out, if that's what you mean. Truth was, I liked the time we spent at your place better. I thought Max had it all. Fancy house, two parents, annoying little sister."

She gave him a playful swat.

"Enough money that he didn't have to worry about anything. I wanted what he had. I wanted to be like him. Your dad was this formidable guy who seemed so in charge of everything. I admired that."

"Yeah, well. Appearances can be deceiving."

He ran his fingers along the back of the hand she'd splayed on his chest, tracing the delicate ridge of her knuckles.

"They can. And I learned that lesson well enough. But at the time, my father was in a downward spiral. He lost his job because of the drinking and the gambling. Between that and the medical bills, we didn't have as much money left over as he'd hoped. I did my best to take care of him. And then your dad gave him a job. We used what was left of my mom's money to send him to rehab, and he managed to help me pay for college. He really got his life together. For a while, things were good."

She'd still been away at university at the time, but she knew about the accident that had ended his father's life, of course. "And then they weren't."

He nodded at the assessment, appreciating her tact. "I wish I'd...been around more. There are a lot of things I wish I'd told him."

"I'm sure he knew," she assured him, obviously assuming he meant heartwarming things, like how much he loved and respected John Beckett. Aidan didn't bother to correct her. He preferred to keep his anger and resentment toward his father, toward the choices he'd made, buried as deeply as possible.

"I wish I could have met him."

God, she was sweet. "He would have liked you."

"How do you know?"

"Because I like you."

The compliment earned him a lazy kiss that didn't last nearly long enough.

"Anyway, long story short I fixed this place up after he died, turned it into a living space so I'd have a place to stay when I'm in town."

"But you're not in town much anymore?" she asked, and he didn't like where the question was taking them. Because this was leading into a question about Max. And him. And he didn't want to fuck up this thing he and Kaylee had going by getting into nitty-gritty details. Time for a subject change.

He picked up her hand, kissed her fingers.

"Your turn to spill. Last time I saw you, you were a ballerina. What changed?"

Kaylee shook her head. "I was never a ballerina, much to Sylvia's dismay. But when I was in college, a group of friends dragged me to this burlesque workshop one weekend and I was enamored."

There was a spark in her when she talked about it, Aidan noticed, still tracing a finger across her knuckles.

"It makes me feel in control of things. I pick the music, I pick the costume. It's a way to be creative and a way to direct people's attention however I want to. I can seduce them, tease them."

"Sounds a lot like PR."

She laughed at the observation. "I never really thought of it like that, but I guess it is." She shrugged, propping her head up with her hand, and stared down at him. "It makes me feel sexy. I like having secrets. I always have. Knowing I'm doing something I shouldn't be, something my mother would disapprove of, is a turn-on."

An angel trying her hand at rebellion. It kind of worked for her. It definitely worked for him.

"Oh yeah?"

She nodded.

"Well, I know for a fact that your mom would hate it if you kissed me right now."

Something sultry sparked at the implied dare, and she leaned down and pressed her mouth to his. Her nipples were tight beads when they pressed into his chest, and his body reacted to the stimulus with gut-clenching speed.

"And she'd really hate it if you put your hands on me."

Her smile was dangerous to his equilibrium. "You think?"

Aidan nodded, stifling a groan as she tugged her fingers free of his and slid them across his chest. She teased his nipple before retreating so she could trace his sternum, down to his abs, lower, until they flirted with the Egyptian cotton that bisected his hips and did little to hide the effect she was having on him.

"What would she think if I did this?" she asked, shoving her hand under the sheet and palming the growing length of him. Her fingers were driving him crazy, and Aidan squeezed his eyes shut at the pleasure.

"Stern disapproval," he ground out, even as she circled her thumb over the head of his cock. "No doubt about it." God, he was desperate for her again. Just like that.

"Well, if she's going to disapprove anyway, we might as well give her something to disapprove of," she purred as she slid down his body, and Aidan half swore, half laughed as she bypassed further teasing and swallowed him deep.

It was soul destroying to have her mouth on him like this and the pain-edged pleasure of it built fast and hard. She alternated between licking and sucking until sensation turned sharp, undeniable, and he couldn't keep his hips still.

"Jesus, Kaylee." He reached down. Fisted his hand in her hair. To what end, he didn't know. "You're gonna make me come."

She obviously took his words as a challenge, and Aidan groaned as she massaged his balls and sped the bob of her head.

"I can't… You need to stop or I…"

He fucking lost it under the onslaught, his hips jerking as his climax pounded through him.

CHAPTER FOURTEEN

Kaylee stretched languorously, a slight smile curving her lips as the scent of coffee and the sounds of someone moving around in the kitchen woke her from sleep.

Someone wickedly sexy who'd kept her up all night driving her body to the edge of pleasure and beyond.

It had been the most incredible sex of her life, and she allowed herself a moment to savor her sore muscles and the erotic memories of the man who'd made them that way before she finally pushed off the covers and swung her legs over the side of Aidan's bed.

Cool air rushed across her bare skin. The bag containing the change of clothes she always took with her to the club was downstairs, abandoned at some point between the thrilling motorcycle ride that had brought her here and the halcyon glow of lust and need that had blurred last night into this morning.

Her corset and pasties and the underwear he'd ripped off her—her stomach clenched at the delicious memory—were downstairs, too.

Left with no other option, Kaylee grabbed the gray T-shirt draped over the arm of the chair in the corner of the room and pulled it over her head. It smelled like Aidan, and she inhaled deeply as she padded across the floor. In the upstairs bathroom, she took a moment to smooth her sleep-tousled hair and remove her disposable colored contacts before staring at herself in the mirror.

Some tiny part of her, the part that had written Kaylee Beckett in various notebooks, was expecting to see a different person in the reflection. But she was still her, Kaylee Jayne Whitfield. Perhaps her smile held a sensual smugness now, but overall, nothing had changed, and she was relieved to see it. Because that meant there was nothing magical about what had happened last night. That girlish dreams and womanly desires could collide in several earth-shaking orgasms without requiring overanalyzing or second-guessing.

She'd had a sexy secret liaison with a wild, handsome man, and now life could go back to normal.

Kaylee headed back into the bedroom and caught sight of the clock next to the bed. She was due at the country club for her weekly brunch with her mother in an hour and a half, and she still had to get back to her car and then home to change. Apparently life would be going back to normal more quickly than she'd hoped.

She hurried down the metal stairs.

Clad in nothing but low-slung jeans, Aidan Beckett was a sight to behold. Add the fact that he was holding a mug of coffee in her direction, and she'd never seen a more perfect sight in her life. Kaylee accepted it gratefully, indulging in a sip of caffeinated heaven. She couldn't help a little moan of contentment.

"This coffee is everything."

"You think that's good, you should try my world-famous omelet. You want one egg or two?"

Kaylee shook her head, taking a gulp of incredible java before setting her mug on the counter. "None. I can't stay." She stole a raspberry from the bowl to his right and popped it in her mouth.

Her answer made him frown. "What's the rush?" He grabbed her hand and tugged her between his body and the edge of the counter, pinning her there with his hips.

"I have to go change before I meet my mother for brunch," Kaylee told him, but despite her words, her hands migrated up his bare chest to twine around his neck. Her fingers toyed with the ends of his hair.

"Why? You look great."

Kaylee glanced down at herself and laughed. Her mother would go apoplectic if she showed up at the club wearing anything as plebeian as a T-shirt, let alone *just* a T-shirt. "Sylvia Whitfield, though she has not yet seen me, disagrees vehemently with your assessment."

"I love it when you use big words." He grabbed her hips and hoisted her up onto the granite countertop, stepping between her legs.

"Oh yeah?"

He nodded, running his hands up her torso. "Apparently women with extensive vocabularies really turn me on."

Kaylee gave a playful moue, injecting a little Marilyn Monroe into her voice. *"Dodecahedron."*

Aidan shot her that sexy smirk of his, lifting his eyebrows. "Mmm. That's the stuff," he teased, leaning forward and burying his face in her neck. Her head lolled back, granting him unfettered access, and her exhalation was shaky as he dragged his lips along the underside of her jaw.

"Sesquipedalian," she whispered.

"Yes, baby. Just like that."

She wanted to laugh, but the hot swipe of his tongue over her thudding pulse undid her, and despite the ticking clock of her looming brunch, Kaylee's arms tightened around his neck, pulling him closer.

"Antidisestablishmentarianism."

Aidan groaned as he finally gave her his mouth, and she sighed at the perfection of the endless, drugging kiss. Soft but with an edge of desperation, one that begged her to stay and see what happened next.

It took everything Kaylee had to pull back. "Hold that thought, for now I must embark on my peregrination." She planted a final kiss on his lips, one that lasted several beats longer than she meant it to, and hopped down from the counter.

"Mean," he chastised, and Kaylee giggled when Aidan's big palm landed on her ass with a loud smack.

How he could be so sexy and so fun at the same time was a mystery to her. She realized suddenly that he'd always been a bright spot in her life. Max never teased her or commiserated with her. Her mother made the things she loved, like dance and music, feel like a heavily regimented burden. Her father casually doled out scraps of attention between bouts of ignoring her completely.

But Aidan had always made time for a quick greeting to let her know she wasn't invisible. Whether it was a teasing wink, a sympathizing eye roll, or a story to distract her, he always seemed to know just how bring a smile to her face. It was one of the reasons she'd looked forward to his visits, hormones aside.

"Hey, you want backup?"

The softly worded offer snapped Kaylee's spine straight, and she turned to find him leaning a hip against the counter, his arms crossed over his beautiful bronze chest. She searched his face for some sign that he was still kidding around.

His gaze was steady. Scrupulous. Serious.

Something quaked through her body, but unlike a few moments earlier, this wasn't lust; it was fear. She tried to imagine her and Aidan arriving at the country club on his bike. Him sitting across from her mother in his jeans and T-shirt, looking defiant and bored and so sexy it made it hard to breathe.

The Dragon Lady wouldn't care that his bank account could back up his membership. That he'd grown from a troubled boy to a self-assured man. All she cared about were the optics. She'd be eating with the son of a former Whitfield Industries employee, one who'd never had fancy letters behind his name, like CFO or even VP. It was why she'd barely tolerated Max and Aidan's friendship back in the day. And why she would ruin Kaylee and Aidan's relationship now.

No. Not a relationship. Sex. A tryst. He wasn't her boyfriend.

"What? That's not… You don't have to do that." Her voice was strained. Everything in her rebelled at the idea. "You don't want to have brunch with my mom."

"That—" Aidan looked like he was going to deny it for a second, but sanity prevailed "—is true."

Kaylee's laugh lodged in her throat when he added, "But I want to have brunch with you."

The words made her ribs feel too tight for her lungs, for the hard beat of her heart—prison bars for the emotion trying to push out of her chest.

What the hell was he doing?

They'd just shared a perfect night, made even more incredible by not having to pretend to be Lola this time. And it was everything she'd hoped it would be. Why did he want to ruin their clandestine affair by taking it public?

She smiled, hoping it looked more natural than it felt. "Then let's do that sometime when we don't have a chaperone."

"Yeah. Okay." He nodded, but the air felt infinitesimally colder. "Some other time."

Despite Aidan's agreement, there was a tightness to his jaw and a stiffness to his shoulders as he turned away from her that made her doubt his sincerity. That he wanted to come with her made her anxious. That he was angry she wasn't going to let him made her wary.

"Aidan…"

"I get it. You don't want her to know."

"It's not that."

"Then what's the problem?" he asked, turning to face her.

Kaylee exhaled, trying to find the words to explain the phenomenon that had been leeching her joy since childhood. The reason she wasn't ready to share him yet. Not with the world at large and most especially not with her mother.

"My family ruins everything I care about. They pick it apart and judge it and tell me the reason that what I want is fanciful or silly or impractical. And I don't want… I'm not ready to have them dissect whatever it is that we're doing. I don't want their opinions on us. I just want it to be you and me for as long as this lasts. I just want it to be ours."

It wasn't the answer he was expecting.

Aidan refused to acknowledge that his earlier annoyance had loosened its grip on his chest. He should be irritated that she wanted to sneak around like goddamn teenagers. He was too old for games. So was she, for that matter. But he'd always been a sucker for KJ. He couldn't remember a time when he didn't care about her, when there was nothing he wouldn't do to put the sparkle back in those pretty hazel eyes.

"So don't go." Seemed simple enough to him.

Her whole body deflated on a sigh. "I have to."

"Why?"

Kaylee looked genuinely stymied for a minute, like she'd never considered the question. He could see the unguarded flash of possibility that sparked before she tamped it down and smothered it. "Because my mother and I always brunch on Saturdays. And today is the first day she's going back to the club since my dad…since what happened."

Aidan kept his face neutral, pushing down the satisfaction he got from imagining Charles Whitfield wearing an ankle monitor.

"Rebel a little." He walked forward until their bodies collided, until she rolled her eyes at him and a tiny smile curved her lips as he backed her into the edge of his dining room table—one of his father's stainless-steel workbenches that he'd had cut down and converted during the renovation.

"It'll do you good."

Before she could protest, he picked her up and set her on the cool metal.

"You just want to get laid," she teased. "And for the record, I'm excellent at rebelling. I've been doing it since I came out of the womb."

He reached down and fisted his hands in the hem of the soft gray material that covered her body. "Name one rebellious thing you've done in your entire life," he challenged.

"My tattoo." Her answer was muffled behind fabric as he dragged his T-shirt up and off her. And there she was, she and her attempt at rebellion, bared to his gaze.

A tiny butterfly that had caused a tsunami in his life.

Chaos theory made manifest. An unexpected series of events that had started the first night he'd seen her and led them to this moment.

Kaylee was perched naked on the edge of his table, looking like his fantasies, dark hair spilling over her shoulders and flirting with the tops of gorgeous breasts that were full and high and begging for his mouth.

He wanted to look at her, but he needed to touch her more. Aidan reached out and dragged his fingers across the tiny winged tattoo, reveling in the rash of goose bumps that flooded her skin in the wake of his touch.

She closed her eyes and bit her lip and his whole body throbbed with need.

"When'd you get it?"

Her eyelashes fluttered open, revealing an intricate pattern of brown and gold and green that eclipsed the flashier fake blue contacts—less showy, maybe, but more interesting, more captivating. He could get lost in those eyes.

"On my sixteenth birthday. Right after my mom said she thought tattoos on women were vulgar. She still doesn't know I have it."

Her voice was soft. Low. Laced with sex. He could feel it in his balls.

He placed a hand on either side of her jaw and buried his fingers in her hair as he angled her face up. "You're not a rebel." Aidan leaned forward and caught her bottom lip between his teeth. The sharp intake of her breath tightened his body. "Rebelling is about doing what you want to do and not giving a damn about the consequences. You're just good at keeping secrets," he challenged against her lips. "It's not the same thing."

He captured her protest with his mouth, kissing her deep and wet until she kissed him back. Until her body went pliant. Until she pushed her breasts forward in search of contact and sighed into his mouth.

Then he pulled his hands from her hair. Stepped back from her. It was the hardest fucking thing he'd ever done. His body clamored in protest, and her look of wounded confusion made it worse.

"Why a butterfly?" he asked, fisting his hands, resisting the temptation to move forward, to drag her against him and forget everything but how good it felt to be buried inside her as she clung to him and whispered sexy words against his skin. Because he had something to say, and if he gave in to impulsive lust, he might never get it out.

CHAPTER FIFTEEN

Kaylee didn't want to talk about her tattoo anymore.

Or be told she wasn't a rebel.

She didn't know why the hell the topic was so important to Aidan, either. The sizeable bulge in his jeans let her know that she wasn't the only one interested in putting his dining room table to X-rated use. Still, something reared up inside her, demanding she defend herself.

"Because my childhood felt like a prison, schedules and straight lines. And I wanted to remind myself that one day I would fly wherever I wanted to. I'd break out of that chrysalis and take to the skies. Live the life I always wanted. Do my own thing. This butterfly is why my stage name is Mariposa. This butterfly reminds me who I want to be."

Aidan nodded like he was absorbing that. "You ever heard the story about how they tether elephants?"

Kaylee frowned at the non sequitur.

"They put a post in the ground when the elephant is little, and they chain her to it. And no matter how much she pulls, she can't get free."

Kaylee shivered as an eerie dread flooded her skin. She didn't like this story.

"But then the elephant grows up, and pretty soon she's strong enough that she could pull that post right out of the ground with one good yank. Thing is, by that point she's used to her boundaries. She doesn't realize that it's not the chain holding her where she is. It's that she doesn't even try to escape anymore."

Everything in Kaylee went still. Got small. It was hard to swallow. "What are you trying to say?" she asked, her voice tight.

"I'm saying maybe you're not a butterfly. Maybe you're an elephant."

Aidan's words were matter-of-fact, with no particular emphasis, but they punctured like broken glass, jagged and misshapen, leaving her chest raw and gaping. She was already naked, but he'd just stripped her bare.

"Fuck you, Aidan." She made a move to shove herself off the table, but he was there caging her in, his palms flat against the table beside her hips.

"You say you're sick of your family taking advantage of you, of giving everything and getting nothing back." There was heat in his voice now. "So don't let them. Don't go for brunch with her. Spend the day with me instead."

"Why? Because you're horny and you want to christen your dining room table?" she spat, using her anger as a shield to keep his words from piercing her skin.

With a curse, he stepped back and ran a hand through his hair with obvious frustration. "Because she doesn't own you, KJ. Because she makes you miserable and you don't owe her anything."

"She's my mother."

"So?"

Why was he being such a dick?

"You know what? I don't have time for this right now. I have to see if I can catch an Uber to the club and I'm going to be late as it is." She twisted around to grab his T-shirt from the table.

"Don't fucking move." The words were hot, ringing out like a gunshot.

Kaylee froze. She hated that her body betrayed her, obeying without her brain's consent. Hated that his imperious tone sent a thrill through her, that it made her wet.

Her chin notched up as she turned back to him, her nakedness forgotten in the flash of rage. "Who the hell do you think you are? You don't get to tell me what to do."

He'd seemed furious a second ago, but it wasn't that now. Something shifted in his expression and she blinked at the dark, dangerous energy that crackled between them. No, not anger. Not exactly. Her body buzzed with it like she'd just been granted superpowers from a downed electrical wire. Like there was lightning in her veins.

His breathing turned harsh. Too fast. Hypnotic. Her palms itched to feel the rise and fall of it, to feel the heat of his skin and the hard muscle beneath. He stood close, but not close enough. She could probably skate her fingertips along his abs if she leaned forward, reached for him.

She didn't.

There was something feral about the sudden tilt of his lips, and she had the odd feeling that she'd somehow impressed him. That he was proud of her for yelling back. Warmth spread through her limbs.

"What do you want?"

"What?" The rapid shifts in conversation had her a little off balance.

"Tell me what you want."

She wanted to slap his face. She wanted to pull him close.

"I want to make you feel good."

"One wish and you want to use it to give me an orgasm?" Aidan shook his head. "Forget about me. What do *you* want?"

"I want you inside me." She spread her knees apart. Liked that his gaze dipped between her legs. Desire ratcheted higher and her fingers tightened on the edge of the table.

"Why?"

"I don't understand what you're asking."

He stepped closer. "It's not deep. It's not a mystery. You know exactly what your body is craving right now. Why your muscles are quivering and you're breathing harder. All you need to do is admit it, and I'll make it happen for you."

Jesus. Her breasts were heavy with want, her nipples so tight it almost hurt.

"You want me to make you come, KJ?"

Yes. All the yes. The answer shuddered through her, loosening her limbs, sparking a heat in her belly. She managed a nod.

"Then fucking say that. Own it."

She was so wet. So desperate that her inner muscles clenched, and she whimpered at the pressure. "I want to come."

"How?"

The question invaded her blood.

"I want your mouth on me."

He invaded her space, placing his hands on the table on either side of her hips. Leaned in close. He smelled warm and primal, like the promise of sex.

"Here?" He brushed his lips over hers.

She shook her head.

"Here?" He dragged his mouth across her cleavage and her head tipped back at the delicious sensation.

"Lower."

"Tell me what you want," he challenged again, lowering her onto the table. She shivered as the cool steel pressed into the hot skin of her back.

"Lick me."

He ran his tongue along the crease of her hip and she shifted restlessly. Unsatisfied. He was so close to where she needed him. She moved her hips, but he just chuckled and dragged his tongue a little farther from the mark.

Frustration made her bold.

"Lick my pussy." She'd never said the word before. Not aloud. But it felt a little bit shocking on her tongue, risqué for her, one step past her comfort zone. And she found it exhilarating. Especially when Aidan swore under his breath and pushed her back against the table.

"Don't ask me," he growled. "Make me."

She fisted her hand in his hair and pushed him right where she needed him. The first brush of his mouth made her hips buck.

Her mind went blank with pleasure, and it took her several moments to realize that whenever she quit directing the action, the action quit.

"Don't you dare stop now."

He chuckled as she tightened her fingers in his hair. Her breath came sawed from her lungs as he worked her over with lips and tongue, responding perfectly to her hand on his head. It was a revelation, being in charge of her own pleasure, taking what she wanted. What she needed.

Having Aidan's head between her legs was almost too much, and the need inside her spiraled out of control in record time.

The sharp catch of her orgasm tugged her under, and her back arched off the table as she drowned in the waves of pleasure racking her body.

The satisfied grin that tilted Aidan's sinful mouth made her feel wanted and wanton and a little bit wicked.

"That was…" She didn't really know how to finish the thought as she reached behind her to grab the T-shirt.

"It definitely was," he agreed.

God, he was beautiful. Broad shouldered and slim hipped, his arms corded with muscle.

Kaylee hopped off the table. She dropped her gaze

to the substantial bulge in the front of his jeans. Her hands fisted, balling the material of the shirt.

"Looks like it's my turn to ask you what you want," she teased, cocking an eyebrow. He shook his head, surprising her.

"I'm good. That was about you."

She frowned. "Are you sure? Because—"

"You need to be selfish sometimes. That's what being a rebel is all about. Saying what you want. Taking what you want. You know?"

She didn't. Not really. The idea detonated in her brain, leaving her confused, disoriented by how bright and loud it was.

"Be the motherfucking butterfly."

Sage. Profane. Simple. The advice was so perfectly Aidan.

To Kaylee, life was complicated. Intricate. Like making her way through a minefield of people's expectations and feelings and desires. She'd spent her whole life navigating that way, trying to keep the peace, to live up to expectations, to not bother anyone, to earn her place.

Aidan made everything seem so easy. He'd offered to come with her. And then he'd told her not to go. Two choices. Black or white. Nothing gray. No elephants.

All she had to do was pick one.

Her bag was on the couch, where she'd left it the night before. With a gut full of trepidation, she walked over and dug her phone out from beneath her change of clothes. Her fingers shook as she swiped through to her mother's contact information and connected the call.

Sylvia Whitfield picked up on the first ring. "Traffic's a mess. You should probably avoid taking the—"

"I'm not coming, Mom."

Eerie silence, the kind that warned of an impending jump scare in a horror movie, made Kaylee's hand tighten on the phone.

"Pardon me?" Her mother's voice was terrifyingly calm. Never a good sign.

"Something came up."

"Something randomly came up? At the exact same time as our standing weekly brunch?"

Kaylee winced under the censure, but her gaze snagged on Aidan's, and just like that hug he'd given her when she was seventeen and heading off to Oxford, she found strength there that she could borrow. She took a deep breath.

"Are you bleeding, Kaylee Jayne? Is it some sort of emergency? Because a lady doesn't cancel plans without adequate notice unless—"

"There's no emergency. I'm not coming because I don't want to." Finally saying the words aloud was like standing at the edge of a cliff. Terrifying and exhilarating. To be honest. To tell her mother the truth.

"Kaylee, if you do not show up for—"

Static surged over the line and then there was no sound. "Mom?"

Kaylee pulled the phone from her ear, checking the screen. The call time was still ticking away steadily, so she tried again. "Mom? Are you there? Can you hear me?"

There was no response. With a sigh, Kaylee disconnected. For a brand-new phone it sure glitched a lot. "Great. Now she's going to think I hung up on her."

"That's probably the least of your worries after that performance. You did good."

"You won't think so when it starts raining fire and the locusts show up."

His grin made her heart stutter. "C'mere."

He pulled her against his chest and she tucked in, listening to his heartbeat. "I'm proud of you."

Tears formed at the foreign words, at the realization no one had ever said that to her before, but she willed them away. Today was her emancipation, and she wasn't going to spend it crying. "Talk is cheap, Beckett." She leaned back in his arms. "I'm gonna need you to back it up with action."

He lifted his brows. "Name it. Your wish is my command."

"Good. Because I like my omelets made with two eggs."

CHAPTER SIXTEEN

"So? What do you think?"

Kaylee pulled off her motorcycle helmet and stood beside Aidan on the cracked pavement. "When you said you wanted to spend the day together, I definitely wasn't expecting *this*." She cocked her head contemplatively. "It's nice, as far as abandoned buildings go."

Aidan rolled his eyes and grabbed her hand, pulling her with him toward the door. Even now, the thrill of his touch made her skin prickle. She wondered idly if it would ever go away, the jolt of his presence, the way every cell in her body vibrated when he was near.

Aidan let go of her hand and passed her his helmet so he could unlock the door, and then she found herself inside a high-ceilinged industrial space. It still had the faint smell of fresh paint and old sweat. And the front reception area was obviously next on the list for renos, as the walls were stripped bare and there were patches of plaster where repairs were being made.

Aidan relieved her of the helmets, setting them on the counter to the left before ushering her farther inside. "Welcome to Sal's."

Two boxing rings, a gauntlet of heavy bags, an assortment of speed bags, and a bunch of other specialized equipment that Kaylee couldn't identify filled the massive space.

"And Sal doesn't mind us being here?" she asked, meandering toward a wall that had obviously not undergone any recent painting. It was full of names and dates scrawled in black marker, some dating back to the '70s.

"He doesn't have much say considering I own the place."

The announcement pulled Kaylee's attention from the signatures.

"Sal's retiring, so I partnered up with his son to keep it open. Just doing a little cosmetic stuff before it reopens next month. This is where I learned to box."

There was a note of pride in Aidan's voice, a boyish excitement, as he surveyed the wall. "Here, look."

He pointed at one of the lower signatures, and Kaylee did a double take at the boyish printing that read Aidan Beckett.

"Everyone gets to sign when they win their first bout in the ring." He rubbed his finger almost reverently across the date beside his name. Kaylee did some quick math.

"You had your first boxing match when you were twelve?"

Aidan laughed as he walked along the wall. "No. I *won* my first boxing match when I was twelve. After my mom got sick, I developed a bit of an attitude. It was...highly recommended that I find healthier ways to channel my aggression. Sal kind of took me in. I learned a lot from him."

Aidan tapped on the wall. "Check this out."

Kaylee walked over to join him. The sight of her brother's name in his bold, slanting scrawl took her aback. The date beside his name made him fifteen when he'd signed.

"This is the year we met," Aidan told her, making his way toward the closest speed bag.

"At Harvard-Westlake?" Kaylee prodded, naming their high school in a desperate attempt to keep Aidan reminiscing. She'd never actually heard their origin story.

Aidan nodded as he lifted his elbows and sent the speed bag dancing beneath his steadily rolling fists. The rhythmic thwapping echoed through the cavernous space. "I punched a guy for calling me a scholarship kid, and then Max had my back later when a bunch of actual scholarship kids tried to jump me. Which, for the record, I probably deserved. But Max and I held our own against the four of them, and they left me alone after that."

Aidan gave the bag a final punch and turned to face her.

"I remember that day! Max came home with his face all messed up, and my mother was beside herself yelling at him because she was hosting a party that night. 'Do you want the neighbors to think I've raised a common street thug?'"

Aidan grinned at her impression of her mother. Kaylee had to admit, it *was* pretty good.

"He was banned from making an appearance that night. I remember being kind of jealous about that. That was because of you?"

Aidan nodded slowly. "Friendship forged in blood and split knuckles. Max and I used to spend a lot of time here."

"You did?" There was so much she didn't know.

"Max never told you any of this?"

She shook her head. "Max and I aren't close. Not like the two of you were." There was a sadness to her voice, Kaylee realized. One that Aidan had obviously recognized, because when he spoke again, there was a cajoling tone in his voice that she recognized from their past and his youthful attempts to cheer her up.

"All right, KJ. No more talking. Let's get you in the ring and see what you're made of."

"You're never going to make the wall if you keep hitting like that."

She laughed at the smack talk. Aidan liked the way she crinkled her nose before she punched.

"I'm trying. This is harder than I thought."

"Remember, elbows in and hands up."

The stubborn set of her chin when she concentrated reminded him of Max. She reset into the stance he'd taught her earlier.

Aidan slapped the focus pads together with a loud *thwap* and held his hands up as targets. She landed three decent jabs and one really good one. "There you go! Now you're on a roll. Try that again."

His phone buzzed in his back pocket and he dropped

his guard, intending to answer it. Kaylee punched him in the shoulder with a pretty respectable shot. "Whoa. Easy there, Fists of Fury."

Her gloved hands flew to her mouth, eyes wide with horror. "You moved your hand! I'm so sorry."

Aidan grinned as he pulled off the focus pads and tossed them onto the stool in the corner of the ring. "I'll live," he assured her, extricating his phone.

His easy dismissal stoked her competitive streak. "Well, sure, but you might have a bruise, right? That was a solid punch."

"Bloodthirsty," he admonished, but he was still chuckling at Kaylee when he answered the call. "Hello?"

"Just got the results back from the coding analysis. You said you wanted to know right away."

The words stiffened Aidan's shoulders. He nonchalantly angled his body away from his boxing protégée and lowered his voice. "And?"

"Coding bingo, just like you thought. The Whitfield and Cybercore products are both built on the original sample you provided."

His dad's work. Aidan let the news sink in. He had all the proof he needed to ruin Whitfield Industries. To gain control of the patent for code he could put in the hands of Endeavor Tech, the start-up he'd just backed, to give them a foothold in a tough market—one he truly believed they could dominate if given the chance.

"Say the word and I'll turn the results over to the lawyers."

Aidan glanced over his shoulder at Kaylee. Ever the vigilant student, she was shadowboxing, practicing the combination he'd taught her. "You know what? Hold off on that."

"Sorry?"

"I want to look it over before we take the next step."

"Uh, okay. Whatever you say, sir."

Aidan disconnected the call and shoved his phone back in his pocket. "Sorry. Business," he said vaguely as Kaylee bounced over to him in an exaggerated impression of a boxer.

"Sounds like a convenient excuse from a man who knows he's about to have his ass handed to him," she taunted, raising her gloves. "Jab, jab, hook."

She named the punches as she threw them, and Aidan couldn't help his smile as he raised his bare hands to block.

"I've got you on the ropes now," she jeered when he took a step back. "What are you gonna do?"

God, she was gorgeous. Flushed with laughter and exercise, her dark ponytail swinging, Aidan wanted her more than his next breath.

"That's easy," he said, and in a lightning-quick move he'd reversed their positions, caging her in with her back to the ropes. He captured her gasp of surprise with his mouth, kissing her deep and hard, the same way he wanted to fuck her. Only when she moaned under the onslaught did he let up and break their kiss. "First I'm going to overpower you, and then I'm going to distract you."

Kaylee swallowed as he stepped closer so their chests touched. "I think it's working."

He grabbed the hem of her T-shirt, and she raised

her arms so he could pull it off. The sleeves got stuck on her boxing gloves, but it was nothing an impatient tug couldn't fix, and then she was free, despite the protest from the stitching.

He'd buy her a new one later.

The rest of her clothes came off without the slightest objection, and his followed suit.

"Hold on to the top rope," he ordered as he sheathed himself with a condom from his wallet. Kaylee obligingly spread her arms along the top rope and hooked the gloves around it.

Fuck.

Aidan stroked himself at the sight of her, spread out before him wearing nothing but boxing gloves. His blood thundered in his veins as he stepped toward her, so close that his cock rested against her stomach, and her nipples grazed his chest.

Her tongue darted out to moisten her lips and his hips gave an involuntary jerk at the visual stimulus.

"You make my knees weak," Kaylee said softly, and the romantic words, so out of place in the middle of a boxing gym, made him want to claim her more. He pushed down on the white rope, second from the top, and hooked it under the sweet curve of her ass. Kaylee's eyes flew wide as he used the recoil of it to lift her up. Her legs wrapped around his hips instinctually, an attempt to steady herself that aligned their bodies in a way that made his hips jerk again.

Aidan gave her a second to catch her breath and adjust her grip on the top rope. Once she'd stabilized herself, he reached between them, guided his cock inside her, getting off on her dreamy look and the way she bit her lip as her body opened to take his length. She felt so goddamn perfect stretched around him.

"Better hold on tight," he warned before grasping the rope on either side of her hips and giving it a quick bounce.

Their bodies came together with a force that wrenched a startled cry from her lips, and Aidan worked them into a rhythm, pushing down on the rope before pulling her back to him, their bodies colliding again and again, until he couldn't see straight. He was so fucking turned on by her, the bounce of her breasts as she rode his cock, the sound of her pleasure as their bodies slammed together.

"I'm so close, Aidan. I'm going to come. Make me come."

He wasn't sure if it was his name on her lips or the dirty words that followed, but everything in him drew tight in preparation for her orgasm, and the second her body spasmed around him he abandoned his control and let the sparks racing through his veins ignite.

She dropped her forehead to his sweat-slicked shoulder, and he slid his hand under her ponytail, letting the soft strands tickle his knuckles as he processed the fact that she made his knees weak, too.

CHAPTER SEVENTEEN

KAYLEE HAD SPENT a dreamy weekend in Aidan's arms, wearing Aidan's T-shirts, and eating Aidan's food. The man really was a genius at omelets. And life advice.

This morning, she was going to implement it by walking into Max's office and unquitting.

As she rode the elevator to the top floor of Whitfield Industries, she felt like a new woman. And it wasn't because her muscles were deliciously sore or her smile was sensually satisfied. Well, it wasn't *just* that.

In a single weekend, she'd given voice to her sexual desires and erected a massive boundary with her mother, and for the first time in her life, she wasn't afraid to stand up for herself. To say exactly what she wanted. To claim some of the self-assurance she felt in her job and onstage and translate it into her personal life.

The delightful haze of secret sex and rebellious confidence dissipated the second the elevator doors slid open.

Max was back.

Kaylee could feel the difference in the building the second she stepped onto the floor.

The office was robust with purpose, as though her brother had brought with him a burst of diligence and sharpened focus that had been missing in his absence.

Not that she hadn't done a kick-ass job of handling things while he was gone, because she had. But Max *was* Whitfield Industries. The company in its current form was the result of his vision. And he'd put his blood, sweat, and tears into it. Figuratively, of course. Emotional robots like her older brother didn't lower themselves to such human weaknesses as feelings.

Ignoring her shaking hands and pounding pulse, she strode straight up to Sherri, Max's hyper-efficient executive assistant. "I need to see him."

"So does everyone. But unfortunately for all of you, the FBI has requested the honor of his and Emma's presence today to talk about the case against your father, so you're out of luck. At least until after four o'clock."

Kaylee wasn't sure if her exhale was one of relief or resignation. "I guess I'll check back later, then."

She wished it inspired more shock, the idea that her father had committed a felony, exploited Emma Mathison for information about SecurePay in return for financing hospice care for her dying mother. Sadly, it was far too easy to believe.

Kaylee had always liked Emma. Pleasant, professional, incredibly dedicated.

When the news of her father's indictment had broken, Kaylee remembered the one time she'd seen the two of them together. She'd been down in the lobby, where her father was supposed to meet her so they could go for lunch, and Emma and Charles had stepped out of the elevator together. Her father had looked so… predatory, but it was Emma who really stuck out in her mind. The woman's posture, her smile, her voice. Everything about her had been brittle. At the time, Kaylee had brushed it off, but in retrospect, it never ceased to haunt her.

"Did you need something else?" Sherri's voice startled Kaylee from her thoughts, and she shook her head.

The day sped by with a million fires to put out, so her ability to *check back later* didn't present itself until seven o'clock that evening.

Kaylee made a point of not knocking as she walked into his office. "Got a minute?"

The sky outside had gone dark, and Max had removed his suit jacket, rolled up his sleeves, loosened his tie. Despite the familiar tableau, Kaylee couldn't help but feel that something had shifted in him. He seemed different. And she wondered exactly what had happened while he'd been in Dubrovnik.

"Not really."

"Well, you need to make one."

Max lifted an eyebrow at her imperiousness, and with a deceptively casual flick of his wrist, his computer screen went dark. He gestured at the chair across from his desk before he leaned back in his own.

Waiting.

A frisson tingled up her spine.

Max was most terrifying when he was silent. Still.

Just say what you want. Be the butterfly.

She was surprised that it was Aidan's voice in her head, and not her mother's.

Kaylee lifted her chin as she strode toward him, pretending that her heart wasn't climbing up her throat.

Show no fear.

"Tomorrow will be two weeks since I quit."

"And?"

The bland question was enough to shake her out of the normal pattern of sit and wait she so often fell into with her brother. She remembered how he used to be, how they used to be together. And sometimes she found herself sitting quietly around him, hoping that one day he might just look over and see her again. Remember how it was when they were kids.

But he never did.

And she wasn't willing to wait for him anymore.

"And you haven't said a word about it."

"You didn't answer any of my texts or calls." His tone was sharp.

Kaylee allowed herself a moment of petty satisfaction. "I've been a little busy around here doing both our jobs. And while you were gone, I realized something. I'm really good at what I do. So I'm here to unquit. I want my job back."

Pride blazed along her nerve endings. She was triumphant and ready for a fight.

"Fine."

"I'm not taking no for an ans—fine? Fine?"

She should have been thrilled. Instead she was furious.

"That's all you have to say? Do you know how much

courage it took for me to walk in here and stand up to you?"

Max dragged a hand down his tie. "I ceded to your demand. Mission accomplished. What more do you want from me?"

"I want you to be a goddamn person instead of a robot for once in your life!"

She'd surprised him. And what shocked her even more was that he let her see it. He didn't temper his flinch at her outburst, the widening of his eyes.

Max's legendary poker face was gone, and years of bearing his cold distance had her ire up, now that she'd pierced his armor. Now that she could watch her barbs land.

"This isn't the time or the place for this discussion."

"That's exactly the problem! It's never the time or the place. You can't put me off because the timing's bad. Because guess what? The timing's always going to be bad. There's always something else that needs taking care of. That's why PR departments exist! And I know this SecurePay stuff is the most important thing in the world to you, but I'm your sister! I know you got stuck with me when Dad retired, but—"

"Fine. You want to have this out now?" Max reached forward, and with the press of a button hidden somewhere on the bottom of his desk the glass wall of his office frosted over. "Let's do it."

"You turned Dad in to the FBI and left the country. I've been dealing with the fallout and acting as the de facto Whitfield while you've been on vacation. Everything fell apart, and I got blindsided. And I quit just to make you see me. But you didn't. You just walked out."

Max stared at her, looking a little blindsided himself, but she didn't back down. She wouldn't let him off the hook this time. The six feet or so that separated them felt like an unbroachable chasm. And what hurt most was that he didn't even make a move to try.

"I don't understand you, Max. It's just so easy for you to cut people out of your life, to shut down. Even Dad. I mean, I know all this shit is bad, but he's our father. And you have to accept some responsibility for your crappy relationship because you never tried to fix it. You just…did nothing. Iced over. Like always."

She ignored the sudden sting of tears. He didn't deserve them anymore. She wasn't the little girl he'd cut out of his life. The one who cried herself to sleep. She was a woman. And Aidan was right. She was done letting her family have all of her just because she was too scared to stand up to them.

With as much dignity as she could muster, she stood but his voice stopped her before she took a step.

"Do you remember Arlo?"

Kaylee frowned at the unexpected question. "Our *dog*?" she asked, stressing the words so he knew what a stupid question it was. "The one who died, after which we never had another pet even though I spent the entirety of my adolescence begging for one? Yeah. I remember." Arlo's death was also the last time Max had hugged her. The beginning of the breach that stretched between them now.

"He didn't die."

"What?"

"Dad got rid of him to teach me a lesson."

Kaylee dropped back into the chair. "He was old. He died."

"He was five."

"But you told me…" Kaylee remembered Max's solemn face when he told her that Arlo had died, that she wouldn't see him again. The way she'd crawled into his arms and cried because her chest hurt so badly. She was eight, and she didn't remember a time without Arlo there. Max had been twelve at the time, and she'd thought he was so grown up. He wasn't crying. It had struck her as odd because Max had loved that dog with everything in him.

"I lied to you because I didn't want you to know what had happened. Mom was so hard on you, and I knew you were closer to Dad."

"I was close to you, Max. At least I used to be."

That muscle in his jaw ticked, and Kaylee hated him for his restraint just then. That icy facade that he used to keep her out.

"That's the last day you ever hugged me, do you know that? After that you were different. Distant. You stopped teasing me. You looked right through me."

"I was trying to keep you safe."

She scoffed. "From what? The emotional trauma of being an outcast in my own family? Because you failed, big brother."

"From Dad!"

The heat of his words flared like a volcano, and Kaylee flinched. She'd never seen Max's rage flare hot before. Cold reserve was his MO. But right now, he was here in the room with her. Fighting with her. Seeing her. And as pissed off as she was, it felt good to have this out with him.

"He got rid of the dog because he said it made me weak. I couldn't let him hurt you to get to me. I promised myself I wouldn't let him know that you were important to me."

A little pinprick of hope burned in her chest at the idea that Max cared about her, but she squashed it with brutal ruthlessness. Words were easy to throw out as placation. Action was what mattered. Aidan was right about that.

"Okay, this is getting way too 'poor little rich kid' for me. You were worried he'd send me away? Like, to boarding school in the Swiss Alps? Because I would have loved to be free of the Dragon Lady for ten months of the year. Of feeling so goddamn lonely in my own house that I used to cry myself to sleep."

"I wasn't worried he would send you away."

Something about the haunted look on Max's face checked her sarcasm. She could feel him slipping away, retreating, even though he hadn't moved a muscle.

"So long as he kept his focus off you and on me, I knew he wouldn't take anything out on you."

The weird choice of words penetrated her anger. Something terrifying slithered through her brain. She wanted to ignore it, but she couldn't. "What did he do to you?"

Max dropped his head. It was so out of character that Kaylee's lungs flooded with dread, pushing the air out of them.

"Max, what did he do?"

She didn't recognize him when he lifted his head. There was anger edging his voice, but it was the shame in his amber eyes that put her heart in a vise. He didn't look like the formidable man he was. Her imperturbable older brother. He looked…haunted. And starkly human.

"First he'd send me to the closet. I always got to pick which belt he was going to use."

Kaylee hands flew to her mouth. *No. Please no.* Her stomach churned.

He relayed the horror with such cold detachment that it made everything worse. Because she recognized it now. The shift that had happened when he was just twelve years old. A boy who had burned so bright in her memory, his fire snuffed out in a cowardly act of violence.

The tears she wouldn't let fall for herself earlier now spilled down her cheeks with abandon. "I didn't know. I swear I didn't know."

Max's expression was glassy-eyed, like he wasn't quite in the room with her. He was staring at memories somewhere over her right shoulder. "I didn't want you to."

"Why not? I'm your sister. I love you."

"Because there was nothing you could have done. And it stopped. I got big enough and it stopped, Kale.

I didn't want you to have to worry about me. I know you love him."

"I'm so sick of everyone trying to protect me! What about you, Max? Maybe I could have helped, but you cut me out. He hurt you like that, and you let me go on thinking he was good? Let me pander for scraps of his attention?" She knew her ire was misplaced, but she was so angry. At her father. At her mother. At Max. "I thought Dad was great, and you let me think it! I defended him to you. I took his side against you."

"I just wanted you to have a parent who didn't treat you like garbage."

"I didn't have a parent. I had a monster, and everyone knew it but me. No wonder you pushed me away! You probably see him every time you look at me."

Numbness tingled through her body. She would have picked Max over her father, but she'd never had a chance. Because Max chose to deal with it alone rather than have her on his side. Maybe not in the moment. She understood how a twelve-year-old boy might think he was saving his little sister. But they weren't children anymore.

And it hurt so much to know he didn't trust her enough to tell her the truth, no matter how soul shattering.

"Kaylee…"

She shook her head. "I can't… I'm sorry he hurt you. I'm sorry I…" Oh God. She wanted to vomit at the thought of Max being whipped.

Kaylee lurched to her feet. "I have to go."

"Kale, wait!"

His voice, her childhood nickname, the truth. It all collided in her chest, spinning like a tornado that took all her memories and upended them, reordered them. It was disorienting to see the events that had shaped her though a totally different lens. To realize that her allegiances were based on lies, that the choices she'd made teetered on a crumbling foundation.

"I didn't mean to—"

She blocked out Max's voice. If he apologized for being the victim of abuse she might throw up all over his office. "I have to go," she repeated, a reminder to her stultifying muscles. Now was not the time and this was not the place for her to lose it. *A lady is always in control of herself.*

She made it to the elevator, relieved to see that Max had paused at his office door, that he wasn't going to follow her. She dropped her head in shame at her own cowardice as the silver door slid shut.

Kaylee made it to her car on wooden legs, and when she dropped into the Audi's leather bucket seat, her only thought was of escape. She jammed her key into the ignition and made her way out of the underground parking garage. Max's confession was like a pickax in her brain, and instead of turning toward home when she reached street level, she turned in the opposite direction. She thought she was driving aimlessly until she recognized her surroundings. She'd driven straight to him—to the last person Max would want her to find comfort with.

One more secret between them, but she couldn't help herself.

She was tired and emotionally drained, and her hands were shaking as the adrenaline that had carried her out of her brother's office dissipated. And now, alone, without shock and pride to keep her emotions in check, the tears she'd managed to outrun caught up with her, stinging the bridge of her nose as she did battle with them again.

Her father had hit Max. With a belt. For years.

It was horrifying. Gut-wrenching. And she didn't doubt Max's story for a second.

Her heart twisted. She thought of all the time she'd wasted trying to please her father, to make him proud. And now... Now she questioned those choices. Because her brother wasn't the man she'd thought he was. And her father wasn't the man she'd thought he was. And if all the choices she'd made in life were based on those misconceptions, what kind of woman did that make her?

She unfastened her seat belt. Pushed open the door.

Not the time for thinking, she reminded herself. Action. She wanted action.

She knocked with enough force that her knuckles stung.

It was getting hard to breathe again. The waiting made her restless, like her skin was shrinking. Thoughts crowded her brain, but she pushed them aside. Feelings warred in her chest, but she shoved them down.

I'm fine, she reminded herself sternly, the way her mother would. *A lady never feels too much in public.*

The sound of the door opening snapped her head up, and then Aidan was there.

"Kaylee?" Aidan grabbed her shoulders, searched her face. "Jesus Christ. What happened to you?"

"Max just…" They were the only words that came out before the sobbing broke loose as he pulled her close, cradled her against his chest as she wrapped her arms around him.

He felt solid in a world that had just tipped off its axis. Max. Her father. But even as sobs racked her body and her chest ached so badly she thought she might split in two, there was comfort in having Aidan's arms around her.

He held her close, stroked her hair.

"Breathe, baby. I need you to breathe, okay?"

The rumble of his deep voice soothed her, even though her mind was spinning in a million different directions. She managed to nod, to heed his words. She gulped in some air.

Max had been trying to keep her safe. It was sweet and heartbreaking and infuriating and sad and all sorts of things that she couldn't put a name to.

Because it meant that her father, the man she'd been so desperate to please, was a monster.

Aidan pulled her tighter.

Jesus, she needed him right now. Needed him to stop the maelstrom of colliding facts imploding in her brain. Her brother was a good man. Her father did a bad thing.

She curled into him, tucking her face into his chest, greedily taking all the comfort that came from his heart beating beneath her cheek, the way his hand cupped the back of her head. Safe.

"What the hell happened?" His voice rumbled through his chest, deep and sure. She knew why she'd come here now. Because Aidan knew her better than anyone. It was an odd realization, that a man who'd only stumbled back into her life by accident after a ten-year hiatus would hold that honor, but he did.

He was the one who'd caught her rolling her eyes when her mother nagged her about her posture or her hair, the one who'd shared commiserating glances when she was being dragged to violin lessons or ballet class. He knew about her secret life as Lola, knew what it took to make her come, knew what she looked like when her heart was broken.

Things she'd never let anyone else see.

Because she trusted him. She always had.

And right now she trusted him to make her feel better. Because no one else could.

Pulling back, she curled her fingers into the softness of his T-shirt. "I don't want to talk, Aidan. I want to forget."

He frowned at that, just the slight dip of his eyebrow and a tightness in his mouth that let her know he wasn't happy with her nonanswer. But she couldn't. Not yet. Not when she didn't understand herself. Everything she'd thought was real had shifted just enough to make her lose her footing. She was too scattered to dissect it right now.

She just needed something solid to hold on to, and Aidan was her anchor of choice.

Imploringly, she lifted her mouth, tasting the salt of tears on her lips a split second before she tasted him.

He filled her senses, filled up all the empty spots inside her, and she wrapped her arms around his neck, pressing against him, letting the pleasure of touching him distract her.

To her infinite relief, he accepted that. He didn't protest or push her away. He just let her kiss him, kissed her back as she clumsily yanked off her jacket and they stumbled through his place toward the stairs, banging into the railing as they undressed each other in her quest to get him to the bedroom. She just needed to get to the bedroom.

He left her for only a second, to grab a condom, and then he was right where she needed him, in her arms, between her legs, over top of her, inside of her.

Yes.

He rocked his hips, pushing deep, and her world narrowed to the rasp of his beard against her neck, the rush of his breath across her skin. Kaylee closed her eyes and let herself feel everything, letting the grind of their bodies push her higher.

He made it good for her. Even as she broke, he kept pumping his hips. She couldn't stop kissing him, touching him. She didn't want to stop. She wanted this forever—her body trembling under his, her fingers in his hair, holding him close as he came.

He stayed over her, staring down at her as they both caught their breath. She felt safe there, with his body caging her in, his weight braced on his elbows and forearms, their legs tangled together. There were a million questions in his eyes, but he didn't ask them. And she appreciated that most of all. That he understood she wasn't ready.

And when he lay down beside her, she tucked herself against Aidan's body and stole the warmth and strength of being held by him until sleep came and gave her temporary respite from the horrors of the day.

CHAPTER EIGHTEEN

AIDAN BANGED ON the door, hoping to hell his intel guy had him at the right place. Resting his hands on either side of the jamb, muscles flexing as he tried to stay calm, he reminded himself to breathe.

Just breathe.

Kaylee might have drifted off into a fitful sleep, but Aidan was too wound up to do the same. She'd been shattered when she'd shown up at his place, and he wasn't going to let that stand.

He banged his palm on the door again, jarring the bones in his hand, and he relished the moment of pain.

Then the door opened, and Aidan came face-to-face with his hated nemesis.

His oldest friend.

Aidan had already moved before he realized it, his left hand gripping Max's T-shirt, his right forearm angled across the man's collarbone. He used his momentum and the surprise of his attack to spin Max and shove him hard against the wall beside the door.

"What the fuck did you do?"

Those cold amber eyes clashed with the fire in his

own, once again reminding Aidan how different they were. Every muscle in Max's body was coiled tight but on lockdown.

"You're going to want to back off, Aidan."

"Not until you tell me what you did to her."

"What I did to whom?"

Aidan shoved Max into the wall again before he let go of him.

To whom.

Fucking Max.

"I'm asking why Kaylee came home crying her goddamn eyes out."

Max went eerily still. "What did you say?"

Maybe he should have seen it coming, but in all the years he'd known Max, the guy had never punched first.

Aidan's head snapped back and the familiar crunch of knuckles versus cartilage accompanied the pain that bloomed behind his nose, but he shook it off. Instinct brought his fist up in a right hook that caught Max hard in the jaw and sent him staggering under the weight of the blow. Aidan flexed his hand as he stepped back, lungs heaving thanks to the cocktail of adrenaline and testosterone that had flooded his body like a shot of nitrous oxide. He shifted his weight to the balls of his feet, ready if his opponent wanted to take this to the next level.

Max drew up to his full height, also sucking in oxygen. His bottom lip was busted up and starting to swell. "You want to come after me, that's fair game. But stay the fuck away from Kaylee, you son of a bitch. Don't drag her into this."

Aidan smirked at the warning because he knew it would piss Max off.

"What the hell is going on? It's after midnight and—oh my God, Max! You're bleeding."

Both he and Max turned their attention to the gorgeous blonde in the tank top and boxers who'd just emerged from what Aidan presumed was the master bedroom.

"I'm fine," Max told her, wiping his mouth with the back of his hand. It came away smeared with blood.

"You're not fine," she said pointedly, the slight rebuke obviously aimed at Aidan. Not that he gave a damn if Max's latest piece of ass didn't approve of his manners.

"Aidan's always had shit for timing, but we have some things to discuss. Go back to bed."

The animosity cooled, but her look turned speculative. Instead of following orders, she headed toward the tricked-out kitchenette and pulled open the freezer.

Aidan frowned at that. Conquests, as a rule, disappeared when you told them to.

So not just a piece of ass, then.

Interesting.

Aidan sniffed, and the metallic tang of blood registered in the back of his throat. He grabbed the hem of his T-shirt and wiped his face before prodding gingerly at his nose. It didn't feel broken.

The blonde returned with a makeshift ice pack in each hand—ziplock baggie, ice cubes, dish towel—and, surprising the hell out of him, held one out to Aidan.

"I'm Emma."

Aidan took it, a platitude. She obviously had no idea who he was and how her boyfriend felt about him.

"Max has told me a lot about you."

Or he was wrong on all counts.

He rested the ice on his aching knuckles, his surprised gaze sliding to Max. "I didn't know he'd ever told anyone a lot about anything, let alone about me."

She smiled at that, stepping close to Max, cupping his jaw tenderly as she pressed the ice pack to his injured face. It was almost a protective gesture, and the way Max lifted his hand to cradle hers was not lost on Aidan. It made him uncomfortable, like he was intruding on something private.

He dropped his gaze, focusing instead on the throbbing in his sinuses. Despite himself, he was a little impressed. Max had landed a hell of a jab.

"Okay. You two obviously have a lot to discuss, and since that is the extent of my nursing skills, I'm going to make myself scarce." Emma lifted onto her toes and pressed a kiss to Max's cheek, but when she turned her gaze on Aidan, there was a warning there.

Ballsy as hell. He liked her despite himself.

"I'll just be in the bedroom," she announced, walking away from them. "Watching TV. With 911 on speed dial. Play nice, boys."

Aidan waited until she'd pushed the bedroom door closed behind her before he turned his attention to Max.

"How much did you tell her about me?"

"Everything."

"Are you fucking serious?"

Max shrugged, but there was nothing apologetic about it. "I love her."

The admission caught Aidan off guard. It was totally out of character for Max. Well, for the Max he'd known. But he supposed he wasn't the only one who had changed in the last five years. He because he'd lost his father and his friend in one fell swoop. Max because he'd gained ownership of a multimillion-dollar tech company, finally gotten rid of the son of a bitch who'd raised him, and apparently found true love, as well.

Everything was coming up fucking roses.

Aidan let his anger reignite, tightening his muscles, reerecting the emotional wall he'd had in place before Max had opened the door.

As if Max had read his posture, he sighed. "Am I going to need a drink for the rest of this conversation?"

"Probably."

"You want one?" Max offered, heading for the bar cart on the far side of the room.

Civilized. So very Max. "Sure."

Aidan wandered deeper into the suite, down the three steps that led to the sunken living room, stopping in front of the floor-to-ceiling windows that overlooked the city. Los Angeles looked damn good at night—sexy and inviting, an inky sky twinkling with lights. "So... you live in the penthouse of a hotel? Isn't that a bit pretentious, even for you?"

Max shot him a wry glance as he set down his ice pack and pulled the stopper from a crystal decanter. "I like to stick to my strengths."

Silence stretched between them as Aidan surveyed the city below and Max poured.

"This isn't exactly how I imagined this moment."

Aidan glanced over at him. "Been dreaming about me again, huh?"

"Glad to see you haven't changed." Max grabbed the drinks and joined Aidan by the window. "Still as gloriously humble as ever."

Aidan accepted the tumbler and the gibe with a tip of his head. "Well, if it's any consolation, this isn't how I thought this would play out, either." He took a swallow of scotch, and it went down smooth.

Max had always had a knack for the finer things in life.

"I mean—" Aidan gestured at his friend with the glass in his hand "—I definitely thought I'd throw the first punch."

The corner of Max's mouth pulled up as he took a sip of his drink, and he winced, prodding at his busted lip. For a moment, he stared contemplatively at the cityscape. When he spoke, none of that spark of humor was evident in his voice. "She was crying?"

Aidan nodded.

Max sighed. "Then I guess this is the part where I let you explain why the hell she's coming to you in times of emotional turmoil."

Aidan hadn't dissected it much past he was glad she had. But he should have known Max would parse it for meaning. Aidan rushed in hot, ready for action, and Max hung back, assessing the situation. It was how it had always been with them.

He shrugged, sipped his drink. "What can I say? Ladies love a good listener."

Max's flat, subzero stare got under his skin. Made him want to move, pace it out.

"So after five years of this silent feud of ours, you roll back into LA and just happen to start seeing my sister? Who apparently means so much to you that you've come over here to try and kick my ass? That's what I'm supposed to believe?"

The question hit dead center. Max had the precision of a sniper.

"Just to be clear, if I'd meant to kick your ass, you'd be laid out on the ground right now."

"Maybe. But I swear to God, man, if you're using her to get back at me…" Max let the threat hang as he took a swig of scotch. The accusation prickled along Aidan's spine.

"How long have you two been together?"

Shit. Aidan shifted his shoulders. He should have expected the inquisition. Max liked to dismantle things to find out how they worked.

"I'm through answering questions until you tell me what you did to her."

Max's jaw tensed, and it felt good to shift the momentum. To put him on defense. "Let it go, man."

"You know I'm not going to do that."

The man beside him at the window was quiet for so long that Aidan was surprised when he finally spoke. "I told her my dad used to hit me and I let him to keep her safe. And it made her feel like shit because apparently it's the only thing I'm good at with her."

"Jesus Christ." Now it was Aidan's turn to take a swill of premium liquor. Pieces of their past clicked into place. Max asking him for pointers after their schoolyard brawl. The way he'd tagged along to Aidan's neighborhood boxing gym, despite the dozen or so snooty health clubs that would have bent over backward to count the Whitfields among their ranks. How hard he worked to bulk up the summer after they met. "While we were in high school?"

"It stopped by junior year. No point mentioning it after that."

"Fists?"

"Belt."

Shit.

"You shoulda told me." Anger tightened Aidan's shoulders, and his hand flexed around his empty glass. "I could've helped."

Max's glance darted to him, then back to the city. "You did help. You and Sal. I took care of the rest. And you wouldn't have understood. You had a great dad. A dad who cared about you. Loaned you start-up capital for your business. Was proud of your accomplishments."

Aidan's laugh was bitter. "What after-school-special version of my life were you watching?"

The question got Max's attention.

"My dad was a drunk, Max. A high-functioning one at work, most of the time. The rest of the time he was passed out or betting on whatever odds he could find. It got really bad when my mom got diagnosed and worse after she died. He started to slide. Lost his job. By the time I was thirteen, I spent more time taking care of him than he did taking care of me."

"How did I not know that?"

"Because by the time we met, he'd started to pull it together a little. He was obsessed with the idea that you two turned into SecurePay. You saw the good part of him. The coding-genius part. He saved the 'passed out in his own puke after dropping fifty grand on the ponies' part for after hours." Aidan ran a hand down his beard. "And he really cleaned his act up when you got him that job at Whitfield Industries. For a while anyway. I could tell things were getting worse toward the end. I knew I should have come back."

The guilt that always flared in Aidan's gut when he remembered that moment—the moment he'd decided *fuck the old man, let him take care of himself for once*—struck again. His dad had been ranting on the other end of the phone, a sure sign he was a few drinks too deep. Aidan had been in Spain, some five-star hotel in Pamplona, celebrating the milestone of making his first million and not in the mood to babysit. It was complicated, loving someone and hating them in equal measure.

"I didn't want to deal with his drunk ass, so I stayed away. And now I have to live with that choice."

Max's face turned stony. Unreadable. "That's on me. That's not on you. I'm the one who put John on my father's radar. You asked me to look after him, and I let you down."

"Turned out okay for you, though, huh? Ended up pushing Charles out of the way and taking over the family business. Now you're going to make millions off my dad, and you don't have to share the spoils or the credit."

Max grew still, but Aidan knew he was leaving a mark. Knew his words were well-placed knives. Knew it cost Max not to wince. Aidan itched to deepen the wound, to get a rise. He was more comfortable fighting.

Max's smile was bitter. "So that's what this is about. Revenge."

"I know that SecurePay and Cybercore's knockoff are built on the same code. That you shared it somehow and violated the exclusivity clause in Dad's contract. And I will prove it in court, Max."

He'd been expecting fury. Threats. Bribes. Another punch. Pretty much anything but the way Max stared out the window, at the ceiling, at his bare feet—anywhere but at Aidan.

After years of covering for his father, of letting people believe what they wanted, of lying by omission or through silence, Aidan recognized the signs. A cold sweat broke out across his back and the world shifted under his feet, the realization making him motion sick. He'd blamed Max and Charles for years for pushing John Beckett past his breaking point, and if that wasn't how it had happened...

He tasted bile as he leaned forward. *Just breathe.*

"What did he do?"

Max shook his head. "Don't do this, Aidan. Don't open this wound. Charles is going to jail. It's over."

The advice didn't make him feel better. *"What did he do?"* he repeated.

Max stared into his glass for a moment, and when

he raised his eyes, they were older, calmer than Aidan had ever seen them. Five years hadn't quite made him a stranger, but he wasn't the same man Aidan remembered, either.

"When you asked him for that loan to start your business, John didn't have what you needed. So your dad broke his contract and sold the patented code to Liam Kearney to get the money."

Corporate-fucking-espionage.

"No." That couldn't be true. If it was, nothing in his world made sense.

It's okay, Aidan. I got a bonus at the last minute. Take it. It would make your mother happy.

"When your dad got wasted, told me what he'd done, we tried to cover it up so my father wouldn't find out. And I told John he should tell you, that you'd understand. But he didn't want you to know. He felt losing your mother was hard enough on you, and he didn't want you to feel like you'd lost him, too."

Aidan had poured all his rage and hatred and guilt on Max for so long that it felt weird to believe him. But he knew in his gut that what Max had just told him was the truth. Knew how much it must have hurt Max to discover his mentor had let him down.

"It wasn't until after the accident that I discovered my father knew what John had done, that he'd already taken his revenge. In the original contract, your dad held on to a percentage of the SecurePay profits for as long as the code was exclusive to Whitfield Industries. Since John had violated the agreement, Charles forced him into signing away all his rights to the SecurePay code along with any intellectual property developed during his tenure at Whitfield Industries. Threatened your dad with jail time, and said he'd go after you as well, since your company was founded on dirty money. My father fucked him over completely. That contract is the reason your dad was drunk the night he died."

Everything in Aidan went still, but his heart began to race. His blood thundered in his ears as Max's words landed with all the impact of a detonating bomb.

"You were right when you accused me of being selfish. I didn't want to lose Whitfield Industries. My grandfather built this company, and my father almost destroyed it. I didn't want to let him. I wanted my birthright, my chance at the helm. But I hope you can believe, at some point, that it's not the only reason I didn't turn him in for what he did to John. To you."

Max faced him now. "I didn't want your dad's name dragged through the mud. I didn't want your memory of the man he was to be ripped apart because my father is an asshole. And I didn't want my dad to make good on his threat to come after you."

So like Max, really. Just like he'd protected Kaylee. Taking the brunt of the punishment and the blame.

"I've spent a long time hating you for that."

Max finished his drink. "I know."

Something inside Aidan's chest unlocked. Breathing didn't seem so hard anymore. "It wasn't your job to save me."

"You're not the one I was trying to save. Your father, the version of him I knew anyway, was an incredible man who made a mistake. But he did it for you."

Do this for me, Dad. Ninety days to dry out. It'll go by fast.

Eat something, Pop.

Damn it, Dad. The track? Again?

I'll make it up to you, Aidan. I swear.

He stared at Max, who looked as drained and as bleak as he felt. Five fucking years of secrets had taken their toll.

"I'd rather have had you in my life for the last five years than a slightly less tarnished memory of my dad." The truth of that made Aidan feel better and worse. They'd lost a lot of time, missed out on a lot of things.

The thaw in the room wasn't large, but it was noticeable. And uncomfortable.

"I should go." He placed his empty glass in the hand Max had extended. He didn't want Kaylee to wake up alone after everything she'd been through.

Max didn't say anything, just followed him to the door. Aidan stopped with a hand on the knob, one foot in the hallway, and looked over his shoulder. "This thing with Kaylee? It's new. And I have no idea what's happening. But if you make her cry again, I won't stop after one punch."

Max's answering nod was tight and controlled. "Same goes."

The door snicked shut behind him, and for the first time in years, Aidan let himself miss the friendship that had preceded all the pain and guilt that had consumed him since his father's death.

CHAPTER NINETEEN

Aidan was tinkering with his bike when he heard Kaylee moving around upstairs. Max's questions had pounded in his brain all night, which, along with the throbbing in his face, made sleep an elusive bitch. He was tired and moody and disgusted with himself.

What the hell was he doing with Kaylee? He wasn't back in LA to stay. He'd come here to fuck Max over and get the patent on his father's code. And now that there was neither vengeance nor legal rights for him to claim, he should get the hell out of Dodge.

Because the one thing he wanted to stay for had *disaster* written all over it.

Aidan sighed and dropped his wrench on the concrete floor with a clatter.

His father had put alcohol and gambling above all else, and it had cost him everything.

And now it had cost Aidan everything, too. His friendship with Max. Any chance of something real with Kaylee.

She trusted too easily, cared too much about people who didn't deserve her loyalty.

And he counted himself among them.

"Morning."

Her voice made his abs draw tight, a kick of lust he'd given up trying to control. He kept his head down, focused on his bike. "Hey. You're up early."

"I have to get home and change before I go to work. You want coffee?"

"I'm good, but thanks."

He ignored the part of him that liked the sound of her in his kitchen, and that she knew which cupboard to open to find a mug. It wouldn't do him any good to realize how long it had been since he'd had someone consistent in his world or how comforting it was to think of a place as *home*.

"Can you believe this battery is dead already? No wonder Wes gave it to me. This phone is a piece of crap."

"There should be a charger in that drawer." Aidan glanced over his shoulder as he pointed at the cabinet closest to the door, not realizing his mistake until Kaylee had already banged her mug onto the counter.

"Oh my God, Aidan! What happened to your face?"

Phone woes forgotten, she rushed toward him and he swore under his breath and straightened up from his crouched position to his full height. "It's nothing," he protested.

"You have a black eye. It's not nothing."

"Tool slipped while I was working on the bike earlier."

"Hold still and let me see." She set her hand on his

face, and it was so reminiscent of the private moment he'd witnessed between Emma and Max that he winced.

Kaylee's brow crumpled with concern. "Does it hurt?"

Aidan had to remind himself that she was talking about his eye and not the sudden lurch of his heart.

I love her. Max had said the words so simply. No emphasis. No uncertainty. A statement of fact.

Aidan managed the slightest shake of his head.

"I could get you some ice," she offered, but this time she licked her lips, letting him know that the sudden heat kindling in his belly wasn't one-sided.

Her hand still rested on his cheek.

"I could kiss it better." Her voice was barely more than a whisper, but it didn't lessen the impact on his body. He was ravenous for her, instantly ready, desperately hard.

Aidan ran his hands over her ass and down her thighs before he hitched her up his body and she locked her heels across the small of his back. Kaylee pressed her mouth to his, first sweet, running her tongue along his bottom lip, then not so sweet, catching it between her teeth.

He loved having her mouth on him.

"Is this working?" she asked, dropping a kiss against his jaw and another on the side of his neck. "Because if you don't feel better yet, I do have a couple of more advanced techniques that might help you forget about the pain," she teased.

He wanted to take her up on the offer.

Christ, did he ever.

But he couldn't. Not like this. Not until he made things right.

"You still have to get changed and get to work," he reminded her. "You're going to be late if we try out your advanced techniques. And even later if we try out some of mine."

"My name is on the building. What are they going to do, fire me?"

"All the more reason to set a good example," he joked.

Kaylee gave an exaggerated moan of protest as she unhooked her legs from around his waist so he could lower her back to the floor. "Adulting sucks."

Almost as much as watching her walk away from him, Aidan thought.

"Leave your phone when you go. I'll take a look at it." He did his best to pass it off as a casual offer, hoping the waver his voice didn't betray him.

Kaylee arched an eyebrow at him as she grabbed her purse. "Oh, you fix cell phones now?"

"What can I say? I'm good with my hands."

She grinned at that. "Says the man who clocked himself in the face."

Aidan's response was a wounded frown. "That sounds like both a slur on my manhood and an undeniable challenge. And when you get home from work, I'll be happy to prove just how good I really am with my hands. As many times as you want."

"Well, in that case," she said, grabbing her phone from the counter and handing it to him on her way to the door, "you'd better limber up those fingers while I'm gone, because I feel a bout of skepticism coming on."

When Kaylee arrived at work an hour later, her heels clicked against the tiled floor that made up the lobby of the PR department. Thanks to the communal working space, it wasn't a sound she usually heard above the day-to-day chatter, and it definitely wasn't a sound she should be hearing now, considering Whitfield Industries was still digging out from the perfect storm of scandals that had plagued them lately. To say the PR department was abuzz with activity right now was a massive understatement. Or at least it should be.

That was why the clack of her pumps unnerved her. Along with the surreptitious glances her team was throwing her.

Things made sense when she arrived at her office. Nothing like an unannounced visit from the boss to put people on edge.

"Max? I thought we weren't meeting until..." She trailed off as he turned from his inspection of one of the paintings on her wall. He was dressed impeccably as ever, his Windsor knot crisp and precise. Even the slight wave of his ebony hair was perfect. Perhaps that was what made his fat lip so out of place.

The sight of it hit her like a bucket of cold water.

Tool slipped while I was working on the bike earlier.

No. Aidan wouldn't have gone to Max. They hated each other.

And she'd made it clear to Aidan that she wasn't

ready for her family to know about…whatever was going on between the two of them.

"What happened?" But she knew. God help her, she knew.

The realization that Aidan had lied to her struck hard and with disorienting speed.

Max's eyebrow lifted. "Aidan didn't—well, that's not a surprise, I guess."

"He hit you."

The summation made him frown. "I hit him first," Max clarified before releasing an uncharacteristic sigh. "What are you doing with him, Kale?"

This. This was the very reason she'd wanted to keep Aidan from her family. The inquisition. The censure. The justification.

"You don't get to go all big brother on me now, Max." Kaylee stood her ground as he approached. "I'm sorry about what Dad did to you. Truly I am. And I wish that you'd told me earlier, that I'd been able to help you somehow. But what I do with my life is my own concern. We're long past your chance to have a say in who I date."

Even if she wasn't doing such a bang-up job when left to her own devices.

"I just don't want to see you get hurt. You know Aidan has a tendency to bail. And he came here to ruin SecurePay."

"He told you that?" No wonder they'd come to blows. That goddamn app was the most important thing in Max's world. And right now, Aidan had full access to it because she'd left her phone with him. *Shit.*

She reversed direction, opening her office door and focusing on the elevator across the sea of worried glances.

"Where are you going?" Max asked.

"I'm taking lunch." Fixing her error. Taking charge of her life. Maybe giving Aidan matching black eyes.

"It's nine in the morning."

"Call it brunch, then. I have something I need to deal with."

CHAPTER TWENTY

AIDAN THUMBED OPEN the spyware app he'd gotten from Cybercore as soon as the phone had enough charge to turn it on. This was it. He was going to end this right now. He didn't want any more secrets between him and Kaylee—he wanted a fresh start. A chance to see if what she made him feel stood a chance at becoming something real or if it was doomed to fail beneath the lies and deceit that had stained their relationship before it had even started.

Only one way to find out.

Aidan hit the uninstall button.

Uninstall failed.

What the fuck? Kearney had assured him that was all he had to do. He touched it again.

Uninstall failed.

And again.

Uninstall failed.

Shit. Shit, shit, shit. He dialed Liam Kearney.

"You said this thing would self-destruct."

"It will."

Aidan's grip tightened on the phone. *Prick.* "I wouldn't be calling you if it had."

"Hey, I get it. My tech's too complicated for a lot of people."

"I can handle the uninstall button, asshole. Too bad I didn't make you prove your garbage tech before I paid for it."

"If I were you, Beckett, I might keep a civil tone. You're the one who came begging favors from me."

Kearney was baiting him and he knew it, but it still took everything in him to keep his cool. "Hey, if I'd begged for this, I'd expect what I got, but since you took my money, yeah, I'm feeling a little uncivil about shitty tech that either sounds like static or cuts out. If my father was polite in his dealings with you, it's only because he didn't know what a hack you are."

Aidan hadn't meant to go there, but some part of him needed to know. Needed to confirm what Max had told him.

"Oh, I see. We've got daddy issues. I'll tell you what, because John was nothing but a gentleman during our dealings and because he was a true craftsman, I'm going to overlook your slur on my tech."

Aidan stood up. He needed to move. An outlet. He started to pace. He felt like a caged tiger—dangerous and inclined to rip someone's throat out but with no chance of getting his hands on his prey. And because he knew it, Kearney was poking a verbal stick through the bars.

"Don't even say his name, you hear me? Now, I think you were about to tell me how you were planning to fix this issue I have."

"I'll take a look remotely after my meeting. It'll be fine."

The word set his fucking teeth on edge.

"Do not tell me this is going to be fine, Kearney. People always say that, and it never is. I want the malware you sold me off Kaylee's phone. Right. Fucking. Now."

He hung up, his blood thundering through his veins. But despite the clamor in his head, a soft sound behind him prickled up his spine, froze him. Time slowed as he turned toward the door. The betrayal on her face almost sent him to his knees.

Kaylee's purse slipped from her limp fingers, and it hit the ground with a thump.

One minute, she was charging back home—back to his place, she corrected herself—to give Aidan hell for lying to her about his black eye, and the next minute her whole world was crashing down around her.

"You've been spying on me?"

The words didn't make sense. It was like parroting a language she didn't actually speak.

"I wasn't spying on you!" His exhalation deflated his battle stance. "I was spying through you."

"What?" She shook her head, but even through her shock, the pieces were starting to click into place. "That's why you wanted my phone. Because you... Oh God. You bugged my phone? When?"

Aidan broke eye contact, looked down. "The night we went for drinks."

The first night. The first fucking night. He hadn't wanted *her* at all.

"My God, Aidan. Do you know what I thought when I turned around and saw you in that coffee shop?" Something—part laugh, part cry, and all self-recrimination—burst from Kaylee's lips. It was a harsh, wounded sound that made her flinch. "I thought it was fate."

And the whole time, she'd just been an easy mark. The weak link. The one who used to hang on his every word. No wonder he'd targeted her. And she'd fallen for it. Hell, she'd instigated it! "Max. My dad. Your dad. None of this was about me at all."

The unthinkable occurred then, and it killed her that—in light of what she'd just learned—it wasn't actually unthinkable anymore.

"Did you hack my brother's company?"

Aidan frowned, gave a curt shake of his head. "I had nothing to do with that."

Emotion bubbled up in her throat. She was vaguely relieved when it manifested as a scoffing laugh instead of a strangled sob. "Forgive me if I don't just take your word on that."

"KJ…"

She stepped back from the pleading tone, the intimacy of the name only he called her. "Just swooping in like a vulture then, biding your time. Waiting for the death throes to end."

"It's not like that. Not anymore."

"Oh? And what's it like now, Aidan? What's changed, besides the fact that I caught you?" She shook her head at her own stupidity. "You were just using me to get information. You wanted the goddamn app." The truth cut swift and deep. There was a moment of blessed numbness before pain bloomed in her heart, almost overwhelming with its intensity. She braced her hand on the counter, lifted the other to massage her temple. "None of this was real." Another laugh escaped her, but this one held an edge of hysteria and burned her throat raw.

"It wasn't supposed to be, but it is now." He stepped closer. His voice was raspy, like he was being tortured to divulge state secrets. "Being with you is the realest fucking thing that's ever happened to me."

"There's nothing real about any of this!" Her attention landed on the dining room table, where things had been so different a few days ago. When he'd made her believe she was worth standing up for. Had that all been part of the ruse?

"Don't say that."

He reached for her. She hated that the brush of his fingers on her skin felt so good. Hated that his touch calmed her. Now was not the time for calm.

She stepped back, and his hand fell away from her arm. Cool air swept over her skin where his fingers had been, and she shivered. "Why were you at the burlesque show that night?"

"I was looking for you."

In any other context, the words would have been a dream come true. But not now. Not this context. "Why?"

"My PI tracked your car there."

"That was your plan all along, wasn't it?" It was hard to breathe through her outrage. "I wasn't just a convenient mark you happened to run across at the coffee shop and chose to exploit. You recruited me. You were just using me, right from the start."

Aidan's eyes flashed fire. "Well, you know all about that, don't you?"

The words cracked through the room with the ferocity of a whip.

"What the hell is that supposed to mean?"

"You knew who I was that night in the supply closet. I'm just one more of your dirty little secrets, right? Who are you using me to get back at? Max? Your mom? Or hell, maybe it's all intensely meta, and younger you is proving something to younger me, punishing me for not seeing what an incredible woman you were destined to become. Maybe D? All of the above?"

The charges punched through her chest with devastating precision. It sounded so ugly when he put it that way. But was he wrong? Hadn't she thought each and every one of those things that night in the club, when their gazes had collided? When she'd acted out her most cherished fantasy in that supply closet? When she'd accepted his offer for drinks, all the while hoping he'd figure out she and Lola were one and the same?

"You want to talk truth? Here's one for you. Are you here with me? Or are you here because they wouldn't want you to be?"

Kaylee didn't want to think about it. Not when it didn't matter anyway. He was here only because he was using her. And she'd let fanciful teenage emotions make her think this was something…what? Real? Special? Fated?

She should have known better. No one who meant anything to her ever felt the same way back.

"Jesus Christ, Kaylee. You say that secrets make you feel alive, but all you've managed to do is set your life up as a grenade, rigged to inflict maximum damage on anyone who's wronged you."

"What?"

He pinned her with a measured look. "Your mom lost her senatorial bid when your dad cheated on her with a stripper."

"She cheated on him first!" The defense of her father was automatic, as old as the scandal Aidan had referenced, and her gut lurched with disgust. She pushed the queasy feeling aside as she remembered the horrors Max had endured at Charles Whitfield's hand. She couldn't think about that right now. "And I'm not a stripper. I dance burlesque, and I'm not ashamed of it. Burlesque is art. It's dance as social commentary."

"Tell yourself that all you want. Hell, maybe it's true. But if this hits the media, you know how it will play."

She hated that she had no defense for that. That maybe it was a little bit true. That she'd taken that burlesque class for the wrong reasons, not the least of which was Sylvia Whitfield's disapproval. But no matter why she'd started, she'd grown to love burlesque. The girls. The art of it. It meant everything to her now.

Kaylee raised her chin. "You're hardly in a position to give me life advice, Aidan. You've never stuck around long enough to deal with the intricacies of relationships. Whenever things get hard, you claim wanderlust and disappear on another adventure."

The barb landed. She could tell by the way Aidan's hands fisted, his automatic reaction to every blow, be it physical or verbal, but Kaylee got no joy from it.

"You know what? You're right." He grabbed his leather jacket from the back of the dining room chair. "It's definitely past time that I got out of here."

Kaylee watched him go, flinched as the door slammed in his wake. Further proof that fight or flight was the extent of Aidan's operating capacity.

The rumble of his motorbike confirmed which option he'd chosen to apply to her.

Kaylee's bottom lip trembled, a precursor to the tears scalding the backs of her eyes. But she blinked them back and swallowed the lump in her throat. She needed to get back to work.

CHAPTER TWENTY-ONE

Heartache hangovers were so much worse than their tequila counterparts, Kaylee decided the next morning. Her eyelids felt like they were lined with gravel as she dragged them open to check the time. It took a moment for the numbers to register.

Shit. It was almost eight o'clock! Her alarm was supposed to go off an hour and a half ago.

She grabbed her phone with such ferocity that the charging cable came loose from the wall. Everything looked fine, but three attempted swipes later, Kaylee realized the stupid thing was frozen. No wonder the alarm hadn't rung.

Stupid piece of crap.

She held down the power button, forcing a restart before she dropped the phone on her comforter and got to her feet. If she skipped the shower and breakfast, she could probably make it to the office by—

Her plans were cut off by a cacophony of buzzes and dings as hundreds of push notifications and texts and missed calls flooded her phone.

What the hell?

She walked back over to the bed to investigate, but what she saw on the screen in her hand stopped her dead. A litany of words she'd hoped never to see strung together.

Kaylee.

Lola.

Burlesque.

Whitfield Industries.

Scandal.

Stripper.

The phone slipped from her numb fingers.

Everyone knew. Her parents. Max. The people who worked for her. All of Los Angeles. The world. But it wasn't embarrassment that quaked through her at the realization. It was betrayal.

Because burlesque was the one thing in her life that was just hers.

The one thing she hadn't shared with anyone else... except Aidan.

Her heart keened at the idea that he could be so cruel. Her head told her to grow the hell up. He'd bugged her phone with the express purpose of hurting Max, of ruining her family. It was naive in the extreme to think he wasn't capable of this.

Whitfield Industries had been plagued with disgrace of late.

First a security breach had raised questions about the safety of their flagship product—an app designed to keep information secure.

Then her father, the former CEO, had been turned in

to the FBI by his son, the current CEO, for blackmailing a key member of the SecurePay team.

Somehow, Kaylee and her team had managed to juggle and avoid the full brunt of either crisis, but how long was that going to last now that she was the latest scandal? How did you spin the fact that the woman in charge of spin was about to be shamed for taking off her clothes in public? All the plates she'd set spinning to keep people looking where she wanted them to would come crashing down around her.

And much as it pained her, Kaylee knew there were many who would see her "transgression"—being female *and* embracing her sexuality publicly—as the worst of the three offenses.

If her credibility was shot, she couldn't effectively do her job.

Looked like Aidan was right after all. She was a grenade.

She'd done all the work for him. All he'd had to do was pull the pin.

Boom.

With a resigned sigh, she ignored the part of her that wanted to crawl back into bed and pull the covers over her head and grabbed the phone instead. Between the beeps and the buzzing, she managed to text her assistant.

Announce a press conference at 10 a.m.

Then Kaylee walked over to her closet to pick out some appropriate armor for the battle ahead.

***

Aidan wasn't sure what he was expecting to see after the shit show that had erupted overnight, but if he'd thought that having her burlesque career splashed all over the internet and the local papers would cow her, well, he'd been all kinds of wrong.

Kaylee strode toward the entrance of the building, looking every inch the competent PR director in her sleek gray pantsuit and heels with her dark hair pulled back in a no-nonsense ballerina bun, and nothing like her alter ego, the blonde bombshell who'd caused all this trouble in the first place. And while Aidan had enjoyed every second of watching her dance, he found he preferred this Kaylee. Her certainty, her determination, her general kick-assiness. No secrets. No flash. Just her.

She was spectacular.

Her stride faltered as she caught sight of his bike, parked near the entrance of her building. He stepped forward, and their gazes collided. His body came alive as though she'd touched him. But instead of altering her direction to meet him, she headed for the entrance, dismissing him completely.

Shit.

He started toward her, and she sped up, but there was no way she'd make it into the lobby before their paths intersected. She beat him to the door by a fraction of a second, pulling it open without breaking stride, so Aidan followed her into the building.

"I'm not leaving until you hear me out."

She shook her head, kept walking. "There's nothing left to talk about. You should go. In case you haven't heard, I have a huge press conference to manage this morning."

"I didn't do this, KJ."

She whirled on him, eyes flashing. "Right. You're the only one who knows about...my secret identity."

"Ms. Whitfield? Everything okay?"

Aidan's shoulders stiffened at the threat of confrontation. Some rent-a-cop trying to impress Kaylee was the last thing he needed to deal with.

Kaylee nodded, waving off the approaching security guard. "I'm fine, Roy."

The burly man sent a pointed glare at Aidan before he turned and headed back to the crescent-shaped desk to the left of the elevators.

"That's what I'm trying to tell you. I don't think I'm the only one who knows about Lola." Aidan held a hand out, palm up. The static, the interference, the quick drain on the battery, and now the leak. And all of it would benefit Liam Kearney. "I need to see your phone."

"After what happened last time? No way."

"Give me the phone, KJ. I think someone bugged it."

She frowned at that. "Oh, no kidding?"

"I think someone *else* bugged it."

After a beat of stunned silence, Kaylee took off toward the elevators again, leaving him no choice but to follow.

"If you'd just let me explain, I—"

"Explain what? Some giant conspiracy theory? Do you have an evil twin I don't know about?"

"Hey." He reached for her, but his fingertips barely

brushed her arm before he thought better of it, pulled his hand back.

She stopped, though, and dropped her head. Her shoulders curled forward as though he'd popped the bubble of her confidence. It tore him apart.

The pretty, studious girl he'd known had withstood the constant nagging of her mother, the emotional abandonment of her brother, and the calculated disinterest of her father, and still she'd grown into a beautiful, brave woman who continued to believe in people. Who looked at him like he was something special. At least she used to.

And he'd ruined it. He hadn't wanted her trust, had actively warned her not to give it to him. But now that he'd lost it…

It felt like forever until she turned to face him, even longer until she lifted her head. "How could you do this to me?" She shook her head. "How could I let you do this to me?"

That spark of fire in her eyes was a relief, even if it was aimed at him. Mad was better than broken.

"You really think I leaked this to the press? You know me better than that, KJ."

For a fraction of a second she looked like she wanted to believe in him again, but then the elevator dinged and the doors slid open and she was back to glaring at him. He followed her inside. Briefly, Aidan thought they might luck out and get the elevator to themselves so he could warn her about the tech glitch, or beg her to forgive him, or push her up against the wall and kiss her until she was too breathless to be mad at him anymore. But before he could do any of those things, they were joined by three women and two dudes in suits.

Aidan exhaled. Despite the easy chatter of the rest of the occupants, the silence between him and Kaylee was oppressive. Thick. He didn't like being around her without being able to touch her.

Not that he deserved to. Or that she'd have let him, even if they were alone. He'd really fucked things up. But at least if they were unaccompanied he could try to fix it.

Two of the women got out on the sixth floor, the other woman on the fourteenth. The guys, it seemed, were in it for the long haul.

They kept whispering to each other. Shoulders shaking with laughter as they alternated covert looks at Kaylee. And Aidan knew he wasn't just imagining it. He could feel her shrinking beside him. Head down, shoulders hunched, like she was trying get small enough to escape their notice.

By the time they got to the top floor, Aidan was strung tight.

If the guy in front of him had known that, he might not have raised his voice slightly as the silver doors slid open. The words *continuing the family legacy* were unmistakable. His buddy laughed.

Aidan's blood ran hot as he and Kaylee followed them off the elevator. "We got a problem here?"

The guy turned around and smirked at him. "Nope. No problem."

"You sure? Because it sounded like maybe you had something you wanted to say."

The tenseness of the interaction was starting to draw the attention of nearby employees.

"Is this..." The asshole glanced at Kaylee, then back at Aidan. "Are you trying to impress her, tough guy? Is that what this is?"

Kaylee's hand on his arm was all that stopped Aidan from ending him, but his fists drew tight anyway, every muscle in his body aching to wipe that damn smirk off the guy's face.

"Because from what I've heard, you don't have to try too hard to get her clothes off. Like father's hooker, like daughter, I guess."

The asshole's head snapped back as blood gushed all over his skinny hipster tie, and with the amount of satisfaction that roared through Aidan's body at the contact, it took his brain a second to realize he hadn't thrown the punch.

Kaylee cradled her fist in her other hand, swearing softly, and Aidan had never been prouder of anyone in his whole damn life.

"You fucking cow!"

The asshole lurched forward, one hand still cradling his bleeding nose, and this time Aidan did step forward, angling his shoulders so Kaylee was slightly behind him. It was only a courtesy, though. Since her punching hand was sore.

"I wouldn't." Aidan's warning was soft and low.

"Jones, c'mon man." His buddy grabbed him and pulled him back, and Aidan was a little disappointed in his good sense.

The guy swore again, drawing even more of a crowd.

Blood spatter dotted the tiles in the reception area like a macabre Jackson Pollock painting.

"What the hell is going on here?"

The air changed around Aidan at the sound of Max's voice, and the gathered spectators snapped to attention, suddenly remembering everything they should have been doing.

"This crazy bitch punched me!"

Icy rage flattened Max's features. "What did you say?"

"Look, Max. Uh, Mr. Whitfield. I—"

"Security will meet you at your desk, Jones."

Max glanced behind him, but his admin already had the phone to her ear.

"Sir, I think…" Wisely, Jones's sidekick stopped thinking when Max levelled that subzero stare at him.

"I'll be at my desk if you need me," he spluttered before hurrying away.

Fucking coward.

Kaylee's punching bag seemed mostly recovered, though his complexion was mottled with anger, blood still trickled from his swollen nose, and his mouth kept opening and closing like a dying fish's. "Are you kidding?" he finally stammered. "You can't fire me!"

"I just did. Take it up with my lawyer if you don't like it."

Jones bit back whatever else he was about to say at the deadly look on Max's face—obviously the guy wasn't a complete moron—and turned around.

Aidan needled him with a cocky grin and a casual press of the down button.

Max waited until Jones had disappeared from sight behind the silver doors—united front and all that—before he spoke in that clipped, all-business tone that Aidan had always associated with him, even in their teens. "You two, in my office."

Kaylee bit her lip like she was trying not to cry.

"You okay?" he asked, his hand automatically lifting to her back in a comforting gesture. Relief surged through him when she didn't shake him off.

"I punched him." Her hazel eyes were wide, like she didn't quite believe it.

He was so fucking in love with her in that moment that he thought his ribs might crack. Still, he managed to keep his voice even. "Yeah you did. Like a heavyweight champ."

Kaylee looked down at her hand, then back at him. "I didn't think it would hurt this much."

Me neither. But it did. It hurt worse than anything he'd ever felt.

Aidan exhaled as they headed for Max's office. "C'mon, Slugger. Let's get you some ice."

CHAPTER TWENTY-TWO

"Somebody had better start talking."

Kaylee followed Max all the way to his desk, dropping into the visitor chair across from him, but Aidan hung back a little, under the guise of taking in the office's killer view and swanky furnishings.

In truth, he was waiting for Max's executive assistant to show up with the ice he'd asked her for.

"Martin Jones called me a hooker and I hit him."

Max's frown darkened, but Aidan didn't get a chance to revel in it, because Max's EA had poked her head into the office. Aidan grabbed the official first-aid-kit-issued ice pack and strode toward Kaylee.

"Where the hell did you learn to punch like that?"

In answer to her brother's question, Kaylee's gaze met Aidan's as he knelt in front of her chair and reached for her injured hand. She was still pissed at him, not that he'd expected less. But when she didn't pull away, he counted it as a win and pressed the cold pack to her battered knuckles, using the opportunity as an excuse to keep touching her, even for just a second or two longer.

"Never mind."

Aidan could hear the eye roll in his friend's voice. Former friend. Whatever.

"You wouldn't say that if you'd seen her jab. She probably broke that asshole's nose. You didn't even draw blood." Aidan got to his feet and turned to face Max. "You should get her to give you some pointers."

The taunt ran out of heat when his gaze fell on a familiar piece of metal, and it drew him forward.

He picked up the little statue of the horse with the flaming mane. His father had given it to Max, and seeing it here, in this office, surprised him. That Max not only had kept it but had it prominently displayed. Aidan set it back on the edge of the desk and cleared his throat. "Nice digs. Looks like the rumors are true—it's good to be king."

Max opened his mouth to reply, but before he managed a word, the door to his office swung open.

"Would you mind explaining why I just got a call from Martin Jones's attorney about a wrongful termination and assault case? And Kaylee's...extracurricular activity is all over social media. Maybe we should move up the press conference before—oh. I'm sorry to interrupt. Vivienne Grant. Head counsel. You must be the reason I'm earning my money today."

The woman was sharp. Or perhaps *precise* was a better term. He almost expected her hand to feel cold and angular, but her palm was surprisingly warm.

"Aidan Beckett, innocent bystander. Assault is over there icing her knuckles, and the wrongful termination part is all on that guy." He tipped his head at Max. The slight twitch of the man's mouth was not lost on him.

Damn it felt good, the two of them on the same side of trouble again.

Then Max iced over, and Aidan recognized the glint of danger in his friend's expression, the one that always sparked when Max dropped the *civilized* in preparation for battle.

"The press conference can wait until its scheduled time. Have Sherri get you the camera footage from the reception area and tell Jones's lawyer to cool his heels. We'll deal with him tomorrow. Right now, I have important things to worry about."

Vivienne's perfectly arched brow lifted, and her gaze fell on Kaylee. "I don't mean to be indelicate, but are you sure Kaylee is the best person to deal with the fallout from this?"

That same spark of danger was all over Kaylee's face when she stood and stared down Max's head counsel. She was fucking magnificent.

"Are you questioning my ability to do my job?"

Aidan got the impression that maybe Vivienne was a little impressed with Kaylee, too. "Not at all. Merely suggesting that some distance might be the best course of action in this case."

"Kaylee can handle it." Max glanced at his lawyer. "If that's all?" Her dismissal was clear in his tone.

Vivienne's nod was sharp. "I'll take care of Jones."

"You always do," Max added, softening the exchange.

Aidan crossed his arms, surprised. That Emma was having more of an effect on Max than he'd realized the night he'd met her.

"Now," Max said, taking a seat behind his desk, "where were we?"

Kaylee tossed Aidan a look that dripped with disdain. "Before this morning's brawl, Aidan was telling me how he bugged my phone yet has nothing to do with the burlesque leak."

Oh, she was in the mood for a fight, then. He was more than happy to oblige.

"Hey, you're the one who started throwing punches. And I wasn't telling you that I bugged your phone. I was telling you that I thought someone else bugged your phone. And if I'm right, they could be listening to us right now, so hand it over."

Kaylee frowned, leaned back in the chair, and readjusted her ice pack. "Once again, I respectfully decline."

So damn stubborn.

"Remember what you said to me when you found out about the malware? You asked if I hacked Whitfield Industries. I didn't," he stressed at the identical dark looks of the Whitfield siblings. "But I did get the spyware I used from Cybercore."

"Jesus Christ. Give him the damn phone, Kaylee."

Aidan hated that Max's order held more weight for her than his request, but he supposed he deserved it. She dug it out of her pocket with her good hand and held it toward him. Aidan popped out the battery before placing both pieces on Max's desk.

"The program I uploaded wouldn't uninstall properly, so it should still be on there. But just in case Cybercore removed it remotely..." Aidan reached into his pocket, pulled out the cell Kearney had given him, and tossed it to Max. "Here's what I used to deploy the malware in the first place."

Max caught the phone easily. "And to what do I owe this sudden show of transparency and goodwill?"

"I'm not doing it for you."

"He's trying to save his ass," Kaylee snarked from her chair, flexing her knuckles under the ice pack.

He was trying to save more than that.

"Probably worried you'll charge him with corporate espionage before he manages to tear us apart from the inside."

Aidan hated the hard edge to her words, the grim set to her mouth. He'd done that to her and he accepted the pain under his ribs as his penance.

"That's not why I'm here," he said, focusing on Kaylee, though his words were meant for Max, too. "Not anymore."

He'd come back for revenge, for that damned code, for answers. He'd expected to leave victorious.

Instead, he was broken in every way a man could be.

"Just go, Aidan. Whitfield Industries is reeling. You got what you came for." Her words were harsh, but Kaylee's eyes showed every bit of the hurt and confusion he'd inflicted.

"You're right. I did get what I came for. But I didn't get what I want."

Her laugh was tinged with bitterness. "And what is it you want?"

"You," he said simply.

Her throat worked, and her grip crushed the ice pack.

"I'm in love with you, KJ."

He'd never said those words to a woman, and he hadn't really expected to say them to her now, and certainly not across a fucking office, but if boxing had taught him anything, it was that sometimes you had to improvise and roll with the punches.

Max's chair creaked in the continued silence, and Aidan spared him a glance. "Maybe I should give you two a minute."

Aidan shook off the courtesy. "No. Stay. I'm done with secrets."

He waited until Kaylee looked at him before he spoke again. "I know you think I'm a bad bet. I used you to get back at Max, and I'm going to regret that for the rest of my life. But I swear to you, I didn't leak your burlesque to the press."

Aidan paced the front of Max's desk, three steps one way, three steps back, a futile attempt to burn off the excess adrenaline in his muscles. He needed to get this out.

"I've spent a lot of time running, trying to escape bad situations and avoid dealing with the hard stuff. I always thought that's just how I was built. But I realize now it's because I've never had a home I wanted to be at."

Aidan drew to a stop in front of Kaylee's chair.

"Until you. You feel like home. And I'm going to prove it to you, KJ. The only way I know how. By sticking around and letting my actions speak for me."

Her face had gone slack, and he couldn't get a bead on what she was thinking, but her knuckles were white against the blue ice pack clutched in her hand.

"You can be mad at me for as long as you need to. But I'm not going anywhere. So when you're ready, come find me, okay? I'll be at home."

And with a nod at Max and a long look at Kaylee, Aidan walked out the door.

CHAPTER TWENTY-THREE

Kaylee dragged a deep, shuddering breath into her lungs.

Aidan *loved* her.

It wasn't…she couldn't…he didn't…

Some random beeping pulled her out of the processing loop she was stuck in, and she looked up as Max removed a sleek black cell phone from the bottom drawer of his desk. It wasn't the one he used day to day, the silver one she knew was tucked away in the breast pocket of his Burberry suit jacket.

Desperate for distraction, for anything that would knock the maelstrom that was Aidan out of her thoughts, Kaylee stood and rounded his desk for a better view. "What are you doing? Deploying the Bat-Signal?"

"In a manner of speaking…" Max hit Redial on a blocked number, and after a couple of rings, a woman's face appeared on the screen, her light brown skin wreathed in a halo of bouncy raven curls, already talking as though she and Max were in the middle of a conversation.

"I'm gonna guess you finally read the info I sent you

about the real reason the government is putting fluoride in the—"

"Not now, AJ. I need you to analyze some spyware," Max interrupted.

Kaylee had a vague impression of a brick wall behind the woman, similar to the one in Aidan's kitchen, before AJ leaned closer, her face filling up the entire screen as she lowered her voice conspiratorially.

"Uh, boss. You know you're not alone, right? Ixnay in front of your ister-say."

Max glanced over his shoulder, and Kaylee turned away to save him the trouble of dismissing her. She almost jumped out of her skin when Max's fingers brushed her wrist, staying her. She stared at the point of contact, then raised her gaze to his.

"You can speak freely in front of her." Max didn't break eye contact with her as he spoke. "Kaylee and I are trying something new."

"And what's that?"

The question came from the woman on the screen, but Kaylee might as well have voiced it herself.

"Honesty."

AJ scrunched her nose up and leaned back. "Sounds pretty fucked up to me, but whatever floats your ocean liner. I assume that since you're bringing this to me instead of your pet security wizards over at Soteria, you're thinking it's linked to the mole who installed the program on Emma's computer."

Max nodded. "A reliable source tells me that one of the programs on this phone is Cybercore issue, but the CEO is playing stupid about the competing malware."

"You think Kearney's playing the ol' double cross on your *reliable source* then?"

"It crossed my mind."

"And how did the dueling malware manifest?"

Max gestured toward the phone and moved slightly to his right. Surprised, Kaylee leaned forward so she was fully in the frame.

"Frozen screen, garbled calls, trouble closing apps. The battery life is nonexistent," Kaylee answered.

AJ nodded. "And where'd you get it?"

"The phone? Wes Brennan gave it to me after my old one broke. Said he didn't need it."

"And how soon after you got it did the glitching start?"

Kaylee bit her lip, thought back. "The next day, I guess." Right after Aidan had installed the spyware. She tried to summon some of her earlier outrage at the thought, but it only made her heart feel raw.

"Well, color me intrigued. I'm all over it, boss. Let's nail this bastard."

"I'll leave the phone in the usual spot?" Max resumed his spot on the video call.

"Correct. Give me forty-eight hours with it and you'll be begging me to accept the ridiculously generous bonus I will so rightly deserve." And with that, AJ disconnected.

Kaylee glanced at Max. Who knew the king of stoicism had so many surprises in him? "Do I even want to know that that's about?"

"What are you still doing here, Kale?"

She didn't like the question. Didn't like the meaning

behind it, or the concern in her brother's eyes. Kaylee set the mangled ice pack on the edge of his desk.

Work. She just needed to focus on work. It was the one thing in the whole world that made sense to her right now. "What do you mean, *what am I doing here?* We have a press conference in under an hour. And I was thinking maybe we should—"

"I was an asshole the day you quit, distracted. I'd lost Emma."

Kaylee's mouth snapped shut at the interruption. She had to lift her chin to maintain eye contact as he stood.

"I'm in love with her, Kale. I thought I'd never see her again, and I couldn't let that happen. So I just walked out and left you to clean up the SecurePay mess. And I'm sorry about that."

Kaylee's eyes widened with astonishment. Her robotic older brother was in love? And with the woman who'd almost ruined SecurePay, the project Max had poured all of his focus into for the last five years and counting?

"I never would have done it if you weren't so damn good at your job."

Kaylee's heart stopped at the compliment. The one she'd been waiting to hear from him for her entire professional life.

"I know you said it was too late for me to play the 'big brother' card, and maybe it is, but I can still play the 'boss' card. And right now I'm telling you—no, I'm ordering you—to take the rest of the day off work."

"But the press conference is—"

"I'll handle it."

"You don't have any talking points and—"

"Not only is Kaylee Whitfield an adult, capable of making her own decisions, but she's done nothing for which she needs to be ashamed. Her personal life is of no concern to us insofar as it does not affect her job performance. Whitfield Industries stands by our director of public relations. And more important, I stand by my sister."

Tears stung her eyes at her brother's words, even though she didn't want them to.

Max put his hands on her shoulders, and she started at the foreignness of the touch. "Do you love him?"

Yes.

Her heart answered before her brain could kick in, and the realization shook her to her core. "So much it's hard to breathe sometimes."

Max let go of her, tipped his chin in the direction of his office door. "Then go *home*."

CHAPTER TWENTY-FOUR

THE ELEVATOR GODS smiled upon her, and instead of a million stops on her way to the lobby, there was only one. Kaylee silently cursed the giggly girls who boarded on the sixth floor as she pressed the close-door button with the speed and voracity of a particularly single-minded woodpecker. With any luck, Aidan hadn't gotten too much of a head start.

She burst into the lobby the second the doors opened, scanning the anonymous, business-suited workday crowd.

Relief and adrenaline, and maybe a little fear, flooded her veins when she spotted him near the security desk, being hassled by Roy. She had a sneaking suspicion that Max had something to do with the stalling tactic, and she made a mental note to thank her brother later.

"Aidan!"

Her half scream echoed and bounced across every hard surface. Everyone loitering in the lobby turned to face her, whether curious about her outburst or because they recognized her from the burlesque scandal, she didn't know.

Didn't care.

Because right now, she had only one concern—winning back the gorgeous, infuriating badass with the golden-blond hair and the black leather jacket who'd turned to face her at the sound of his name.

Kaylee's fingernails dug into her palms as she stood there, frozen, waiting to see what he would do. And then she realized only an elephant would wait.

And she was a motherfucking butterfly.

Her pulse slammed in her ears, sounding a lot like the speed bag at Sal's, but Kaylee ignored it and walked toward him, one step at a time. She didn't falter, didn't stop until Aidan was directly in front of her.

He was still the sexiest man she'd ever seen, the cocky swagger of his stance, the set of his big shoulders, a slight arch in the eyebrow above his bruised eye. "What are you doing down here? You've got a press conference to—"

He stopped talking when she fisted her sore hand in his T-shirt and yanked him close. There was nothing soft about the way she kissed him, commandeering his mouth with the unrestrained hunger he so easily stoked in her. A clash of lips and teeth and tongues that dared him to keep up. Telling him with her body how much she needed him, how much she wanted him, how much she loved him.

He growled as she licked into his mouth, and his hands came up to cradle her head. It was too tender a gesture for the heat of their kiss, love amidst the rush of lust, and it was almost Kaylee's undoing.

They were both panting when the kiss broke, their

foreheads pressed together, his hands fisted in her hair, destroying her bun.

A slight smile toyed with the corner of Aidan's mouth. "What was that for?"

"For being the one person who always saw me, all of me, and never made me feel like I wasn't enough. It's the reason I had a crush on the boy you used to be. And it's why I'm in love with the man you are now."

She placed a hand on his scruffy jaw. "I always thought the reason I kept secrets was because I got off on the illicit thrill of doing something I shouldn't. But I was just hiding. I see that now. I was too scared to stand up for myself and take what I wanted. But I'm not scared anymore."

His hand came up to cradle the back of hers, and he turned his head, pressing a kiss to the middle of her palm.

"I love you, Aidan. And I don't want it to be a secret."

"I love you, too," he said, lacing his fingers through hers and pulling her hand down from his cheek. "And I intend to spend the rest of my life proving it to you, but right now, you've got a job to do." He made a move for the elevator, but she tugged him back.

"Actually, Max is taking care of that. He owes me a press conference. So I thought maybe you could take me home instead."

A beat slipped by as her words landed, and then he squeezed her hand. "It would be my honor," he said softly as they started toward the exit doors.

"Everyone's staring at us."

He glanced around. "Yeah, well, people are perverts,

and you just tongue fucked me in the middle of the lobby."

Kaylee laughed. For the first time in recent memory, she felt light inside. Happy.

"Besides, they've probably never seen a burlesque legend so close up before. With all this publicity, you should have a full house for your show this week."

"Actually, I've been thinking that maybe it's time for Lola to retire, hang up the old pasties."

The announcement stopped him dead. Aidan's frown was full of concern as he searched her face, and it warmed her to know she had that kind of support in her corner.

"What are you talking about? You don't have to give up burlesque. This bullshit media stuff is going to blow over. Even if it doesn't, fuck what they think."

"It's not that. I just don't need her anymore. I don't need to put on a blond wig and blue contacts to feel like myself. Don't get me wrong—I love Lola. I love the confidence she gave me. But right now, I just want to be myself for a while."

Aidan pulled her into his arms, lifted her up his body. Kaylee locked her legs around his waist.

"I love you so fucking much, KJ."

She licked her lips, and his eyes darkened with need as she twisted her hips against his growing erection. "I love you more. And if we weren't in the middle of the lobby, I'd prove it to you."

"Jee-zus. You can't say shit like that to me in public." Aidan's fingers dug into her ass as he did an about-face and headed away from the doors.

Kaylee giggled at the sudden change in direction. If they weren't getting looks before, they definitely were now. "What are you doing?"

"You said Max had everything under control. And just because we're being honest with each other doesn't mean we can't still have some secrets."

She moaned at the delicious friction when he hitched her up his body without breaking stride.

"There's got to be a supply closet around here somewhere."

She was never going to get enough of this man, Kaylee realized, lowering her head until her lips brushed his ear. "Hang a left at the security desk. It's the third door on the right."

* * * * *

AWAKENED BY THE SCARRED ITALIAN

ABBY GREEN

This is for Sharon Kendrick, whose advice I should have taken about two months before I did.

I got there in the end!

Thanks, Sharon!

CHAPTER ONE

LARA TEMPLETON WAS glad of the delicate black lace obscuring her vision and hiding her dry eyes from the sly looks of the crowd around the open grave. They might well suspect that she wasn't grieving the death of her husband, the not so Honourable Henry Winterborne, but she didn't want to give them the satisfaction of confirming it for themselves. So she kept herself hidden. Dressed in sober black from head to toe, as befitting a widow.

A grieving widow who had been left nothing by her husband. Who had, in fact, been little more than an indentured slave for the last three months. A detail this crowd of jackals would no doubt crow over if it ever became public knowledge.

Her husband had had good reason to leave her with nothing. She wouldn't have wanted his money anyway. It wasn't why she'd married him, no matter what people believed. And he hadn't left her anything because she hadn't given him what he wanted. *Herself.* It was her fault he'd ended up injured and in a wheelchair for the duration of their marriage.

No, it wasn't your fault. If he hadn't tried to—

Lara's churning thoughts skittered to a halt when she

realised that people were looking at her expectantly. The back of her neck prickled.

The priest gave a discreet cough and said, *sotto voce*, 'If you'd like to throw some soil on the coffin now, Mrs Winterborne...'

Lara flinched inwardly at the reference to her married name. The marriage had been a farce, and she'd only agreed to it because she'd been blackmailed into it by her uncle. She saw a trowel on the ground near the edge of the grave and, even though it was the last thing she wanted to do, because she felt like a hypocrite, she bent down and scooped up some earth before letting it fall onto the coffin. It made a hollow-sounding *thunk*.

For a moment she had the nonsensical notion that her husband might reach out from the grave and pull her in with him, and she almost stumbled forward into the empty space.

There was a gasp from the crowd and the priest caught her arm to steady her.

Unbelievable, thought the man standing nonchalantly against a tree nearby with his arms crossed over a broad chest. He fixed his gaze on the widow, but she didn't look his way once. She was too busy acting the part—practically throwing herself into the grave.

His mouth firmed, its sensual lines drawing into one hard flat one. He had to hand it to her. She played the part well, dressed in a black form-fitting dress that clung to her willowy graceful frame. Her distinctive blonde hair was tied back in a low bun and a small circular hat sat on her head with a gauzy veil obscuring her face. Oh, he had no doubt she was genuinely grieving...but not for her husband. For the fortune she hadn't been left.

The man's mouth curved up into a cruel smile. That

was the least Lara Winterborne, née Templeton, deserved.

The back of Lara's neck prickled again. But this time it prickled with heat. Awareness. Something she hadn't felt in a long time. She looked up, shaking off the strange sensation, relieved to see that people were moving away from the grave, talking in low tones. It was over.

A movement in the distance caught her eye and she saw the tall figure of a man, broad and powerful, walking away towards the cars. He wore a cap and what looked like a uniform. Just one of the drivers.

But something about his height and those broad shoulders snagged her attention...the way he walked with loose-limbed athleticism. More than her attention. For a fleeting moment she felt dizzy because he reminded her of... *No.* She shut down the thought immediately. It couldn't be him.

Snippets of nearby whispered conversation distracted Lara from the stranger, and as much as she tried to tune it out some words couldn't be unheard.

'Is it really true? She gets nothing?'
'Never should have married her...'
'She was only trying to save her reputation after almost marrying one of the world's most notorious playboys...'

That last comment cut far too close to her painful memories, but Lara had become adept at disregarding snide comments over the past two years. Contrary to what these people believed, she couldn't be more relieved that she'd been left with not a cent of Winterborne's fortune.

She would never have married him in a million years if she hadn't been faced with an impossible situation. A heinous betrayal by her uncle. Nevertheless, she wasn't such a monster that she couldn't feel some emotion for Winterborne's death. But mostly she felt empty. Weary. Tainted by association.

The grief she *did* feel was for something else entirely. Something that had been snatched away from her before it had ever had a chance to live and breathe. *Someone.* Someone she'd loved more than she'd ever thought it possible to love another human being. He'd been hurt and tortured because of her. He'd almost died. She'd had no choice but to do what she had to save him further pain and possibly worse.

Swallowing back the constriction in her throat, Lara finally turned away from the grave and started to walk towards where just a couple of cars remained. She wasn't paying for any of this. She couldn't afford it. As soon as she returned to the exclusive apartment she'd shared with her husband there would be staff waiting with her bags to escort her off the premises. Her husband had wanted to maintain the façade as far as the graveside. But now all bets were off. She was on her own.

She clamped down on the churning panic in her gut. She would deal with what to do and where to go when she had to.

That's in approximately half an hour, Lara!

She ignored the inner voice.

One of the funeral directors was standing by the back door of her car, holding it open. She saw the shadowy figure of the driver in the front seat. Once again she felt that prickle of recognition but she told herself she was being silly, superstitious. She was only thinking of *him* now because she was finally free of the burden that had been thrust upon her. But she couldn't allow her thoughts to go there.

She murmured her thanks as she sat into the back of the luxurious car. It was the last bit of decadence she'd experience for some time. Not that she cared. A long time ago, when she'd lost her parents and her older brother in a tragic accident, she'd learnt the hard way that nothing external mattered once you'd lost the people you loved most.

But clearly it hadn't been enough of a lesson to protect her from falling in love with—

The car started moving and Lara welcomed the distraction.

Not thinking of him now.

No matter how much a random stranger had reminded her of him.

Unable to stop her curiosity, though, she looked at the only part of the driver's face she could see in the rear-view mirror. It was half hidden by aviator-style sunglasses, but she could see a strong aquiline nose and firm top lip. A hard, defined jaw.

Her heart started to beat faster, even though rationally she knew it couldn't possibly be—

At that moment he seemed to sense her regard from the back and she saw his arm move before the privacy window slid up. Cutting her off.

For some reason Lara felt as if he'd put the window up as a rebuke. *Ridiculous.* He was just a driver! He'd probably assumed she wanted some privacy…

Still, the disquieting niggle wouldn't go away.

It got worse when she realised that while they were headed in the right direction, back to the Kensington apartment she'd shared with her husband, they weren't getting closer. They were veering off the main high street onto another street nearby, populated by tall, exclusive townhouses.

Lara had walked down this street nearly every day for two years, and had relished every second she wasn't in the oppressively claustrophobic apartment with her husband. But it wasn't her street. The driver must be mistaken.

As the car drew to a stop outside one of the houses Lara leant forward and tapped the window. For a moment nothing happened. She tapped again, and suddenly it slid down with a mechanical buzz.

The driver was still facing forward, his left hand on the wheel. For some reason Lara felt nervous. Yet she was on a familiar street with people passing by the car.

'Excuse me, we're not in the right place. I'm just around the corner, on Marley Street.'

Lara saw the man's jaw clench, and then he said, 'On the contrary, *cara*. We're in exactly the right place.'

That voice. *His voice.*

Lara's breath stopped in her throat and in the same moment the man took off the cap and removed his sunglasses and turned around to face her.

She wasn't sure how long she sat there, stupefied. In shock. Time ceased to exist as a linear thing.

His words from two years ago were still etched into her mind. *'You will regret this for the rest of your life, Lara. You belong to me.'*

And here he was to crow over her humiliation.

Ciro Sant'Angelo.

The fact that she'd said to him that day, *'I will regret nothing,'* was not a memory she relished. She'd regretted it every second since that day. But she'd been desperate, and she'd had no choice. He'd been brutalised and almost killed. And all because she'd had the temerity to meet him and fall in love, going against the very exacting plans her uncle had orchestrated on her behalf, unbeknownst to her.

If she was honest with herself, she'd dreamed of this moment. That Ciro would come for her. But the reality was almost too much to take in. She wasn't prepared. She would never be prepared for a man like Ciro Sant'Angelo. She hadn't been two years ago and she wasn't now.

Panic surged. She blindly reached for the door handle but it wouldn't open. She tried the other one. *Locked.* Breathless, she looked back at him and said, 'Open the doors, Ciro, this is crazy.'

But nothing happened. He responded with a sardonic twist of his mouth. 'Should I be flattered that you remember me, Lara?'

She might have laughed at that moment if she hadn't been so stunned. Ciro Sant'Angelo was not a man easily forgotten by anyone. Tall, broad and leanly muscular, he oozed charisma and authority. Add to that the stunning symmetry of a face dominated by deep-set dark eyes and a mouth sculpted for sin. A hard jaw and slightly hawkish profile cancelled out any prettiness.

He would have been perfection personified if it wasn't for the jagged white ridge of skin that ran from under his right eye to his jaw. She could only look at it now with sick horror as the knowledge sank into her gut: she was responsible for that brutal scar.

He angled the right side of his face towards her, a hard light in his eyes. 'Does it disgust you?'

She shook her head slowly. It didn't detract from his beauty, it added a savage element. Dangerous.

'Ciro...' Lara said faintly now, as the truth finally sank in, deep in her gut. This wasn't a dream or a mirage...or a nightmare. She shook her head. 'What are you doing here? What do you want?'

I want what's mine.

The words beat through Ciro Sant'Angelo's body like a Klaxon. His blood was up, boiling over.

Lara Templeton—*Winterborne*—was here. Within touching distance. After two long years. Years in which he'd tried and failed to excise her treacherous, beautiful face from his mind.

A face he needed to see now more than he needed to acknowledge her question. 'Take your hat off.'

Her bright blue eyes flashed behind the veil. He could see the slope of her cheek down to that delicate jaw and the mouth that had made him want to sin as soon as he'd laid eyes on it. Full and ripe. A sensual reminder that beneath her elegant and coolly blonde exterior she was all fire.

Her lips compressed for a second and then she lifted a trembling hand—*another nice dramatic touch*—and pulled off the hat and veil.

And even though Ciro had steeled himself to face her once again she took his breath away. She hadn't changed in two years. She was still a classic beauty. Finely etched eyebrows framing huge blue eyes ringed with long dark lashes… High cheekbones and a straight nose… And that mouth… Like a crushed rosebud. Promising decadence even as her eyes sent a message of innocence and naivety.

He'd fallen for it. Badly. Almost fatally.

'Not here,' he said curtly, angry with himself for letting Lara get to him on a level that he'd hoped to have under control. 'We'll talk inside.'

Inside where? Lara was about to ask, but Ciro was already out of the car and striding towards an intimidating townhouse. Her door was opened by a uniformed man—presumably the real driver?—and Lara didn't have much choice but to step out of the back of the car.

As she did, she noticed two or three intimidating-looking men in suits with earpieces. *Security.* Of course. Ciro had always been cavalier about his safety before, but she could imagine that after the kidnapping he'd changed.

The kidnapping.

A cold shiver went down her spine. Ciro Sant'Angelo had been kidnapped and brutally assaulted two years ago. Lara had been kidnapped with him, but she'd been released within hours. Dumped at the side of a road outside Florence. It had been the singularly most terrifying thing they'd ever experienced and *she'd* been the reason it had happened.

For a moment Lara hesitated at the bottom of the steps leading up to a porch and an open front door. She could see black and white tiles in the circular hallway. A grand-looking interior.

'Mr Sant'Angelo is waiting.'

One of the suited men was extending his arm towards the house. He looked civil enough, but she imagined it was a very superficial civility.

She went up the steps and through the door. A sleek-looking middle-aged woman approached her with a polite smile. 'Miss Templeton, welcome. Please let me take your things. Mr Sant'Angelo is waiting for you in the lounge.'

Numbly, Lara handed over her hat and bag, barely even noticing the use of her maiden name. She wore a light cape-style coat over her shift dress and she left it on, even though it was warm. She followed the woman, not liking the sensation that she was walking into the lion's den.

The sensation was only heightened when she saw the tall figure of Ciro, his back to her as he helped himself to a drink from a tray on the far side of the room.

'Would you like tea or coffee, Miss Templeton?'

Lara shook her head at the question from the woman and murmured, 'No, thanks.' The housekeeper left the room.

The muted sounds of London traffic could be heard through the huge windows. It was a palatial lounge, beautifully decorated in classic colours with massive paintings hanging on the walls. The paintings were abstract, and a vivid memory exploded into Lara's head of when Ciro had taken her to an art gallery in Florence, after hours.

They'd only just met a few days previously, and she'd been surprised enough at his choice of gallery to make him say with a mocking smile, 'You expected a rough Sicilian to have no taste?'

She'd blushed, because he'd exposed her for assuming that a very alpha Italian man would veer towards something more…classical, conservative.

She'd turned to him, still shy around him, wondering what on earth he was doing with her, a pale English arts student. 'You're not rough…not at all.'

He'd been like a sleek panther, oozing a very lethal sense of coiled sensual energy.

The gallery had been hushed and reverential. She could still remember the delicious knot of tension deep in her abdomen, and how she'd thought to herself, *How can I not fall in love with this man who opens art galleries especially for me and makes me feel more alive than I've ever felt?*

They hadn't even kissed at that stage...

Ciro's voice broke through her reverie. 'Would you like something stronger, Lara? Perhaps some brandy for the overwhelming grief you must be feeling?'

Lara's nerves were jangling. He'd turned to face her now, and she noticed that he'd taken off the jacket and wore dark trousers and a white shirt open at the throat. Her mouth went dry. She knew how he tasted there. She could still remember how she'd explored that hollow with her tongue—

Stop.

She ignored his question. 'How long have you lived here?' Had he been here all this time? Just seconds away from where she'd been existing so miserably?

Lara thought she saw Ciro's hand tighten on his glass, but put it down to her overwrought imagination. He said, 'I bought it months ago but the renovations have only just been completed.'

So he hadn't been living here. Somehow that thought comforted Lara. She didn't know if she could have borne being married to Winterborne while knowing Ciro was so close. Even the thought of seeing him with another woman coming out of this house made her insides clench. *Crazy.* She had no jurisdiction over this man. She never had. She'd been dreaming. Delusional.

She lifted her chin. 'I don't have time for this, Ciro... whatever it is that you want. I have to be somewhere.'

Evicted. She ignored the fresh spiking of panic.

Ciro lifted his tumbler of golden liquid and downed the lot in one go. For a second Lara wished she'd asked for a drink.

Then he said slowly, 'But that's just it, Lara. You don't have anywhere to go, do you?'

She actually felt the blood drain from her face. How could he possibly...?

'How can I know?'

He read her mind. Speared her with that dark gaze. Maybe she'd spoken out loud. She felt as if she were slipping under water, losing all sense of control.

He lifted a brow. 'The guests at the funeral were a hotbed of gossip, but I also have my contacts, who've informed me that Winterborne left everything to a distant relative and that as soon as you collect your things from the apartment, you're out on the streets. As for your trust fund—apparently you've blown through that too. Poor penniless Lara. You should have stayed with me. I'm worth three times as much as your dead husband and you wouldn't have had to put up with an old man in your bed for the past two years.'

Lara's head hurt to think of how he'd obtained all that information about her trust fund, and her insides churned at the mention of *old man*.

Any money left to her by her parents had been long gone before she'd ever had a chance to lay her hands on it. 'It was never about the money.'

Ciro's mouth tightened. 'No. It was about class.'

No, Lara thought, *it was about blackmail and coercion*.

But, yes, it had been about class too. Albeit not for her; she couldn't have cared less about class. She never had. Not that Ciro would ever believe her. Not after the way she'd convinced him otherwise.

She clamped her lips together, resisting the urge to defend herself when she knew it would be futile. She hardly knew this person in front of her, even though at one time she'd felt as if she'd known every atom of his being. He'd disabused her of that romantic notion two years ago. Yet, she couldn't deny the rapid and persistent spike in her pulse-rate ever since Ciro had revealed himself. Her body *knew* him.

Something caught her eye then, and she gasped. His right hand...the one holding the glass...was missing a little finger.

He saw where her gaze had gone. 'Not very pretty, eh?'

Lara felt sick. She remembered Ciro lying in that hospital bed, his head and half his face covered in bandages...his arms... She'd been too distraught to notice much else.

'They did that to you? The kidnappers?' Her voice was a thread.

He nodded. 'It amused them. They got bored, waiting for their orders.'

Lara realised that he was different. Harder. More intimidating. 'Why am I here, Ciro?'

'Because you betrayed me.' He carefully put down the glass on the silver tray. And then he looked at her. 'And I'm here to collect my due.'

My due. The words revolved sickeningly in Lara's head.

'I don't owe you anything.' The words felt cumbersome in her mouth.

Liar, whispered a voice.

'Yes, Lara you do. You walked out on me when I needed you most, leaving me at the mercy of the press, who had a field day reviving all the old stories about my family's links to the Mafia. Not only that, you left me without a bride.'

A spark of anger mixed with her guilt as she recalled the lurid headlines in the aftermath of the kidnapping and her subsequent engagement to Henry Winterborne. She focused on the anger.

'You only wanted to marry me to take advantage of my connections to a society that had refused you access.'

Ciro hadn't loved her. He'd wanted her because at first she'd intrigued him, with her naivety and innocence, and then because of her connections and her name.

Over the last two years, with the benefit of distance and hindsight, Lara had come to acknowledge how refreshing someone like her must have been for someone as jaded as him. She'd been so trusting. *Loving.*

If they had married it never would have lasted. Not beyond the point where her allure would have worn off and he would have become disenchanted with her innocence. Not beyond the point at which her name and connections would have served their purpose for his ambitions. Of that she had no doubt.

Of course he wasn't going to forgive her for taking all that away from him. He was out for revenge.

For a heady moment Lara imagined telling him exactly what had happened. How events had conspired to drive them apart. How her uncle had so cruelly manipulated her. She even opened her mouth—but then she remembered Ciro's caustic words. They resounded in her head as if he'd said them only moments ago.

'Don't delude yourself that I felt anything more for you than you felt for me, Lara. I wanted you, yes, but that was purely physical. More than all of that I wanted you because marrying you would have given me a stamp of respectability that money can't buy.'

Ciro's voice broke through the toxic memory as he said coolly, 'I prefer to think of it as a kind of debt repayment. You said you'd marry me and I'm holding you to that original commitment. I need a wife, and I've no intention of getting into messy emotional entanglements when you're so convenient.'

Lara's blood drained south. 'That's the most ridiculous thing I've ever heard.'

'Is it? Really? People have married for a lot less, Lara.'

She looked at him helplessly, torn between hating him for appearing like a magician to turn her world upside down and desperately wanting to defend herself. But she'd lost that chance when she'd informed him coldly that she'd never had any intention of going through with their marriage because she was already promised to someone else—someone eminently more suitable.

She'd told him that it had amused her to go along with his whirlwind proposal, just to see him make a fool of himself over a woman he could never hope to marry. She'd told him all her breathy words of love had been mere platitudes.

She'd never forget the look of pure loathing that had come over his face after she'd spoken those bilious words. That had been the moment when she'd realised how deluded she'd been. And on some level she'd been glad she was playing a role, that at least she knew how he'd really felt.

He was almost killed because of you.

Lara felt sick again. He hadn't deserved that just for not loving her. And he hadn't deserved her lies. He'd saved her from the kidnappers. He'd offered up his life for hers. And then she'd learned she'd never really been in danger. He didn't know that, though. And right now the thought of him ever finding that out made her break out in a cold sweat. However much he hated her already, he would despise her even more.

Suddenly a ball of emotion swelled inside her chest. Lara couldn't bear it that Ciro thought so badly of her, even if it *was* her fault that she'd convinced him so well. Seeing him again was ripping open a raw wound inside her, and before she knew what she was doing she took a step forward, words tumbling out of her mouth.

'Ciro, I *did* want to marry you—more than anything. But my uncle…he was crazy…he'd lost everything. He didn't want me to marry you—he saw you as unworthy of a Templeton. He forced me to say those awful things… They were all lies.'

Lara stopped abruptly and her words hung in the air. The atmosphere was thick with tension. Taut like a wire. Ciro was expressionless. She could remember a time when he'd used to look at her with such warmth and indulgence. And *love*, or so she'd thought. But it hadn't been love. It had been desire. Physical desire and the desire for success.

He lifted his hands and did a slow and deliberate hand-clap, the sound loud in the room. Lara flinched.

He shook his head. 'You really are something, Lara, you know that? But the victim act doesn't suit you and it's wasted on me. You really expect me to believe you were *coerced* into marrying a man old enough to be your father and rich enough to pay off the national debt of a small country? You forget I've seen your extensive repertoire of guises, and this innocent, earnest one is overdone and totally unnecessary.'

Her belly sank. She'd known it was futile to try. How could she explain how her uncle had manipulated and exploited her for his own gain since the moment he'd taken over her guardianship after her parents had died? The extent of his ruthlessness still shocked her, even now.

And she should recognise ruthlessness by now. She should have known Ciro hadn't been making idle threats two years ago. After all, he was Sicilian through every fibre of his being. He came from a long and bloody tradition of men who meted out revenge and punishment as a way of life, even if they had tried to distance themselves from all that in recent generations.

Ciro had told her once that his ancestors had been Moorish pirates and she could well believe it. She could see that he'd been wounded beyond redemption—not in his heart, because that had never been available to wound, but in his fierce Sicilian pride. Wounded when she'd walked away, and by the ruthless kidnappers when they'd physically altered him for ever and demonstrated that even he wasn't invincible.

She did owe him a debt. But it was a debt she couldn't afford to pay emotionally.

Lara's sense of self-preservation kicked in and she cursed herself for even trying to defend herself. She couldn't bear for him to find out just how vulnerable she really was—how nothing had really moved on for her since she'd known him. How the last two years of her life had been a kind of lonely torture.

She ruthlessly pushed aside all those memories and shrugged one shoulder minutely, affecting an air of boredom. She'd played this part once before—she could do it again.

'Well, it's been interesting to see you again, Ciro. But quite frankly you're even more pathetic now than you were two years ago, if this is how little you've moved on. What would you have done if Henry hadn't died? Kidnapped me? Seduced me away and then meted out your punishment?'

Lara's words fell like stinging barbs onto Ciro's skin.

They cut far too close to the bone. He had been keeping tabs on her. Getting reports on her whereabouts and her activities—which, as far as he could see, had consisted of not much at all. Not even socialising. Her husband had monopolised her attention, kept her all to himself.

Ciro hadn't articulated to himself exactly what he was going to do where Lara was concerned, but he'd known he had reached some kind of nadir when he'd bought this house, sight unseen, because it was around the corner from where she lived. He'd known that he was reaching a place where he simply could not go on without exacting retribution.

Without seeing her again.

He crushed that rogue thought.

In the past few months, as a restless tension had increased inside him, he'd found himself contemplating seducing Lara Winterborne. He'd told himself it would be to prove just how duplicitous she was. But he knew that his motivations were murkier than that. Embedded in a place he'd locked them away two years ago, when she'd morphed into a stranger in front of his very eyes.

When she'd shown him up as a fool who had cast aside his well-worn cynical shell in a fit of blind lust and something even more disturbing. *Emotion.* A yearning for a life he'd never known. For a woman who was pure and who would be faithful. Loving. Loyal. A good mother. Fantasies he'd never indulged in before he'd met Lara and she'd exposed a seam of vulnerability he'd never acknowledged before.

The fact that he'd even considered seducing her away from her husband was galling for a man who had always vowed to conduct his life with more integrity than his mother—never to stoop to her level of betrayal. And yet he'd had to face the unwelcome realisation that his desires were no less base than his weak and adulterous mother's.

Lara watched a series of expressions flicker across Ciro's face. They gradually got darker and darker, until he was glaring at her as if she was the sum of all evil. He started moving towards her then, all coiled lethal masculinity, and Lara took an involuntary step back.

She wasn't scared of his physicality—not even with this tension in the air. She was scared of something far more ambiguous and personal deep inside where she knew he had the ability to destroy her. Where he'd already destroyed her.

He stood in front of her, his scent winding around her like invisible captive threads. He asked with lethal softness, 'Are you suggesting my life has been on hold?'

Before she could respond, a sound halfway between a sneer and a laugh came out of Ciro's mouth.

'Oh, *cara,* my life hasn't been on hold for one second since you decided to take that old man into your bed.'

Lara winced inwardly. She already knew that Ciro's life hadn't been on hold. Far from it. As much as she'd tried to block him out of her consciousness, it had been next to impossible. Since his kidnapping he'd become even more infamous and sought-after. He'd tripled his fortune, extending the wildly successful Sant'Angelo Holdings, which had been mainly focused on real estate, to encompass logistics and shipping worldwide.

And he hadn't been seen with the same woman twice—which was some feat, considering the frequency with which he'd been photographed at every ubiquitous glamorous event on the European and the worldwide circuit.

The gossip about his hectic love-life had quickly eclipsed any rumours about why his wedding to Lara hadn't taken place. Most people had assumed exactly what her uncle had wanted them to assume—that the kidnapping and fresh stories of his links to the Mafia had scared off Lara Templeton, one of Britain's most eligible society heiresses.

If anything the tone of the gossip about her had been as sneering as about Ciro—especially when she'd got married so quickly after the event, to a man more than twice her age. It was as if she'd merely proved her own snobbishness. As if she hadn't been woman enough to handle Ciro Sant'Angelo.

Certainly all the women he had been photographed with since then had run to a type that was a million miles from Lara's cool blonde, blue-eyed looks. Women with flashing dark eyes and glossy hair. With unashamedly sexy and curvaceous bodies and an effortless sensuality that Lara could never hope to embody. She was too self-conscious. Too...inexperienced.

Ciro was shaking his head now, a look of disgust twisting his features and making his scar stand out even more. 'Did you keep up the virginal act with your husband? Or did you fake it right up until—?'

'Stop it!' The sharp cry of Lara's voice surprised even herself. She felt shaky. 'That wasn't an act.'

Ciro made a rude sound, dismissing her words. More proof that she'd been utterly naive to try and defend herself. All she could hope for was that Ciro would get bored and ask her to leave.

'Look, what do you want, Ciro?' Lara's voice had a distinctly desperate tone that she didn't even try to disguise now.

'It's very simple. I want *you*, Lara.' He folded his arms across his formidable chest. 'It's time to pay your debt.'

CHAPTER TWO

Lara's sense of panic and desperation increased. 'I told—you I don't owe you anything.'

Ciro responded, 'We've been through this and, yes, you do. You owe me a wedding.'

Lara fought to stay calm. To appear unmoved. 'Don't be ridiculous. I'm not going to marry you.'

He shook his head. 'Not ridiculous at all. Very practical, actually. Like I said, I'm in need of a wife, and as you deprived me of one so memorably two years ago, you can step up now and honour the commitment you made when you agreed to marry me in the first place.'

Vainly scrabbling around for something—anything to make sense of Ciro's crazy suggestion, Lara asked, 'Why do you need a wife so badly?'

'The circles I'm moving in… Let's just say things would be better for me if I had an appearance of stability. Settling down. Conforming to societal norms of what people expect of a man my age.'

'An appearance… So this would just be a sham…a fake marriage?'

'Call it a marriage of convenience.'

'But it'll mean nothing.'

Ciro's lip curled. 'As if *that* was a concern in your first marriage… As if you *cared* about Winterborne.'

Lara had to hide her flinch at that.

Ciro continued, 'It'll be a lesson in learning that your actions have consequences.'

She took a step backwards, surprised that her legs were still working. 'This is beyond crazy. If marriage is so important to your image then I'm sure there are many more suitable women who would be happy to become your wife.'

Like any of the hundreds of women she'd seen on his arm over the past twenty-four months, for a start.

'I don't want any of them. I want *you*.'

Ciro was finding it hard to maintain his composure. Lara was right—there were plenty of women he knew who would jump at the opportunity to become his wife. He'd found himself seeking out women who were the antithesis of this woman's cool blonde looks, but none of them had made his blood run hot as she could, just by standing in front of him.

For two years his bed had been lonely and he had been frustrated. Not that the world would believe it. But he hadn't wanted any of them. He wanted Lara. And now, after two years of a kind of purgatory, hating her and wanting her, she was finally within reach again.

He would be the first to admit that his pride had suffered a huge blow when she'd walked away from him and from their marriage commitment. He was, after all, descended from a long line of proud Sicilians.

She'd accused him of only wanting to marry her to further his ambitions for social acceptance and he hadn't been able to deny it. But it hadn't been as much to the forefront of his desire to marry her as he'd let her believe. However, he had to admit that it had always been in the back of his mind...her strategic connections.

But, more than that, he hadn't been done with her.

When she'd told him she was a virgin—most likely a lie—Ciro had been stunned. To think that she was untouched...a rare novelty in his jaded world, had been, surprisingly, and seriously, erotic. The prospect that he would be her first lover had tipped Ciro over the edge of his restraint where Lara was concerned.

He'd always been traditional and Sicilian enough to envisage taking an innocent wife some day, but also cynical and experienced enough to know that it was next to impossible in this modern world. And yet there had been Lara, with her huge innocent blue eyes that had looked at him sometimes as if he was a hungry wolf, and her body with its slender lines and lush curves, telling him that she was this rare thing. An innocent in a world of cynics.

She'd led him a merry dance. Convincing him that she had something he'd never seen before in his life: an intoxicating naivety. But it had all been an act. For her own amusement. Because she'd been bored. Or as jaded as him.

Lara stood in front of him now, tall in her heels, but she'd still only reach his shoulder. For a second something inside him faltered.

Had her eyes always been so blue and so huge? She was pale now, her cheeks and lips almost bloodless. Because she was disgusted by his proposal? Good.

Ciro had to forcibly curb the urge to clamp his hands around her face, angle it up towards him and plunder that mouth until she was flushed and her mouth was throbbing with blood.

No other woman had ever had the same effect on him. Instantaneous. Elemental. He vowed right then that she would never see how easily she pushed him to the edge of his control.

He took a step back. Lara had denied him before but she wouldn't deny him now. She owed him. Owed him her body and the connections a marriage to her would bring him.

'Well, Lara?'

'This is the day of my husband's funeral...have you no sense of decency?'

Ciro could have laughed at her dogged refusal to stop acting. 'Are you telling me you really *cared* about the old man?'

The thought that she might actually be grieving for her husband slid into his mind for a second before he brutally quashed it. *Impossible*.

She flushed. With guilt. Ciro didn't like the rush of relief he felt. 'Save your energy, *cara*. Your acting skills are wasted on me.'

'Stop calling me that. I'm not your *cara*.'

Her hands were balled into fists by her sides and her eyes were bright blue.

Ciro uncrossed his arms. 'You never minded it before... If I remember correctly you used to love it.' He mimicked her breathless voice, *'"Ciro, what does it mean...? Am I really your* cara?"'

'That was before.' Lara's cheeks had lost their colour again.

'Yes,' Ciro said harshly, angry that he noticed so much about this woman. Every little tic. 'That was when you were only too happy to court infamy by becoming engaged to me to alleviate your boredom. What I can't quite understand, though, is the virginal act? That was a touch of authenticity that deprived us both of mutual pleasure.'

It was excruciating to Lara that Ciro remembered how ardently she'd loved him. How much she'd wanted him.

Without thinking about it, just needing to wound him as he was wounding her, she let words tumble out of her mouth. 'I never wanted you.'

As soon as she'd said the words she realised her mistake. Colour scored Ciro's cheekbones, making the scar stand out even more lividly. His eyes burned a dark brown, almost black. She was mesmerised by the fierce pride she could see in his expression. He was every inch the bristling Sicilian male now.

'Little liar,' he breathed. 'You wanted me as much as I wanted you. *More.*'

He came towards her, closing the gap. Lara's feet were frozen to the floor. He reached for her, hands wrapping around her waist, pulling her towards him, until she could feel the taut and unforgiving musculature of his body. But not even that could break her out of this dangerous stasis. She was filled with a kind of excitement she'd only ever felt with this man.

She'd thought she'd never feel it again, and something exultant was moving through her, washing aside all her reservations and the sane voices screaming at her to wake up. Pull back.

Ciro's hands tightened on her waist and his head came down, blocking out the room, blocking out everything but *him*. Lara's breath was caught in her throat, nerves tingling as she waited for that firm mouth to touch hers. It was so torturous she made a small sound of pleading...

Ciro heard the tiny sound come from Lara's mouth. He knew this was the moment when he should pull back. He'd already proved his point. She was practically begging him to kiss her... But his body wouldn't follow the dictates of his mind. She was like a quivering flame under his hands. So achingly familiar and yet utterly new.

He could feel the press of her high firm breasts, the flare of her hips, the cradle of her pelvis. He burned for her. He'd been such a fool to believe in her innocence. He'd held back from indulging in her treacherous body. But no longer.

Ciro gave in to the wild pulsing beat of desire in his body and claimed Lara's mouth with his. For a second he couldn't move—the physical sensation of his mouth on hers was too mind-blowing. And then hunger took over. He could feel her breath, sharp and choppy, and he deepened the kiss, taking it from chaste to sexual in seconds.

Lara was wrapped in Ciro's arms, and for a moment she happily gave up any attempt to bring back reality. His touch and his kiss, that masterful way he had of touching her and bringing her alive—she'd dreamed of this so often.

His taste was heady and all-consuming. She barely noticed his hands moving up her body, cupping her face so he could angle it better and take the kiss deeper, make it even more explicit. She craved him. Pressed herself even tighter against him.

The knot at the back of her head loosened and the sensation of her hair falling around her shoulders finally broke through enough for her to falter for a moment. And a moment was all she needed to allow enough air back into her oxygen-starved brain to recall what Ciro had called her. *Little liar.* And she'd just proved him right.

She stiffened and pushed against Ciro. He let her go and stood back, but it was no comfort. Lara already ached for him. The glitter of triumph in his eyes only added salt to the wound she'd opened.

She felt totally dishevelled and unsteady on her feet. Her cheeks were hot and her mouth felt swollen. She'd just humiliated herself spectacularly.

She lifted a shaking hand to her mouth. 'You had no right to—'

'To what?' he said silkily. 'To demonstrate that our chemistry is still very much mutual and alive?'

It wasn't much of a consolation that Ciro didn't look overly thrilled about that fact.

He shook his head, his dark hair gleaming. 'In this at least you can't hide your true nature.'

He started to walk around her and Lara's skin prickled. Her pulse was still pounding. She felt raw.

'How could you do it?' he asked from close behind her. 'How could you take that man into your bed every night and let him—?'

Lara whirled around, bile rising. 'Stop it! I won't discuss my dead husband. Not on the day of his funeral. It's…immoral.'

Ciro emitted a harsh bark of laughter. '*Immoral*, is it? More immoral than promising yourself to a man only to leave him by the wayside as soon as you realise how close you've come to sullying the perfect Templeton family line with a brood of half-Sicilians?'

Lara's heart squeezed painfully. At one time she had fantasised about the children she would have with Ciro, wondering if they'd inherit their father's dark good looks and vital charisma. The fantasy mocked her now. She'd been so deluded.

Her voice trembling slightly, she said, 'You accuse me of being immoral, but you admitted that your motive for marriage was nothing but a cold calculation to improve your social standing.'

Ciro stood back and his dark gaze narrowed on her. She immediately felt exposed.

'There was nothing immoral about seeking out a union that would benefit us both. You really didn't have to go so far as to feign feelings for me, *cara*. It was entertaining, but unnecessary.'

Lara smarted as she recalled yet again how naive she'd been. Because it wasn't as if he'd led her on—he hadn't professed any feelings for *her*. Instead she'd pathetically read too much into every tiny gesture and word, building up a very flimsy belief that he was falling for her too.

Ciro continued. 'Why didn't you try to secure your future by giving Winterborne an heir? Is that why he left you with nothing? Because you didn't fulfil your wifely duty?'

Lara shook her head to negate what he'd said. She couldn't seem to formulate words. Memories were rushing at her in a jangled kaleidoscope of images—Ciro proposing, down on one knee in the middle of a *piazza* in Florence, with everyone looking on and clapping, the pure joy she'd felt in that moment.

And then another memory—the awful dark, dank smell of fear as she'd been jostled in the back of that van with a hood over her head. Ciro's arms had been around her and she'd clung to him with a death grip…

'I don't… I never wanted to marry—'

'Me,' Ciro interjected. 'Yes, I know.'

Lara swallowed. He'd misunderstood her. She'd wanted to marry Ciro so desperately that she was afraid if she opened her mouth now it might all spill out and then he would tear her to shreds.

She couldn't imagine—didn't want to—what he would do if he ever found out that her uncle had been behind the kidnapping in an elaborate bid to show Lara the lengths to which he would go to ensure she married someone 'suitable'.

She had to regain control of this situation and of her fraying emotions. She injected all the *froideur* she could muster into her voice. 'You've proved your point, Ciro. You haven't forgiven me for leaving you. But if it's a wife you need I suggest you look elsewhere. I'm not available.'

She turned away to leave, but before she could take a step her arm was taken by a firm hand. She stopped, every part of her body tense against the inevitable effect Ciro had on her.

He drew her back around to face him. 'Please do tell me what it is you're so busy with now that you're a free woman again?'

He dropped her arm, but the imprint of his fingers lingered. She rubbed it distractedly. She looked at him, but the truth was that she was busy with nothing, because she literally *had* nothing—as he well knew.

She had just enough money in her account to see her through a week, maybe, in an inexpensive hostel. And that was it. She had nowhere to go. No one to go to.

The stark reality of just how isolated she was hit her like a body-blow.

'The fact is you're not busy—isn't that the truth, Lara?'

It was as if Ciro was delving casually into her mind and pulling out her innermost humiliation for inspection.

She tipped up her chin. 'I'll keep myself busy finding a job, somewhere to live.'

Ciro snorted. 'A *job*? You wouldn't know a job if it jumped up and bit you. I doubt an art history degree gets you very far these days. You were bred to fulfil a role in society, Lara. Anything else is beneath you.'

Hurt hit Lara squarely in the chest. She'd once confided in Ciro about wanting to do more than what was expected of her. No doubt he thought she'd been lying.

She lashed out. 'You mean like marrying you? We went through this once before—do you *really* want to be humiliated again, Ciro?'

This was the Lara that Ciro remembered. Showing her true haughty colours. He could recall only too easily how two years ago she'd morphed in front of his eyes into someone distant and calculating. Utterly without remorse.

It had shocked him. And yet it shouldn't have. Because it wasn't as if he hadn't already learnt how beautiful women operated at the hands of his brittle, self-absorbed mother. She'd made a fool of his father over and over again in her bid for desperate validation that she was desired.

His father had put up with it because he'd loved her, and Ciro had believed from an early age that if that was what love meant, he wanted none of its ritual humiliation.

And yet Lara had sneaked under his defences before he'd known what was happening.

His first image of her was still etched into his memory, no matter how much he'd tried to excise it. She'd been standing just a few steps from Ciro on a busy street in Florence, a hand up to her face, shading her eyes, seemingly entranced by an ornate building. She'd been like a vision of a Valkyrie princess against the ancient

Florentine backdrop. Long bright blonde hair falling to the middle of her back... Acres of pale skin...

She'd been oblivious to the attention she was drawing. *Or so Ciro had believed.* But now he knew she must have been aware of exactly what she was doing, with that face of an angel and the body of a siren.

Suddenly someone had jostled her from the pavement and she'd stumbled into the busy road. She would have been hit by a car if not for Ciro grabbing her and pulling her to safety. She'd landed against him, all soft lithe curves. Silky hair under his hands. And her scent... lemon and roses. Huge shocked blue eyes had stared up into his and he'd fallen into instant lust, for the first and only time in his life. Captivated.

But memories were for fools and he would never be such a fool again. He knew who—*what*—Lara was now. He would make use of her and then discard her, exactly as she had done with him when he'd literally been at his lowest point.

'You're really not in a position to bargain, Lara. You have nowhere to go and no one to turn to. You wouldn't survive half an hour outside that door.'

Lara clenched her hands into fists. The only thing stopping her making a vociferous defence was the fact that Ciro was speaking her fears out loud. What skills did she have? What meaningful education? Where would an interesting but useless degree get her in this new digital age? Some menial job in an art gallery if she was lucky? She could probably plan and host a diplomatic function for fifty people, but in reality domestic cleaners were more highly qualified than she was.

Taking advantage of her silence, Ciro said, 'This is what I'm proposing. We will get married in Rome, exactly as we planned two years ago. I think a year of marriage should suffice, but we can review it after six months. During our marriage you will perform social duties as my faithful and loyal wife. You will open doors for me that have remained resolutely shut. And once we agree to a divorce settlement I will make you a very rich woman.'

Lara was incredulous. 'You're serious.'

'Deadly.'

He looked at his watch then, as nonchalantly as if he hadn't just made such a preposterous suggestion. 'My driver will take you back to your apartment, where you will pack up your things, and then you will return here to me. We leave for Rome this evening.'

Lara's head was spinning. Too much had happened in such a short space of time. Her husband dying. Ciro reappearing in her life. His crazy proposal, which made a mockery of his first proposal. The prospect of having to learn how to survive on her own. And now the opportunity for something else entirely.

Something ridiculous. Gargantuan. *Impossible*.

And yet all she could think of to say was, 'Why did you pretend to be a driver?'

Ciro's jaw clenched. 'Because it amused me to see you in action among your peers. Behaving true to your nature. The nature you hid from me when we first met.'

Her chest ached. The woman she'd been when she'd met Ciro—that *had* been her. Infinitely naive and innocent. But she'd learnt many harsh lessons since then, and she had to protect herself around this man or he would annihilate her.

She said, with as much coolness as she could muster, 'This conversation is over, Ciro. You've played your little stunt but I'm not interested.'

He merely lifted a brow. 'We'll see.' He extended his

hand towards the door. 'My driver is ready to take you to the apartment, where he will wait for you outside.'

Without a word Lara turned and walked out. The woman who had shown her into the room was waiting with her things. Lara murmured a distracted thank you and went to the front door, where Ciro's car and driver were indeed waiting. Along with the security men.

Another shiver went down her spine as she recalled that awful moment when Ciro had gathered her in his arms to kiss her on that quiet Florentine side street and all hell had broken loose as they'd been ripped apart and then bundled into the back of a van…

She was tempted to ignore the car and walk around the corner to her apartment, but the driver was waiting with the door open and Lara's innate sense of politeness and a wish to not cause conflict made her get into the back of the vehicle. Also, although she was probably being paranoid, she could imagine Ciro standing at a window, silently commanding her to do as he'd bade.

The journey was short and she got out again only a couple of minutes later. She noticed that Ciro's security detail hadn't followed her to her apartment. *And why would they?* she scolded herself. She was nothing to Ciro except someone he wanted to toy with for his own amusement.

And revenge, whispered a voice.

She hurried inside, needing the time alone. To her relief the apartment was empty of staff. Her few meagre belongings were packed into two suitcases, which were standing neatly in the entrance hall. A reminder to leave as quickly and quietly as possible. But Lara needed time to process everything that had just happened.

She wandered around the apartment that had been like a prison to her in the past two years. She still couldn't quite believe the sequence of events that had led her to this place: marriage to an odious man old enough to be her father.

Of course she hadn't wanted to marry him. When her uncle had suggested it she'd laughed. But then he'd revealed to her that he'd been behind the kidnapping and that he would do worse to Ciro unless she married Henry Winterborne.

Lara sat down blindly on the end of the bed for a moment, overcome with the weight of the past.

Her uncle had been in debt to the tune of millions. His entire fortune gambled away. When she'd told him defiantly she didn't need him, that she had her trust fund, which was due to come to her on her twenty-fifth birthday, he'd told her that that was gone too. He'd had access to it, in order to manage it on her behalf, and he'd gambled it away.

Even then—after his threats and after he'd revealed how far he was willing to go to stop her from marrying Ciro—Lara had still hoped that perhaps if she told Ciro he would be able to protect them. So she'd gone to the hospital where he'd been recuperating and she'd asked him if he loved her—because she'd known that if he loved her then she was willing to do anything to defy her uncle. She'd believed that once Ciro knew about the threat surely he'd be powerful enough to protect himself—and her?

But Ciro had looked at her for a long moment and hesitated. And in that moment she'd known she'd been ridiculously naive.

He must have seen her expression, because he'd said quickly, 'Love? *Cara*, I never promised you love. But I am prepared to commit to you for ever, and I respect you... Isn't that enough? It's a realistic foundation for a life together.'

He hadn't loved her. And so she'd followed the dictates of her uncle in order to protect a man she loved who didn't love her.

Lara had come back to London where she'd been introduced to Henry Winterborne and the marriage had been arranged. Her uncle had made a deal. Henry would bail him out of his debts, restore his reputation, in return for marriage to Lara. A medieval and Machiavellian arrangement.

Lara had been in a fog for days. Lost. Alone. And all the time she was being reminded by her uncle that if she didn't comply he would hurt Ciro.

It had been on their wedding night that Lara had returned to this apartment with her new and very drunk husband and reality had finally broken through the numbing shell in which she'd encased herself.

To this day she had no real memory of the wedding, or saying her vows. It was all a blur. But on that night she'd heard her husband thrashing about the apartment, shouting at the staff to get him drinks. She'd hidden in the bedroom, telling herself that she would leave, escape...send a warning to Ciro somehow... Anything had to be better than this.

And then Henry had come into her room. Crashed through the door.

Lara had tried to get away, but he'd caught her and tried to rip her nightdress. He'd shoved her down on the bed and instinctively Lara had lifted her legs to kick him off. His bulk and his inebriated state had made him fall backwards, and he'd hit his head on the side of a dresser.

The fall and his general bad health had resulted in

him being put into a wheelchair. The shock of the accident, and Lara's uncle's persistent reminders of his threats, had stopped her initial thoughts of trying to escape.

That was when she'd started to see pictures of Ciro, out and about, getting on with his life. The beautiful women on his arm didn't seem to be put off by the livid scar. It only enhanced his charismatic appeal. And seeing Ciro like that... It had broken something inside Lara. Broken any will to try and escape her situation. Any sense of optimism that perhaps she'd been wrong about him not loving her dissipated.

All hope had gone.

With the threat of physical violence from her husband negated, Lara had sunk into a routine of sorts. Days had passed into weeks, and then months, and before she'd known it a year had gone by. Henry Winterborne had got rid of his staff by then, had begun using Lara as an unpaid housekeeper and carer.

When her uncle had died, three months ago, Lara's will to leave her husband had been revived. The threat hanging over Ciro was finally gone. But without any funds of her own she'd been in no position to take legal action.

Before she'd had a chance to assess her options Henry Winterborne had had a stroke, and he'd spent the last two months of his life in hospital. For the first time in two years Lara had had a sense of autonomy again. Albeit within her gilded prison.

She caught sight of her reflection in a mirror on the wall opposite her. She took in her pale and wan features. Why on earth would a man as vital as Ciro Sant'Angelo still be remotely interested in marrying her?

An inner voice answered her: *For revenge.*

And because he had her right where he wanted her. Vulnerable and desperate. Or so he thought.

Lara might have qualms about navigating the world on her own after a lifetime of not being prepared for it, but she'd do it. She'd longed for months just to walk out of this apartment and not look back. To take her chances. But the blackmail her uncle had subjected her to and the guilt of Henry Winterborne's accident had kept her a prisoner.

And there was still guilt. Because the threat to Ciro might be gone, but it had been *her* involvement with him that had led to his kidnap in the first place. If she hadn't ever met Ciro he would never have come to her uncle's attention and would never have been put in danger.

She'd *known* that her uncle had plans for her to marry someone 'suitable'. He'd spoken of little else since she'd left school and gone to university—which he hadn't approved of at all. But Lara had never taken him seriously. It had sounded so medieval in this day and age, and at one time she'd told him so.

He'd reminded her of how much she owed him. Asked her where she would have ended up if he hadn't been there to take her in after his dear brother's tragic death. He'd reminded her of how he'd put his life on hold to make sure she was educated and looked after. He'd reminded her that his brother's death had been a devastating shock for him too, and yet he'd had no time to grieve—he'd been too busy making sure Lara was all right.

Little had she realised how deadly serious he was about marrying her off, and by the time she'd met Ciro, Thomas Templeton had been in dire straits—which had turned Lara into an invaluable commodity. And even though Ciro was a wealthy man, it hadn't been enough for Lara's uncle. He'd needed her to marry a man of *his* choosing, from the *right* side of society.

Lara willed down the nausea that threatened to rise. She needed to focus on the present. Not on the painful past.

She stood up from the bed, immediately agitated. *Ciro.* Back and looking for revenge. And could she even blame him? No. She couldn't. She'd single-handedly brought terror into his life. Forced him to live under the shadow of personal protection. Because he'd been shown to be vulnerable. Something she knew he must *hate.*

She also owed him for the resurgence in the rumours about his family's links to the Mafia, who people believed had been responsible for his kidnapping. Not to mention the humiliation of walking out on him days before they were due to be married under the spotlight of the world's media.

One of the many headlines had read *Sicilian Millionaire to Wed English Society Fiancée!* The article underneath had been less flattering, snidely suggesting that Ciro had been trying to marry far above his station.

The fact that Ciro had managed to ride out the storm of headlines and speculation to thrive and survive only demonstrated the scale of his ambition. But clearly that wasn't enough for him.

Her guts twisted. She'd loved him so desperately once. She would have done anything for him. And she had. Could she sacrifice herself again just to allow him to feel some measure of closure? To allow him the access he craved to a level of society that would bring him even more success and acceptance?

'A year of marriage...review it in six months.'

Ciro's cold proposal was daunting. Could she possibly even contemplate such a thing? Subject herself to Ciro's bid for revenge?

Lara stopped pacing and caught her reflection in the mirror again. Her cheeks were flushed now. Eyes over-bright.

Would it really be a sacrifice when he still stirs up so many powerful emotions and desires? questioned a snide inner voice.

She saw the buildings and the skyline of London behind her, reflected in the mirror through the window. There was a back way out of the apartment. She knew she could leave if she wanted to. Slip away into the millions of anonymous people thronging London's streets. Get on with her life. Try to put all this behind her.

But Ciro would come after her. Just as he'd pursued her once before. Relentlessly. Seductively.

She'd kept refusing his advances at first, intimidated by his charismatic masculinity and his playboy reputation. But in the end he'd won her over, when he'd taken her to that gallery after hours.

She shook her head to dislodge the disturbing memory. All it had been was an elaborate seduction ruse. She'd been different from his other women. Naive, wide-eyed. Except now he thought it had all been an act.

Lara had already been through worse than a marriage of convenience to one of the world's most notorious playboys. Far worse. She'd lost her entire beloved family overnight. She'd been heinously betrayed and exploited by her uncle, her last remaining family member. She'd been belittled and bullied by her husband. And she'd had her heart broken already by Ciro Sant'Angelo, so she had no heart left to break.

Realising that Ciro hadn't ever loved her had made it easier for her to do what she'd had to. To be cruel. To walk away. And yet now she was contemplating walking back to him?

A voice in her head queried her sanity. After everything she'd been through at the hands of her uncle and her deceased husband she should be running a million miles from this scenario. And yet despite everything the pull she felt to go back into Ciro's orbit was strong. Too strong to resist?

Lara knew she had only one choice. She had to do what was best for her and her future, so that she could get on with her life with a clear conscience and leave her past behind once and for all.

CHAPTER THREE

CIRO FELT THE tight knot inside him ease. Disconcertingly, it was the same sensation he'd felt when one of his assistants had informed him of Henry Winterborne's death. Except that had been more acute, and quickly followed by a sense of urgency. Find Lara. Track her down. Bring her to him.

She was his now.

His driver had just rung to say that Lara had asked for help with her bags. Which meant she hadn't tried to run. She was coming back to him.

It irked him that he hadn't been sure, when he was so sure of everything else in his life. Nothing was left to chance. Not since the kidnapping.

His little finger throbbed. The missing finger. They called it phantom pain. Pain even though it wasn't there any more. A cruel irony.

He found most women boringly predictable, but Lara Templeton had never been predictable. Not even now, when she was penniless and homeless. A woman that resourceful and beautiful? He had no doubt that she could slip out of his grasp and then he would encounter her at some future event, with another man old enough to be her father.

So why had he given her the opportunity to run if she

so wanted? Because a perverse part of him wanted to prove to himself how mercenary she was. She wouldn't get a better deal than the one he was offering: a marriage of convenience for a year, maximum. Minimum six months. And when they divorced she would be set for life.

He'd laid it out for her and she'd taken the bait. It was perverse to be feeling...*disappointed*. Especially when he had lived the last two years in some kind of limbo. Unable to move on. To settle.

He'd worked himself to a lather, tripling his fortune. Earning respect. But not the respect he craved. The respect of polite society. The respect of the upper echelons of Europe, who still saw him as little more than a Sicilian hustler with a dubious background. Especially after the kidnapping, which remained a mystery to this day.

His best friend, an ex–French Foreign Legionnaire who worked in security, and who had courageously rescued Ciro with a highly skilled team of mercenaries, had told Ciro that they might never find out who had orchestrated it. But one day Ciro would find out, and whoever was responsible would pay dearly.

At that moment he saw his car pull up in front of the house again. There was a bright blonde head in the back. Ciro's blood grew hot. Lara Templeton would be his. *Finally.* And when he'd had his fill of her, and had achieved what he wanted, he would walk out and leave her behind—exactly as she'd done to him in his weakest moment.

Within hours Lara was sitting on Ciro's private jet, being flown across Europe to Rome. She'd just declined a glass of champagne and now Ciro asked from across the aisle, 'Don't you feel like celebrating, darling?'

She looked at him suspiciously. He was taking a sip of his own champagne and he tipped the glass towards her in a salute. He'd changed into dark grey trousers and a black polo shirt. He looked vital and breathtakingly handsome. From this angle Lara couldn't see the scar on the right-hand side of his face—he looked perfect. But she knew that even the scar didn't mar that perfection; it only made him more compelling.

'Surprisingly enough, not really.'

She'd wanted to sound sharp but she just sounded weary. It had been a long day. She couldn't believe the funeral had been that morning; it felt like a month ago. She'd changed out of her funeral clothes into a pair of long culottes and a silk shirt which now felt ridiculously flimsy.

Ciro responded. 'Your marriage to Winterborne might have left you destitute, but fortunately you still have some currency for me. You must have displeased him very much.'

Lara had a sudden flashback to the suffocating weight of the drunken Henry Winterborne on top of her and the sheer panic that had galvanised her into heaving him off.

She swallowed down the nausea and avoided Ciro's eye. 'Something like that. Maybe I will have that champagne after all...' she said, suddenly craving anything that might soothe the ragged edges of her memory.

Ciro must have made a gesture, because the pristine-looking flight attendant was back immediately with a glass of sparkling wine for Lara. She took a sip, letting it fizz down her throat. She took another sip, and instantly felt slightly less ragged.

'Here's to us, Lara.'

Reluctantly she looked at Ciro again. He was facing

her fully now, and she could see the scar. And his missing finger. And the mocking glint in his eye. He thought he was unnerving her with his scars, and he was—but not because she found them repulsive.

He was holding out his glass towards her. Lara reached out, tipping her glass against his, causing a melodic chiming sound which was incongruously happy amidst the tension.

It was a cruelly ironic echo of another time and place. A tiny bustling restaurant in Florence where they'd toasted their engagement. Lara could recall the incredible sense of love she'd felt, and the feeling of security. For the first time in her life since her parents and her brother had died she'd felt some measure of peace again.

A sense of coming home.

The sparkle of the beautiful ring Ciro had presented her with had kept catching her eye. She'd left that ring in his hospital room when she'd walked out two years ago.

As if privy to her thoughts, Ciro reached for something in his pocket and pulled out a small velvet box. Lara's heart thudded to a stop and her hand gripped the glass of wine too tight.

Ciro shrugged. 'Seems an awful waste to buy a new ring when we can use the old one.'

A million questions collided in Lara's head at once, chief of which was, *How did he still have the ring?* She would have thought he'd thrown it away in disgust after she'd walked out.

He started to open the box, and Lara wanted to tell him to stop, but the words stuck in her throat. And there it was—revealed. The most beautiful ring in the world. A pear-shaped sapphire with two diamonds on either side in a gold setting. Classic, yet unusual.

Lara looked at Ciro. 'I don't want this ring.' She sounded too shrill.

Ciro looked at her. 'I suppose you hate the idea of recycling? Perhaps it's too small?'

'No, it's not that... It's...' She trailed off ineffectually.

It's perfect.

Lara had a flashback to Ciro telling her that the sapphire had reminded him of the colour her eyes went when he kissed her... *That* was why she didn't want it. It brought back too many bittersweet memories that she'd imbued with a romanticism that hadn't been there.

She managed to get out, 'Is this absolutely necessary?'

Oblivious to Lara's turmoil, Ciro plucked the ring out of the box and took her left hand in his, long fingers wrapping around hers as he slid the ring onto her finger, where it sat as snugly as if it had never been taken off.

'Absolutely. I've already issued a press release with the news of our re-engagement and upcoming marriage.'

There was a sharp cracking sound and Lara only realised what had happened when she felt the sting in her finger. She looked down stupidly to see blood dripping onto the cream leather seat, just as Ciro issued a curt order and the flight attendant took the broken glass carefully out of Lara's grip.

She was up on her feet and being propelled to the back of the plane and into a bathroom before she'd even registered that she'd broken her champagne glass. Ciro was crowding into the small space behind her, turning on the cold tap and holding her hand underneath.

The pain of the water hitting the place where she'd

sliced herself on the glass finally made her break out of her shocked stasis. She hissed through her teeth.

'It's a clean cut—not deep.' Ciro's tone was deep and unexpectedly reassuring.

He turned her around to face him and reached for a first aid kit from the cabinet above her head, pulling out a plaster which he placed over the cut on the inside of her finger with an efficiency that might have intrigued Lara if she'd not been so distracted.

He said with a dry tone, 'While I will admit to relishing your discomfort at the prospect of marrying me, Lara, I'd prefer to keep you in one piece for the duration of our union.'

Lara's finger throbbed slightly, and just when she was going to pull her hand back he stopped her, keeping her hands in his. He was frowning, and Lara looked down. He was turning her hands over in his and suddenly she saw what he saw. She tried to pull them back but he wouldn't let her.

The glittering ring only highlighted what he was looking at: careworn hands. Hands that had been doing manual work. Not the soft lily-white hands she used to have. Short, unvarnished nails.

Suddenly he let her hands go and said curtly, 'You've been neglecting yourself. You need a manicure.'

Lara might have laughed if the space hadn't been so tiny and she hadn't been scared to move in case her body came into contact with Ciro's. Panic rose at the thought that Ciro might kiss her. She didn't need her dignity battered again.

She scooted around him and into the relative spaciousness of the plane's bedroom, hiding her hands behind her back. She wasn't unaware of the massive bed in the centre of the room but she ignored it.

'You could have told me you were putting out a press release. This affects me too, you know.'

Ciro looked unrepentant. 'Oh, I'm aware of that. But as soon as you agreed to marry me you set in motion a chain of events which will culminate in our wedding within a week.'

'A week!' Lara wanted to sit down, but she didn't want to look remotely vulnerable. So she stayed standing.

Ciro shrugged. As if this was nothing more to him than discussing the weather. 'Why not? Why drag it out? I've got a busy schedule of events coming up and I'll need you by my side.'

Lara felt cornered and impotent. She'd walked herself into this situation after all. 'Why not, indeed.'

A knock came on the door and a voice from outside. 'We'll be landing shortly, Signor Sant'Angelo.'

Ciro took Lara's arm in his hand, as if to guide her out, but when he didn't move she glanced at him and saw him direct an expressive look from her to the bed.

'Pity,' he said silkily. 'Next time.'

An immediate wave of heat consumed Lara at the mere thought of such a decadent thing, and she pulled her arm free and muttered a caustic, 'As if...'

All she could hear as she walked back up the plane was the dark sound of Ciro's chuckle.

Lara was very aware of the ring on her finger. She turned it absent-mindedly as she looked out of the window at the view of Rome.

She was glad they were here and not in Florence. Florence held too many memories...and nightmares.

It was where she'd met Ciro on a street one day and her world had changed for ever. He'd been in Florence to close a major deal which would convert one of the city's oldest *palazzos* into an exclusive hotel. Something the Sant'Angelo name was famous for.

Not that she'd had any clue who he was at first.

She'd been pushed into the road by another tourist, blind to everything but the beauty of Florence, when someone had grabbed her and pulled her back from the oncoming cars.

She'd looked up to see who was holding her arm with such a firm grip and laid eyes on Ciro Sant'Angelo for the first time. He'd fulfilled every possible cliché of tall, dark and handsome and then some. And, even though Lara had seen plenty of tall, dark, handsome Italian men by then, it had been this one who had stopped her heart for a long second. When it had started beating again it had been to a different rhythm. Faster.

Lara had been excited and terrified in equal measure. Because no one had affected her heart in a long time. She'd locked it away after losing her family. Closed it up tight to protect herself. And yet, in that split second, on that sunny day in Florence, she'd felt it start to crack open again. Totally irrational and crazy. But it had opened and she'd never managed to close it up again.

She'd looked him up on the internet a couple of days after meeting him and absorbed the full extent of his fame and notoriety as a playboy who came from a family steeped in Sicilian Mafia history.

She'd told him that she'd looked him up. His expression had shuttered immediately, and she'd seen him drawing back into himself.

He'd said to her, 'Find anything interesting?'

She'd known instinctively that the moment was huge, and that she trusted him. So she'd said, 'I'm sorry. I just wanted to know more about you, and it was hard to resist, but I should have asked you about yourself face-to-face.'

After a long moment he'd extended a hand and said, 'Ask me now.'

She'd taken his hand and asked him about Sicily, about his business. His deep voice had washed over her and through her, binding her even tighter into the illusion that there was something real, palpable, between them.

Lara turned away from the bird's eye view of the iconic Colosseum, visible in the distance, and looked around the bedroom. When they'd arrived yesterday evening every bone in her body had been aching with fatigue. They'd eaten a light meal of pasta, prepared by Ciro's unsmiling housekeeper, and Lara had been glad that conversation had been kept to a minimum.

It had been an ironic reminder of other meals with Ciro, when they'd been happy just to be near each other. Not speaking.

That had always surprised her about him—that he didn't feel intimidated by silence. It had reminded her of when her brother would tug playfully on her hair and say, 'Earth to Lara—where are you in the world?' because she'd used to get so lost in her daydreams.

She diverted her mind away from the painful memory of her brother. And from daydreams. They were a thing of the past. A vulnerability she couldn't indulge in. She didn't believe in dreams any more. Not after losing her entire family in one fell swoop. Not after being betrayed by her uncle. And certainly not after having her heart broken into a million pieces by Ciro Sant'Angelo.

The bedroom was spacious and luxurious without being ostentatious—much like the rest of the apartment. A pang gripped her. She knew how hard Ciro had worked for this—to show the world that he was different from the Sant'Angelos who'd used to rule and succeed through crime and brute force.

Lara sighed. She hated it that she still cared enough to notice that kind of thing.

She caught her reflection in a full-length mirror and considered herself critically, noting the puffiness under her eyes. She'd had a shower in the en suite bathroom and was dressed in slim-fitting capri pants and a T-shirt. No make-up. Totally boring. Not designed to attract the attention of a playboy like Ciro.

Surely when he saw her in the cold light of morning he'd wonder what on earth he'd done?

After pulling her hair back in a low ponytail and slipping on flat shoes, she went in search of Ciro, vaguely wondering if it had all been a dream and she'd find herself back in London.

Liar, whispered an inner voice, *you don't want it to be a dream.*

She ignored it.

But when she walked into the big living and dining area reality was like a punch to the gut. This was no dream.

Ciro was sitting at the top of a huge table with breakfast laid out before him, reading a newspaper. His legs were stretched out and crossed at the ankle and he was looking as relaxed as if it was totally normal to have whisked your ex-fiancée off to another city straight after the funeral of her husband because you were bent on retribution.

He looked up when she approached the table and Lara immediately felt self-conscious. She wished she had some kind of armour to protect herself from that laser-like brown gaze.

He stood up and pulled out a chair to the right of his. Ever the gentleman. Lara murmured her thanks and sat down. The housekeeper appeared and poured her some coffee. Lara forced a smile and said her thanks in Italian, but the housekeeper barely acknowledged her.

'She's deaf.'

It took a second for Lara to realise that Ciro had spoken. She looked at him. 'What?'

'Sophia…my housekeeper. She's deaf. Which is why it can sometimes feel like she's being rude when she doesn't acknowledge you.'

'Oh.'

'I'm telling you because I don't want you to upset her.'

Affronted, Lara said, 'Why would I upset her?'

'Just don't.'

It struck at Lara somewhere very vulnerable to hear Ciro defend his housekeeper. It struck her even deeper that he would think her capable of being rude to someone with a disability. But then, she'd given him that impression, hadn't she? When she'd convinced him she'd been with him purely for her own entertainment.

'You didn't have much luggage.'

Lara felt a flush working its way up her body. A burn of shame and humiliation. 'I brought what I needed.'

Ciro inclined his head. 'And I guess you're counting on me buying you an entirely new wardrobe of all the latest fashions.'

She hated the smug cynicism in his voice, but she wasn't about to explain that once her husband had become incapacitated, and blamed her, she'd been reduced to being little more than unpaid help. With very little money of her own, and none from her husband, Lara had had to resort to selling her clothes and jewellery online to try and make money when she needed it.

At one point when she'd needed money for something she'd had to sell her mother's wedding dress—a beloved heirloom that she'd always hoped to wear when she married for love, and not because she was being forced into it. The fact that it was gone for ever seemed darkly apt.

Ciro took a sip of coffee. 'You'll need to look the part as my wife. I have standards to maintain.'

Lara realised that she wouldn't survive for a week, let alone months, if she didn't do something to distance herself from Ciro's caustic cynicism and bad opinion of her. She needed to develop a hard shell around her heart. He mustn't know how deeply he affected her or his revenge would be even more cruel.

She shrugged and affected a look of disdain. 'Well, you couldn't very well expect me to wear clothes two seasons out of date, could you?'

Ciro took in Lara's expression. *There she was.* The Lara who had shown her true face in his hospital room two years ago. Making him the biggest fool on the planet. And yet it didn't make him feel triumphant. Because there were those disconcerting moments when for a second she looked—

He shook his head. *This* was Lara Templeton. Spoilt and manipulative. Prepared to marry a man just because he was from the right side of society.

'I've arranged for a stylist to come and take you shopping today. You'll also be fitted for your wedding dress. I've pre-approved the design, so you don't have a choice, Lara. I want to make sure you're suitably attired for this wedding.'

Suddenly the disdain was gone. 'What will people think of me? Marrying again so soon?'

'They'll think you're a woman who has a strong sense of self-preservation. And they'll think you're a woman who knows she made a bad choice and is now rectifying the situation.'

'They'll think I'm nothing but a gold-digger.'

Ciro tensed. 'You walked out on your injured fiancé to marry a man old enough to be your father within weeks of the day our own wedding was due to take place, so don't try to pretend a sudden concern about what people think.'

Lara's cheeks whitened dramatically, but Ciro put it down to anger at the fact that he could see right through her.

He hated it that he was so aware of her with every pulse of blood through his veins. He had no control over it. It hardened his body, made him a slave to his libido.

She wasn't even trying to entice him. He wasn't used to women not preening around him. Or he hadn't been until he'd met Lara and she'd stunned him with her fresh-faced beauty.

She was fresh-faced this morning, with not a scrap of make-up, right down to the slightly puffy eyes. Something about that irritated him intensely. It was as if she was mocking him all over again. As if she knew that she didn't even have to make an effort to have an effect on him.

He gestured towards her with a hand. 'I don't know what you're angling for with this lack of effort in your personal appearance, Lara. But after you've met with the stylist, and once we are married, I'll expect a more… *polished* result.'

Her eyes flashed bright blue at that. And then she lowered them in a parody of being demure. 'Of course.'

That irritated him even more. It was as if there was some subtext going on that he wasn't privy to.

He stood up. 'I have back-to-back meetings all day at my head office. If you need anything, this is my private secretary's number.'

He put a card down on the table in front of her. Lara picked it up. Was it his imagination or was there a slight tremor in her hand?

She still didn't look at him as she said, 'So not even your fiancée gets your personal number?'

He reached down and tipped up her face with a finger under her chin, 'Oh, some people have my personal number, Lara. The people I trust most in the world. I have a business dinner this evening, so don't wait up. The marriage will take place this Saturday, so you'll be kept busy between now and then.'

This Saturday.

Lara jerked her chin away from Ciro's finger. Even that small touch was lighting her insides on fire. Not to mention the nearness of the whipcord strength of his body, evident even though he was dressed in business attire of dark trousers and a white shirt. It was as if mere clothes couldn't contain the man.

'Worried I'll abscond?'

Ciro stepped back and put out his arm. 'You're not a prisoner, Lara. You're free to leave. But we both know that you won't—especially when you see the very generous terms of the pre-nuptial contract. I know the real you now. You don't need to pretend to be something else. This will be a very mutually beneficial arrangement.'

And she knew the real him. The man who wanted her

only for her connections and her class. She was tempted to stand up and walk out with her head held high. Claim back her life. But she'd agreed to this because she knew what had been done to this man was her fault.

He might not have loved her, but he hadn't deserved to be treated the way she had treated him, and he certainly hadn't deserved to be kidnapped and almost killed. She had no choice but to stay. Not if she wanted to live the rest of her life with a clear conscience.

Ciro looked at his watch. 'The stylist will be here at midday and some of my legal team will come before that with the pre-nuptial contract. An assistant will set you up with a mobile and laptop—whatever you need.'

Then he was gone, striding out of the room before she could say anything.

Lara looked at the delicious array of food on the table and her stomach churned. The coffee she'd drunk sat heavily in her stomach.

The housekeeper came back just as Lara was standing up and Lara touched her arm gently. The woman looked at her questioningly and Lara smiled and said *grazie*. The woman smiled widely and nodded, and Lara felt for a second as if she'd scored some kind of tiny victory.

Ciro might think the worst of her but *she* knew who she was. She just needed to remember that.

By the time Lara had walked from the car and up the steps to the porch of the cathedral on Saturday afternoon she was shaking. There were what looked like hundreds of people lining the steps, calling out her name, and the flashes of cameras.

The wedding dress that Ciro had picked out was stunning, but far more extravagant than Lara would have ever chosen for herself. Designed to get as much attention as possible with its long train and elaborate veil. Not unlike the dress she'd worn to marry Henry Winterborne.

Her mother's dress had been simple and graceful. Whimsical and romantic. But then it had been a dress worn for love. Lara was almost glad it was gone now. Hopefully some other woman had married for love in it.

She was not unaware of the irony that for the second time in the space of a couple of weeks she was glad of a veil to hide behind.

The aisle looked about a hundred miles long from where she was standing. And she was going to walk down it alone. She wanted to turn and run. But instead she squared her shoulders, and as the wedding march began she started walking, spine straight, praying that no one would see her bouquet shaking.

The back of Ciro's neck prickled. *She was here.*

He'd heard the cacophony of shouts outside just before a hush rippled through the church. He knew she would be walking down the aisle alone—she hadn't requested any bridesmaids or attendants. She had no family. Something about that lonely image of her caught at his gut but he ignored it.

She was the type of woman who could bury one man one week and marry another a week later. She was not shy or vulnerable.

You offered her little alternative, pointed out the voice of his conscience.

Ciro ignored it. Lara might not like what people thought of her, but she'd soon forget it when she got used to the life of luxury Ciro could offer her.

He fought the desire to turn around, not liking the sense of *déjà vu* washing over him as he thought about how this day should have happened two years ago. And how it hadn't.

In the lead-up to that wedding he'd been uncharacteristically nervous. And excited. Excited at the thought of unveiling his virginal bride. Of being the first man who would touch her, make her convulse with pleasure. And at the thought of the life he would have with her—a different life from the one he'd experienced with his parents.

But she hadn't been that woman.

Suddenly Ciro felt hollow inside. And exposed. As if he was making a monumental fool of himself all over again.

The wedding march grated on his nerves. For a moment he almost felt the urge to shout out, *Stop!* But then Lara's scent reached him, that unique blend of lemon and roses he would always associate with her, and the urge drained away.

He turned to look at her and his breath caught. Even though he'd chosen the dress for its classic yet dramatic lines—a full satin skirt and a bodice which was overlaid with lace that covered her arms and chest up to her throat—he still wasn't prepared.

He'd always known Lara was beautiful, but right now she was...*exquisite*. He could just make out the line of her jaw, the soft pink lips and bright blue eyes behind the veil. Her hair was pulled back into a chignon.

His gaze travelled down over her slender curves to where she held the bouquet. There was an almost imperceptible trembling in her hands, and before he could stop himself Ciro reached out and put a hand over hers. She looked at him, and a constriction in his chest that he hadn't even been aware of eased.

Instead of the triumph he'd expected—*hoped*—to be

feeling right now, the residue of those memories and emotions lingered in his gut. And relief.

It was the relief that made him take his hand off hers and face forward. The scar on his face tingled, as if to remind Ciro why they were there. What she owed him. And any sense of exposure he'd felt dissipated to be replaced by resolve.

The wedding service passed in a blur for Lara. She wasn't even sure how she'd made it down the aisle. The mass was conducted in English, for her benefit, and she dutifully made her vows, feeling as if it was happening to someone else.

Her second wedding to a man who didn't love her. At least she'd never been deluded about Henry Winterborne's feelings for her.

Every time she looked at Ciro she wanted to look away. It was like looking directly at the sun. He was so...*vital*. He wore a dark grey morning suit with a white shirt and tie. His dark hair was gleaming and swept back from his face.

But now she had to face him, and she reluctantly lifted the veil up and over her head. There was nothing to shield her from that dark, penetrating gaze. Hundreds of people thronged the cathedral but suddenly it was just her and him.

Before, she'd imagined this moment so many times... had longed for it. Longed to feel a part of something again. A unit. A unit of love.

And now this was a parody of that longing. A farce.

Suddenly Lara felt like pulling away from Ciro, who had her hands in his. As if sensing her wish to bolt, he tightened his grip on her and tugged her towards him.

'You may kiss the bride...'

One word resounded in Lara's head. *No!*

If Ciro touched her now, when she was feeling so raw— But it was too late. He'd pulled her close, or as close as her voluminous skirts would allow, and his hands were around her face. He was holding her as tenderly as if she really meant something to him. But it was all for show.

Past and present were blurring. Meshing.

Ciro's head came closer and those eyes compelled her to stay where she was. Submit to him. At the last moment, in a tiny act of rebellion, Lara lifted her face to his. She wasn't going to submit. She was an equal partner.

Their mouths met and every muscle in Lara's body seized against the impact of that firm, hot mouth on hers. But it was useless. It was as if a hot serum was being poured into her veins, loosening her, making her pliant. Making her fold against him, letting her head fall back so he could gain deeper access to her mouth.

It was only a vague sound of throat-clearing that made them break apart, and Lara realised with a hot flush of shame just how wantonly she'd reacted. With not one cell in her body rejecting his touch. She pushed back, disgusted with herself, but Ciro caught her elbows, not allowing her to put any distance between them.

'Smile, *mia moglie*, you've just married the man you should have married two years ago.'

Lara dragged her gaze away from Ciro's and looked around. A sea of strangers' faces looked back at her, their expressions ranging from impassive to downright speculative. And there were a couple of murderous-looking beautiful women who had no doubt envisaged themselves becoming Signora Sant'Angelo.

Ciro tucked her arm into his and led her back down

the aisle to a triumphant chorus of Handel's 'The Arrival of the Queen of Sheba'.

Lara somehow fixed a smile to her face as they approached the main doors, where Rome lay bathed in bright warm sunshine—a direct contrast to her swirling stormy emotions. She was Ciro Sant'Angelo's wife now, for better or worse, and the awful thing was Lara knew without a doubt that it was going to be for worse…

CHAPTER FOUR

'Well, you certainly had us all fooled.'

Lara's fixed-on smile slipped slightly when she saw who was addressing her. Lazaro Sanchez. Probably Ciro's closest friend. She'd met him a few times two years ago, when he would often look at her speculatively and say, 'You're not like Ciro's other women.'

Lara had used to joke with him that he and Ciro had a warped sense of what was normal and what was not, given their astounding good-looks and success in life. Lazaro Sanchez was every bit as gorgeous as Ciro, with messy overlong dark blond hair and piercing green eyes.

Yet in spite of the Spaniard's devastating charm he'd never made her pulse trip like Ciro had. *Did.* She could still feel the imprint of his kiss from the church on her mouth and had to resist the urge to touch it.

Lara decided to ignore his barbed comment. 'Lazaro, it's nice to see you again.'

Lazaro folded his arms. His expression was not charming now. Far from it. 'I'm afraid I can't say the same. You know, two years ago, when you left Ciro in the hospital, I've never seen him so—'

'Filling my wife's head with stories like you used to?'

Lazaro scowled at Ciro, who'd interrupted them and who was now snaking a possessive arm around Lara's waist. She was intrigued to know what Lazaro had been about to say but suspected she never would now.

Then she registered what Ciro had said—*my wife*. With such ease. As if this was all entirely normal.

He turned to Lara. 'We'll be leaving shortly to take our flight to Sicily. You should go and change—there's a stylist waiting for you upstairs.'

The manager of the exclusive Rome hotel that Ciro owned, where Lara had stayed the night before and got ready earlier, escorted her to the suite where the stylist was waiting. Lara welcomed he opportunity to get away from the hundreds of judgemental eyes. Lazaro's in particular.

In the past week, along with the wedding dress, Lara had been fitted for dozens of other outfits. Evening wear, day wear. Night clothes. Underwear. Now, as the woman and her assistant helped Lara out of the elaborate wedding dress and veil, she felt a pang of regret that this wasn't a normal wedding or marriage and never would be. She'd always fantasised about a small and intimate wedding, and the fantasy had included staying in her wedding dress all night, until her groom lovingly removed it as he took her to bed.

But she had to remind herself that she'd only ever been a means to an end for Ciro. Access into a rarefied world. So she needed to forget about fantasies of small, intimate weddings. If life had taught her anything by now it was that she was on her own and had to depend on herself.

'*Bellissima, Signora Sant'Angelo.*'

Lara's attention was directed back into the room, where the stylist was standing back and looking her up and down.

The wedding dress was on its hanger again, and Lara

now wore a sleeveless mid-length shirt dress in the softest blush colour. It had a high ruffled neck and was cinched in at the waist with a belt. She wore strappy high-heeled sandals. Her hair was left down, to tumble over her shoulders, and a make-up artist touched up her make-up.

For a hysterical moment she felt like an actress, about to take her cue to go on stage.

Ciro was waiting outside when she emerged. His dark gaze swept her up and down. 'You look beautiful.'

The immediate flush of warmth that bloomed inside Lara felt like a betrayal. She didn't want his words to have any effect on her. They weren't infused with emotion. They were purely an objective assessment. She was a commodity. Just as she'd always been.

He'd changed into a dark grey suit and white shirt, open at the neck. Elegantly casual. They complemented each other. He extended his arm and she took a breath before putting her arm in his, so he could lead her down the stairs to the main foyer, where people were waiting.

The crowd parted to let them through, and a few people clapped Ciro on the shoulder as they passed. Lara caught Lazaro's eye. He still had that grim expression on his face. She felt like pulling free from Ciro, so she could go over and tell him that he had it all wrong. Ciro had hurt *her*, not the other way around…

And then she glanced up and saw Ciro's scar, standing out so lividly, and fresh guilt for her responsibility in that made her keep her eyes forward until they were outside and in the back of a sleek SUV. Lazaro Sanchez was right to look at her the way he did.

'Try to smile, hmm…*cara*? You've just married the man of your dreams and you will never have to lift a finger again if you are wise with your divorce settlement when it comes.'

Lara's rattled emotions bubbled over. She turned to Ciro as the vehicle pulled into the traffic. 'I couldn't care less about the money, Ciro. You, on the other hand, are obsessed by it. I pity you—because if it all went tomorrow, what would you have?'

Stupid question, Lara.

She realised that as soon as the words were out of her mouth. He'd have the towering Sicilian pride and immense self-belief that had brought him to where he was today.

But he merely shrugged lightly and said, 'I'd start again and be even more successful.'

That stopped anything further coming out of Lara's mouth.

Ciro conducted some phone calls in Italian while they were en route, and soon they were pulling into a private part of the airport where a small silver jet was waiting.

The pilot and staff welcomed them on board and Lara accepted a glass of champagne when they were airborne. Below them Rome was bathed in a magical golden sunset.

She sneaked a look across the aisle to see Ciro holding his own glass of champagne, which didn't look at all ridiculous in his big hand. Her belly fluttered with nerves and awareness. Would he expect her to sleep with him tonight? Take it as his due? Would he force her?

She shivered. He wouldn't have to. Not like her first husband. She diverted her mind from that bilious memory.

As if sensing her regard, Ciro turned and looked at

her. She cast around for something to say—anything but what was on her mind. 'All those people at the wedding and afterwards...do you know them?'

Ciro's mouth twitched slightly. 'Of course not. They're mostly peers...business acquaintances. A small number of friends and staff whom I trust.'

Whom I trust.

Lara smarted at that. Even though he'd married her, he didn't trust *her*. She thought of the pre-nuptial agreement and how it had specified that no children were expected from the union.

They hadn't really discussed children before. Lara had just assumed Ciro would want them, as he was the last in the Sant'Angelo line.

However, for her it had been more complicated. The memory of losing her own parents and her brother had been so painful she'd always believed she couldn't have borne that kind of loss again, or inflicted it on anyone else... And yet after meeting Ciro, she'd found herself yearning to be part of a family again. He'd made her want to risk it for the first time.

Ciro was still looking at her, as if he could probe right into her brain and read her thoughts. Terrified in case he might ask her what she'd been thinking about, she scrabbled around for the first thing she could think of.

'Where are we going in Sicily?'

'My family's *palazzo*. Directly south from Palermo—on the coast.'

'Does anyone live there?'

He shook his head. 'Not since my grandfather passed away a few years ago. It was his property and he left it to me because he was afraid my mother would persuade my father to sell it or turn it into a resort. She never liked Sicily.' Ciro's jaw clenched. 'As you might have noticed from her absence at the wedding, we're not really in contact.'

Lara said nothing. He'd told her before of his mother's serial philandering, and the way his father had devoted himself to her regardless of the humiliation. How his mother had persuaded his father to move to Rome, away from his homeland of Sicily. But Ciro had spent a lot of time there with his grandfather.

Lara had always believed that his experience at the hands of his mother had explained the ease with which Ciro had believed in Lara's duplicity and betrayal. He had told her once that when he was very small she'd used to make him collude with her in hiding the evidence of her infidelity from his father. Making him an accomplice. Lara could understand how her own betrayal must have been a huge blow to his pride, and more.

But while knowing all that was very well, it didn't really do much to help her now. Ciro's beliefs were entrenched, and what she had done had merely confirmed for him that women were not to be trusted.

Lara was quiet. Unnervingly so. Ciro remembered the way she'd used to chatter when they'd first met. She'd ask him so many questions that he'd resort to kissing her to stop them. And yet there'd been those moments when no conversation had been required and she hadn't filled the silence with nonsense. She'd been just as happy not to talk. Something he'd found refreshing.

This time around he was under no illusions.

He thought of the moment just a few hours before, when he'd emerged from the cathedral with Lara on his arm. When the paparazzi's cameras had exploded into life he'd felt her flinch ever so slightly on his arm, and the sense of triumph which had been so elusive had finally oozed through his veins.

He'd envisaged that moment—the beauty marrying the beast. And yet when he'd looked down at her she hadn't had a look of revulsion on her face at being photographed with Ciro and his livid scar—she'd looked haunted by something else entirely and he hadn't liked that...

In fact, since they'd met again he'd never got a sense from her that she considered him some sort of monster—which was how he felt sometimes, when people looked at him with horror or fascination. In her eyes there was something else...something almost like... sympathy. Or guilt. Which made no sense at all.

Ciro looked over Lara's form broodingly. Her head was turned away, as if the shape of the clouds outside the window was utterly fascinating. The silk of her dress clung to her slim curves in a way that made his hands itch to uncover her inch by inch and see the bounty he had denied himself before...

He'd been such a fool. Lust had clouded his judgement the first time around. Of *course* a woman as beautiful as Lara couldn't have been a virgin. Or if she had been she wasn't one now.

No matter. Tonight she would be his in every way— wife and lover. Tonight he would slake the hunger he'd felt since the moment he'd laid eyes on her. Tonight he might finally feel some measure of peace again.

The late summer dusk was tipping into night as they made the journey up a long and winding driveway to Ciro's Sicilian *palazzo*. All Lara could see was the wide open lavender sky full of bright stars and acres and acres of land rolling down to the sea. It was quiet.

They climbed an incline, and when they reached the top she sucked in a breath.

The *palazzo* seemed to rise out of nowhere and cling to a cliff-edge in the distance; a soaring cluster of buildings with a tower that looked like something from a movie. As they got closer she could see just how massive it was. Lights shone from high windows, and they drove into a huge courtyard with a fountain in the middle. Wide steps led up to a huge open door where light spilled out. It looked incongruously welcoming in spite of the intimidating grandeur of the building.

'You said once that you spent a lot of time here growing up?' Lara said as Ciro drew the SUV to a stop at the bottom of the steps.

He cut the car's engine and put both hands on the steering wheel. Lara was conscious of the missing little finger on his right hand. It made her chest ache. She looked away.

'Yes. We were mainly in Rome, after my parents moved there, but I spent most holidays here with my grandparents. My *nonna* died when I was small, but my grandfather was alive until not long ago.'

'Were your mother's parents alive?'

His mouth compressed. 'They lived in Rome and they didn't approve of her choice of husband. They had nothing to do with me or my father—even though my father moved to Rome to keep my mother happy.'

'That was harsh.'

She'd never really realised how lonely Ciro must have been as an only child. Or how it must have looked to a young boy to see his father giving up his own heritage to keep his selfish mother happy.

Just then a young woman in jeans and a white shirt appeared at the top of the steps. Ciro saw her and uncurled his large frame from the SUV, calling out a greeting in Italian.

The young woman flew down the steps and hurled herself at Ciro, who chuckled, wrapping her in his arms. Lara's breath stopped as something very sharp pierced her heart. She hadn't seen Ciro so relaxed and easy since they'd met again. He'd been like that with her, once...

She got out of the car slowly, and as she came around to where Ciro was extricating himself from the woman's embrace Lara could see that she was a girl of about eighteen, extraordinarily pretty with long dark hair and dark eyes. She was looking up at Ciro as if he was God.

Then she saw Lara and stepped back, clapping a hand to her mouth. Her eyes were sparkling and she took her hand down, smiling so widely and infectiously that Lara couldn't help but respond.

Lara held her hand out, but the girl ignored it and embraced her warmly too. When she pulled back she said, *'Scusi...'* and then she rattled off some words in Italian that Lara had no hope of understanding.

Ciro said something and the girl stopped talking, looking embarrassed.

'Lara, I'd like you to meet Isabella. She grew up here on the estate with her family, who have cared for the *palazzo* for generations.'

Lara smiled. 'It's nice to meet you.'

Isabella smiled again. 'And you, Signora Sant'Angelo. Please excuse me. I do speak English but I forget when I am excited.'

The obvious warmth flowing between Ciro and this young woman was as unexpected as it was heartening. Lara had never seen him look so relaxed.

Isabella took Lara's arm. 'Roberto will come and

get the bags—he's my twin brother. Let me show you around!'

Lara didn't think she had much choice, so she let herself be led up the steps and into the *palazzo* on a wave of Isabella's exuberance. In all honesty she was glad of a moment's respite—glad to get away from Ciro and stop overthinking everything that was to come that night.

Their wedding night.

About half an hour later Lara was led out onto an open terrace, overlooking the sea below. She could see another terrace further down, set precipitously right over the cliff. All was calm now, but she could imagine how dramatic it must be in a storm.

The rest of the *palazzo* was seriously impressive. Apparently it had undergone a major renovation in recent years, and now it was a byword for elegant sophistication and comfort.

It had an opulent cinema room, and a gym with an indoor pool. There was an outdoor pool set into its landscaped grounds. Too many bedrooms to count. Formal and informal dining rooms. A kitchen to die for. And there was even a quaint old church on the property.

Isabella had confided in Lara that Ciro was sponsoring her and her twin brother to go to university in Rome in the autumn. This was a side to Ciro that Lara hadn't seen before—philanthropic.

Isabella said now, 'I'll show you up to your suite. Ciro has asked that dinner be served here on the terrace in half an hour, but I'm sure you'd like to freshen up first?'

Lara nodded gratefully. She couldn't believe that the wedding had been earlier that same day. It felt like a lifetime ago.

She followed Isabella up the main staircase to the

first floor, where the bedrooms were situated. At the end of a plushly carpeted corridor she opened a door on the right and led Lara into an exquisitely decorated bedroom suite, complete with walk-in wardrobe and en suite bathroom. There was even a balcony through a set of French doors, overlooking the sea. It was sumptuous.

Isabella left her alone and Lara slipped off the light jacket she'd been wearing over her dress and took off her shoes, sighing with relief as her bare feet sank into the carpet.

She padded over to the balcony and looked out, drawing in a lungful of fragrant warm air from the Mediterranean Sea. Dozens of different scents tickled her nostrils…lemons…bergamot? The salty air from the sea. It was paradise, and in spite of everything Lara could feel something inside her loosen and untangle.

'Surprised that the uncouth Sicilian has some taste after all?'

Lara jumped nearly a foot in the air and slapped a hand over her racing heart. Ciro was standing on a similar balcony she hadn't noticed, just a few feet away. He'd lost his jacket too, and the sleeves of his shirt were rolled up, revealing strong muscled forearms.

Lara struggled to process his words. 'No…not at all.' She was irritated that she was so skittish around him. 'I always knew you had taste. I never called you uncouth.'

Or had she?

In those awful moments two years ago in the hospital… She'd been so desperate to get out of there before he'd seen what a fraud she was…

Ciro made a noise. 'Maybe not, but as good as.'

It was impossible not to notice how right Ciro looked against the dramatic backdrop of *palazzo* and cliffs and sea. As if he'd been hewn out of the very rock beneath them.

He straightened up from where he'd been leaning against the door. 'I'll take you down to dinner.'

He disappeared, and Lara was confused until she heard a door opening back in her suite and went in to see Ciro standing in an adjoining doorway. An interconnected but separate suite. She could see his bed in the background.

All at once she felt a conflicting and humiliating mixture of relief and disappointment. She knew she wasn't ready to share such an intimate space with Ciro yet. If ever. But she had expected him to want to project a united front. Ever mindful of people's opinion.

'Won't people expect us to…?'

'Be cohabiting?'

Lara shrugged, embarrassed. Maybe this was new etiquette and she was being incredibly unsophisticated to assume that all couples were like her parents, who had shared a bedroom. After all, her first experience of marriage had hardly been conventional.

'I have every intention of this being a marriage in all senses of the word, but we don't need to share a bedroom for that.'

Lara felt that like a slap in the face. Ciro would sleep with her but not *sleep* with her.

He came into the room. 'Dinner will be ready—shall we?'

Lara was about to follow him out of the room when she saw her shoes and slipped them on again, wincing slightly as they pinched after the long day. She also pulled her jacket over her shoulders, feeling a little exposed in the silk dress.

When they went out onto the terrace Lara couldn't

stop an involuntary gasp of pleasure and surprise from leaving her mouth. There were candles flickering in little jars all along the wall and fairy lights strung into the leaves and branches that clung to the *palazzo*'s ancient walls.

With the moon shining on the sea in the distance and exotic scents infusing the air, it was magical. The thought that Ciro might have gone out of his way to—

'Don't get any ideas. This is all Isabella's idea. She's a romantic.'

Lara's heart sank and she berated herself. What was *wrong* with her? Throw a little candlelight on the situation and she was prepared to forget that this was a marriage of convenience built on her sense of guilt and responsibility. Built on Ciro's need for retribution.

A table had been set for two with a white tablecloth and silverware. A champagne bottle rested in a bucket of ice. Out of nowhere a handsome young man appeared to open the champagne. Ciro introduced him as Roberto, Isabella's twin brother.

Ciro lifted his glass to Lara when they were sitting down. It was a mockery against the flickering lights of all the candles. 'Here's to us, and to a short but beneficial marriage.'

Lara longed to put down her glass and make her excuses, but Isabella was back with the first course, and she looked so happy to be serving them that Lara didn't have the heart to cause a scene.

When she'd left them alone, Lara leaned forward. 'You didn't have to marry someone you despise, you know. There are plenty of women who I'm sure would have loved to be in my position.'

Ciro took a drink. 'Ah, but they weren't you, *cara,*

with your unique qualities. You've been a thorn in my side for two years. I need to exorcise you to move on.'

'You mean take your revenge and in the process exploit my connections as much as possible?' She added, 'I hate to break it to you, but I don't wield half the influence my father and uncle did.'

Ciro appeared totally unperturbed by that. He flicked open his napkin. 'You wield influence just by being a Templeton. Marriage to you has automatically given me access to an inner circle that no one admits exists.'

Lara knew he was right on some level. As much as she hated to admit such hierarchical snobbishness existed. Impulsively she asked, 'Why does it matter so much to you?'

Ciro sat back, not liking his sense of claustrophobia at her question. But then he considered it. Why *shouldn't* he tell her? It wouldn't change anything. It wouldn't give anything away. It might actually show her just how determined he was to make this work. And how clinically he viewed this marriage. Even if his thrumming pulse told another story that was a lot *less* clinical.

'My father had a bad experience in England. He went to talk business with a number of potential partners. One by one they smiled to his face but refused to do business with him. He heard later that they had decided to close ranks against him. It wasn't just that he was new money—it was the rumours of where that money had come from. Had it been laundered? Did it come from the money made out of violence and crime by previous generations? He was humiliated. Angry. He made me promise to do better. To get myself a seat at the table so that the Sant'Angelo name could finally be free of negative associations.'

'Was your father the first one to try and break away?'

Ciro shook his head. 'It was his father. My grandfather desperately wanted to remove the stain of infamy from our name. He knew the world was moving on and he had ambitious plans for the Sant'Angelos. To go beyond these small shores, and Italy. He was sick of how our name engendered shock and derision. No respect. Not *real* respect. He wanted us to be accepted outside our narrow parameters. He craved the ultimate acceptance from a world that had always shunned us. But to do that we had to change our ways completely.'

Lara's eyes were wide. 'Where did he get his drive from? Presumably it would have been easier to keep things as they were?'

Ciro had been about to bring this line of conversation to an end—he'd said enough already—but some rogue urge compelled him to keep going, as if to impress upon Lara how determined he was.

'My grandfather's mother had wanted to marry a man she'd fallen in love with but he wasn't from the right family—in other words a family that the Mafia approved of. Her family threatened to kill him if she eloped with him. So, she stayed and married the man chosen for her—my great-grandfather. They had nine children and a perfectly cordial marriage, but she never forgave her family for doing that to her. She hated all the violence and oppression. She rebelled by passing on a new message to her own children—to my grandfather. A message to do things differently.'

Lara had stopped breathing. Ciro's ancestors had threatened to kill a man because they didn't sanction the relationship. History had repeated itself right here and the parallel was too cruelly ironic.

A little shakily she asked, 'What happened to the man she loved?'

Ciro waved a dismissive hand, as if it was of no importance. 'He left—emigrated to America. Does it matter?'

Lara curbed her urge to shout *Yes, of course it matters!* 'Not now, I guess, no.' She avoided Ciro's eye, not wanting him to see how this was affecting her.

'That's why it matters to me,' Ciro said. 'The Sant'Angelo name no longer has anything to do with those old and lurid tales of violence and organised crime, but the stain of infamy is still there. That kind of infamy only disappears completely with acceptance—true acceptance—in a very visible and public way. By association, you will bring a new kind of respect to the Sant'Angelo name that we've never had.'

Lara recalled how sick she'd felt when she'd seen the headlines after the kidnapping: *Mafia Heir Kidnapped and Held for Ransom... Sant'Angelo Kidnapping Proof He's Still Target for Criminals... Sant'Angelo Stocks Plummet After Kidnapping!*

She had brought that infamy into his life. And she hated to admit it but he was right, even though status meant nothing to her. She had to recognise that she'd been born into privilege—what did she know of his family's struggles to prove that they'd moved on from a violent world?

She had made the decision to do this—to make some redress for what had happened to Ciro, for what she had done. It was too late to turn back now.

He gestured to her plate. 'Eat up. Isabella's mother Rosa is a sublime cook.'

Lara saw the delicious-looking pasta starter on her plate but her appetite had fled. She forced herself to eat, not wanting to upset Isabella or her mother.

They conducted the rest of their meal in relative civility, sticking to neutral topics. When the plates for dessert had been cleared away Ciro got up with his coffee cup and went over to the wall of the terrace. Lara couldn't help drinking in his tall, powerful form. The broad shoulders and narrow hips. His easy graceful athleticism. The thought of going to bed with him...of seeing him naked...was overwhelming.

She realised she wasn't remotely prepared for such an intimate encounter with Ciro. What would he do when he discovered she was still a virgin?

A spark of panic propelled her from the chair to stand. 'I think I'll go to bed, actually. I'm quite tired.'

She winced. Her voice was too high and tight. She sounded so prim. A world away from the kind of woman who would undoubtedly be twining herself around Ciro right now, whispering seductive things in his ear.

He turned and leant back against the wall. Supremely nonchalant. He put down the coffee cup and looked at her. 'Come here, Lara.'

There was a sensual quality in his voice that impacted directly on her pulse, making it go faster. Afraid to open her mouth again, in case she sounded even more panicked, Lara reluctantly went towards Ciro. Her jacket had fallen off her shoulders and she shivered slightly in the night breeze.

'Cold?'

She rubbed her arms. 'No, I'm fine.'

I'm not fine.

Lara's hip bumped against the terrace wall. Ciro reached out and caught a strand of her hair, tugging her a little closer. The air between them grew taut. Expectant.

He looked at her hair as it slipped through his fingers, and then he said musingly, 'I don't despise you,

Lara. I will admit that I felt humiliated by you for some time, but then I had to acknowledge that it was my own fault for having believed the façade you'd projected when I should have known better. No woman had ever managed to fool me before you.'

Lara's heart squeezed. It hadn't been his fault at all. 'Ciro, I didn't—'

He put a finger to her mouth. 'I don't care about that any more. All I care about is that I've wanted you since the moment I saw you and I should never have denied myself this…'

'This' was Ciro putting his hands to Lara's waist and urging her towards him. Unsteady in her heels, and taken by surprise, Lara fell into him, landing flush against his body.

The effect was instantaneous. From the moment this man had first touched her, kissed her, two years ago, it had been like this. She cleaved to Ciro like a magnet drawn to its true north. His mouth touched hers and she gripped his shirt to stay standing. When she felt the slide of his tongue against the seam of her mouth she opened it instinctively, allowing him access.

Sicily and this place, even in such a short space of time, had touched something raw inside her. She could no more deny herself or Ciro this than she could stop breathing.

He gathered her closer and she could feel every ridge and muscle of his chest against hers, through the thin silk of her dress. And, down further, the press of his arousal against her belly. Desire pulsed between her legs. She wanted this man with a ferocity that might have scared her if she'd been thinking rationally for a moment. It was as if she was embracing the carnal to avoid thinking about anything rational.

Ciro's whole body was taut with the effort it was taking him not to swing Lara up into his arms and take her to the nearest horizontal surface, so he could lay her down and banish the demons that had been stalking him for two long years.

She felt like liquid fire in his arms. The soft contours of her body melted into his as if they'd been made especially for him. A ridiculously romantic notion that he didn't even have the wherewithal to reject right now, because he was so consumed with desire and need.

She tasted of sparkling wine and something much sweeter. And she exuded a kind of blind trust in Ciro, following and mimicking his movements. Darting out her tongue to touch his, as if she was afraid of what might happen if she was bolder. It ratcheted up his levels of arousal to a point where he had to bite back a groan. It reminded him of how she'd been before…which *had* to be his fevered imagination…

Her effect on him was as explosive as it always had been. Even though he now knew who she was and what she was capable of. It was as if that knowledge had added a darker edge to his desire. Because she was no longer an innocent—if she ever had been.

His hands couldn't rest on her waist. He had to explore her or die. Tracing over the curve of her hip, and up, he felt the silk of her dress slide over her body under his hand.

Ciro held his breath for a moment when he found and cupped her breast, felt its lush weight filling his hand, the press of her nipple against his palm. He wanted to taste her there, explore the hard nub with his tongue and teeth, make her squirm with pleasure. Make her moan…

Lara was drowning in heat and sensation. She'd never felt so many things at once. It was overwhelming, but utterly addictive. The rough stroke of Ciro's tongue on hers made her yearn to know what his tongue would feel like on her breast. He squeezed her there and her body vibrated with pleasure. It was too much. It wasn't enough.

Lara knew that she should pull back, put a stop to this, but some vital part of her resolve was dissolving in Ciro's arms and a fatal lethargy was taking over. A strong desire to put herself in the hands of this man. To capitulate to his every command.

'I've wanted you from the moment I saw you.'

She'd wanted him too—even though it had terrified her. And two years of purgatory had only made that wanting stronger. It was one of her big regrets that Ciro had never made love to her. That she'd had no palpable memory to comfort her in the long and lonely nights of her marriage.

It was also one of the reasons she'd found that superhuman strength to push her husband off her on their wedding night. The thought of any man but Ciro touching her had been utterly repulsive.

And now she was here in Ciro's arms. And she wanted him to touch her so desperately that she blocked out all the inner voices whispering warnings.

But a tiny sliver of oxygen got to her brain and she pulled back with an effort, struggling to open her eyes and calm her thundering heart.

Ciro's eyes were so dark they were fathomless. 'Lara…'

Her tongue felt heavy in her mouth as she said, 'Is this really a good idea?'

CHAPTER FIVE

A COOL BREEZE skated over Ciro's skin and he felt a prickle of exposure. Lara looked utterly wanton with her tousled hair and flushed cheeks. Her too-big eyes. Her plump and swollen mouth.

'Yes. We are consummating this marriage. You want me, Lara. You can't deny it.'

She looked down for a moment and it incensed Ciro. He had seen the way she'd morphed into another person in front of him once before. He tipped her chin back up, expecting to see some measure of triumph or satisfaction because she knew he couldn't hide how much he wanted her, but there was nothing in those huge blue eyes except an emotion he couldn't define. An emotion that caught at his chest, making it tight.

'Say it, Lara. Admit it.'

She bit her lip and looked at him searchingly, as if trying to find the answer to some riddle. Ciro was so used to women jumping into his arms at the slightest invitation that this was a wholly new experience.

Except it wasn't. Lara had been like this before. Hesitant. Shy. *Lying*.

'I do want you, Ciro. I always have.'

Ciro couldn't keep the bitterness from his voice when

he replied. 'That was *one* thing that was honest between us at least.'

Lara didn't want to be reminded of the past. She wanted to stay in this moment. *This* moment, when she could almost pretend the previous two years hadn't happened.

A sense of urgency gripped her and she pressed against Ciro, spreading her hands on his chest. 'Please, make love to me.'

Ciro looked down at her for such a long moment that Lara instinctively started to pull back, suspecting that perhaps this was all part of his plan to humiliate her when she was at her most vulnerable, but then he made a small rough sound and grabbed her hand, entwining his fingers with hers to lead her back into the *palazzo*.

Her heart was thundering so loudly she was sure he must be able to hear it. There wasn't any sign of Isabella or Roberto and Lara was glad. This moment was too raw to be witnessed. This was no benign wedding night consummation.

Lara's hand felt tiny in Ciro's and he instinctively tightened his grip, even as he rejected the notion that she was somehow vulnerable.

Disconcertingly, it reminded him of how fragile and delicate she'd felt during the kidnapping. How he'd been afraid he'd hurt her because he was holding her so tight. But they'd ripped her out of his arms anyway, and in that moment Ciro had known—

He shut his rogue thoughts down right there. *Not now.* Never would he think of that again.

He pushed open his bedroom door and looked at Lara. She met his gaze and there was something indecipherable in her expression. Determined.

She took her hand out of his and walked into the room

and over to the bed, kicking off her sandals as she went. She had her back to him and he could see her hands move. The silk dress started to loosen around her body.

She made a movement and he watched her shrug the dress from her shoulders so that it landed in a silken ripple by her feet. He was frozen to the spot, taking in the naked contours of her body covered only by the tiniest wisps of lace across her back and bottom. Nothing—no amount of anticipation—could have prepared him for this moment.

Ciro was glad she was facing away from him because he was convulsed with need and desire. Once again she was reaching inside him and turning his guts inside out—except this time he would slay the dragon, and once he'd had her she would lose the hold she'd had over him since they'd met.

Lara was practically naked, dressed only in her panties and a flimsy lace bra. She could sense Ciro behind her. Looking at her. She wasn't sure what had possessed her. A moment ago she'd been filled with a sense of bravado, but now little tremors were going through her body at the thought of facing Ciro like this.

And then she heard a rough-sounding, 'Lara…'

Swallowing her fear, she slowly turned around and Ciro filled her vision. She could see the tension in his body, making him loom even larger than he normally did. Suddenly self-conscious, she crossed one arm over her breasts and covered herself between her legs with the other hand.

Ciro shook his head. 'No…let me see you. I've waited for this for so long.'

After a moment Lara did as he asked, dropping her hands to her sides, clenching them into fists. In the dim light of the room she couldn't see where Ciro's dark gaze touched her. But she could feel it. On her breasts, her belly, waist, thighs...between her legs.

Her skin broke into goosebumps.

Ciro walked towards her, his usual grace absent. When he stood in front of her she could see the stark expression of pure need on his face. His eyes were blazing.

'You are more beautiful than I ever imagined.'

Lara ducked her head, overwhelmed by what she saw in his eyes. 'I'm not...truly...'

He tipped up her chin and there was something else on his face now, an expression she couldn't decipher. Something like frustration.

'Yes, you are. You really don't have to put on this act, Lara. It's just us here now.'

He thought she was acting coy. She was stripped bare, save for some scraps of material. She'd never been more exposed. And he couldn't see it.

She realised she couldn't entirely blame him. After all, she'd done her best to convince him she was someone else. Someone who cared more for prestige and social standing than anything else.

'Lara.'

She looked at him and her whirling thoughts stopped. She sucked in a breath.

'I need to hear you say it again.'

Lara's heart squeezed. There was no going back. She needed this as much as he did.

She stepped closer, until they were touching and his clothes caused friction against her naked skin. She went up on her tiptoes and pressed her mouth to his neck. 'Please...' she said.

She trailed her mouth along his jaw, up to where she could feel the rough edges of his scar on the right side of his face. He tensed, and then he put his hands on her arms, hauling her up and closer, before his mouth found hers and the whole world burst into flame.

Lara sensed Ciro shedding his clothes, but while his mouth was on hers she couldn't focus on anything except his intoxicating scent and the dark sensuality of his kiss. Deep and drugging.

When his hot bare skin met hers she stopped and drew back, dizzy from the kiss, and even dizzier when she saw that Ciro was completely naked. The breath left her body as she feasted unashamedly on his perfect form.

She'd never seen him fully naked. Broad shoulders, a wide, powerful chest with a dusting of dark hair that dissected his abdominals in a tantalising line all the way down to where his arousal jutted proudly between his legs. Her gaze stopped there, heat rising inside her at this very potent evidence of his desire for her.

'*Cara mia*...if you keep looking at me like that we won't make it to the bed.'

With difficulty, Lara raised her gaze to Ciro's again.

He took her hand and led her over to the bed. 'Lie down,' he instructed.

Lara lay down on the bed, hoping that he hadn't noticed the tremor in her limbs. Ciro stood for a long moment, his dark gaze moving up and down her body. Then he sat on the bed and lifted a hand, tracing the shape of her jaw and her mouth, which was still swollen from his kisses.

He trailed his hand down, dipping his fingers into the hollow at the base of her throat, and then over her chest to her breasts. Her nipples were two hard points, pressing against the delicate lace of her bra.

Ciro tortured her slowly, trailing his fingers between her breasts, under one and then the other, before covering one breast with his palm, its heat and weight making Lara bite her lip. She could feel the point of her nipple stabbing Ciro's palm, and instinctively she arched her back to push herself into his hand.

His mouth quirked. With an expertise that spoke of his experience he undid the front clasp of her bra and peeled the lace squares back, baring her to his gaze. He squeezed her breast gently and Lara's breath hitched. She was unprepared for the spiking of pleasure deep down in her core. Then he took his hand away and placed both hands either side of her body, so he could lower his head and...

Lara nearly jack-knifed off the bed when she felt the potent drugging sensation of Ciro's hot mouth closing over first one nipple and then the other.

He put a hand on her belly, as if to calm her. She was breathing so fast it hurt—but not nearly as much as the exquisite torture of his mouth on her flesh...the hot, wet heat, teeth tugging gently at her sensitised flesh.

Lara's whole body was on fire now, as the bed dipped and Ciro moved to lie alongside her. The hand on her belly moved down until it rested at the juncture of her legs. With the same expert economical touch he dispensed with her panties, throwing them to the floor. He touched her thigh.

'Open for me, *bella*.'

Lara opened her legs and Ciro's hand slid down to explore where she was so aroused. It was excruciating. It was exquisite. She'd never known anything like it before.

Ciro had been a model of restraint two years before, when he'd discovered she was a virgin. So much so that she'd begun to feel seriously insecure. She'd ached with wanting him but he'd always seemed so in control.

Not any more.

Lara's nails scored her palms as Ciro massaged her throbbing flesh with his fingers before sliding one deep inside her. The sensation was electrifying. Lara instinctively reached for his wrist but he was remorseless.

'Trust me, *cara mia*.'

In the midst of this sensual onslaught Lara felt a dangerous bubble of emotion rise up. She *did* trust Ciro. Perhaps not with her heart any more, but in a very deep and fundamental way. She'd never expected to see him again, be with him again. Certainly not like this. But she'd fantasised about it in her lonely bed so many times…

Shocked and aghast at the welling of emotion—she shouldn't be feeling *emotion* right now!—she almost cried out with relief when Ciro took his hand away and replaced it with his body, settling between her legs as if it was the most natural thing in the world. As if they'd done this dance a million times before.

His weight was heavy and she revelled in it, widening her legs so that he came into closer contact with the cradle of her femininity, where every nerve-ending was pulsating with need.

Ciro had to take a breath and resist the urge to drive deep into Lara's willing body. He could feel the pulse of her desire against him, and the way she was opening like a flower under his body. He couldn't remember ever wanting a woman like this. Lovemaking for him had always held a certain amount of detachment. But here, right now, he was…*consumed*.

But then he'd always known instinctively that Lara had a different kind of hold over him. Something he hadn't encountered before. Something that made him nervous. But right now nerves were gone.

Ciro reached for and found protection, miraculously thinking of it at the last second, rolling it on with uncharacteristic clumsiness.

He positioned himself at the juncture of Lara's legs and looked down into her eyes. It was another thing he usually avoided with lovers, but with Lara he couldn't seem to move unless his gaze was locked onto hers.

Her expression was soft, unfocused. Her cheeks were flushed. Damp strands of her hair clung to her forehead. She was biting her lip.

'Ciro...please.'

In this there was no *other Lara*. He had undone her, exposed her.

He felt her move beneath him and couldn't hold on. He plunged deep inside her, feeling every muscle in his body spasming with pleasure at the sheer sensation of his body moving deep into the clasp of hers.

The very *tight* clasp...

It took a second for him to register in his overheated brain that Lara had tensed, and now she looked anything but unfocused. There was an expression of shock on her face. Awe. And...*pain*?

Ciro moved slightly and she sucked in a breath. His brain didn't seem to be working properly. He knew he was big but he'd thought she'd be experienced enough...

'Lara, am I hurting you?'

'It's okay...don't stop now. Please don't stop.'

She sounded breathless.

She put her hands on his hips, and even as a very uncomfortable truth made itself graphically known to him Ciro could no more deny his primal urge to move than he could stop breathing.

Lara consciously relaxed her muscles, and for a second she almost cried out because the sensation was so intense. But as Ciro started to move again she could feel the pain easing, her body adapting to his, softening around him. And then, pleasure became the dominant sensation as the steady, rhythmic glide of Ciro's body in and out of hers led to a rising excitement, a sense of urgency and desperation that made her reach around to clasp his firm muscular buttocks, silently pleading with him to go deeper, faster…

Lara wasn't prepared for the sudden rush of intense pleasure. It was so unexpected and overwhelming that it was all she could do to cling on to Ciro as his body bucked into hers, again and again, as he too was torn apart and lost all control, finally slumping against her, his head buried in her neck, his ragged breath warm against her damp skin.

For those few moments while they were still intimately joined, their pulses racing, Lara knew complete contentment. Something she hadn't experienced in a very long time. But then Ciro moved, and she winced slightly as he extricated himself from her embrace. Her muscles were tender.

Ciro wasn't looking at her. He sat on the edge of the bed, his back to her, head downbent. His breathing was still uneven. Lara felt a chill skate across her bare flesh and instinctively reached for a sheet to cover herself.

After a moment he got up without a word and went into the bathroom. Lara heard the hiss of the shower. She lay in bed with the sheet pulled up over her chest, totally unsure of herself and not knowing how to behave.

Should she join Ciro in the shower? It seemed like the kind of thing a sophisticated lover would do… But he hadn't said anything and perhaps he wanted to be alone.

He suddenly emerged from the bathroom, taking Lara by surprise. He had a towel slung around his waist and his skin glistened with moisture. For a second she was breathless at the mere thought that moments ago they'd been joined as intimately as it was possible to be joined with another person.

He said, 'I've run you a bath. You'll be sore. Then we need to talk.'

Lara swallowed. Had it been that obvious? Had he noticed she was—*had been*—a virgin?

Feeling totally exposed, and far too vulnerable after what had just happened, Lara got up from the bed as elegantly as she could and went into the bathroom, trailing the sheet behind her.

After the bath, which soothed her tender muscles and her skin, Lara got out and dried herself perfunctorily. She pulled on the voluminous terrycloth robe hanging on the back of the door and steeled herself before going into the bedroom.

But it was empty.

She went out through the door and took a deep, shaky breath before going in search of her husband.

Lara had been a virgin. Innocent. Untouched.

Ciro was feeling such a conflicting mass of emotions and sensations that he couldn't quite pin down what was most prominent: anger, confusion…or, worst of all, a humiliating level of relief at knowing that *he* had been Lara's first lover and not that old man.

With that relief came more confusion and anger, and in the midst of it all was a residual heavy feeling of sexual satisfaction on a level he'd never experienced.

Before, it had been a fleeting thing. Soon forgotten. Much like the women he'd slept with, *before*. But this satisfaction felt as if it was seared into his bones and as his hunger grew for her again. Already. Insatiably.

There had been a moment out on the terrace, after Lara had said, *'Please make love to me...'* when for a split second Ciro had been tempted to reject her. As she'd rejected him. And yet even though he might have fantasised about such a moment in the previous two years, when it had been there, right in front of him, he'd been aware of how petty it was.

And also that he didn't have the strength to reject her. Not when his mouth had been full of her taste and his hands imprinted with the shape of her body.

Madre di Dio.

He heard a noise at that moment.

Lara.

Ciro's whole body tensed against the inevitable reaction his new bride would precipitate. His new *virgin* bride.

Lara tracked Ciro down to a room she hadn't yet been in. A state-of-the-art modern study with humming computers and shelves full of books and periodicals.

He was standing at a window which looked out over the sea. He'd dressed in low-slung faded jeans and a T-shirt. Bare feet. Messy damp hair. She could see his face reflected in the window. The long white line of his scar. His hands were shoved deep in his pockets, which pulled the material of his jeans taut across the perfect globes of his bottom.

Her heart thumped. 'Ciro...look...'

He turned around and she saw the full extent of his anger on his face. '*Dio,* Lara. How the *hell* were you still a virgin?'

'How did you know?'

Even as she asked the question she wanted to kick herself for being so stupid. A man as experienced as Ciro? Of *course* he'd known. He wasn't some boorish bully like her first husband had been.

He emitted a harsh-sounding laugh. 'How did I *know*? I felt it in your body and there was blood on the sheets.'

A hot wash of humiliation rushed up under Lara's skin. She hadn't even noticed the blood. She felt utterly gauche. She pulled the robe around her, tightening it.

Ciro sent her a dark look. 'It's a bit late for that.'

Lara noticed a drinks cabinet in the corner of the room. 'Can I have a drink, please?' She needed something if this was going to be the tone of their conversation.

Ciro went over and asked tightly, 'Brandy?'

Lara shook her head. 'No—anything but that.'

He poured something into a glass, then came and handed it to her. 'It's whisky. What do you have against brandy?'

Lara took the glass, relieved that Ciro was distracted from his inevitable questions for a moment. 'Brandy reminds me of funerals. When my parents and brother died my uncle made me drink some. He said it was for the shock but it made me sick.'

She took a sip of the whisky, wincing at the tart, acrid taste. It slid down her throat and landed in her stomach, sending out a glow of warmth. But she knew it was just illusory and wouldn't last.

'How old were you?'

Lara glanced at Ciro warily. 'Thirteen.'

'You were close as a family?'

Lara nodded, her hand clasping the glass. 'The closest. My parents loved each other and they loved me and Alex. We were a very happy family.'

Ciro surprised her by saying, 'You were lucky to have had that, even if only for a short while. My father loved my mother, but it was a suffocating love and she wasn't happy to be adored by just one man. After he died she remarried within a month. She's now on husband number three—or four. I've lost count.'

The careless tone in Ciro's voice didn't fool Lara. He couldn't be immune to the fact that his mother had failed to be the kind of mother every child deserved. No wonder he was so cynical.

Ciro sat back against his desk, and folded his arms. The reprieve was over. 'So. Are you going to explain to me how you were married but still a virgin?'

Lara took another fortifying sip of whisky and sat down on a chair behind her. Her legs didn't feel steady all of a sudden. She looked up at Ciro and then away. She didn't want to see his expression.

'On our wedding night Henry came into my bedroom expecting to—' She stopped.

'Go on.'

Lara felt sick. She looked at him. 'Do we really have to discuss this now?'

Ciro nodded. Grim.

He stood up and pulled over a chair so that he was opposite Lara, sat down. She knew he wouldn't budge until she'd told him the ugly truth.

'On our wedding night he came into my bedroom... He...we'd agreed that we wouldn't share a room. I somehow...obviously naively...assumed that would mean he wouldn't try to...' She faltered and stopped.

'Try to...*what*? Sleep with his new *wife*? A natural expectation, I would have thought.'

Lara hated Ciro's faintly scathing tone. It scraped along all the raw edges of the memories crowding her head. She stood up and went over to where he'd been standing, at the window. She could see dark clouds massing over the sea and the white edges of rough waves. There was a storm approaching.

It was easier to talk when Ciro wasn't looking at her. 'He came into the bedroom. He'd been drinking all day so he was very drunk. He grabbed my nightdress and ripped it. Before I could stop him he'd pushed me backwards onto the bed. I was in shock... I couldn't move for a moment... He was so heavy and I couldn't breathe...'

Lara didn't even hear Ciro move. He caught her arm and turned her around to face him. She'd never seen that expression on his face before—disgust mixed with pure anger.

'He tried to rape you?'

Lara nodded. 'I thought we had an agreement...that he was just marrying me for appearances. He was old... I didn't think...' She trailed off, humiliated by her naivety all over again.

Ciro was grim. 'Old men's libidos can be voracious.' Then he shook his head. 'Did you really think he wouldn't demand sex from you?'

Lara pulled her arm free and moved away. Some liquid slopped out of her glass and she looked at the carpet in dismay.

'Leave it—it's nothing.'

Ciro took the glass and put it down. Lara flinched minutely at the clatter against the silver tray.

'But he didn't rape you?'

Lara looked at Ciro, remembering how thinking of him had given her the strength to deal with Henry Winterborne. 'No. I managed to kick him off me...somehow.

He was unsteady from the drink. He fell backwards. He injured himself badly in the fall...and he was in a wheelchair for the rest of our marriage. Eventually he had a stroke—that's how he died.'

Lara couldn't excise the memory of Henry Winterborne's bitter words from her head. *'You little bitch— you'll pay for this. Your only currency is your beauty and innocence. Why the hell do you think I paid so much for you?'*

Fresh humiliation washed over her in a sickening wave. She hadn't even known until then the full extent of her uncle's machinations—that he'd actually sold her like a slave girl. Ciro didn't know the half of it.

Ciro was reeling. All he could see in his mind's eye was that paunchy old man shoving Lara down onto a bed and then climbing on top of her like a rutting bull. Anger bubbled in his blood. No, worse—a ferocious fury that she had put herself in harm's way like that.

'Was the prospect of marrying me really so repulsive that you would choose a man capable of rape over me? *Dio,* Lara...'

He turned around and speared a hand through his hair, not wanting her to see the emotions he couldn't control. He'd thought he'd underestimated her before. This put a whole new perspective on her ambition.

She stayed silent. Not responding.

Ciro steeled himself before turning. Wild dishevelled blonde hair trailed over her shoulders. The robe had fallen apart slightly, to reveal the plump globes of her high firm breasts. Breasts he could still feel in his hands and on his tongue...

Her eyes were huge and he hated her ability still to look so...*innocent*. Even when he'd just taken that innocence in a conflagration that had left him feeling hollowed out and yet hungry for more.

He felt the need to push her away. Gain some distance. He couldn't think when she was so close. When she was telling him things...putting images into his mind that made him want to go out and put a fist through the face of a man who was already dead.

Her silence grated on his nerves. It was as if there was something she was withholding.

'Was it that important to you? Status?'

Her eyes flashed. 'You have some nerve when you've admitted you only wanted to marry me for one thing—my connections.'

Ciro's gut was a mass of tangled emotions he really didn't want to investigate. But this woman had always touched more than just his body. A minute ago he'd wanted to put push her away and now he needed to touch her. *Damn her.*

He closed the distance between them, noting with satisfaction how a line of pink scored each of her cheeks. She couldn't hide her reaction. It was the only honest thing between them.

He slid a hand around the back of her neck, felt the silky fall of her hair brushing his hand. 'Not just for your connections, *cara mia*, but also because I wanted *you*. Your social connections and impeccable breeding were a bonus.'

Ciro's words dropped like the poisoned barbs they were into Lara's heart. And yet could she blame him when she'd convinced him that she'd never intended to marry him?

She pulled away, hating the way her body was reacting to his proximity. Excitement was building already, heat melting her core. She was still so sensitised she was afraid that if he even kissed her it would be enough to send her over the edge.

'Well, you've had me now. I'm sure the novelty is already waning.'

Ciro easily closed the distance between them again, and this time he took Lara's elbows in his hands, tugging her towards him. All she could see was that wicked sculpted mouth, and all she could think about was how it had felt on her body. Against her skin.

'Waning? I've wanted you since the moment I laid eyes on you, *cara*, and you've haunted me for two years. Believe me, once is nowhere near enough to sate my appetite.'

His mouth was on hers and Lara couldn't formulate another word. All she knew was that for a while at least there would be no more cruel words. Her heart was pounding, blood flowing to every tender part of her...

Ciro swung Lara up into his arms as if she weighed no more than a bag of flour. She knew she should protest, try to reclaim some minute modicum of dignity, but as he carried her back upstairs she couldn't help but think of how she'd endured two barren years of regretting the fact that she hadn't slept with Ciro.

So she wasn't going to regret a single moment now. No matter how much Ciro might resent her for this inconvenient desire he felt. It would burn out, sooner or later, and this time, when Lara walked away, she would have no regrets.

When Lara woke the following morning she was in her own bed. Naked. The French doors were open and the white drapes were moving gently in a warm breeze. She grabbed for a sheet, pulling it up over her chest even though she was alone.

She had a very vague memory of Ciro carrying her into this room as dawn had been breaking over the horizon, the storm clouds of the previous night banished.

Silly to feel bereft when he'd told her he didn't think it necessary for them to share a room. After all, he wasn't interested in morning-after intimacy. In a way, Lara should be grateful that this time around all the romantic illusions she'd harboured were well and truly shattered.

She tried to absorb everything that had happened in the space of twenty-four hours but it was overwhelming. This time yesterday she'd still been a single woman, on her way to get married.

She'd still been a virgin.

And now…she felt transformed.

She didn't want to admit that Ciro's touch had had some kind of mystical effect on her—but it was true. In spite of the way he felt about her, his touch had soothed something inside her—the lonely place she'd retreated to for the past two years in a bid to survive an impossible situation.

She heard a familiar low rumble and got out of bed to investigate, pulling on a robe as she did so. She went over to the French doors that led out to the balcony, knotting the robe around her.

Hesitantly she peeked over the railings, to see Ciro standing on the terrace below. He was dressed in those faded jeans and another T-shirt and Lara's mouth dried. He reminded her too painfully of when they'd first met in Florence and he'd been casually dressed. When she'd fallen in love with him.

At that moment Ciro turned around and looked up. Lara stepped back hastily, her heart spasming. *Love.* Did she still *love* him?

No. The rejection of such a disturbing thought was swift and brutal.

How could she still love a man who had betrayed her as much as he believed she'd betrayed him? After years of protecting herself from the pain of loss Ciro had come along and smashed aside her petty defences. Leaving her vulnerable all over again. She'd never forgive him for that.

Enduring all the things she had, had made her strong. Strong enough to withstand this marriage so she could finally move on with her life, her conscience salved. But the little whispers of that conscience told her that as much as she might try to justify why she was doing this, she wouldn't be here unless deeper motives were involved. Far more personal motives.

After all, if she'd really wanted to she could have told Ciro the full truth from the start. Or even last night, when she'd had a chance. But she hadn't. *Why?*

She knew the answer. Because however much he disliked her now—resented her, even, for this desire that burned between them—he would truly despise her if he knew about her uncle and his involvement in the kidnapping and ruination of their wedding. In the very public humiliation Ciro had gone through.

Lara knew that after eroding Ciro's trust in her so effectively he would never believe she hadn't had a part in it... She also knew it would be another huge blow to his pride to find out that she'd known who was behind the attack. He'd never forgive her for that.

There was a peremptory knock at her door and Lara whirled around, expecting to see Isabella. But it was Ciro. Immediately her belly clenched at the memory of how he'd felt between her legs, surging into her body over and over again.

'Buon giorno, mia moglie.'

There was something so palpably satisfied about his tone that Lara injected as much coolness into her voice as she could when she answered. 'Good morning.'

'I've decided that we're leaving today. We've been invited to an event in London tonight.'

Feeling prickly at how cool he appeared to be after a night in which her world had been seismically altered, she said, 'You mean *you've* been invited.'

Ciro leant against the doorframe and folded his arms. 'No, *we've* been invited. To the Royal Opening of the Summer Exhibition at the Longleat Gallery.'

Lara was impressed. Henry Winterborne had been incandescent with rage last year when he hadn't received an invitation to the opening. He'd blamed *her*, of course.

Ciro straightened up. 'Isabella is on her way up with a breakfast tray. We'll leave in an hour. I've arranged for a stylist to deliver some clothes to the townhouse in London, so you don't need to pack.'

He walked away and Lara breathed out slowly, her pounding pulse mocking her attempts to affect the same coolness as Ciro exuded so effortlessly. But then what had she expected? Morning-after cuddles and tender enquires as to how she might be feeling?

Lara turned around to the view again. She would be sorry to leave Sicily so soon, but at the same time she was a little relieved. It had been a cataclysmic twenty-four hours and it would surely be easier to deal with Ciro and try to maintain some emotional distance from him in a busy city surrounded by people, than here, in this effortlessly seductive and intimate environment.

CHAPTER SIX

CIRO WAS AWARE that he should be feeling more satisfied than he was. And that irritated the hell out of him.

Lara was standing a few feet away, a vision in a long yellow evening dress. She effortlessly stood out from the crowd. The dress was one-shouldered, revealing the alluring curve of her bare shoulder and the top of her back. A decorative jewel held the dress over her other shoulder. All it needed was a flick of his fingers and it would be undone, letting the dress fall down to expose her beautiful breasts—

Basta! Ciro cursed his overheated imagination.

Her hair was smoothed back and tied low at the nape of her neck in a loose bun. Long diamond earrings glittered from her ears. She wore minimal make-up. She epitomised cool elegance, and yet all he could think about was the fire that lay under her pale skin. The ardent passion with which she'd made love to him last night. It was hard to believe she'd been a novice...but she *had* been. And that bugged him like a thorn under his skin.

How had he missed it? He who considered himself a connoisseur of women?

He didn't like getting things wrong. Underestimating people. He'd learnt a harsh and brutal lesson at the hands of those kidnappers. The kidnappers who'd yet to be caught and whom he was still investigating—with not much luck.

Until that day he would have been the first to admit that life had always come easily to him. Blessed with good looks, a keen intellect and a sizeable family fortune, he'd lacked for nothing. But since those days at the hands of violent thugs Ciro had learnt not to be so complacent. And since the day Lara had informed him she'd never had any intention of marrying him he'd learnt not to underestimate anyone.

His cynicism had become even more pronounced. Any kind of easy charm he'd displayed before had become something much darker.

Unbidden, a memory resurfaced at that moment. Lara, not long after they'd met, admitting to him sheepishly that she'd looked him up on the internet. He'd immediately felt betrayed. And disappointed. She was like everyone else. Assessing his worth. Looking for the salacious details of his family history.

And then she'd stunned him with an apparently sincere apology, saying that she should have asked him face to face. Normally he abhorred women trying to get him to reveal personal details, but within seconds he'd been saying to Lara, 'Ask me now.'

That was the night she'd confided in him about her family and their history. How she had a trust fund worth millions. For the first time in his life someone had surprised Ciro. And it had only added to her allure.

Until she'd pulled the rug out from under his feet.

For the first time in a long time he wanted to know *why* she'd done it. Created that persona. But something held him back. Some sense of self-preservation.

A feeling that he'd be exposing himself if he asked the question.

As if sensing his brooding regard, she turned and looked at him, and for a second Ciro couldn't breathe. She was so beautiful. And the memory was so vivid. He could almost imagine that the previous two years hadn't happened.

But they had.

He cast aside memories and nebulous dangerous thoughts. She was here by his side. *His*. That was all that was important.

He lifted his hand and crooked a finger, silently commanding her to come to him. He saw the way her eyes flashed, the subtle tensing of her shoulders. The resistance to his decree. But then she came. Because she was here in her own milieu and of course she wouldn't cause a scene.

It was time to remember why he had spent two years keeping tabs on her and why he'd married her at the first opportunity. For revenge, yes, but so much more. He caught Lara's hand in his, very aware of the absence of his little finger. The reminder firmed his resolve to stop thinking of the past.

He bent his head close to hers, inhaled her scent drifting up to tantalise his nostrils and threatening to dissolve that resolve. He directed Lara to look across the lawn to where heads of state, royalty and A-list celebrities sipped champagne and mingled. 'Do you see Lord Andrew Montlake over there?'

Lara nodded.

'He was a friend of your father's, yes?'

Lara nodded again. 'Yes—a good friend.'

Ciro smiled. 'Good, then introduce me. I've been trying to get a meeting with him for months, to discuss the chateau he's selling outside Paris.'

***

A few hours later Lara's feet were aching almost as much as her facial muscles ached from smiling and pretending that it was totally normal to be back in London society with a new husband just over a week after burying her previous husband. She'd felt every searing look and heard every not so discreet whisper and had held her head high with a smile fixed in place.

They were in the back of Ciro's car now, and she looked out of the window at the streets of London bathed in late summer sunshine. Young couples stood hand in hand outside pubs, drinking and laughing. Carefree.

She'd never had the chance for a life like that. As soon as her uncle had taken over his role as guardian he'd had his nefarious plan mapped out for Lara and she'd been totally unaware of it.

Pushing down the uncharacteristic welling of self-pity, Lara thought of the event they'd just been to. As much as *she'd* been the centre of attention, so had Ciro. Lara had noticed the looks and whispers directed his way too, the way people's eyes had widened on his scarred features. It had made her want to stand in front of him and stare them down. Shame them for their morbid fascination.

She'd seen the masterful way he'd operated, winning people around, charming them into submission. He might have needed someone like her for access into this rarefied world, but it wouldn't be long before he became an indelible part of it. And then her role would be obsolete.

Ciro turned to look at her then, as if aware of her regard. The back of the luxury car suddenly felt tiny. All evening Lara had been acutely aware of Ciro, of his every movement as he'd taken her hand, or touched her arm, or the small of her back. Her skin felt tight and sensitive. Her body ached with a wholly new kind of yearning. And her lower body tightened with need every time his dark gaze rested on her. Like now.

She didn't feel in control of herself at all any more. If she ever had around this man. And she hated it that he seemed so cool, calm and collected.

If he so much as touched her right now she knew she wouldn't be able to control her reaction, but he surprised her by saying, 'We're going to stay in London for a few days. I have some meetings lined up.'

Lara hid her skittishness and said, 'Fine.'

And then, just when she thought she could gather herself, he reached for her, taking her hand and tugging her across the divide in the seat, closer to him.

'What are you doing?' Lara cast a glance at the driver in front.

Ciro said something in Italian and the privacy window went up, cocooning them in the back of the blacked-out car. The streets outside faded into insignificance as Ciro's hand sneaked around the back of Lara's neck, where with deft fingers he loosened her hair so it tumbled over her shoulders.

Lara's heart rate increased as Ciro's fingers massaged her neck—and then his hand moved to where the dress was held up by the jewel over one shoulder.

Excitement curled low in her abdomen as she protested weakly, 'Ciro...we're in the back of the car...'

He said, 'Do you know how hard it's been for me to keep my hands off you all evening?'

She shook her head, mesmerised by the look on his face. She could see it now—the desire bubbling just under the surface, barely restrained—and she felt it reach out and touch her.

With a flick of his fingers the dress opened and loosened around her breasts. She gasped and put a hand up, but Ciro caught her hand and said roughly, 'Leave it.'

Ciro peeled her dress down, uncovering her breasts. Lara shivered with a mixture of arousal and illicit excitement, aware of the people outside the car on the pavement, where they were stopped at some lights. Only the blacked-out windows and some steel and glass separated her from them and their eyes.

Ciro looked at her and cupped her naked breasts, thumbs moving back and forth over her nipples. 'So beautiful,' he breathed.

'Ciro…' Lara was almost panting. She stopped talking, afraid of exposing herself even more.

His dark head bent towards her, and when his mouth closed around one tight tingling nipple the spiking pleasure was so intense she speared her hands in his hair. She quickly got lost in the maelstrom Ciro had unleashed in her body, knowing that she was showing her weakness but unable to do anything about it…

Ciro looked at himself in the mirror of his bathroom and took in his glittering eyes and the still hectic colour on his cheekbones. When they'd returned to the townhouse a short while before Lara had all but fled up the stairs, holding up the top of her dress with one hand, her hair in a tangle.

Ciro had let her go, even though he'd wanted to carry her straight to his bedroom and to his bed. The only thing that had stopped him was the awful suspicion that he'd just exposed himself spectacularly.

Just an hour before he'd been talking with one of

Europe's heads of state, and within minutes of getting into a car with Lara he'd been all over her like a hormone-fuelled teenager.

He splashed cold water on his face, as if that might dilute the heat raging in his body. After a moment he went into his bedroom, restless and edgy. He looked at the interconnecting door between his and Lara's rooms for a long moment before going over and opening it quietly.

She was in bed. Curled up on one side in a curiously childlike pose, her hair spread out on the pillow. Her breaths were deep and even.

Something about the fact that she could find the equilibrium of sleep so easily made him feel even more exposed.

He went back into his bedroom and closed the door. And then he did the only thing he could do to try and dilute the sexual frustration in his body. He headed for the gym.

As soon as Lara was sure that Ciro had left her room she turned on her back and sucked in a deep, shuddering breath. She looked up at the ceiling.

She was in her underwear under the covers. She'd heard Ciro moving about next door, and after coming so spectacularly undone in the back of his car had felt far too raw to be able to deal with seeing him again. So she'd dived under the covers and feigned sleep even as her body had mocked her, aching for Ciro's touch. For him to finish what he'd started.

This evening had been a salutary lesson in the reality of how this marriage would work. Ciro had used her with a ruthless and clinical precision to seek out meetings with the various people he was interested in talking to. She had to remember that was the focal point of the marriage—her desire to make amends to Ciro for what her uncle had done to him.

What she *had done to him.*

And the other stuff? The physical chemistry? The aching desire he'd awoken in her body?

A man of his extensive experience would surely lose interest soon. Wouldn't he? And when he did she'd have to live with that. She'd lived with far worse, so she would cope. She'd have to.

The following days brought a reprieve of sorts for Lara. Ciro was out at meetings all day, and each evening he had a business dinner to attend, where she wasn't required.

Like a coward, she'd taken the opportunity to make sure she was in bed by the time Ciro came home, pretending to be asleep if he came into her room.

She'd got used to her surroundings—just a stone's throw from the old apartment she'd shared with Henry Winterborne—but she deliberately made sure to avoid that street if she was out of the house, and she knew the security men must think she was mad, taking such a long way round to go to the shops.

Ciro had issued her with a credit card, and Lara had swallowed her pride and taken it. After two years of feeling trapped, due to her lack of personal finances, she was embarrassed at being beholden to someone else. More than ever she wanted to make her own money. Be independent.

And yet there was something about Ciro handing her some economic freedom that made her feel emotional. A man who had a lot less reason to trust her than her previous husband was trusting her with this.

She'd also got to know the staff who worked in the house: the housekeeper was called Dominique, and there was a groundsman/handyman called Nigel. Dominique hired in staff as and when it was required for entertaining or cleaning, she'd told Lara. But as yet Ciro hadn't actually ever entertained in the house.

Fleetingly Lara wondered again at the coincidence that had Ciro's new house right around the corner from where she'd been living.

One evening it was Dominique's night off—she lived close by, so didn't stay over at the townhouse—and Lara went into the kitchen, feeling restless.

She'd always loved to cook, so when Henry Winterborne had maliciously turned her from wife into housekeeper she'd welcomed it, far preferring to be in the kitchen than to share space in his presence.

She'd learnt to cook in the first instance from her parents' housekeeper—a lovely warm woman called Margaret, who had been more like a member of the family than staff. And then over the years she'd continued to cook...usually surreptitiously, because her uncle hadn't approved of her doing such a menial thing.

'You were not born to cook and serve, Lara,' he'd said sharply.

No, she thought bitterly, she'd been born so he could exploit her for his own ends.

She shook her head to get rid of the memory and looked around the gleaming kitchen, instinctively pulling out ingredients from the well-stocked cupboards and shelves.

As she cooked from memory she felt a peace she hadn't experienced in weeks descend over her. She tuned the radio to a pop station and hummed along tunelessly.

In a brief moment of optimism she thought that if things continued as they were going, and if she could maintain her distance from Ciro, she might actually survive this marriage...

Ciro had returned home early, to change for a dinner event. He was irritable and frustrated—which had a lot to do with the workload he'd taken on and the fact that he'd barely seen Lara since that first night in London.

Somehow she was always conveniently in bed when he got home, and he was not about to reveal how much he wanted her by waking her up like some kind of rabid animal to demand his conjugal rights.

He wasn't sure what he'd expected to see on his arrival this afternoon, but it involved an image along the lines of Lara being ready and waiting for him to take her to his bed when he got in.

He set down his briefcase in the hall and loosened his tie. For the first time in his life a woman wasn't throwing herself at Ciro.

He scowled. *The second time in his life.*

The first time had also been with Lara. She'd been like a skittish foal around him when they'd first met. It had taken him weeks of seducing her on a level that he hadn't had to employ for years. If ever.

After she'd revealed herself so spectacularly, and walked out of his hospital room, he'd put it down to being part of her act, but now he had to acknowledge that she *had* been a virgin. She hadn't lied about that. At least.

He was about to head up the stairs when a smell caught at his nostrils. A very distinctive smell. Delicious. Mouth-watering. Evocative of his childhood.

He went towards the kitchen, expecting to find Dominique cooking, but when he opened the door it took a second for his eyes to take in the scene.

Lara was bent down at the open oven door, taking something out. She was dressed in jeans and a loose shirt. Bare feet. Her hair was up in a messy knot, and as she turned around with the dish in her hands he saw how the buttons of the shirt were fastened low enough to give a tantalising glimpse of cleavage.

Tendrils of hair framed her face and flushed cheeks. He heard the music. Some silly pop tune. Then realised that Lara was smiling, bending down to sniff the food in the dish. Lasagne, he guessed. It reminded him of the famous lasagne his *nonna* used to make when he was small, hurtling him back in time.

Ciro was rendered mute and frozen, because he couldn't deny the appeal of the scene, nor that it had already existed in the deepest recesses of his psyche, even as he would have denied ever wanting such a domestic scenario in his life. At least until he'd met Lara that first time around and suddenly his perspective had shifted to allow such things to exist.

She'd cooked for him one evening; a spaghetti *vongole*. So mouthwatering that he could still recall how it had tasted, and the look of uncertainty on her face until he'd declared it delicious.

He'd totally forgotten about that until now.

At that second she looked up at him, catching him in a moment between past and present. Between who this woman was and who she wasn't.

Ciro felt as if there was a spotlight on his head, exposing every flaw—and not just the very physical ones. His scar felt itchy now, compounding his sense of dislocation and exposure. The scar that didn't seem to bother her in the slightest.

'What do you think you're doing?'

Lara looked as frozen as he felt. 'Cooking.'

'For who? Your imaginary friends?'

Ciro didn't have to see the rush of colour into Lara's cheeks to know he was being a bastard, but this whole scenario was unacceptable to him on a level that he really didn't want to investigate too closely.

Lara cursed herself for having given in to this urge to do something so domestic, but she refused to let Ciro's palpable disapproval intimidate her. She wouldn't let another man tell her she couldn't cook.

'It's lasagne, Ciro, not some subversive act.'

A suspicious look came over his face as he advanced into the kitchen. 'Why are you doing it, then? Angling to forge a more permanent position in my life by showcasing your domestic skills? As if they might hide your true nature?'

Lara pushed the dish away from the edge of the island, curbing the urge to lift it up and throw it at Ciro's cynical head. She said through gritted teeth, 'I really hadn't thought about it too much. I merely wanted to cook. It's Dominique's night off—how else am I going to feed myself?'

Ciro was so close now that Lara could see his long eyelashes casting shadows on his cheeks. They should have diminished his extreme masculinity. They didn't.

Feeling exasperated now, as well as jittery that Ciro was so close, Lara said, 'You've been out for dinner every night, Ciro. Did you really expect that I'd be sitting here pining away for your company?'

He flushed as if she'd hit a nerve. 'Clearly I made a mistake in not taking you along to those dinners with me.'

Lara started backing away around the kitchen island,

her jitteriness increasing as Ciro advanced. 'No, it's fine—honestly. I know those things are work-related... not interesting. I'd only cramp your style.'

Then, as if she hadn't spoken, Ciro said almost musingly, 'I had no idea you liked going to bed so early. I seem to remember you telling me that you loved the night-time—after midnight, when everyone else is asleep and the world is finally quiet and at peace.'

Now Lara flushed. He'd remembered that romantic stroll when he'd taken her through deserted Florentine squares under the moonlight? She'd been such a sap, believing he wanted to hear all her silly chattering about everything and anything.

He waved a hand. 'None of that's important. There's only one thing I'm interested in right now, and that's repairing an area of our marriage that seems to have become neglected, thanks to my workload and your proclivity for early nights.'

Lara could see the explicit gleam in his eye and felt herself responding as if she literally had no agency over her own body.

'Actually, I think this week is a good example of how this marriage will succeed,' she blurted out with a sense of desperation. 'You know, if you want to take a mistress then please go right ahead. It might be better, actually, if we're to keep things clear and separate. After all, my worth is only really in helping you to network.'

Ciro barked out a laugh and shook his head. 'Take a mistress and give you grounds for divorce? I don't think so, *cara mia.* And you do yourself down. Your worth isn't only for your social standing and connections—it's also in the place where I want you right now.'

Lara stopped moving, feeling a sense of inevitability

washing over her that, treacherously, she didn't fight. 'Where's that?'

Ciro came and stood in front of her. 'My bed...under me.'

The lasagne growing cool on the island was forgotten. Everything was distilled down to this moment and the way Ciro was looking at her.

He reached out and she felt air caress her skin. He was undoing her shirt and she slapped at his hands. 'Stop! What if someone comes in?'

Ciro was spreading her shirt apart now, his hands spanning her waist. She was finding it hard to focus as he tugged her forward.

'Dominique isn't here and Nigel has gone home. I passed him on my way in.'

Lara knew all that. They were entirely alone in this vast townhouse. She was so close to his body now that she could smell his scent. It reminded her of Sicily, of the sun baking the ground and something far more sensual and musky. *Him*.

She knew he was distracting her, and also punishing her on some level for having had the temerity to bring domesticity into this situation, but all she could think about was how she had denied herself his touch all week.

His head was coming closer, and Lara fought a tiny pathetic internal battle before she gave up and allowed Ciro's mouth to capture hers. He pressed her back against the island but Lara didn't even notice. Nor did she notice when Ciro pulled off her shirt and undid her bra, freeing her breasts into his hands, bringing her nipples to stinging life.

She squirmed against him, instinctively seeking flesh-on-flesh contact. He smiled against her mouth and Lara felt it, just as he broke the kiss and trailed his mouth down over her jaw and her chest to her breasts, tipping up first one and then the other, so that he could feast on them, sucking and licking and biting gently, causing a rush of hot blood to flow between Lara's legs, damp and hot.

Suddenly she was being lifted into Ciro's arms and he was carrying her out of the kitchen and up through the house. Lara's breathing was uneven. She realised she was bare from the waist up, but she could feel no shame, only a sense of rising desperation.

When they got to Ciro's bedroom he shed his clothes with indecent haste. Lara was equally ready, pulling off her jeans and panties, her skin prickling with need as she lay back and took in the sight of Ciro standing proudly by the bed, every muscle bulging and taut as he rolled protection on.

She wanted to weep because she was so ready. It made a mockery of the nights when she'd feigned sleep and believed herself to have scored some kind of victory. It had been a pyrrhic victory. Empty.

Ciro came down on the bed by Lara and she bit her lip. He put a thumb there, tugging her lip free, before claiming her mouth in a drugging, time-altering kiss. Ciro's hands explored every inch of her body until she was incoherent with need, past the point of begging.

But he knew. Of course he knew. Because he was the devil.

He settled his body between her spread legs, and in the same moment that he thrust deep, to the very core of where she ached most, he took her mouth and absorbed her hoarse cry of relief.

It was fast and furious. Lara reached her peak in a blinding rush of pleasure so intense she blacked out for a moment. Ciro's body locked tight a moment after, his huge powerful frame struggling to contain his own climax. It gave Lara some small measure of satisfaction to see his features twisted in an agony of pleasure as deep shudders racked his frame.

One thing was clear in her mind before a satisfaction-induced coma took her over. Ciro had just demonstrated very clearly where the parameters of this marriage lay: in the bedroom and on the social circuit. Not in the kitchen.

When Lara woke the next morning she was back in her own bed. She really hated it that Ciro did that. *What was he afraid of?* she grumbled to herself. Was he afraid he'd wake up and she'd have spun a web around his body, turning him into a prisoner?

The image gave her more than a little dart of satisfaction. The thought of Ciro being totally at her mercy…

She didn't hear any sounds coming from his bedroom and checked the time, realising that Ciro would have gone to the office already.

After showering and dressing she went downstairs to find Dominique in the kitchen. The woman turned around and smiled widely, and it was only at that moment that Lara had a mortifying flashback and saw her shirt and bra neatly folded on a chair near the door.

She grabbed them, her face burning, gabbling an apology, but the older woman put up a hand.

'Don't apologise. It's your home. I might have been married for twenty years, but I do remember what that first heady year was like.'

Lara smiled weakly, welcoming the change in subject when Dominique said, 'The lasagne—did you cook it? It smells delicious. I've put it in the fridge but I can freeze it if you like.'

Lara had been taught a comprehensive and very effective lesson last night in not expecting to see Ciro sitting down to a home-cooked meal any time soon, so she said, 'Actually, do you want to take it home with you this evening for you and your family? I thought we'd have a chance to eat it but we won't.'

Dominique reached for something and handed a folded card to Lara. 'That reminds me—Ciro left this for you. And, yes, I'd love to take the lasagne home if you're sure that's all right? It'll save me cooking!'

Lara smiled and retreated from the kitchen. 'Of course. I hope you enjoy it.'

She looked at the card once she was out of sight. The handwriting was strong and slashing.

Be ready to leave for a function at five this evening. Dress for black tie.

No, she could be under no illusions now as to where her role lay.

On her back and at Ciro's side as his trophy wife.

Ciro's driver came for Lara at five. She checked her appearance in the mirror of the hall one last time. The long sleeveless black dress had a lace bodice and a high collar. She'd pulled her hair back into a sleek ponytail and kept jewellery and make-up to a minimum.

The car made its way through the London traffic to one of the city's most iconic museums. She saw Ciro before he saw her in the car. He was standing by the kerb, where cars were disgorging people in glittering finery.

For a moment Lara just drank him in, in his classic

tuxedo. He must have changed at the office. He was utterly mesmerising. She could see other women doing double-takes.

Then he saw the car and she saw tension come into his form. She felt a pang. They might combust in bed, but he still resented her presence out of it. Even if he did need her.

The car drew to a stop and Lara gathered herself as Ciro opened the door and helped her out. Even her hand in his was enough to cause a seismic reaction in her body. But she felt shy after what had happened last night.

Ciro said, 'You look beautiful.'

She glanced at him, embarrassed. 'Thank you. You look very smart.'

A small smile tipped up his mouth. 'Smart? I don't think I've been called that before.'

Lara felt hot. No... Ciro's lovers would have twined themselves around him and whispered into his ear that he was magnificent. Gorgeous. Sexy.

She felt gauche, but he was taking her elbow in his hand and leading her towards the throng of people entering the huge museum near Kensington Gardens, one of London's most exclusive addresses.

It was only when they were seated that Lara realised it was a banquet dinner to honour three charities. One of which had Ciro Sant'Angelo's name on it.

She read the blurb on the brochure.

The Face Forward Charity. Founded by Ciro Sant'Angelo after a kidnapping ordeal left him facially disfigured.

There was an interview with Ciro in which he explained that after his injury he'd realised that any physical disfigurement, not just facial, was something that affected millions of people. And that a lot of disfigurement came about due to birth defects, injuries of some kind—whether through accident, war or gangs—or domestic violence.

His mission statement was that no one should ever be made to feel 'less' because of their disfigurement. His charity offered a wide range of treatments, ranging from plastic surgery to rehabilitation and counselling, to help people afflicted. To help them move on with their lives.

Lara looked at Ciro. She was seated on his right-hand side and his scar seemed to stand out even more this evening. A statement.

He glanced at her and arched a brow. She felt hurt that he hadn't mentioned this before. 'I didn't know you'd set up a charity.'

He shrugged minutely. 'I didn't think it relevant to tell you.'

Something deeper than hurt bloomed inside Lara then. Something she couldn't even really articulate.

She stood up abruptly, just as they were serving the starters, and almost knocked over the waiter behind her. Apologising, she fled from the room, upset and embarrassed.

Once outside, in the now empty foyer, she stopped. She cursed herself for bolting like that. The last thing Ciro would want was for people's attention to be drawn to them.

She heard heavy footsteps behind her. Ciro caught her arm, swinging her around. 'What the hell, Lara?'

She pulled free, her anger and hurt surging again at the irritated look on his face. 'I know you don't like me very much, Ciro, but we're married now. The least you could have done is tell me what this evening is about. *You're* the one concerned with appearances. How do you think it would look if someone struck up a conversation with me about your charity which I know nothing about?'

Ciro felt a constriction in his chest. Lara was right. But he hadn't neglected to tell her about it in a conscious effort not to include her. He hadn't told her because he didn't find it easy to mention the kidnapping. Even now. Even here, where he was in public and talking about something that had arisen out of that experience.

Lara looked...*hurt*. And then she said, 'I was there too, you know. I didn't experience what you experienced, and I'm so sorry that you went through what you did. But they took me too, Ciro. So I do have some idea of what you went through, even if it's only very superficial. I might not have any physical scars to prove I had that experience, but I had it.'

She turned and went to walk back into the room, but Ciro caught her arm again. For the first time, he felt the balance of power between them shift slightly.

She looked at him, her full mouth set in a line. Her jaw tight.

'You're right,' he said, and the words came easier than he might have expected. 'I should have told you—and, yes, you *were* there too.'

'Thank you.'

Ciro realised in that moment that she had all the regal bearing and grace of royalty, and something inside him was inexplicably humbled. She'd been right to call him out on this. And he wasn't used to being in the wrong. It was not a sensation he'd expected to feel in the presence of Lara.

Lara felt shaky after confronting Ciro, but his apology defused her anger. She realised now that she'd been hurt because she'd felt left out, which was ridiculous when Ciro had set up the charity well before they'd met again.

After the meal people got up to give speeches, and Lara was a little stunned when Ciro was introduced and he got up to go to the podium. He was a commanding presence. The crowd seemed far more hushed when he spoke. And how could she blame them? He stood out.

His scar also stood out, in a white ridged line down the right side of his face. Most people probably wouldn't even notice his missing finger, too transfixed by that scar.

He spoke passionately about the psychological effects of being scarred and how, with pioneering plastic surgery treatments, people could have the option of going on to live scar-free lives. Especially children.

There was a slideshow of images of some of the children and people his charity had helped so far, and Lara had tears in her eyes by the time he was finished.

When he came back to the table Lara felt humbled. She'd seen a new depth to Ciro tonight. Ever since she'd met him he'd always projected a charming, carefree attitude to life. He was someone who'd been graced with good looks, wealth and intellect. Taken for granted—as his due. Not any more. That much was blatantly obvious.

When they had returned to the townhouse Lara said, 'I think what you're doing is amazing. If there's ever anything I can do… I'd like to be involved.'

Ciro turned to face her. 'There is something you can do…right now.'

He took her hand and tugged her towards him.

Instant heat flooded Lara's body at the explicit gleam in his eyes. 'Ciro...' she said weakly.

'Lara...' he said, and then he stopped any more words by fusing his mouth to hers.

It was only much later, when Lara was back in her own bed, her body still tingling in the aftermath of extreme pleasure, that she realised he'd effectively dismissed her desire to help with the charity.

Clearly it was an arena, along with the kitchen, that she wasn't allowed to enter. Which only made Lara determined to do something about it.

CHAPTER SEVEN

'She's *where*?'

Ciro stood up from his chair and stalked over to the window, which took in a view of the Thames snaking through London.

The voice on the other end of the phone sounded nervous, 'Er...she's in one of the Face Forward charity shops, boss. It looks like she's helping with the display in the window.'

Ciro was terse. 'Send me a video and stay with her until she leaves.'

About a minute later there was a *ping* on his phone and he played the video. There was Lara, in jeans and a sweatshirt, hair pulled back, helping to dress and accessorise a mannequin in the window of one of his charity's shops on the King's Road.

She looked about sixteen. He saw her turn and smile broadly at a young staff member. She looked...*happy*. Happier than he'd seen her since they'd met again.

Something dark settled into his chest. A heavy weight. And confusion. Who the hell was she doing this for? What was she up to?

'What do you mean, what was I up to? *Nothing!* I wanted to prove that I was serious about helping with the charity. Or do you expect me to sit around all day waiting for the moment you decide to dress me up and take me out as your trophy wife?'

Ciro had been festering all day and he'd come home in a black mood. Which had got even blacker when he'd found Lara in the kitchen again, cooking.

'I thought I told you that I don't expect you to cook?'

She smiled sweetly at him, which made his blood boil even more, because it only reminded him of the very real smile he'd seen on that video earlier.

'I'm not cooking for you. I'm cooking for me. And Dominique. She can take the leftovers for her and Bill.'

'Bill?'

'Her husband. He's not well.'

'And you know this...*how*?'

Lara looked at him now as if he was a bit dense. 'Because I have conversations with her.'

Ciro was aware that he was being totally irrational and ridiculous. His wife was cooking in the kitchen. Most men would be ecstatic. Especially as it smelt so delicious.

Lara said, 'I know there's nothing on tonight, thanks to the helpful events calendar your assistant installed in the phone you gave me. Unless that's changed?' She suddenly looked less happy.

'No,' Ciro bit out. 'It hasn't changed. The evening is free.'

'Well,' Lara said, sounding eminently reasonable, and far calmer than Ciro felt, 'have you made plans for dinner or would you like to join me? It's *boeuf bourguignon*.'

Ciro forced himself to stop being ridiculous. He had no idea what Lara was up to with this little charade— helping at the charity shop and revealing her domestic goddess side—but he wasn't foolish enough to cut off his nose to spite his face.

'That would be nice, thank you. I'll have a shower and join you.'

Ciro left and Lara took a deep breath. She regretted cooking now. Dominique had left a perfectly serviceable stew she could have heated up, but she'd needed the ritual of cooking to centre herself.

She guessed Ciro's security guy would have been on the phone to him earlier, about her going to the charity shop, and she'd expected his suspicious mind to spin it into something nefarious.

She knew he expected her to be like some kind of ice princess, waiting obediently for his instructions, but since they'd begun sleeping together it was harder and harder to maintain that kind of façade. And any emotional distance.

So Ciro could just *be* perplexed and suspicious. He didn't really care who she was, after all. So why not be herself?

The following morning Lara was surprised to see Ciro in the kitchen, chatting to Dominique over a cup of coffee. She felt exposed when she thought of the previous evening, and how Ciro had quickly and efficiently dispensed with dinner so that he could remind Lara of one of her primary functions in this marriage. Being in his bed.

He'd said it to her again as they'd finished eating. 'I really don't expect you to be in the kitchen, Lara.'

She shrugged. 'I know I don't have to do it, but I like it.'

He'd looked at her as if she'd spoken in some kind of riddle and then, when she'd been getting up to clear the plates, he'd pulled her down onto his lap. 'I'm drawing the line here. You do *not* clear up.'

Lara was blushing now because she was thinking of Dominique finding their detritus. Again. But the woman was looking twinkly-eyed. The inevitable effect of Ciro on most people.

She wondered what Dominique thought of their separate beds...

Ciro looked at her then. 'You need to pack. We're leaving for New York this morning. Some business has been moved forward. We'll be there a couple of weeks. Don't worry too much about what to bring—a stylist will stock your wardrobe there. They've been given a list of the functions we're due to attend.'

Ciro walked out the kitchen with his coffee cup and Dominique sighed volubly. 'What I wouldn't give to have my wardrobe stocked for me.'

Lara forced a smile and desisted from saying something trite. She knew she was incredibly lucky. Even if it *did* feel as though she were a bird in a gilded cage.

As she packed her modest suitcase a little later she told herself she was being ridiculous to suspect that Ciro had brought forward the New York trip to keep her in her place, because things were getting a little too domesticated in London.

Ciro seemed to be in a state of permanent frustration around Lara. He watched her broodingly from his side of the private plane as she did a crossword puzzle. A pen was between her teeth and her brow was furrowed. Why wasn't she flicking through a magazine? Or drinking champagne? Or trying to seduce him?

He turned away, angry that he couldn't seem to focus on his own work. And also angry because he'd acted impulsively, deciding to come to New York ahead of schedule purely because the previous night and that dinner had impacted on him somewhere he didn't like to investigate.

He hadn't married Lara so she could be of actual help in any aspect of his life other than in the social arena. And in his bed. Yet she was starting to inhabit more parts of his life than he liked to admit.

Apart from the dinner last night he'd noticed soft touches around the house in London. Flowers. Throws. Shoes left discarded. Unintentional little feminine touches. Not even anything concrete he could point to.

Ciro had never lived with a woman. Lara would have been the first and she was still the first. In spite of what had happened.

Because of what had happened.

He found that as much as it made him feel exposed and discombobulated he couldn't say that he didn't like it. He just hadn't counted on Lara's softness. Her ability to converse with the staff. Her...*niceness*.

She'd been nice before. And then she'd changed. So he wouldn't believe it. He had to believe she was up to something. It was easier.

Lara could feel Ciro's eyes on her. She could almost hear his brain whirring. She knew how he worked. He problem-solved. And she was a problem because she wasn't behaving as he thought she should. As he thought the Lara who had rejected him should.

She felt something well up inside her. The urge to just turn around and let it all spill out. The full truth about her treacherous uncle. About what had happened. She even opened her mouth and turned to Ciro...and then promptly shut it again.

His head was thrown back and his eyes were closed.

She'd never seen him asleep. He looked no less formidable.

The urge to talk drained and faded. It would be self-serving. She might want to be absolved of all her sins in his eyes, but was she really ready to face his disgust? He would get rid of her immediately, of that she had no doubt. As it was, the ties binding them were incredibly fragile.

Ciro was so proud. It would kill him to know that she knew the truth about the kidnapping. That it had been done to him by *her* family. He would blame her. No doubt. *She* blamed herself. Why wouldn't he?

She got up from her chair and pulled a blanket over Ciro's body. Immediately his eyes opened and he caught her, bringing her down onto his lap. She was instantly breathless.

She looked at him accusingly. 'I thought you were asleep.'

'Are you finished pretending to be uninterested?'

She saw something in his eyes then—very fleeting. It almost looked like vulnerability.

Lara might have made some trite comment or pushed herself away from Ciro, fought to keep the distance between them, but instead she said, 'You're not a person who would ever inspire a lack of interest, Ciro.'

'That's more like it.'

He pulled her head down and kissed her.

Lara fought to retain a little bit of resistance, but it was futile. Within minutes Ciro was carrying her through the cabin to the back of the plane, where the bed awaited.

New York felt different from London. Where London felt intimate, New York felt expansive and impersonal.

Ciro had a townhouse there too—which was some feat in a city full of soaring buildings and massive apartment blocks. It was nestled between two huge buildings by Central Park, on the Upper East Side.

His staff there were polite and impersonal. Lara couldn't imagine getting to know them all that well. And from the day they arrived she was sucked into a dizzying round of events and functions.

The days took on a rhythm. Ciro would get up and go to his office downtown. Lara would get up, have breakfast and then go to the park for a run. Invariably she found herself sitting on a bench watching other people—couples, dog-walkers, children and their nannies.

She saw a family one day—father, mother and two children. A boy and a girl. It made her heart ache, and she cursed Ciro for making that pain real again even as she denied to herself that she was still in love with him.

Their evenings were spent either at banquet dinners or less formal functions. Lara had lost count of all the people she'd met. There was no time here for cooking cosy dinners in the kitchen. It was as if Ciro was purposely not letting her have the opportunity.

But even he hadn't been able to complain when they'd been passing a famous pizza place a couple of nights ago and Lara had asked if they could stop. She'd been starving, and so, it turned out, had been Ciro, his driver and his security team. So they'd all stood around the high tables, eating slices of pizza. Ciro in his tuxedo with his bow tie undone and Lara in a glittering strapless silver sheath dress.

It had been a very private personal victory for Lara.

And then the nights...

Ciro would take her to bed in his room, shatter her into a million pieces over and over again and then deposit her back in her own bed. Sometimes Lara was glad, because the intimacy felt too raw. But other times she despised him for the way he seemed to find it so easy to despatch her.

His determination to keep her confined to the box in which he'd kept her since he'd married her was very apparent. She knew it wasn't a real marriage, but their physical intimacy was wearing her down and making it harder and harder to keep her guard up. And she hated him for that. Because he seemed totally impervious to it.

That evening they had yet another function to attend and Ciro knocked on Lara's door.

Feeling incredibly weary, she called out, 'I'm ready.'

He opened the door and came in, his dark gaze sweeping her up and down. It turned hot as he took in her light blue silk evening gown. It was one-shouldered, and fell in soft fluid folds around her body—which came to humming life under Ciro's assessing look. *Damn him.*

Her hair was up in a loose chignon and she'd chosen dangling diamond earrings. The only other jewellery she wore was her engagement and wedding rings.

'Stunning,' Ciro pronounced. And then, 'Let's go. The car is waiting.'

For a second Lara wanted to stamp her feet and refuse to follow him, but she swallowed the urge. This wasn't a real marriage. Ciro didn't care if she was feeling weary from the constant socialising. He didn't care because this was all about work for him—a means to an end. And essentially she was just an employee. With benefits.

At the function that evening—there had been so many of them that even Ciro felt as if all the faces and places were blurring into one mass of people—he felt disgruntled. When he had no reason to do so.

Lara was at his side, conversing in Spanish with a diplomat. She was fulfilling her role as corporate wife with absolute perfection. She wasn't behaving like a spoilt petulant princess, demanding attention, or moaning because her feet hurt from standing too long.

But he sensed it. Her discomfiture. He saw it when she moved her weight from foot to foot, or when she winced slightly as someone shook her hand too hard. He saw it when she quickly masked a look of boredom. The same boredom he was feeling.

He'd seen it in her eyes earlier—a kind of fatigue along with the slightest of shadows under her eyes. After all, they weren't falling asleep until near dawn most nights.

Ciro had been feeling more and more reluctant to take Lara back to her own bed after making love to her, and was doing it out of sheer bloody-mindedness—so she didn't get ideas and think that their mind-blowing sex was leading to any deeper kind of intimacy.

She'd asked if they could stop on their way home the other night. For pizza. The gratitude on his staff's faces had made Ciro feel guilty about how hard he was working them. Not to mention the almost sexual look of pleasure on Lara's face as she'd bitten into a slice. It had been the best damn pizza he'd ever tasted. And he'd eaten pizza in Naples.

It had been fun. Unexpected. And it had reminded him so much of when he'd known Lara *before* that past and present had blurred painfully.

There were too many of those moments now. Moments that made him doubt his sanity. His memory.

Maybe that was why he'd insisted on such a punishing pace. So as not to give himself a chance to stop and think for a second.

'Do you think we could go now? I'm quite tired.'

Ciro looked around. He hadn't even noticed most of the other guests leaving. Lara looked pale, the shadows under her eyes more pronounced.

A dart of guilt lanced Ciro before he could stop it. 'Of course, let's go.'

They got outside and even he was grateful for the fresh air. He wondered if all this endless networking was really worth it. That would have shocked him if he'd thought it before.

Suddenly his thoughts came to a standstill as Lara stopped beside him and then darted towards a dark alleyway nearby. All he could see was her light blue dress disappearing like an aquamarine jewel into the dark night.

'What the...?'

Ciro flicked a hand to tell his security team that he would get her. As he walked towards the alleyway, though, he felt his insides curdle at the thought that she might be trying to run.

This was it. What she'd been up to.

He'd given her a credit card—maybe she'd just been biding her time. Maybe she'd met a man at one of these functions and devised a plan to escape with someone more charming than him. Someone who would offer her a lifetime of security and not just a year or six months. Someone who didn't have their tangled history...

But at that moment Lara appeared again, in the mouth of the alleyway, and he came to a stop at the same time as his irrational circling thoughts.

He frowned at the sight before him.

She was holding something in her arms against her

chest. Something that was moving. Shaking uncontrollably. She came forward, her eyes huge and filled with compassion. 'It's a puppy... I heard it crying. It needs help. It's been attacked by someone, or another dog. It's bleeding.'

Ciro could see it now—an indeterminate bundle of matted hair and big wounded-looking eyes. Dark blood was running down Lara's dress along with muck and dirt. There was a streak of something dark along her cheek and he could smell the dog from here.

For a second he couldn't compute the scene. Lara, dressed in a couture gown, uncaring of the fact that she was holding a mangy dog covered in blood and filth.

'Please, Ciro, we need to take him to a vet. He'll die.'

A memory blasted Ciro at that moment. He'd been very small. Tiny. Holding his mother's hand as she'd walked along the street. Which had been odd, because generally she hadn't taken him with her anywhere, not liking to take the risk that he would do something to show her up in public.

But on this day he'd been with her, and as they'd passed a side street he'd seen some older boys pelting a cowering dog with stones. He'd stopped dead, eyes wide on the awful scene. He could remember trying to call *Mamma!* but his mouth wouldn't work. Eventually she'd stopped and demanded to know why he wouldn't move.

He had pointed his finger, horrified at what he was witnessing. Such cruelty. He'd looked up at her, tears filling his eyes, willing her to do something. But she had taken one look, then gripped his hand so tightly it had hurt and dragged him away.

The piteous yelps of that dog had stayed with him for a long time. And he'd forgotten about it until this moment.

'Ciro...?'

He moved. 'Of course. Here—let me take him.'

She clutched the animal to her. 'No, it's fine. He's not heavy. There's no point two of us getting dirty.'

Ciro just looked at her. And then he said, 'Fine. We'll find the closest vet.'

Lara got into the back of the car carefully, cradling the bony body of the dog, which was still shaking pitifully. There was no way she could have ignored the distinctive crying once she'd heard it. She adored dogs.

She heard Ciro on the phone, asking someone to find them a vet and send directions immediately. She imagined a minion somewhere jumping to attention.

Ciro's phone rang seconds later and he listened for a second before rattling off an address to the driver.

He said to Lara, 'We'll be at the vet's in ten minutes—they're expecting us.'

'Thank you. I'm sorry, but I couldn't just...'

'It's fine.' Ciro's voice was clipped.

Lara said, 'If you want you can just leave me at the vet with the dog... I can call a taxi to get home.'

Ciro looked at her. She could see the dark pools of his eyes in the gloom of the back of the car.

'Don't be ridiculous. I'll wait.'

After that Lara stayed silent, willing the dog to survive. When they got to the vet Ciro insisted on taking the dog into his arms, and Lara was surprised to hear him crooning softly to it in Italian, evidently not minding about getting dirty himself.

There was a team waiting when they got inside—the power of Ciro's wealth and influence—and the dog was whisked away to be assessed. Lara felt something warm settle around her shoulders and looked up. Ciro had given her his jacket. She realised that it was chilly inside, with the air-conditioning on, and she'd been shivering.

'Coffee?'

She nodded, and watched as Ciro went to the machine provided for clients. He handed her a coffee and took a sip of his own. It was only then that Lara caught a glimpse of herself in the reflection of a window and winced inwardly. Her hair was coming down on one side and she had streaks of dirt all over her face and chest. And her dress was ruined.

She gestured with her free hand. 'I'm sorry... I didn't mean to ruin the dress.'

Ciro looked at her curiously. 'It's not as if you would have worn it again.'

She thought of how much a dress like this might have fetched in an online auction, like when she'd been reduced to selling her clothes while married to Henry Winterborne. She couldn't ever imagine telling Ciro that story. He wouldn't believe her.

She said, 'Of course not,' and sat down on a plastic chair, the adrenalin leaving her system. They were the only people at the vets. The harsh fluorescent lighting barely dented Ciro's intensely gorgeous looks. He caught her eye and she looked away hastily, in case he saw something on her face. She felt exposed after her impetuous action. Less able to try and erect the emotional barriers between her and Ciro.

If she ever had been able to.

'Lara...'

Reluctantly she looked at him.

He shook his head. 'Sometimes you just...confound me. I think I know exactly who you are and then—'

At that moment there was a noise and Ciro stopped

talking. Lara welcomed the distraction, not sure if she wanted to know what Ciro had been about to say.

The vet walked in and looked at them both before saying, 'Well, he is a she and it's lucky you found her when you did. She wouldn't have survived much longer. She's about five months old and as far as we can tell she hasn't been microchipped. She's probably from a stray litter or got dumped.'

Lara said, 'Is she okay?'

The vet nodded. 'She'll be fine—thanks to you for bringing her in. She's obviously been in a scrap, but it's just cuts and bruises. Nothing too serious. She needs some TLC and some food. We can microchip her and keep her in overnight to clean her up, then you can take her home tomorrow, if you like?' He must have seen something on their faces because then he said, 'I'm sorry, I just assumed you'd want to keep her, but I can see I shouldn't have.'

Lara didn't want to look at Ciro, but all of a sudden it seemed of paramount importance that she got to keep the dog. As if something hinged on this very decision.

Without looking at Ciro, she said, 'I'd like to keep her.'

The vet looked at Ciro, who must have nodded or something, because he said, 'That's good. Thank you.' The vet was just turning to leave and then he said, 'You should probably think of a name.'

Lara sneaked a look at Ciro, who was expressionless. But she could see his tight jaw.

'We'll let you know,' he said.

The vet left and Lara said, 'If you don't want to keep her I'll look after her and take her with me when I leave. You won't even know she's there.'

She. Her.

As if they were discussing a person.

Ciro wasn't sure why, but he had an almost visceral urge *not* to take this puppy. A puppy smacked of domesticity. Longevity. Attachment.

'It's fine. You can keep her.'

Ciro told himself that Lara would soon tire of the dog and then he would arrange for it to go to a new home. A home with a family who would appreciate it.

But even as he thought that he felt some resistance inside him. He was losing it. Seeing how Lara had been with the dog had made him feel as if he was standing on shifting sands.

'Thank you.'

'Let's go.'

Lara walked out ahead of Ciro, his jacket dwarfing her slender shoulders. She should have looked ridiculous. Her hair was all over the place and she was smeared in dubious-smelling substances. Not to mention the blood. Yet she seemed oblivious to it.

When they were in the back of the car Lara said, 'Sorry—I know I stink.'

Ciro looked at her in the dim light. Even as dishevelled as she was, she was stunning. More so, if possible. As if this act of humanity had added some quality to her beauty.

'I wouldn't have had you down as a dog-lover.'

Her mouth curved into a small smile. 'My parents got a rescue Labrador puppy when I was just a toddler. We called her Poppy, we were inseparable.'

'What happened to her?'

The smile faded. 'After my parents and brother died my uncle had her put down. She was old… She probably only had another year at the most.'

Ciro absorbed that nugget of information. He could hear the emotion she was trying to hide in her voice.

'Have you thought of a name for this one?'

She turned to look at him and he could see the gratitude in her eyes. He really didn't want it to affect him, but it did. He couldn't imagine another woman looking so pleased about taking on a mongrel of dubious parentage.

'Maybe Hero? I've always liked that name. After the Greek myth.'

The fact that Hero had been a virgin priestess wasn't lost on Ciro, but he only said, 'Fine. Whatever you want. She's your dog.'

When they arrived back at the house Lara made a face and gestured to her clothes. 'I should clean myself up.'

She handed Ciro his jacket. He took it, and there was something vulnerable about the way Lara looked. He had a memory flash of having her ripped out of his arms by the kidnappers and thrown from the van to the side of the road. She'd been dishevelled then too. And the look of terror on her face had matched the terror he'd felt but had been desperate not to show.

'Of course,' he said tersely. 'Go to bed, Lara, it's been a long night.'

Ciro went into the reception room and dropped his jacket on a chair, loosening his bow tie. Except he knew it wasn't the fault of his tie that he felt constricted. It was something far more complicated.

He poured himself a whisky and downed the shot in one go, hoping to burn away the questions buzzing in his head. Along with the unwelcome memories.

He forced his mind away from the past and the image of Lara's terror-stricken face to think of her as she was now—standing under a shower, naked. With rivulets of water streaming down over her curves, her nipples hard and pebbled. The soft curls between her legs would be wet, as wet as she always was when he touched her there—

Dio! He had a wife, willing and hot for him, one floor above his head, and he was down here, torturing himself, when he could be burying himself inside her and forgetting about everything except the release she offered.

Ciro slammed down the glass and went upstairs, taking two stairs at a time. When he got to Lara's bedroom door he stopped, his sense of urgency suddenly diminishing when he thought of how vulnerable she'd looked. What she'd told him about her family dog. Her uncle had had her put down. Just after her family had been taken from her.

Ciro had had his hand lifted, as if to knock on her door, but he curled it into a fist now, and walked away.

CHAPTER EIGHT

It seemed to take an age for Lara to fall asleep. She could have sworn she heard Ciro outside her bedroom, and even as she'd longed for him to come in she'd known that if he did she wasn't sure she'd be able to maintain the façade that she was as cool and impervious to their intimacy as he was.

So when he didn't appear in her doorway she couldn't help a tiny dart of relief.

She slept fitfully, and when she woke at some point in the night she wasn't sure if she'd been asleep for hours, or had only just fallen asleep.

And then she heard it—the sound that must have woken her. A shout. A guttural shout drawn from the very depths of someone's soul.

Ciro.

The tiny hairs stood up all over Lara's body as he shouted again—something indeterminate. Half English, half Italian. She realised she was getting out of bed before she'd even decided to do so, and she went to the adjoining door to Ciro's room.

And then he unleashed a cry that she did understand.

'No—stop!'

Lara didn't hesitate. She opened the door and flew into Ciro's room, where he was thrashing in the bed.

Naked. A sheet was tangled around his hips and legs, and his hands were balled into fists at his sides. His skin was sheened with sweat. His hair was damp.

Lara went into the bathroom and soaked a cloth with cold water. She brought it back and sat beside Ciro on the bed, pressing the damp cloth to his forehead. She desperately wanted to ease his pain without waking him, if she could help it. She knew he wouldn't thank her for seeing him in such a vulnerable state.

But then one of his hands caught her wrist and suddenly she was looking down into wide open dark eyes. She held her breath. He was breathing as if he'd run a marathon.

'Ciro...?' Lara whispered. 'You were dreaming...'

With a sudden move Ciro had Lara flat on her back and was looming over her, both her wrists caught in his hands. Now *she* was breathing as if she'd been running. She didn't know if he was asleep or awake and he looked crazed. Yet she wasn't scared. She knew he wouldn't hurt her. Even like this.

Ciro was still reeling from the nightmare. So vivid he could still taste it on his tongue. Acrid. He wasn't even sure where he was. All he could see were Lara's huge blue eyes. Soft and full of the same emotion she'd had in them earlier when she'd held the dog. Pity... No, not pity. Compassion.

It impacted Ciro deep inside, and he felt a desperate need to transmute the effects of the nightmare into something much more tangible. He could feel her body against his, all lithe and soft like silk. The press of her breasts...the cradle of her hips.

He was so hard it hurt. Hard and aching. And not just in his body. In his chest, where he felt tight.

He took his hands off her wrists and put them either

side of her head. 'I need you, Lara. Right here, right now, and I can't promise to be gentle. So if you want to go, go now.'

I need this. I need you.

He didn't say the words but they beat so heavily in his brain he wondered if he had said them out loud.

Lara reached up and wound her arms around his neck, bringing her body into close contact with his. 'Take me,' she said, 'I'm yours.'

And in that moment, Lara knew she was done for. She felt Ciro's need as clearly as if it was hers. And all she wanted to do was assuage his pain. She loved him. She still loved him. Had always loved him. Would always love him.

Ciro waited a beat, as if making sure that Lara knew what she was doing, and then with studied deliberation he put his hand to her silky nightgown and ripped it from top to bottom. It fell apart, baring her to his gaze, and Lara found herself revelling in it. She felt the ferocity Ciro felt—it thrummed through her in waves of need, building and building.

Ciro's dark gaze devoured her body and his hands moulded her every curve. His tongue laved her and with big hands he spread her legs so he could taste her there, making her cry out loud when he found and sucked on that little ball of nerves at the centre of her body.

She lifted her head, hardly able to see straight. She was sheened with sweat now too. 'Ciro, I can't wait… please.'

He reached for something and she saw him roll protection onto his length. For the first time Lara wished there could be nothing between them—but this marriage wasn't about that. Procreation. It was just about…

this... She hissed out as Ciro joined their bodies with one cataclysmic thrust.

He was remorseless, using every skill he had to prolong and delay the pinnacle. At one point he withdrew from Lara, and she let out a pitiful-sounding mewl, but he rolled onto his back and urged her to sit astride him, saying roughly, 'I want to see you.'

Lara put her thighs either side of his hips and came up on her knees. She felt Ciro take himself in his hand, and then he guided her down onto his stiff length. She came down slowly, experimentally, savouring the exquisite sensation of Ciro feeding his length into her, and then he put his hands on her hips. 'Take me, *cara mia*...all of me.'

Lara soon found her rhythm, her slick body moving up and down on his, excitement building at her core, making her move faster. The pinnacle was still elusive, though, and she was almost crying with frustration as Ciro clamped his hands on her hips and held her still so that he could pump up into her body.

He pulled her down, finding her breast and sucking her nipple into his mouth as the first wave of the crescendo broke Lara into a million pieces. It went on and on, like waves endlessly crashing against the shore, until she was limp and spent and hollowed out.

In the seconds afterwards it was as if an explosion had just occurred. Her ears were ringing and she wasn't sure if she was still in one piece.

Her body and Ciro's were still intimately joined. She lay on him, exhausted but satisfied, her mouth resting on the hectic pulse-point at the bottom of his neck, and that was all she remembered before she fell into a blissful dark oblivion.

***

When Lara woke she realised she was still in Ciro's bed. Dawn was breaking outside. He lay beside her on his back, one arm flung over his head, the other on his chest. Her gaze drifted down over hard pecs to the dark curls where his masculinity was still gloriously impressive, even in sleep.

She knew she should leave because he would soon return her to her room. She wondered with a pang if he'd ever let a woman spend the whole night in his bed.

She was sitting up when Ciro's hand caught her arm. 'Where do you think you're going?'

Lara's heart thumped. 'Back to my own bed.'

'Don't. Stay here.'

Lara looked at Ciro. His eyes were still closed. Maybe he wasn't even awake, so wasn't aware of what he was saying. She lay down carefully and he rolled towards her, trapping her with a leg over hers. She felt him stir against her. He opened his eyes.

A bubble of emotion rose up in her as she took in Ciro's stubbled face and messy hair. Without thinking she reached out and touched his scar gently, running her finger down the ridged length.

'Does it hurt?'

'Only sometimes… It doesn't hurt… It feels tight.'

'You were never tempted to get it removed? Like the people you help with your charity?'

His mouth firmed. 'No. I think it's important for people to see it—to know that if they want to live with their scars, it's okay. And it's a reminder.'

Lara was touched by his sentiment. Then she frowned. 'A reminder of the kidnapping…? Why would you want that?'

'Not that, specifically, but it's a reminder that I'm

not as infallible as I once believed. And it's a reminder not to trust anyone.'

Including me, Lara thought.

Facing him like this in the half-light, with no sounds coming from outside, made her feel otherworldly. As if they were in some sort of cocoon.

'The dream you were having last night…'

Ciro rolled onto his back again. 'It was a nightmare.'

Hesitantly Lara asked, 'About the kidnapping?'

He nodded, clearly uncomfortable. He probably saw it as a sign of weakness.

'I had them too,' Lara said.

Ciro looked at her.

'For months afterwards. The same one, over and over again… The hoods being put over our heads, then taken off. Realising we were in that van with those men. Being ripped out of your arms…left at the side of the road—' She stopped, shivering at the memory.

Ciro reached for her and hauled her into his arms. He said, 'I would never let that happen again—do you hear me?'

Lara looked at him, saw the determination on his face. She nodded. 'I believe you.'

There was something incredibly fragile about the moment. And then Ciro hauled her even closer and kissed her. Their bodies moved together in the dawn as they reached for each other and their breath quickened. This was nothing like the ferocity of last night—it was slow and sensuous, and so tender that Lara had to keep her eyes closed for fear that Ciro would see how close to tears she was.

'Working from home again?'

Ciro looked at Lara and raised a brow, but there was

no edginess to his expression. 'Do I need to ask permission?' he said.

Lara shook her head and helped herself to some of the salad which had been laid out on the terrace at the back of the house by the housekeeper. Ciro had been joining her for lunch the past few days. It had been a week since that tumultuous night, and since then Ciro hadn't taken her back to her own bedroom once. They woke up together, and usually made love again in the morning.

But Lara knew it was dangerous territory to believe anything was changing.

Ciro sat down and helped himself to some salad and bread. The housekeeper came out and poured them some wine.

There was a mewling cry from down below and Lara looked down to see Hero, looking up at her with huge liquid brown eyes. It turned out that she was been a cross between a whippet and something else. Cleaned up, and getting fatter by the day, she wasn't a pretty dog by any means—but she was adorable, mainly white with brown patches. The vet had said that he figured she was crossed with a Jack Russell.

A couple of times Lara had gone searching for her, only to find her curled up at Ciro's feet in his study. He'd pretended not to have noticed her, and when Lara had carried her out she'd whispered into her fur, 'I don't blame you, sweetheart. I know how it feels.'

Hero would lick her face, as if in commiseration for the fact that they were both in thrall to Ciro Sant'Angelo.

Lara absently stroked Hero and she lay down at her feet, curling up trustingly. She said to Ciro, 'Thank you for letting me keep her.'

Ciro shrugged, and then he looked at his watch. 'You wanted to visit the Guggenheim Museum, didn't you?'

Lara nodded, surprised he'd remembered her saying that the other night at a function.

'I can take the afternoon off—we'll go after lunch.'

Lara felt a dangerous fluttering in her belly and said, 'Oh, it's okay…you don't have to. I can go by myself—'

'Don't you want me to come with you?'

Lara could feel her face grow hot. This teasing, relaxed Ciro was so reminiscent of how he'd been before that it was painful. 'Of course I'd love to see it with you.'

Ciro stood up. '*Va bene*. I've a few calls to make—we'll leave in an hour.'

Lara watched him leave, striding off the terrace back into the house. She took a deep breath—anything to try and get oxygen to her brain and keep herself from imagining impossible things.

Like the fact that Ciro might actually be learning to like her again…

The following day Ciro watched Lara play on the lawn with the puppy from the window in his study. She was wearing shorts and her long slim legs had taken on a light golden glow. She wore a silk cropped top and he could see tantalising slivers of her belly when it rode up as she moved.

He might have cursed her for trying to tempt him, but he knew she wasn't even aware that he'd come home early. *Home early.* Since when had he started to come home early? Or work from home? Or take afternoons off to go to a museum? The only person who'd ever had that effect on him was on her back, laughing as the puppy climbed all over her, yapping excitedly.

There was a bone-deep sense of satisfaction in his body from night after night of mind-blowing sex. He'd stopped sending Lara back to her own bed. She effectively shared his room now—something he'd never done with another woman, far too wary of inviting an intimacy that would be misread, or taken advantage of.

And they'd spent hours wandering around the Guggenheim the day before. It had been one of the most pleasant afternoons Ciro could remember in a long time.

As he looked at Lara now he had to acknowledge that his desire for her wasn't waning. Far from it. It seemed to be intensifying. But if he stuck to his agreement with her they'd be divorcing—at the earliest in only a few months. That thought sent something not unlike panic into his gut.

So far she'd fulfilled her side of the marriage, and introduced him to people who would never have welcomed him into their sphere before. He had a list of new deals to consider. Invitations to events and places he'd never been allowed access to before. All because of her.

But in truth, he found it hard to focus on that when she filled his vision and he spent most days reliving the night before and anticipating the night ahead.

She was not what he'd expected. More like the Lara he'd known first. And if this was an elaborate act, then what was the point? He couldn't figure it out, but something wasn't matching up...

At that moment his phone rang and he answered it impatiently, only half listening as he watched Lara throwing a ball for the puppy.

He turned away from the view, though, after his solicitor had finished speaking. 'Repeat what you just said.'

'I said that we know who was behind the kidnapping, Ciro, and I don't think you're going to like what you hear.'

* * *

The sun was throwing long shadows on the grass by the time Lara picked up Hero and went back inside the house. All was quiet except for the dull hum of Manhattan traffic outside.

But then she heard a sound coming from the main reception room, and put Hero down in her bed before investigating. She walked in to find Ciro throwing back a shot of alcohol. Predictably, her heart rate increased.

'I didn't know you were home.'

Her heart fluttered at the thought that maybe he'd come back early to take her on another excursion. But when he turned around she had to stifle a gasp. He was pale, and she realised he was pale with fury, because his eyes were burning.

'What is it? What's wrong?'

Ciro put the empty glass back on the tray with exaggerated care and then he looked back at Lara. She had only the faintest prickling sense of foreboding before he said, 'So, when were you going to tell me that you and your uncle were behind the kidnap plot?'

Lara's insides turned to ice. 'How do you know about that?'

'I've been investigating the kidnap since it happened. I kept hitting dead ends until now. Is it true?'

Lara felt sick. She nodded her head slowly.

Not exactly, but... 'Yes. My uncle planned it. He didn't want us to marry.'

Ciro's lip curled. 'And so he came up with a lurid plan to have us kidnapped? Or was that your contribution?'

Lara shook her head. She felt as if she was drowning, and moved sluggishly over to a chair where she sat down. 'I didn't know anything about it...not until after.'

Ciro looked at Lara. He couldn't believe it. Couldn't believe that after everything he'd been through with this woman she had done it again. The emotion he felt transcended anger. He was icy cold with it. Far worse than heat and rage.

He could feel the livid line of his scar. The phantom throbbing of his little finger. He wanted to go over and haul Lara up to stand. She looked pathetically, unbelievably shocked.

'I want to know everything. *Now.*'

He saw her swallow. She was so pale he almost felt the sting of his conscience but he ruthlessly pushed it down. This woman was the worst kind of chameleon. And potentially a criminal.

'I was forced to marry Henry Winterborne. By my uncle.'

Ciro shook his head. 'That's ridiculous.'

'I wish it was. My uncle was obsessed with status and lineage. There was no way he was going to allow me to marry you. But it went much further than that.'

Ciro said nothing. He saw Lara clasp her hands together and in that moment had a flashback to how her hands had felt on his buttocks only hours before, squeezing him, huskily begging him for more.

He gritted out, 'Keep going.'

'My uncle was in debt. Serious debt. Millions and millions of pounds. He'd run through his fortune—and my trust fund. I was his only hope of saving his reputation and clearing the debt. He'd had us followed from the moment I mentioned you to him. He knew we were serious.'

Ciro said nothing so Lara continued.

'He knew that I was sheltered…not experienced. He was fairly certain we hadn't…'

Remarkably, colour stained her cheeks, and it made Ciro feel so many conflicting things that he decided to focus on the anger.

'Save your blushes, *cara*. This really is the most intriguing story.'

Lara's mouth tightened for a moment, but then she said, 'He sold me—like a slave girl at an auction. To Henry Winterborne, the highest bidder.'

Ciro struggled to take this in. It was such a far-fetched story. He decided to see how far Lara would go towards hanging herself and pretending she was an innocent player. 'When are you claiming that you knew about this?'

'I didn't know until after the kidnapping. That's when he told me. And that's when he told me he would kill you if I pursued the relationship.'

'So you came to the hospital to convince me you'd never wanted to marry me in order to *save* me? *Cara*, that is the most romantic thing I've heard in my whole life.'

Something occurred to Ciro then, and he went very still.

Then he said, 'I told you that story in Sicily...about my great-grandmother. About how she couldn't marry the man she wanted, how he was threatened. You appropriated it as your own... You didn't even have the creativity to come up with something original. You make me—'

Lara shot up from the chair. 'It's true—I swear. That's just a coincidence. It all happened exactly like I said.'

Ciro forced down his anger. Forced himself to stay civil just for a little longer. 'So why didn't you tell me this when you had the chance at the hospital? We were alone—no one to hear you tell me the gory details.'

He held up his hand when she opened her mouth.

'I'll tell you why, shall I? Because even though you might not have liked the idea of marrying an old man, it was still preferable to marrying a man of no lineage except a dubious one, hmm?'

She shook her head. 'No. I would never have wanted to marry that man—not in a million years. He disgusted me.'

'So why didn't you leave him? He was in a wheelchair—he could hardly run after you.'

He saw Lara flinch minutely at that and he crushed the spark of emotion when he thought of her being threatened. For all he knew that was an elaborate fabrication.

'My uncle was alive until three months before Henry Winterborne died. The whole time he held the threat of doing you harm over my head. I had nothing—no money and nowhere to go. I felt guilty because I had put Henry in a wheelchair. And then, after he had the stroke, it was clear he was dying, so I felt even less able to try and leave.'

Ciro snorted. 'No money? The man was a millionaire.'

Lara avoided his eye. 'After the accident…he was angry. He gave me nothing.'

Ciro's fury increased—she was manipulating him again with this wildly elaborate tale. He wasn't even sure to what end, but he felt sure it couldn't be as simple as she was making out. And he'd had enough.

Ciro's voice was low and lethal. 'I don't know why you're doing this, Lara, but it serves no purpose.'

Lara could see the total rejection of what she'd said on Ciro's face…hear it in his voice. It was exactly as she'd feared. Worse. She could also see the torment of those dark memories in the lines etched into his face.

She'd witnessed his horrific nightmares. Instinctively she reached out towards him. 'Ciro, I'm so sorry. I never meant for any of this to happen—'

He lifted his hand to stop her words. '*Basta*. Enough. My investigative team haven't ruled out your involvement with your uncle. You *do* know you could be prosecuted for this?'

She went pale again—white as parchment. 'Ciro, please, you have to listen to me... I knew nothing. I was as much a victim as you were. I loved you so much... I was terrified of what my uncle might do. I had no choice.'

Ciro's expression turned to one of disgust. 'You *loved* me? You go too far, Lara.' He continued, 'If what you say is true—and I'll verify that myself—how do you explain not telling me all this when we met again?'

She swallowed. 'I was afraid you wouldn't believe me—and apparently I was right.'

Ciro's expression got even darker. 'Not good enough. The truth is that you colluded with your uncle in sending me a message to stay away from you. You could have just *told* me you didn't want to marry me—you didn't have to go to such dramatic lengths.'

Lara realised that further defence would be futile. She said, 'Do you remember I asked you if you loved me, that day in the hospital?'

A flash of irritation crossed Ciro's face. 'What does that have to do with anything?'

'I did want to tell you everything. In spite of my uncle's threats...in spite of the kidnapping... I believed that somehow you'd be able to fight him. But when I knew you didn't feel the same for me as I felt for you, I believed there was no point in risking your life.'

He looked at her for such a long moment that Lara almost believed for a second that she might have got through—but then he said in a toneless voice, 'I've heard enough, Lara. Enough to last a lifetime. This marriage is over—we're done. I want you to leave today. Right now. I'll organise getting you on a flight back to the UK. If you leave with no fuss I'll consider not pressing charges. To be perfectly frank you're not worth the legal hassle or the headlines. Now, get out of my sight.'

A numbness was spreading from Lara's heart outwards to every extremity. She moved jerkily away from Ciro, towards the door. When she got there she stopped and turned around. Ciro was staring at her with such disgust on his face that she almost balked.

She grabbed the door knob to try and stay standing. 'I love you, Ciro. I always have. I did what I thought was best for you and it almost killed me. The last two years have been purgatory. I won't apologise for loving you, whether you choose to believe me or not. And I'm sorry I had to lie to you.'

She left then, before he could say anything caustic. He didn't love her. He'd never loved her, and this was the final lethal blow.

It all happened with military precision. Staff came and helped her to pack, but she insisted on taking just a small case with the belongings she'd arrived with. A car was waiting to take her to JFK, and she was on-board a flight within a few hours.

She'd had to leave Hero behind, as the dog didn't have documentation, and Lara hadn't seen Ciro before she left, so she wasn't even sure he'd still been there. But one thing was certain. She'd never see him again.

* * *

The following evening Ciro sat in the back of his car as it inched its way down Fifth Avenue towards Central Park and his house. His heart was beating a little too fast and he had to modulate his breathing. It was at times like this that he felt most claustrophobic—when he cursed the kidnappers for doing what they had to him, so that no matter how strong he was mentally he still felt a residue of fear that clung to him like a toxic tentacle whenever he was in a small confined space.

He hated it that he couldn't just ease his sense of claustrophobia by jumping out of the car to walk, because he'd spark a massive security alert.

The thought occurred to him that when Lara had been in the back of the car with him he hadn't noticed the claustrophobia as much. He'd been too distracted by her. He scowled at that.

Since the revelations of yesterday, and Lara's departure, he'd been existing in a kind of fog. He couldn't recollect what he'd done today, exactly. The puppy had barked pitifully that morning and Ciro had let her out into the garden, where she'd sniffed around disconsolately in between directing accusatory looks his way.

For a man who was used to thinking clearly he was beyond irritated that he was still thinking of her.

Whether or not it was true that she hadn't colluded with her uncle, she'd *known* about the kidnapping the day she'd come to him at the hospital. He would never forget the blasé way she'd dropped her bombshell that day. When he'd been lying there, beaten and battered. *Because of her!* She'd had her chance and she'd said nothing.

Last night had been the first night he'd spent alone in his bed in weeks. He'd had the nightmare again—except this time he hadn't woken to the cooling touch of Lara's hand or her tempting body. He'd woken sweating, tangled in the sheets, his voice hoarse from shouting. And this time the dream had been slightly different—it had been one moment, repeated over and over. The moment they'd ripped Lara out of his arms and opened the van door to dump her outside.

Her voice drifted into his head then: *'Do you remember I asked you if you loved me?'* He did, actually. He shifted in his seat now, feeling uncomfortable. He did recall it, and he also recalled the feeling of panic that had gripped him.

Love.

He remembered thinking of his father and his slavish devotion to his unfaithful wife, how it had disgusted him. If that was love then, no, he didn't feel that. But there had been something almost desperate on Lara's face and so he'd made some platitude.

What about the terror you felt when she was taken from you by the kidnappers? In that moment you thought you loved her.

Ciro shifted uncomfortably again. He'd always put that surge of emotion down to the extreme circumstances.

His staff had informed him that her flight had left on time yesterday. She'd be back in the UK now. She could be anywhere. For the first time in two years he didn't have tabs on her.

Before the car had even come to a standstill outside his house Ciro got out, not liking the panicky feeling in his gut. He went inside, dropping his things, and the puppy sped across the tiled floor towards him, yapping. It was quickly followed by the housekeeper, apologising profusely. Ciro picked Hero up and waved away the apology.

Feeling restless, he climbed the stairs to the bedrooms. He stood outside Lara's door for a long moment, and then an image of his father came into his head and he scowled and pushed the door open.

It had been tidied, and the bed remade. It was as if she'd never been there. But he could still smell her scent in the air. Lemon and roses.

He put the puppy down on the bed, where she promptly curled up and went to sleep.

Ciro went to the dressing room and opened the doors, expecting to find it empty. But it was full of clothes. He frowned. Everything he'd bought her was there. As was her jewellery. Neatly lined up on velvet pouches under glass display cases.

He went and picked up the phone in the room and rang down to the housekeeper. 'What did Lar— Mrs Sant'Angelo take with her when she left?'

He listened for a moment and then hung up, sitting down on the bed. She'd taken one suitcase. And he knew which one. The one she'd come with. The battered one.

The puppy crept towards him and got into his lap. Ciro stroked her absently. After a while he stood up, taking her with him. He left her with the housekeeper in the kitchen.

Still feeling restless, Ciro went into the reception room. It was filled with priceless paintings and *objets d'art*... Persian rugs. It could be a museum it was so still and stuffy.

When he'd bought this property he'd felt as if he'd reached a pinnacle. One of the many he'd set himself. Then, when he'd proposed to Lara, he'd imagined her here as his wife and hostess. Charming people with her natural warmth and compassion.

Giving you access to a higher level of society, reminded a voice.

A crystal decanter glinted at him from the drinks tray nearby. It seemed to mock him for thinking he'd had it all worked out. For believing that he'd had his fill of Lara. That he was done with her. For believing that all this excess around him actually meant anything.

The tightness in Ciro's chest intensified, and with an inarticulate surge of rage he grabbed the decanter and threw it at the massive stone fireplace, where it smashed into a million pieces.

He heard footsteps running, and for some inexplicable reason he thought it might be—

But when he turned around it was just a shocked-looking staff member.

'Is everything okay, Mr Sant'Angelo?'

He felt ragged. Undone. Empty.

'Everything is fine.'

But he knew it wasn't.

'Two pints of bitter, love!'

Lara forced a smile. 'Coming up.'

After-work drinks on a warm Indian summer evening in London meant packed pubs with people spilling out onto the pavements. Laughing, joking. Delighted that the end of the week had come and they had two days off stretching ahead.

Lara didn't have two days off. At weekends she worked in a small Italian restaurant, near where she was living at a hostel in Kentish Town. But she refused to feel sorry for herself as she went outside with the two pints and collected money and dirty glasses.

A man leaned towards her. 'You're far too pretty to be working here, love. Let me take you out of this cesspit and we'll run away.'

His friends guffawed loudly, but ridiculously Lara couldn't even force a fake laugh. She felt tears sting her eyes. Which was pathetic. She was lucky to have found two jobs. She was earning her own money for the first time in her life. She was finally free... If only that freedom didn't feel so heavy.

She never thought about...*him*. She couldn't. Not if she wanted to keep it together.

'Hey, gorgeous! A pint and a white wine, please!'

Lara looked up at the flushed face of a city boy and forced herself to smile. 'Coming up.'

CHAPTER NINE

A WEEK LATER Ciro was back in London. He was at a black tie event in Buckingham Palace. Lesser members of the royal family mingled with the guests, and he'd just had a long conversation with a man who was in direct line to the throne of England. And it hadn't just been an idle conversation—it had been about business. Ciro's business.

He looked around. This was literally the inner sanctum—the most exclusive group of people on the planet. And he, Ciro Sant'Angelo, a man descended from pirates and Mafiosi, was standing among them. Accepted. Respected. *Finally*.

So why wasn't he feeling more satisfied?

Because he'd just had a call from his solicitor to say that Lara had finally been in touch about going forward with divorce proceedings and had given him a PO box address. She'd told his solicitor that she had no interest in taking the money due to her in the event of their divorce and had named a charity for it to be sent to, if they insisted.

Ciro's charity—Face Forward.

And other things had come to light too—discomfiting things. He'd found the credit card he'd given her on the desk in his study in New York. And her engagement ring and wedding ring, which were both worth a small fortune.

There had been a note.

I'll pay back what I owe.

On inspection, there had been a sum of just a few hundred dollars owing on the card. A laughable amount to someone like Ciro.

She'd also said that once Hero had her papers in order she would appreciate being reunited with the dog. And a parcel had arrived for her. When Ciro had opened it, it had contained a wedding dress. Clearly from the eighties. It wasn't even new.

Nothing made sense.

He had to acknowledge uncomfortably that the Lara who had appeared in his hospital room that day...the unrecognisable Lara...he'd never seen her again. Just flashes at the beginning. If she really was some rich bitch who had only been concerned with status and wealth, then wouldn't she have fleeced him for all he was worth?

Wouldn't she be here right now? Her elegant blonde head shining like a jewel amongst the dross, dressed in a silky evening gown as she hunted for a new husband?

A feeling of clammy desperation stole over Ciro. Maybe she was still playing him. Maybe she *was* here. He looked around, heart thumping, almost expecting to see her blonde head, hear her low, seductive laugh...

'Who are you looking for, Sant'Angelo? Your wife? Have you mislaid her?'

Ciro looked to his right and down into the florid features of a man whose name he'd forgotten and whom he had never liked on previous acquaintance.

'No,' he said tightly. 'She's not here.'

Where the hell is she?

'Pity,' said the man, leaning in a little. 'She's a rare jewel. But I doubt she's *that* rare any more...' He winked. 'If you get what I mean... After all, she's been married twice now. Winterborne got the best of her, lucky sod. If I'd had more money at the time maybe it would have been me.'

Ciro looked at the man with an awful kind of cold horror sinking into his blood. 'What on earth are you talking about?'

The man looked up at him and suddenly appeared uncomfortable. 'Ah... I thought you knew... The auction, of course. I mean, obviously it wasn't a *real* auction. Just something between a few of Thomas Templeton's friends. Girls like Lara are few and far between these days. Innocent. Pure...'

Lara's voice was in Ciro's head. *'He sold me like a slave girl at an auction. To Henry Winterborne, the highest bidder.'*

The man slapped him on the shoulder. 'All right there, Sant'Angelo? You've gone very pale.'

Ciro felt sick to his stomach. 'How many men were involved?' he managed to get out.

Blissfully unaware of the volcano building inside Ciro, the man looked around and said conspiratorially, 'There's always a market for girls like her. With the right breeding. Especially virgins. It's a rare commodity these days, you know.'

Ciro didn't stop to think. His right hand swung back and his fist connected with the fleshy part of the man's face, sending him windmilling backwards into the crowd, where he collided with a waiter holding a tray of glasses, and a woman, who shrieked just before he landed in a heavy heap on the ground.

Instantly security men were beside Ciro, taking his arms in their hands. He briefly caught the eye of the member of the royal family he'd been talking to and saw disdain spreading over his aristocratic features. Everyone was staring at him. Shocked. And then they started whispering as Ciro was led out.

And he didn't give a damn.

For the first time in his life, he didn't give a damn.

It was another hot, muggy evening in the bar and Lara's feet were aching. But at least she wasn't wearing heels any more. She was wiping down the counter under the bar when she heard it.

'Lara.'

She stopped. She'd dreamed about him nearly every night. Was she hallucinating now?

She kept cleaning.

'Lara.'

She looked up and her heart jumped into her throat. *Ciro.* Standing head and shoulders above everyone else around him at the bar.

'Oi, mate—if you're going to take up space at the bar, put in an order for us too, will ya?'

A group of young guys behind Ciro sniggered. He ignored them.

Lara gripped the cloth. 'What are you doing here?'

'Can we talk?'

She noticed that he looked drawn. Dishevelled. 'Is something wrong? Has something happened?'

He shook his head. 'Everything is fine…but we need to talk.'

It was the familiar bossy tone that reassured her in the end—and also told her that this was real, not a fantasy. She was aware of her grumpy boss hovering... aware that no drinks were being served.

Lara sent her boss a reassuring glance and said to Ciro, 'I can't just leave. Sit down and I'll bring you a beer. You'll have to wait until my shift ends.'

'How long is that?'

'Three hours.'

She ignored his look of affront and handed him a pint of bitter, willing him to disappear. Eventually he turned away when she started serving the people behind him.

It was the most excruciating three hours Lara had experienced. With every move she made she was aware of Ciro's eyes burning into her from where he was sitting in a corner. She was surprised she didn't drop every glass, fumble every order.

But finally the pub was empty and she stood in front of Ciro in beer-spattered jeans and T-shirt, a cardigan over her arm and her bag across her body. She felt exhausted, but also energised.

'Where do you want to talk?'

Ciro stood up. 'Do you live near here?'

Lara walked with him out of the pub. She saw Ciro's security team nearby, and his car and driver. She thought of the hostel she called home.

'I don't think you'd like where I'm living. There's a late-night café near here that should still be open.'

'We could go to the townhouse.'

Lara immediately shook her head. *That* London was a million miles from her life now. 'No.'

'Fine—where's this café?'

Lara led him around the corner and into the friendly

café. They were given a booth at the back. Ciro commanded attention and special treatment even here.

Lara ordered tea; Ciro coffee.

When the drinks were delivered, Lara said, 'So what do you want to talk about?'

For a second Ciro looked comically nonplussed, and then he said, 'You left no forwarding address.'

Lara stifled the hurt of recalling that moment in New York. 'You kicked me out, Ciro. I didn't think my forwarding address was high on your list of priorities. I contacted your solicitor with my details.'

'A PO box. What even *is* that?'

Anger surged. If he'd just come here to harangue her because she wasn't following divorce etiquette properly... 'I'm living in a hostel, Ciro. I don't know where I'll be in a month's time. That's why I have a PO box.'

Now he looked horrified. 'A *hostel*?'

Lara nodded. 'It's perfectly clean and habitable.'

Ciro had gone pale under his tan. Lara refused to let it move her.

He put a parcel on the table and said, 'This arrived for you. I opened it. Why did you buy a wedding dress, Lara?'

Lara pulled the package towards her, lifting out the familiar dress. Her mother's wedding dress. She'd tracked it down online and it had only been a couple of hundred dollars to buy it back. Emotion surged in her chest. *She had it back*.

She fought to keep her composure. 'It was my mother's wedding dress. I sold it once.' Tears blurred her vision but she blinked them away, saying as briskly as she could, 'Thank you. I'll pay you back.'

'Why did you sell your mother's dress in the first place?'

Lara avoided looking at him in case he saw how much this dress meant to her. When she felt composed enough, she looked at Ciro. 'I needed the money. After Henry Winterborne got injured I was useless to him. He made me work for him—for free, of course. He sacked his housekeeper. I put up with it because my uncle was still alive and he continued to hold the threat of hurting you over my head. I think he was scared I'd go to you, ask for help. Or that I'd try to warn you. I fantasised about doing that so many times.' Lara touched the package. 'I'd hoped to wear this dress when I married you... it was a connection to my mother. A piece of the past.'

'But you sold it?'

Lara looked at him again. 'The housekeeper who had worked for Henry Winterborne...we'd become friendly. After losing her job she was in dire straits. Her husband had lost his job and was ill... She couldn't find work. I couldn't do much, but I sold this dress and some of my other clothes. Some jewellery. I tried to help her. I felt responsible.'

'Why on earth did you feel responsible?'

Ciro sounded almost angry. Lara avoided his eye. 'If I hadn't injured Henry Winterborne—'

Ciro cut her off. '*Dio*, Lara. The man would have raped you if he could. It wasn't your fault.'

Lara felt a flutter in her chest. *Dangerous*. She looked at Ciro. 'Why are you here?'

'You don't want anything? From the divorce?'

She shook her head, stifling the disappointment. He'd only tracked her down because he needed to discuss this. He probably didn't believe her.

'It was never about money for me. Ever. Not the first time around. Not now.'

Ciro pulled out a tabloid newspaper and handed it to Lara. He said, 'I presume you haven't seen this?'

She looked down and gasped. On the front page there was a picture of Ciro in handcuffs, being put into a police car. His knuckles were bleeding and he looked grimmer than she'd ever seen him. The headline read: *Sant'Angelo Brawls in Palace Amongst Royalty!*

She took in the few words underneath.

You can take the man out of the Mafia...

Lara looked at him, shocked. 'What happened?'

Ciro said, 'I met a man. He was one of the men at the select little auction run by your uncle. One of the men who—' He stopped.

Lara finished for him, feeling sick. 'One of the men who might have become my husband?'

Ciro nodded.

He flexed his hand and Lara reached for it, turning it over to see his bruised knuckles. She said quietly, 'Thank you, but you didn't have to do that. You must hate the press attention.'

Ciro flipped his hand so he held hers. 'I don't care about any of that. Finally I've got it through my thick skull that it doesn't matter. Respect and acceptance come from living with integrity and honesty. I can't do more than that and I'm done trying.'

Lara was almost too scared to breathe for a moment. She looked at Ciro and saw a blazing light in his eyes. Something she'd never seen before. A different kind of pride. It made her emotions bubble up again.

'You've never needed to. You tower above men like my uncle and Henry Winterborne. You always have.

But I can understand your father and his father's desire for acceptance. They deserved better.'

Ciro huffed a laugh. He still held Lara's hand. 'Did they? They had blood on their hands, Lara. We all did, by association—although we've come a long way since those times. I'll never be fully accepted into that world, but what I've realised is that money and commerce talk more than social acceptance. That's all that matters in growing a business and a reputation.'

His scar stood out against his olive skin and Lara's emotions finally got the better of her. Ciro would never have had to come to this painful realisation if not for her.

'I'm so sorry, Ciro. If we hadn't met...if I hadn't fallen in love with you...my uncle never would have—' She stopped, biting her lip to stem the tears threatening to flow down her cheeks.

His grip on her hand tightened. 'You have nothing to be sorry for, Lara. *Nothing*. From the moment we met again you confounded me. I expected the woman who had appeared in my hospital room that day, but I got *you*. The Lara I remembered. Except I couldn't trust it. You. I was afraid to after you hurt me so badly.'

Lara chest seized. '*Hurt...?* But you didn't have any feelings for me.'

Ciro huffed out a sound halfway between a laugh and a groan, his hand still tight on hers. 'I didn't know *what* I was feeling. All I knew was that when you asked me if I loved you I panicked. All I could think of was my father, and his toxic obsessive love of my mother. I knew it wasn't that I felt. But I couldn't deny that I felt obsessive about you, and suddenly I was terrified that I was just like my father—that I would lose myself over a woman and make a fool of myself like he had.'

Before Lara could fully absorb this, or what it meant, Ciro asked her a question.

'Why did you agree to marry me this time?'

She swallowed her emotions. 'I felt so guilty for what had happened to you. I owed you. After everything that had happened...'

Ciro took his hand from hers, his expression changing. 'You felt obliged...' He grimaced. 'And why wouldn't you? I *told* you that you owed me.'

He looked at her and she saw pain in his eyes. The pride was gone.

'You had nowhere to go. No money. You felt guilty already. I left you no choice.'

Lara shook her head. 'Of course I had a choice. I could have walked away... I could have told you everything that day and let the chips fall where they may. But I didn't.'

'Why didn't you?'

She kept looking at him, even though it was hard. 'Because you were back in my life. I didn't tell you because I'd convinced myself I owed it to you. I was afraid that if I told you everything you'd despise me even more than you already did.' She took a deep breath. 'Even though I denied it to myself I still loved you, I would have done anything to be with you—even let you take your revenge out on me.'

Ciro looked shell-shocked. 'What you went through... for two years... When I think of that man and what he could have done to you if you hadn't been brave enough to fight him off...' He stood up abruptly and stalked out of the café.

Shocked, Lara sat there for a moment, before throwing down some cash and grabbing the wedding dress. He was outside on the empty street, a fist up to his mouth. When she got close he turned away from her, but not before she'd seen the agony on his face. Moisture on his cheeks.

'Ciro—'

His voice was thick. 'Don't look at me. I can't bear it, Lara. To know what you went through because I was too much of a coward to own up to my feelings…'

Lara went and hugged him from behind, resting her head against his back. The parcel fell by her feet, unnoticed.

Eventually he turned around and she sucked in a breath at the ravaged look on his face.

'How can you ever forgive me?'

A weight lodged in her gut. She'd never expected to see this: Ciro feeling guilty. *She* was the guilty one.

She reached up and wiped away the moisture on his face, her heart aching, because she knew that even though Ciro might have feelings for her it wasn't love, and she would have to walk away again.

'It was my fault—' she said.

He shook his head. '*No*. Never say that again. It was your uncle. Lara, I've had him investigated. You have no idea how corrupt he was. What he did to you was the tip of the iceberg. He was involved in fraud, and in trafficking women in and out of the UK.'

Lara's hands dropped. 'My God…'

'Lara… I'm so sorry.'

She was unable to speak. She'd never expected the cruel irony of Ciro feeling guilty. Saying sorry.

He took her hand. 'This isn't a conversation for here. Come with me to the townhouse—please?'

Lara knew that she should pull back. She'd heard all she needed to. Ciro was right. It wasn't her fault. Or his. They'd both been used as pawns. But she couldn't pull away—not just yet. Soon she'd have a lifetime to try and forget him.

'Okay.'

Ciro picked up the wedding dress and led her over to his car, where she got into the back. When he got in on the other side, he surprised her by pulling her into his arms, enfolding her close. She closed her eyes and guiltily revelled in his strength. It wouldn't last. He just felt guilty. But she'd take it while she could.

Amazingly, she fell asleep, with Ciro's heartbeat thudding against her cheek. She was only vaguely aware of the car stopping, of Ciro lifting her out and carrying her. There was another familiar voice. And then she was being put down on a soft surface and a warm blanket was being pulled over her.

She struggled to wake up but Ciro's commanding voice said, 'No, go to sleep, Lara. You need to rest.'

When Lara woke the next morning it was early. Just after dawn. It took a minute for her to realise that she wasn't in her disinfectant-scented room at the hostel. She was in a luxurious bed.

Ciro's townhouse.

She sat up and looked down, grimacing. She was still dressed in her T-shirt and jeans. A faint smell of beer and fried food wafted up. She got up and went into the bathroom, stripping off and stepping under the shower.

As the water sluiced down over her body she finally allowed herself to remember the previous cataclysmic evening. The outpouring of emotion. The pain on Ciro's face.

The fact that he didn't love her but that he was sorry.

Lara hugged herself under the water for a long moment, willing back the emotion. She had to hold it in until she left this place. Then she could grieve. *Finally.*

When Lara stepped out of the shower she felt lighter, in spite of the heaviness in her heart. Cleansed. At peace. She had something she could hold to her and cherish, no matter what happened with Ciro.

Because, in spite of the catharsis of the truth finally being revealed, and what he'd said about his priorities, she knew him too well. She knew he would have had time now to assess what had happened, and that he must be mortified by how much he'd revealed. Not to mention the public humiliation of being arrested at a party in Buckingham Palace.

He wouldn't thank her for that when he realised the full extent of the repercussions. He'd worked too hard not to mind.

She pulled on a towelling robe from the back of the door and made her way downstairs to the utility room with her clothes, intending to wash and dry them.

When she was on her way back up she heard a noise in the kitchen and went in. Ciro was there, in jeans and a shirt, sipping a cup of coffee. He turned to face her and she felt shy. Ridiculously.

'I'm sorry about that—falling asleep. I must have been more tired than I thought.'

Ciro looked stern. 'I'm not surprised...working two jobs.'

Lara's mouth fell open. 'How did you know?'

'I tracked you down a few days ago. My investigators told me.'

Lara tried not to sound defensive. 'I need the money.'

Ciro changed the subject. 'Coffee?'

Lara nodded. 'Please.'

She tried to gauge his mood but it was hard. He

wasn't exhibiting any sign of the emotion of last night and her worst fears seemed to be coming true. He was regretting having said anything.

He handed her a cup. 'Let's talk upstairs.'

'We really don't have to. You must be busy. And I have to get to work at the restaurant—'

He stopped her. 'You're not working there again.'

'Ciro, I can't just—'

'Come upstairs with me. Please.'

Lara followed him, trying not to give in to the anger and panic that Ciro was riding roughshod over her life all over again.

He led her into one of the informal living rooms, with soft slouchy sofas and chairs. She took a chair and Ciro walked to the window. She tried not to let her gaze drop to where the material of his snug jeans hugged his buttocks so lovingly.

She took a fortifying sip of coffee and put down her cup. 'As soon as my clothes are dry I'll get out of your hair. I know you mean well, but I really can't afford to lose that job—'

Ciro whirled around, the first crack in his calm façade showing. 'I said you are *not* going back there, Lara. *Dio*.' He put down his own cup and shoved his hands deep in his jeans pockets, as if afraid he might do something bad with them.

Lara was stunned into silence. She saw a muscle beating in his jaw.

'This house is your house, Lara. You have somewhere to live. You don't need to work to put a roof over your head. Ever again.'

She looked at him. Totally confused. 'You're giving me your house?'

'I mean, it's *ours*. My home is your home.'

She shook her head. 'I don't... What are you saying, Ciro?'

He came over and sat down. Stood up. Sat down again. Suddenly she could see the emotion on his face.

'I'm saying that I want us to stay married, Lara. But after everything you've been through... I know you deserve your independence. You've had people—*men*—telling you what to do since you lost your family, and I don't want to just be another man running your life.'

Lara's heart constricted. 'You don't want me to go?'

He shook his head, kneeling down beside her. '*No*. I *don't* want you to leave. *Ever*. But I also don't want you to feel obliged to stay because you feel like you owe me, or because of guilt. I love you, Lara, but I don't want you to feel trapped.'

The world stopped on its axis. 'You...what?'

Ciro frowned. 'I love you... I told you yesterday...'

Lara shook her head. 'No. I'm pretty sure I would have remembered that piece of information. You were upset...feeling guilty... You mentioned *feelings*. But you never mentioned love.'

Ciro took her hand. 'Well, I do love you. I've loved you since the moment I laid eyes on you in that street in Florence. I just didn't know what it was. You were the first woman to get under my skin without even trying, Lara. The first woman I spent a whole night with in my bed. When I proposed to you it was because you were the first woman who made me want more. Who made me hate the cynicism I'd been brought up with.'

Ciro went pale.

'When those kidnappers ripped you out of my arms that day...that's when I knew... But even afterwards I told myself that it couldn't be *love*. I would never be so foolish, such a slave to my emotions—not like my father.'

Lara saw it on his face. Pure emotion. She put a hand to her mouth to stifle a sound of pure joy mixed with shock.

But Ciro took her hand down. 'Please believe me, Lara. I love you more than life itself. Without you the world didn't make sense. I never truly believed you were that person you'd turned into in the hospital, but it was easier to believe that than admit you'd broken my heart.'

Lara touched his face, his scar. Tears blurred her vision. 'Oh, my love...my darling. I'm so sorry.'

He caught her face in his hands. He looked fierce. 'Never say sorry again. *Never*.'

She nodded. 'I love you...so much.'

Ciro shook his head. 'I'm almost scared to believe... We've been through so much—I've put you through so much...'

Lara put a finger to his mouth, stopping his words. 'Don't *you* ever say that again. Neither of us were to blame. We got caught up in events outside our control. I love you, my darling, and that's all you have to believe.'

She bent forward and kissed him. A sweet chaste kiss. Then she pulled back and said shakily, 'Even if you had told me you loved me, and we'd stood up to my uncle, I dread to think what might have happened. He was crazy, Ciro. I was his only hope of redemption and he was capable of anything.'

Ciro was grim. 'Maybe—but he put us through two years of hell.' He said then, 'Do you know why I really bought this house?'

She shook her head, marvelling at how full her heart could feel.

'I kept tabs on you for those two years...hoping for

God knows what to happen. I knew where you lived and I bought this house sight unseen. I think I had nefarious plans to seduce you away from Henry Winterborne. It would have proved that you had no morals, but more importantly it would have brought you back to me. I had no qualms about playing dirty to get you back.'

Lara smiled a shaky smile. 'You have no idea how many nights I dreamed of you coming to rescue me. But then I'd see photos of you, out and about, getting on with your life, with other women...'

The pain of that still made her gut churn. She looked away.

Ciro caught her chin and turned her back to face him. 'I didn't take one of those women into my bed. I couldn't. The thought of you—it consumed me. You ruined me for anyone else. *Ever.*'

Lara couldn't hold back. She flung her arms around Ciro and he caught her. Lifted her up and sat down on the sofa, settling her across his lap. Cradling her.

Lara clutched at his shirt. 'We've wasted so much time...'

He caught her chin again, tipping it up. 'No. We start again now. No more regrets, okay?'

Lara nodded, humbled by Ciro's capacity to forgive and move on.

He sat up then, and put her beside him. Then he got off the sofa and down on one knee in front of her.

'Ciro...'

He drew a box out of his jeans pocket. A familiar velvet box. Her heart tripped. He opened it and she saw her engagement ring and wedding ring.

Ciro suddenly looked anxious. 'Maybe I should have bought new ones.'

Lara touched them reverently. 'No, I love them.'

He took the rings out of the box and looked at her. 'Lara Sant'Angelo, will you please stay my wife—for the rest of our lives?'

She nodded, and got out a choked, 'Yes.'

When the rings were back on her finger, where they belonged, she said, 'I wondered why you hadn't thrown the engagement ring away…'

Ciro looked deep into her eyes and said huskily, 'Maybe because I was already dreaming of this moment.'

He kissed her then, so deeply that he touched her heart and mended all the broken shards back together.

Much later, when they were lying in bed, sated and at peace, Lara said, 'I think maybe that's why I tracked down my mother's wedding dress when I had the chance. Maybe I was hoping for a second chance.'

Ciro caught her hand and her rings sparkled. He kissed her there and she looked at him, caught in those dark eyes that held so much love.

'Second chances and new beginnings.'

'Yes, my love, for ever.'

EPILOGUE

A month later...

DUSK WAS MELTING into night as Lara walked to the entrance of the small chapel in the grounds of the *palazzo* in Sicily. Apparently it was a tradition, marrying at night. She didn't really care.

Lighted torches had guided her from the *palazzo* to the chapel and to Isabella, who was her bridesmaid. The young girl's eyes were suspiciously shiny as she fussed over Lara at the entrance, where flowers festooned the doorway, making the air heavy with a million scents.

Hero danced around their feet, looking up at Lara adoringly. She was attached to Isabella's wrist with a ribbon and had a velvet cushion tied to her collar, upon which was tied a gold wedding band inlaid with sapphires. A new wedding ring to celebrate this renewal of their vows.

'Your dress is so beautiful.'

'Thank you,' said Lara.

She hadn't been allowed to look at herself in a mirror with the dress on—apparently another Sicilian tradition. But she'd had her mother's dress adjusted slightly so that it fitted her perfectly.

It was classically simple and sweetly bohemian, with its high neck and ruffled bodice. She wore her hair down and a garland of flowers adorned her head. No veil. She didn't need to hide any more—from anything.

Isabella pressed a simple bouquet of local flowers into her hands and then stepped in front of her to start her walk down the aisle.

Roberto, her twin brother, was acting as groomsman to Ciro. And Lazaro was there too—Ciro's best friend. His eyes had been suspiciously shiny earlier, when they'd had an informal pre-ceremony lunch.

He'd taken Lara's hands and said, 'I'm sorry for doubting you.'

Lara had shaken her head and said, 'No need to apologise. I'm glad you were there for him.'

Lazaro had grimaced. 'He wasn't a pretty sight the day you got married the first time. I had to peel him off the floor of a bar—'

'Filling my wife's head with stories again, Lazaro?'

Lara had smiled and put her hand over Ciro's, where his arm had wrapped around her waist, leaning back against him and revelling in his solid strength and love. He'd told her about how he'd gone out and got blind drunk the day of her wedding to Henry Winterborne.

She knew everything. And so did he. No more secrets.

Now she hesitated for a moment on the threshold of the small chapel. Hovering between the past and present. Ciro hadn't turned to look at her walk down the aisle at their first wedding ceremony, but even as that thought formed in her head he turned around now.

And even though she hadn't been allowed to look at herself in her wedding dress, she didn't need to. She could see herself reflected in his eyes as she walked towards him and she'd never felt more beautiful or more desired.

Or more loved.

She was home. At last.

Hours later, after the revelry had finally died down and Ciro had picked her up to carry her to their suite amidst much catcalling and cheering, Lara stood facing out to where the dawn was breaking on a new day on the horizon.

Ciro was behind her, undoing each tiny button on the dress—undressing his bride to make love to her, kissing each sliver of exposed skin.

Lara's eyes filled with tears. She whispered, 'I dreamt of this moment but I never dared to believe it might come true. I was so scared to love again after losing my family.'

Ciro's hands stopped and he turned her around to face him. He wiped her tears away. 'It's not a dream… it's real. Because you were brave enough to trust.'

Lara smiled through her tears. 'Because you made me fall for you.'

Ciro smiled smugly. 'That too.'

Then his smile faded and he put a hand to her belly between them. 'And we can have more too, if you trust me.'

She whispered, 'A family…'

He nodded. 'I wouldn't want this with anyone else. Only you.'

'Me too.'

'Let's start now. This morning.'

Lara reached up and put her arms around his neck, pressing her mouth to his before saying emotionally, 'Yes, please.'

* * *

Nine months later, in a hospital in Palermo, Ciro and Lara welcomed a baby son—Carlo—and their family was complete.

At least until Margarita arrived a couple of years later.

And then Stefano.

Then it was complete.

* * * * *

THE SPANIARD'S WEDDING REVENGE

JACKIE ASHENDEN

To Justin Alastair, Duke of Avon,
and Leonie de Saint-Vire.

Thanks for the inspiration!

CHAPTER ONE

THE LAST THING Cristiano Velazquez—current duke of an ancient and largely forgotten dukedom in Spain, not to mention playboy extraordinaire—wanted to see at two in the morning as he rolled out of his favourite Paris club was a gang of youths crouched in front of his limo as it waited by the kerb. He wanted to hear the distinctive rattle and then hiss of a spray can even less.

God only knew where his driver André was, the lazy *bastardo*, but he certainly wasn't here, guarding his limo like he should have been.

The two women on Cristiano's arm made fearful noises, murmuring fretfully about bodyguards, but Cristiano had never been bothered with protection and he couldn't be bothered now. Quite frankly, some nights he could use the excitement of a mugging, and at least the presence of a gang of Parisian street kids was something out of the ordinary.

Although it would have been better if they hadn't been spray-painting his limo, of course.

Still, the youths were clearly bothering his ladyfriends, and if he wanted to spend the rest of the night with both of them in his bed—which he fully intended to do—then he was going to have to handle the situation.

'Allow me, ladies,' he murmured, and strolled unhurriedly towards the assembled youths.

One of them must have seen him, because the kid said something sharp to the rest of his friends and abruptly they all scattered like a pack of wild dogs.

Except for the boy with the spray can, currently graffitiing a rude phrase across the passenger door.

The kid was crouched down, his slight frame swamped by a pair of dirty black jeans and a huge black hoodie with the hood drawn up. He didn't seem to notice Cristiano's approach, absorbed as he was in adding a final flourish to his artwork.

Cristiano paused behind him, admiring said 'artwork'. 'Very good. But you missed an "e",' he pointed out helpfully.

Instantly the kid sprang up from his crouch, throwing the spray can to the right and darting to the left.

But Cristiano was ready for him. He grabbed the back of the boy's hoodie before the kid could escape and held on.

The boy was pulled up short, the hoodie slipping off his head. He made a grab for it, trying to pull it back up, but it was too late. A strand of bright hair escaped, the same pinky-red as apricots.

Cristiano froze. Unusual colour. Familiar in some way.

An old and forgotten memory stirred, and before he knew what he was doing he'd grabbed the boy's narrow shoulders and spun him around, jerking his hood down at the same time.

A wealth of apricot-coloured hair tumbled down the boy's back, framing a pale face with small, finely carved features and big eyes the deep violet-blue of cornflowers.

Not a boy. A girl.

No, a woman.

She said something foul in a voice completely at odds with the air of wide-eyed innocence she projected. A voice made for sex, husky and sweet, that went straight to his groin.

Not a problem. Everything went straight to his groin.

The grip he had on the back of her hoodie tightened.

She spat another curse at him and tried to wriggle out of his hold like a furious kitten.

Cristiano merely tightened his grip, studying her. She was quite strong for a little thing, not to mention feisty, and he really should let her go. Especially when he had other female company standing around behind him. Female company he actually wanted to spend time with tonight.

Then again, that familiarity was nagging at him, tugging at him as insistently as the girl was doing right now. That hair was familiar, and so were those eyes. And that lush little mouth…

Had he seen her before somewhere?

Had he slept with her, maybe?

But, no, surely not. She was dressed in dirty, baggy streetwear, and there was a feral, hungry look to her. He'd been in many dives around the world, and he recognised the look of a person who lived nowhere but the streets, and this young woman had that look.

She had the foul mouth that went along with it, too.

Not that he minded cursing. What he did mind was people spray-painting his limo and interrupting his evening.

'Be still, *gatita*,' he ordered. 'Or I'll call the police.'

At the mention of police she struggled harder, producing a knife from somewhere and waving it threateningly at him.

'Let me go!' she said, and added something rude to do with a very masculine part of his anatomy.

Definitely feisty, and probably more trouble than she was worth—especially with that knife waving around. She was pretty, but he wasn't into expending effort on a woman who was resistant when he had plenty of willing ones who weren't.

Then again, his tastes were...eclectic, and he liked difference. She was certainly that. A bit on the young side, though.

'No,' he said calmly. 'Your customisation of my car I could have ignored. But you have interrupted my evening and scared my friends, and that I simply won't stand for.'

She ignored him, spitting another curse and slashing at him with her knife.

'And now we're dealing with assault,' Cristiano pointed out, not at all bothered by the knife, since it managed to miss him by miles.

'Yes,' she snapped. 'You assaulting me!'

He sighed. He didn't have a lot of patience for this kind of nonsense and now, since it was late—or early, depending on your point of reference—he wanted to get to bed, and not alone. He really needed to handle this unfortunate situation.

So let her go.

Well, he should. After he'd figured out why she was so familiar, because it was really starting to annoy him now.

Though that was going to be difficult with her still swinging wildly at him with a knife.

Amongst the many skills he'd become proficient in on his quest to fill the gaping emptiness inside him was a certain expertise in a couple of martial arts, so it wasn't difficult for him to disarm her of her knife and then bundle her into his limo.

He got in after her and shut the door, locking it for good measure so that she was effectively confined.

Instantly she tried to get out, trying to get the doors to open. It wouldn't work. Only he could open the doors from the inside when they were locked.

He said nothing, watching her as she tried futilely to escape. When it became clear to her that she couldn't, she turned to him, a mix of fury and fear in her big cornflower-blue eyes.

'Let me out,' she demanded, breathless.

Cristiano leaned back in the seat opposite her and shoved his hands into the pockets of his expertly tailored black dress pants. It might have been a stupid move, since it wasn't clear whether she had another knife on her somewhere, but he was betting she didn't.

'No,' he said, studying her face.

Her jaw went rigid, her small figure stiff with tension. 'Are you going to rape me?'

He blinked at the stark question, then had a brief internal debate about whether he should be annoyed she'd even had to ask—especially since the latter part of his life had largely been spent in the pursuit of pleasure, both his own and that of any partners he came into contact with.

But in the end it wasn't worth getting uptight about. If she was indeed on the streets, then not being assaulted was likely to be one of her first concerns. Particularly when she'd been bundled into a car and locked in by a man much larger and stronger than she was.

'No,' he said flatly, so there could be no doubt. 'That

sounds like effort, and I try not to make any effort if I can possibly help it.'

She gazed at him suspiciously. 'Then why did you shut me in this car?'

'Because you tried to stab me with your knife.'

'You could have just let me go.'

'You were graffitiing my car. And it's an expensive car. It's going to cost me a lot of money to get it repainted.'

She gave him a look that was at once disdainful and pitying. 'You can afford it, rich man.'

Unoffended, Cristiano tilted his head, studying her. 'It's true. I am rich. And, yes, I can afford to get it repainted. But it's inconvenient to have to do so. You have inconvenienced me, *gatita*, and I do so hate to be inconvenienced. So, tell me, what are you going to do about it?'

'I'm not going to do anything about it.' She lifted her chin stubbornly. 'Let me out, *fils de pute*.'

'Such language,' Cristiano reproved, entertained despite himself. 'Where did you learn your manners?'

'I'll call the police myself. Tell them you're holding me against my will.'

She dug into the voluminous pockets of her hoodie, brought out a battered-looking cellphone and held it up triumphantly. 'Ten seconds to let me out and then I'm calling the emergency services.'

Cristiano was unmoved. 'Go ahead. I know the police quite well. I'm sure you'll be able to explain why you were crouching in front of my car, spray-painting foul language all over it, and then pulling a knife on me when I tried to stop you.'

She opened her mouth. Closed it again.

'What's your name?' he went on. That nagging familiarity was still tugging at him. He'd seen her before—he was sure of it.

'None of your business.'

Clearly she'd thought better of calling the police, because she lowered her hand disappearing her phone back into her hoodie.

'Give me back my knife.'

Cristiano was amused. She was a brave little *gatita*, asking for the knife he'd only just disarmed her of after she'd tried to stab him with it. Brave to stand up to him, too—especially considering she was at a severe disadvantage. Not only physically but, given her dirty clothes and feral air, socially, too.

Then again, when you lived at the bottom of life's barrel you had nothing to left to lose. He knew. He'd been there himself—if not physically then certainly in spirit.

'Sadly, that's not going to happen.' He shifted, taking his hands out of his pockets and very slowly leaning forward, his elbows on his thighs, his fingers linked loosely between his knees.

A wary look crossed her face.

And that was good. She was right to be wary. Because he was losing his patience, and when he lost patience he was dangerous. Very dangerous indeed.

'I'll ask one more time,' he said, letting a warning edge his voice. 'What's your name, *gatita*?'

The man sitting opposite Leonie—the rich bastard who'd scooped her up and put her in his limo—was scaring the living daylights out of her, and she wasn't sure why.

He wasn't being threatening. He was simply sitting there with his hands between his knees, eyes the same kind of green as deep, dense jungles staring unblinkingly at her.

He was dressed all in black, and she didn't need to be rich to know that his clothes—black trousers and a plain black cotton shirt—had been made for him. Nothing else explained the way they fitted him so perfectly, framing wide shoulders and a broad chest, a lean waist and powerful thighs.

He reeked of money, this man. She could virtually smell it.

And not just money. He reeked of power, too. It was an almost physical force, pushing at her, crowding out all the air in the car and winding long fingers around her throat and squeezing.

There was another element to that power, though. An element she couldn't identify.

It had something to do with his face, which was as beautiful as some of the carved angels on the tombs in the Père Lachaise Cemetery. Yet that wasn't quite it. He seemed warmer than an angel, so maybe more like a fallen one. Maybe a beautiful devil instead.

Night-black hair, straight brows and those intense green eyes...

No, he wasn't an angel, and he wasn't a devil, either. He seemed more vital than a mythical being. More...elemental, somehow.

He was a black panther in the jungle, watching her from the branch of a tree. All sleepy and lazy... Until he was ready to pounce.

That frightened her—but it didn't feel like a threat she was familiar with. Sleeping on the streets of Paris had given her a very acute sense of threat, especially the threat of physical violence, and she wasn't getting that from him.

No, it was something else.

'Why do you want to know my name?'

She wasn't going to just give it to him. She never gave her name to anyone unless she knew them. Over the past few years she'd developed a hearty distrust of most people and it had saved her on more than one occasion.

'So you can call your friends in the police and get them to throw me in jail?'

She shouldn't have vandalised the car, since as a rule she liked to keep a low profile—less chance of coming to anyone's notice that way. But she'd been followed on her way to the little alley where she'd been hoping to bed down and, since being a woman on her own at night could be a problem, she'd attached herself to the crowd of homeless teenagers she'd been with earlier. They'd been out vandalising stuff and she'd had to prove herself willing to do the same in order to stay in their company. So she hadn't hesitated to pick up the spray can.

To be fair, she hadn't minded targeting this man's limo. The rich never saw the people on the streets, and she rather liked the idea of forcing her existence to at least be acknowledged in some way. Even if it did involve the police.

'No.'

His voice was very deep, with a warmth curling through it that made a part of her shiver right down low inside. There was a lilt to it, too...a faint, musical accent.

'But you were vandalising my car. Your name is the least you can give me in recompense.'

Leonie frowned. What had he done with her knife?

She wanted it back. She didn't feel safe without it. 'Why? Don't you want money?'

He raised one perfect black brow. 'Do you have any?'

'No.'

The man shrugged one powerful shoulder in an elegant motion and she found her gaze drawn by the movement. To the way his shirt pulled tight across that shoulder, displaying the power of the muscles underneath.

How odd. She'd never looked at a man that way before, so why was she doing so now? Men were awful—especially rich men like this one. She knew all about them; her father was one of them and he'd thrown her and her mother out on the streets. So no wonder she'd taken an instant dislike to this guy—though maybe it was more hate than dislike.

Hate was the only word strong enough to describe the disturbingly intense feeling gathering inside her now.

'Then, *gatita*,' he said, in his dark, deep voice, 'your name it will have to be.'

'But I don't want to give you that.'

Her jaw tightened. Resistance was the only thing she had on the streets and she clung to it stubbornly. Resistance to anything and everything that tried to push her down or squash her, grind her into the dirt of Paris's ancient cobbles. Because if she didn't resist then what else did she have? How would she even know she existed?

By spraying rude words on a limo?

Yes, if need be. It was all about the fight. That was all life was.

He gave another elegant shrug, as if it was all out of his hands. 'Then sadly I must be recompensed for my inconvenience in other ways.'

Ah, of course. She understood this, at least. 'I'm not paying you in sex. I'd rather die.'

His mouth twitched, which she found disconcerting. Normally men got angry when she refused them, but he didn't seem angry at all. Only...amused.

For some reason she didn't like it that he found her amusing.

'I'm sure you wouldn't,' he said lazily. 'I happen to be very good at it. No one has died having sex with me yet, for example.'

Leonie ignored the way her stomach fluttered. Perhaps that was hunger. She hadn't eaten today, and although a day without food was fairly normal for her, she didn't usually find herself chucked into a limo and kept prisoner by...whoever this man was.

'But,' he went on before she could argue, 'I know what you're talking about, and rest assured my recompense won't be in the form of sex. Though I'm sure you are, in fact, very desirable.'

She gave him a dark look. 'I am, actually. Why do you think I carry a knife?'

'Of course. What man wouldn't want a feral kitten?'

His mouth curved and she found herself staring at it. It had a nice shape, firm and beautifully carved.

She shook herself. Why was she staring at his mouth?

'You'd be surprised what men want,' she said, dragging her gaze to meet his, though quite frankly that wasn't any better.

His amusement abruptly drained away, the lines of his perfect face hardening. He shifted, sitting back against the seat. 'No. I would not.'

Leonie shivered, the interior of the car feeling suddenly cold. 'What do you want, then? I can't pay you, and

I'm not telling you my name, so all you can do is call the police and have me prosecuted. And if you're not going to do that, then isn't it easier to let me go?'

'But then how would I be recompensed for my inconvenience?' He shook his head slowly. 'No, I'm afraid, *gatita*, I can't let you go.' He paused, his green eyes considering. 'I think I'm going to have to put you to work instead.'

CHAPTER TWO

THE LITTLE REDHEAD treated this suggestion without obvious enthusiasm—which Cristiano had expected.

He still didn't know why exactly he'd said it. Because she was right. He could afford the paltry amount it would take to get his limo repainted. And as for his supposed inconvenience...

He glanced out through the window to the two lovely women he'd wanted to join him for the night. They were still out there, waiting for him to give them the word, though for once he felt a lessening of his own enthusiasm for their company.

It was a bit mystifying, since he never said no to anything or anyone—still less two beautiful women. Nevertheless, he found himself more interested in the little *gatita* sitting opposite him. She was a puzzle, and it had been too long since he'd had a puzzle.

He wanted her name. And the fact that she wouldn't just give it to him was irritating. Especially when that familiarity kept tugging on him, rubbing against his consciousness like a burr in a blanket.

Women never denied him, and the fact that she had was annoying.

And then she'd muttered that thing about men, and

he'd realised that letting her go meant letting her go back on the streets at two in the morning. Admittedly she'd been with a crowd earlier, but they'd all vanished, so she'd be on her own.

That she was used to looking after herself was obvious, but it didn't mean he was going to let her. He wasn't a gentleman, despite the fact that he came from an ancient line of Spanish nobility. Not in any way. But he was enough of a man that he couldn't leave this young woman alone in the middle of the night.

Because, no, he wouldn't be surprised at what men wanted from such a delectable little morsel such as herself. He was one of those men after all.

That left him with only one option: to keep hold of her in a way she'd accept.

He could, of course, simply ignore her protests and take her back to his Paris mansion and keep her there. But, again, dealing with the protests that would no doubt entail would be tiresome, and he preferred to avoid tiresome things. Things that left less time to do the things he liked doing. His own personal pleasure always took priority.

It would be easier all round if she agreed, therefore work it was.

If only he had something for her to do...

He had estates and a *castillo* back in Spain—which he avoided going to whenever possible—and numerous companies he'd invested his considerable fortune in. But he already had a number of staff managing all those things—and besides, they weren't the kinds of things a Parisian street urchin could manage, no matter how feisty she was.

No, the only work he could conceivably give her was

domestic, by adding her to his housekeeping staff. He already had a large contingent, but one more wouldn't hurt. House-cleaning, at least, required no extensive training, and it would keep her close until he'd uncovered her mysteries.

Which he was going to do, since he currently had a dearth of mysteries in his life.

'What kind of work?' she asked, still suspicious.

'I need someone to clean for me.' He tilted his head, studying her. 'I have a house in Paris that's very large and needs attention. You may work out what you owe me for the car and my personal inconvenience there.'

'But I—'

'Did I mention that I have rooms set aside for my staff? You will be required to live on-site for the duration.'

'Don't guys like you already have a lot people doing your dirty work for you?'

'Yes.' Her scorn didn't bother him. He tried not to let anything bother him, since it was very dangerous for all concerned when he was bothered. 'But I could always do with one more. Plus, I pay my staff very well for doing my "dirty work".'

At the mention of pay, something changed. Her eyes lost that wary look, and a calculating gleam sparked in their depths.

He knew that gleam and he knew it intimately. It was hunger. And not in the physical sense, of needing food, but in the sense of wanting something you could never have and wanting it desperately.

Money—she wanted money. And who could blame her when she didn't have any? Money was power, and she didn't have any of that, either, he'd bet.

Sure enough, she said, 'Pay? You pay them?'

'Of course. That's why they're my staff and not my slaves.'

She leaned forward all of a sudden, losing her wariness, all business now. Her violet eyes were focused very intently on him. 'Would you pay me? Once I earned back for the car? Could I have a proper job?'

Something shifted in Cristiano's gut. Something that, again, he was intimately familiar with.

She was lovely. And he could imagine her looking at him just like that, with a pretty flush to her pale cheeks and a flame in her eyes and all the beautiful hair spread over his pillow. Hungry for him as he buried himself inside her...

A nice thought, but a thought was what it would stay. She'd never be one of his partners. Apart from the fact that the distance between them in power, money and just about everything else could not have been more vast, she was also much younger than he was.

And he was betting she'd either had some bad experiences with men or she avoided men completely.

Again, dealing with all that sounded like work, and he tried to avoid work whenever he could. He didn't want anything hard, anything difficult, and he avoided complications like the plague.

This small *gatita* was certainly a complication, but he found he was willing to expend a bit of effort on figuring out why she was so familiar to him. After all, it had been a while since he'd let himself be interested in something other than physical pleasure. It certainly couldn't hurt.

'Do you want a job?' he asked, teasing her a little just because he could.

'Yes, of course I want a job.' Her gaze narrowed further. 'How much do you pay?'

A good question—though he was sure she couldn't afford to turn anything down.

'My staff are the best and I pay them accordingly,' he said, and named a sum that made her pretty eyes go round.

'That much?' All her earlier wariness and suspicion had dropped away. 'You really pay people that much just to clean your house?'

'It's a very big house.'

'And you'd pay me that?'

It wasn't a lot of money—at least it wasn't to him. But for her it was clearly a fortune. Then again, he suspected that a five-euro note left on the street would be a fortune for her.

'Yes, I'd pay you that.' He paused, studying her. 'Where do you live? And what are you doing on the streets at two in the morning?'

Instantly her expression closed up, the light disappearing from her face, the shutters coming down behind her eyes. She sat back on the seat, putting distance between them and glancing out of the window.

'I should go home. My...mother will be worried.'

Which didn't answer his direct question but answered the ones he hadn't voiced. Because she was lying. Her slight hesitation made him pretty certain she didn't have a mother and neither did she have a home.

'I think not,' he said, watching her. 'I think you should come directly back to my house and spend the night there. Then you can start work first thing tomorrow morning.'

'I don't want to come back to your house.'

'Like I said, I have quarters for my staff and there will be more than enough room.'

'But I—'

'There will be no argument.' Because he'd decided now, and once he made a decision he stuck to it. 'You have two choices. Either you come back to my house tonight or you spend the night in a police cell.'

'That's not much of a choice,' she said angrily.

'Too bad. You were the one who decided spray-painting my car was a good idea, so these are the consequences.' He liked her arguing with him, he realised. Probably too much—which was an issue. 'So what's it to be, *gatita*?'

She folded her arms. 'Why do you keep calling me that?'

'It means kitten in Spanish.'

'I'm not a kitten.'

'You're small and feral and you tried to scratch me—of course you're a kitten. And a wild one at that.'

She was silent a moment, not at all mollified. Then, 'Why Spanish?'

'Because I'm Spanish.'

'Oh. What are you doing in Paris?'

He stared at her, letting her see a little of his edge. 'That's a lot of questions for a woman who won't even give me her name.'

'Why should I? You haven't given me yours.'

That was true—he hadn't. And why not? His name was an ancient and illustrious one, but one that would soon come to an end. He was the sole heir and he had no plans to produce another. No, the Velazquez line, the dukedom of San Lorenzo, would die with him and then be forgotten. Which was probably for the best, considering his dissolute lifestyle.

Your parents would be appalled.

They certainly would have been had they still been alive, but they weren't. He had no one to impress, no one to live up to. There was only him and he didn't care.

'My name is Cristiano Velazquez, Fifteenth Duke of San Lorenzo,' he said, because he had no reason to hide it. 'And you may address me as Your Grace.'

A ripple of something crossed her face, though he couldn't tell what it was. Then she frowned. 'A duke? Cristiano Velazquez…?' She said his name very slowly, as if tasting it.

He knew she hadn't meant to do it in a seductive way, but he felt the seduction in it all the same. His name in her soft, sweet husky voice, said so carefully in French… As if that same sense of familiarity tugged at her the way it tugged at him.

But how would she know him? They'd never met—or at least not that he remembered. And he definitely hadn't slept with her—that he was sure of. He might have had too many women to count, but he'd remember if he'd had her.

'You've heard of me?' he asked carefully, watching her face.

'No… I don't think so.' She looked away. 'Where is your house, then?'

Was she telling the truth? Had she, in fact, heard of him? Briefly he debated whether or not to push her. But it was late, and there were dark circles under her eyes, and suddenly she looked very small and fragile sitting there.

He should get her back to his place and tuck her into bed.

'You'll see.' Moving over the seat towards the door, he opened it. 'Stay here.'

Not that he gave her much choice, because he got out and shut it behind him again, locking it just in case she decided to make a desperate bid for freedom.

He made excuses to the two patiently waiting women, ensured they were taken care of for the evening, then went to find his recalcitrant driver, whom he eventually found in a nearby alley, playing some kind of dice game with a couple of the kids who'd been standing around his car.

How fortunate.

Getting his wallet out of his pocket, Cristiano extracted a note and brandished it at one of the youths. 'You,' he said shortly. 'This is yours if you tell me the name of the woman with the pretty red hair who was spray-painting my car.'

The kid stared at the note, his mouth open. 'Uh... Leonie,' he muttered, and made a grab for the money.

So much for loyalty.

Cristiano jerked the note away before the boy could get it. 'You didn't give me a last name.'

The kid scowled. 'I don't know. No one knows anyone's last name around here.'

Which was probably true.

He allowed the boy to take the money and then, with a meaningful jerk of his head towards the car for his driver's benefit, he turned back to it himself.

Leonie. Leonie...

Somewhere in the dim recesses of his memory a bell rang.

Leonie blinked as a pair of big wrought-iron gates set into a tall stone wall opened and the car slid smoothly through them.

On the rare occasions when she'd ventured out of the

area she lived in she'd seen places like this. Old buildings surrounded by high walls. Houses where the rich lived.

She'd once lived in a house like this herself, but it had been a long time ago and elsewhere, when she'd been a little kid. Before her father had kicked her and her mother out of their palatial mansion and life had changed drastically.

She still remembered what it had been like to have money, to have a roof over her head and clean clothes and food. Nice memories, but they'd been a lie, so she tried not to think about them. It was better not to remember such things because they only made her want what she could never have—and wanting things was always a bad thing.

She stared distrustfully out into the darkness, where the silhouette of a massive old house reared against the sky.

The driver came around the side of the car and opened the door. The duke gestured at her to get out.

She turned her distrustful attention to him.

A duke. An honest-to-God duke. He didn't look like one—though she had no idea what dukes were supposed to look like. Maybe much older. Although, given the faint lines around his eyes and mouth, he was certainly a lot older than she was. Then again, his hair was still pitch-black so he couldn't be *that* old.

His name had sounded faintly familiar to her, though she couldn't think why. The fact that he was Spanish had given her a little kick, since she'd been born in Spain herself. In fact maybe she'd met him once before—back in Spain, before her father had got rid of her and her mother and her mother had dragged her to Paris.

Back when she'd been Leonie de Riero, the prized only

daughter of Victor de Riero, with the blood of ancient Spanish aristocracy running in her veins.

Perhaps she knew this duke from then? Or perhaps not. She'd been very young, after all, and her memories of that time were dim.

Whatever he was, or had been, she didn't want to remember those days. The present was the only thing she had, and she had to be on her guard at all times. Forgetting where she was and what was happening led to mistakes, and she'd already made enough of those since ending up on the streets.

If she hadn't been so absorbed in getting the lettering just so as she'd graffitied his car, she wouldn't be here after all.

You certainly wouldn't have had a bed for the night, so maybe it wasn't such a mistake?

That remained to be seen. Perhaps she should have fought harder to escape him. Then again, she hadn't been able to resist the lure of a job—if he actually meant what he'd said, that was.

The duke lifted that perfect brow of his. 'Are you going to get out? Or would you prefer to sit here all night? The car is quite comfortable, though I'm afraid the doors will have to stay locked.'

She gave him a ferocious glare. 'Give me back my knife first.' She liked to have some protection on her, just in case of treachery.

He remained impervious to her glare. 'I'm not going to hurt you, *gatita*.'

Kitten. He kept calling her kitten. It was annoying.

'I don't trust you. And I don't want to sleep in a strange place without some protection.'

His jungle-green gaze was very level and absolutely

expressionless. 'Fair enough.' Reaching into the pocket of his jacket, he extracted her knife and held it out, handle first.

She took it from him, the familiarity of the handle fitting into her palm making her feel slightly better. Briefly she debated whether or not to try and slash at him again, then bolt into the darkness. But she remembered the high walls surrounding the house. She wouldn't be able to get over those, alas. She could refuse to get out and sleep in the car, but she didn't like the idea of being locked in. No, it was the house or nothing.

With as much dignity as she could muster, Leonie pocketed her knife then slid out of the car. Behind her, the duke murmured something to his driver and then he was beside her, moving past her up the big stone steps to the front door of the mansion.

Some member of his staff was obviously still up, because the door opened, a pool of light shining out.

A minute later she found herself in a huge vaulted vestibule, with flights of stone steps curling up to the upper storeys and a massive, glittering chandelier lighting the echoing space. Thick silk rugs lay on the floor and there were pictures on the walls, and on the ceiling far above her head was a big painting of angels with white wings and golden haloes.

It was very warm inside.

She was used to being cold. She'd been cold ever since she was sixteen, coming home after school one day to the rundown apartment she'd shared with her mother only to find it empty, and a note from her mother on the rickety kitchen table informing Leonie that she'd gone and not to look for her.

Leonie hadn't believed it at first. But her mother hadn't

come home that night, or the next, or the one after that, and eventually Leonie had had to accept that her mother wasn't coming home at all. Leonie had been evicted from the apartment not long after that, and forced to live on the streets, where she'd felt like she'd become permanently cold.

But she hadn't realised just how cold until now. Until the warmth from this place seeped up through the cracked soles of her sneakers and into her body, into her heart.

Immediately she wanted to go outside again—to run and never stop running. She couldn't trust this warmth. She couldn't let her guard down. It wasn't safe.

Except the big front door had closed, and she knew it would be locked, and the duke was gesturing at her to follow the older woman who stood next to him, regarding her with some disgust, making her abruptly conscious of the holes in her jeans and the stains on the denim. Of the grimy hoodie that she'd stolen from a guy who'd taken it off to fight someone in the alleyway where she'd been sleeping one night. Of the paint stains on her hands.

She was dirty, and ragged, and she probably smelled since she hadn't found anywhere to clean herself for weeks. No wonder this woman looked disgusted.

Leonie's stomach clenched and she gripped the handle of her knife, scowling to cover the wave of vulnerability that had come over her. Never stop fighting. Never show weakness. That was the law of the streets.

'Go with Camille,' the duke said. 'She will show you—'

'No,' Leonie said. 'Just tell me where to go and I'll find my own way there.'

Camille made a disapproving sound, then said something in a lilting musical language to the duke. He replied in the same language, his deep, rich voice making it sound as if he was caressing each word.

Leonie felt every one of her muscles tense in resistance. She couldn't like the sound of his voice. She had to be on her guard at all times and not make any mistakes. And she didn't want to go with this Camille woman and her disapproving stare.

Much to her surprise, however, with one last dark look in Leonie's direction, the woman turned and vanished down one of the huge, echoing hallways that led off the entrance hall.

Without a word, the duke turned and headed towards the huge marble staircase. 'Follow me,' he said over his shoulder.

He didn't pause and he didn't wait, as if expecting her to follow him just as he'd said.

Leonie blinked. Why had he sent the other woman away? Was he just leaving her here? What if she somehow managed to get out through the door? What if she escaped down one of the corridors? What would he do? He wasn't looking at her. Would he even know until she was gone?

Her heartbeat thumped wildly, adrenaline surging through her—both preludes to a very good bolt. And yet she wasn't moving. She was standing there in this overwhelming, intimidating entrance hall, not running, watching a tall, powerful rich man go up the marble stairs.

He moved with economy and a lazy, athletic grace that reminded her even more strongly of a panther. It was mesmerising, for some reason. And when she found herself moving, it wasn't towards the doorway or the corridor, it was towards him, following him almost helplessly.

Was this what had happened in that fairy-tale? Those children following the Pied Piper, drawn beyond their control by the music he made. Disappearing. Never to be seen again.

You're an idiot. You have your knife. Pull yourself together.

This was true. And nothing had happened to her so far. Yes, he'd kept her locked in the car against her will, but he hadn't hurt her. And apart from the moment when he'd grabbed her, he hadn't touched her again.

She didn't trust him, or his offer of a job, but it was either follow him or stay down here in the entrance hall, and that seemed cowardly. She wasn't going to do that, either.

There was a slim possibility that he was telling the truth, and if so she needed to take advantage of it. If she was going to achieve her dream of having a little cottage of her own in the countryside, away from the city, away from danger, then he was her best chance of that happening.

Slowly Leonie moved after him, going up the winding marble staircase, trying to keep her attention on his strong back and not gawk at all the paintings on the walls, the carpets on the parquet floors, the vases of flowers on the small tables dotted here and there as they went down yet another wide and high-ceilinged corridor.

Windows let in the Parisian night and she caught glimpses of tall trees, hinting at a garden outside. She wanted to go and look through the glass, because it had been a long time since she'd seen a garden, but she didn't dare. She had to keep the duke's tall figure in sight.

Eventually, after leading her through a few more of

those high-ceilinged corridors, he stopped outside a door and opened it, inclining his head for her to go on through.

He was standing quite near the doorway, and she wasn't sure she wanted to get that close to him, but she didn't want him to know it bothered her, either, so she slipped past him as quickly as she could. But not quickly enough to avoid catching a hint of his aftershave and the warmth of his powerful body as she brushed past him.

It was only an instant, but in that instant she was acutely aware of his height looming over her. Of the width of his broad shoulders and the stretch of the cotton across his muscled chest. Of the way he smelled spicy and warm and quite delicious.

A strange ripple of sensation went through her like an electric shock.

Disturbed, Leonie ignored it, concentrating instead on the room she'd stepped into.

It was very large, with tall windows that looked out on to trees. A thick pale carpet covered the floor, and up against one wall, facing the windows, was a very large bed, made up with a thick, soft-looking white quilt.

The duke moved past her, going over to the windows and drawing heavy pale silk curtains over the black glass, shutting out the night. The room was very warm, the carpet very soft under her feet, and she was conscious once again of how dirty she was.

She was going to leave stains all over this pretty pale bedroom. Surely he couldn't mean for her to stay here? It didn't look like a cleaner's room. It was far too luxurious.

'This can't be where you put your staff,' she said, frowning. 'Why am I here?'

He adjusted the curtains with a small, precise movement, then turned around, putting his hands in his pockets. 'Not usually, no. But Camille didn't have a room ready for you, so I thought you could use one of my guest bedrooms.'

'Why? Why are you doing this?'

He tilted his head, gazing at her from underneath very long, thick black lashes. 'Which particular "this" are you talking about?'

'I mean this room. A job. A bed for the night. Why are you doing any of it? Why should you care?'

She hadn't meant it to come out so accusingly, but she couldn't help it. Men like him, with money and power, never did things without wanting something in return. Even charity usually came with strings. There were bound to be strings here, if only she could see them.

But the duke merely gave one of those elegant shrugs. 'What else does one do with a feral kitten but look after it?'

'I'm not a kitten,' she said, for the second time that night.

His mouth curved and once again she felt that electric ripple of sensation move through her. It came to her very suddenly that this man was dangerous. And dangerous in a way she couldn't name. He wasn't a physical threat—though those strange little ripples of sensation definitely were—but definitely a threat of some kind.

'No,' he murmured, his gaze moving over her in a way that made heat rise in her cheeks. 'You're not, are you?'

She lifted her chin, discomfited and not liking it one bit. 'And I didn't ask you to look after me, either.'

'Oh, if you think I'm doing it out of the goodness of my heart you are mistaken.' He strolled past her towards the door. 'It's entirely out of self-interest, believe me.'

'Why? Just because I vandalised your car?'

Pausing by the door, he gave her a sweeping, enigmatic glance. 'Among other things. The bathroom is through the door opposite. A shower or a bath wouldn't go amiss, *gatita*.'

'Don't call me that,' she snapped, annoyed that he'd obviously noticed how dirty she was and how she must smell, and then annoyed further by her own annoyance—since why should she care if he'd noticed?

'What else am I to call you?' His eyes gleamed. 'Especially since you won't give me your name.'

Leonie pressed her lips together. He might have strong-armed her into staying in his house, but her name was the one thing he wouldn't be able to force out of her. That was hers to give.

Again, he didn't seem offended. He only smiled. 'Then *gatita* it will have to be.'

And before she could say another word he walked out, closing the door carefully behind him.

CHAPTER THREE

THE LATE-MORNING SUN poured through the big windows of Cristiano's study, flooding the room with light and warmth, but he didn't notice. He wasn't interested in the weather.

He'd got up early that morning, despite not having slept much the previous night, and gone straight to his study to see if the memory that learning Leonie's name had generated was correct. After a couple of calls and a few strongly worded orders he'd had his confirmation.

She was exactly who he'd suspected she was.

Which should have been impossible, considering she was supposed to be dead.

He leaned back in his big black leather chair and stared at the computer screen on the desk in front of him. At the photo it displayed. An old one, from years and years ago, of a tall, dark-haired man, holding the hand of a little girl with hair the distinctive colour of apricots. At the side of the little girl stood a lovely slender woman with hair exactly the same colour.

It was a loving family portrait of the ancient and illustrious de Riero family—Spanish aristocrats who'd fallen on hard times and lost their title a century or so ago.

Leonie had turned out to be Leonie de Riero, Victor de Riero's prized only daughter, who'd disappeared along with her mother fifteen years earlier, rumoured to have died in an apartment fire in Barcelona not long after she'd disappeared.

It was a scandal that had rocked Spain for months and he remembered it acutely. Especially because Victor de Riero, whose family had been blood enemies of Cristiano's, had become his mentor.

Victor had been grief-stricken about the loss of his wife and child—at least until he'd found himself a new family.

Your family.

The deep, volcanic rage that Cristiano had thought he'd excised from his life shifted in his gut, hot enough to incinerate anything in its path, and he had to take a minute to wrestle it back into submission. Because he couldn't allow himself to feel that—not any more. He couldn't allow himself to feel anything any more.

It had taken him years to put that rage behind him, but he had. And he'd thought he'd found some measure of peace. Until Leonie had appeared.

Cristiano pushed his chair back and got to his feet, walking over to the bookshelves opposite his desk before turning and pacing back to the desk again, needing movement to settle himself.

His thoughts tumbled about in his head like dice.

Of course Leonie had been familiar to him. He *had* met her. But it had been years ago, and she'd been that little girl in the photo—a kid of around two or three, initially, when her father had first approached him.

He'd been seventeen at the time, and had just lost both his parents in a car accident. Victor de Riero had paid him a visit not long after the funeral, ostensibly to bury the hatchet on the ancient feud the Velazquez and de Riero families had been pursuing for centuries.

Cristiano had been only too happy to do so, having no interest in old feuds and still grappling with the deaths of his parents and the shock of suddenly having to take on the responsibility of a dukedom. He'd welcomed Victor's interest in him gratefully, listening to the older man's advice and accepting his help, thinking the other man was doing it out of the goodness of his heart.

But he hadn't known then that there was no goodness in Victor's heart, or that the flames of vengeance for the de Riero family still burned in him hot and strong.

In fact it hadn't been until Cristiano had married, three years later, that he'd discovered the truth about Victor de Riero's interest.

In that time, though, he'd met Victor's wife and his small, sparky daughter. Cristiano hadn't taken much notice of the daughter—kids hadn't been on his radar back then—but then Victor's wife had disappeared, taking the girl with her, only for both to be discovered dead in a fire a week or so later.

Cristiano had tried to be there for Victor the way Victor had been for him, after his parents had died, but he'd been in the throes of first love, and then early marriage, and hadn't paid as much attention as he should have.

He hadn't paid attention a year or so after that, either, when he'd gone to Victor for advice when his marriage to Anna had run into trouble. If he had, he might have noticed how much his wife had enjoyed Victor's company—how, at social occasions, she'd spent more time talking to him than she had to Cristiano.

He might have become aware that Victor had never

planned on burying the hatchet when it came to their family feud but had only been lying in wait, lulling Cristiano into a false sense of security, waiting for the right time to take advantage of a vulnerable young man.

And finally he had found that advantage in Cristiano's wife. Because it had been his lovely wife Anna that Victor had wanted, and in the end it had been his lovely wife that he'd taken—Cristiano's already pregnant wife.

Along with Cristiano's son.

Cristiano paced to the bookshelves again, memories he'd long since suppressed flooding like acid through him.

Victor turning up at Cristiano's Barcelona penthouse, flanked by bodyguards and cloaked in triumph, revealing the final piece of his plot like a pantomime villain. Rubbing salt into Cristiano's wound by telling him that his seduction of Anna had all been part of their blood feud, and then rubbing glass into that same wound by telling him that Anna was pregnant and the child was Cristiano's.

He would bring up Cristiano's child as his own, Victor had said. He would take something precious from a Velazquez after a Velazquez had ruined the de Riero family a century earlier, by stealing the dukedom from them.

Cristiano had barely heard the man's reasoning. He'd been incandescent with rage and betrayal. It had been wise of Victor to have brought bodyguards, because he hadn't been at all sure he wouldn't have launched himself at the other man and strangled him.

Your anger has always been a problem.

Yes, and he'd been on fire with it.

For two years he'd used almost the entirety of his

fortune trying to get his son back, but Victor had falsified the paternity tests Cristiano had demanded, paid any number of people off, and Cristiano hadn't had a leg to stand on.

Eventually he'd crashed a party of Victor's, intent on stealing back his son from the man who'd taken him—but when he'd approached the boy, the child had run from him in fear. Straight to Victor.

'This is the reason, Cristiano,' Anna had flung at him, as she'd tried to calm the hysterical child in Victor's arms. *'This is the reason I left you. You're dangerous and you only end up scaring people. Why can't you leave us alone?'*

Well, she'd got her wish in the end. After that—after seeing the fear in his son's green eyes—he'd left the party. Left Spain, vowing never to return.

For his own sanity he'd excised all knowledge of his son from his heart, scoured all thoughts of revenge from his soul. He had found other ways to kill the pain lodged inside him like a jagged shard of broken glass. Pleasure and lots of it had been the key, and soon enough the edges of that piece of glass had dulled, making him look back over the years and marvel at how it had ever been sharp enough to hurt.

But it was hurting now. Because of her.

He came to the bookshelves and turned around, pacing back to the desk once more.

If he'd had any sense he'd have got rid of her the moment that sense of nagging familiarity had hit him, but he hadn't, and now she was here. In his house. And he was certain it was her.

A member of his staff had managed to track down the man who'd told Victor that Leonie and Hélène de Riero had died in a fire, and the man—once some money had been waved in his face—had admitted he'd lied. That Hélène de Riero had paid him to report her and her daughter's death to her ex-husband for reasons unknown.

Of course Cristiano would need DNA confirmation, which he'd get easily enough, but he was sure already. No other woman he'd ever met had had hair that colour or those jewel-bright violet eyes.

He had Victor de Riero's daughter in his grasp.

Tension gathered inside him and a vicious anticipation twisted through it, the rage he'd never been able to conquer entirely burning in his heart. Whether it was fate that had brought her to his door, or merely simple chance, it didn't matter.

What mattered was that here was an opportunity. A very unexpected opportunity.

Isn't revenge a dish best served cold?

After his parents had been killed, the old family feud with the de Rieros had seemed like something out of the Middle Ages. A hold-over from a different time. But he'd been young back then, and naive. He hadn't yet learned that people lied and that they couldn't be trusted. He hadn't yet learned just how far the depths of grief and loss could go.

He'd learned eventually. Oh, yes, he'd learned that lesson well.

And now here was his chance to pay that lesson back in kind.

Tension crawled through him, making his jaw ache as he came to the desk and turned around to the bookshelf again.

He couldn't deny that he liked the thought. Relished it.

Victor de Riero had taken his son, so wouldn't it be

the sweetest revenge of all if Cristiano took his daughter? The daughter who'd been presumed dead for fifteen years?

An eye for an eye keeps the feud alive.

Perhaps he wouldn't have considered it if Leonie hadn't turned up. Perhaps he'd have gone through his life pretending he didn't have a son and that he'd never been married for the rest of his days. But she had, and now he could think of nothing else.

It seemed the old Spanish warlord in him wasn't as dead as he'd thought.

Maybe he'd make her his duchess. Invite de Riero to the wedding. He'd pull up her veil and then there she'd be—the daughter de Riero had thought was dead, marrying the man he'd once thought he could humiliate in front of the entire world.

And maybe to really pay him back Cristiano would have an heir with her after all. Pollute the pure de Riero bloodline with Velazquez blood.

After all, if de Riero could do it, why couldn't he?

He stopped mid-pace, his fingers curling inside his pockets, vicious pleasure pulling tight in his gut.

And then you can move on.

Not that he hadn't moved on already, but that jagged shard of glass was still embedded deep inside his heart, ensuring it could never heal. Perhaps if he took the revenge he was owed it finally would.

Certainty settled inside him like the earth settling after an earthquake, forming a new landscape.

First on the agenda would be Leonie—because she was vital to his plan and would have to agree to it. Which might be a problem when she was so stubborn, wary and distrustful. Not so surprising, given the circumstances under which he'd found her, but not exactly conducive to his plan. Then again, money seemed to motivate her. She could consider being his bride part of her job, for which she'd receive a very healthy bonus.

Revealing that he knew who she was could be a concern, however. She hadn't given him her name for a reason, and everything hinged on how she felt about her father. Had she ever wanted to return to him? Did she even know she was supposed to be dead?

He frowned at the wall opposite. Perhaps telling her about his discovery immediately would be a mistake. Now she was here, within his grasp, he couldn't afford for her to run, and he'd be at risk of scaring her away if he wasn't careful. No, maybe it would be better to gain her trust before he let her in on his secret—an easy enough task to accomplish with a beautiful woman. All it would require was a bit of careful handling.

Galvanised in a way he hadn't been for years, Cristiano turned towards the door, heading out of his study and going in search of the newest member of his staff.

He found her, as he'd expected, in the big library that faced onto the walled garden at the rear of the house. She was kneeling on the floor before one of the big bookshelves with her back to him. Her dirty clothes were gone—clearly Camille had found her something else to wear—and she now wore the staff uniform of plain black trousers and a fitted black T-shirt. Nondescript clothes that should have made her blend in, and yet the skein of silken hair that fell down her back in a sleek ponytail effectively prevented that. The colour glowed against her black T-shirt, a deep red-gold tinged with pink.

Beautiful.

His hands itched with the urge to run his fingers

through it, to see if it felt as soft as it looked. To touch that vibrant colour, wind it round his wrist, examine the contrast against his own skin...

Except that was not what he wanted from her. Her name, yes. Her body, no. He might find her more attractive than he'd expected, but he could get sex from any of the women in his extensive little black book. He didn't need to expend any effort on a skittish, homeless, much younger woman, no matter how pretty her hair was.

But what about your plans for an heir?

Ah, yes, but there would be time for that later.

He hitched one shoulder up against the doorframe and gazed at her.

It was clear she wasn't actually cleaning, since her cloth and polishing spray were sitting next to her. Her head was bent, as if she was looking at something, and it must be very absorbing since it was clear she hadn't heard him and he hadn't exactly been quiet.

That was what had got her into trouble the previous night, hadn't it? She'd been totally caught up in the 'art' she'd been creating on his limo door and hadn't run when she should have.

What would that attention be like it bed? Would she look at you that way? Would she touch you like—?

Cristiano jerked his offending thoughts out of the gutter, irritated with himself. Perhaps he needed to contact those two lovely women he'd been going to take home the previous night and finish what they'd started. Certainly he'd have to do something with his wayward groin—especially if he kept having thoughts like these about Leonie.

He shifted against the doorframe and said finally, 'Find some interesting reading material, *gatita*?'

* * *

The duke's deep, rich voice slid over Leonie's skin like an unexpected caress, making her jump in shock, then freeze in place, the book she'd been reading still clutched in her hands. She stared at the shelves in front of her, every sense she had focused on the voice that had come from behind her.

A small cold thread wound its way through her veins.

Her employer had caught her reading on the job on her very first day. Not a good look. Ugh—what had she been thinking?

Everything had been going extremely well since he'd left her the night before, too. She'd availed herself of the shower, even though everything in her had wanted to spend hours soaking in the vast white marble bath. But it had been very late and she'd needed some sleep. So she'd given her body and hair a decent scrub before falling into that outrageously comfortable bed naked, since she hadn't been able to bear putting on her filthy clothes again—not when she was so clean.

Her sleep had been fitful, due to the comfortableness of the bed—she was used to sleeping on hard surfaces covered with nothing but pieces of cardboard or, if she was lucky and had managed to get a night in a shelter, a hard mattress covered by a thin blanket—and she'd kept waking up. Her sleep was always light, in case of threats, but even so she'd felt okay when she'd woken this morning.

There had been a set of clothes left outside her door, which she'd snatched up and put on, glorying in the feel of soft, clean cotton against her skin. Coffee and a fresh warm croissant had been left along with the clothes, and she'd devoured both in seconds. She had still been hungry, but then Camille had come, a little less scornful than she'd been the night before, and given her an introduction to her duties.

There'd been no time for more food.

She was supposed to have spent no more than half an hour in the library—concentrating on dusting the shelves, since the duke was most particular about them—before moving on to the formal sitting room next door. But she had a horrible suspicion that she'd been in here longer than half an hour. And she hadn't even touched the shelves yet.

She'd just got very interested in some of the books, and hadn't been able to resist taking one off the shelf and opening it up.

Back when she'd been smaller, when her mother had still been around, she'd used to love going to the library and reading, and books were something she'd missed on the streets. And back further still, when she'd been very young, her father had read to her—

But, no, she wasn't going to think of her father.

She needed to be more alert to her surroundings, that was what she needed to be, because this wretched duke was always sneaking up on her.

Quickly, she closed the book and put it back. 'I wasn't reading,' she said, picking up her cloth and polish. 'I was just polishing the shelf.' She ran the cloth over the already gleaming wood a couple of times. 'It's very dirty.'

'Which book was it?'

Again that voice—a deep, dark purr that felt like soft velvet brushing against her skin. It made her shiver and she didn't like it…not one bit.

Clutching her cleaning equipment, Leonie got to her

feet and turned around, only to have the words she'd been going to say die in her throat.

The duke was leaning one powerful shoulder casually against the doorframe, his hands in his pockets. He was in perfectly tailored black suit trousers today, and a pristine white shirt with the sleeves rolled up to his elbows, revealing strong wrists and sleekly muscled forearms. It was plain, simple clothing that set off his sheer physical beauty to perfection, accentuating the aristocratic lines of his face, the straight black brows, the sharply carved mouth and the deep emerald glitter of his eyes.

He seemed different from the man he'd been the night before. There was an energy about him that hadn't been present the previous evening. It was oddly compelling and that made her wary.

Everything about this man made her wary.

He raised a brow in that imperious way he had. 'You were going to say something?'

Leonie was irritated to feel a blush rising in her cheeks, because she had a feeling he'd noticed her reaction to him and was amused by it.

'No,' she said, wishing she had her knife on her. Because although he hadn't made a move towards her, she felt the threat he presented all the same. 'Is there anything you need…uh…*monsieur*?' She couldn't quite bring herself to say *Your Grace*.

A smile curled his mouth, though it didn't look like an amused smile. More as if he was…satisfied.

'Not at all. Just coming to see how my newest staff member is settling in. Is everything to your liking?'

'Yes, thank you.' She kept a tight grip on her cloth and

polish. 'Camille said she would find me another room to sleep—'

'I think not,' he interrupted, with the casual arrogance of a man who was used to his word being law. 'You'll stay in the room you're in.'

Leonie wasn't unhappy with that—especially when she hadn't had a chance to use that amazing bath yet, and also didn't like being in close proximity to a lot of people—but she didn't like his automatic assumption that she could be told what to do.

And your need to fight is what gets you into trouble.

This was very true. And there was also another problem. A problem she'd foreseen the night before and yet had dismissed.

In accepting a bed for the night, and now a job, she'd had a tiny taste of what her life might be like off the streets.

Having a shower whenever she wanted it…having clean sheets and clean clothes. Having food brought to her and having something to do that wasn't figuring out how to shoplift her next meal or begging for coins. Being safe behind walls and locked doors.

Just a tiny taste. Enough to know she didn't want to give it up—not just yet.

This is how they suck you in. You should have run…

She swallowed, clutching her cleaning implements even tighter. It was too late to run now—too late to decide that life on the streets was better than being in this house and working for this duke. Like Persephone from the myth, she'd had a bite of the pomegranate and now she was trapped in the Underworld.

Which makes him Hades.

And a very fine Hades he made, too. No wonder she

found him dangerous. He was the snake in the garden, offering temptation...

'I don't need a special room,' she said, because her need to fight was so ingrained she couldn't stop herself. 'I'm happy to sleep wherever the other employees—'

'As I said, you will stay in the room you've been given.'

'Why?'

'Because I said so,' he replied easily. 'I'm the duke and what I say goes.' That smile was still playing around his fascinating mouth. 'Which reminds me—I usually have a formal job interview with my employees, and since you didn't have one, I suggest we schedule one for tonight. Over dinner.'

Instantly all her alarm bells went off at once. A job interview over dinner? That didn't sound right at all. Not that she had any experience with job interviews, but still...

She gave him a suspicious look. 'Job interviews are usually in offices during the day, not over dinner.'

'Astute, *gatita*. If being in an office would make you more comfortable, I can have dinner served to us there.'

Leonie scowled. 'I'm not sleeping with you.'

He raised both brows this time. 'Have I asked you to sleep with me?'

'No, but when a man asks a woman to dinner he expects certain things. Men always do.'

'You appear to have a very poor opinion of men—though I suppose that's understandable. We're not especially good examples of the human race.' His eyes glittered strangely. 'It's also true that I'm a particularly bad example. But I don't have any sexual designs on you, if that's what you're worried about.'

She *had* been worried about it. The threat of sexual violence was ever-present for a woman on her own on the streets. So why did him telling her that he had no sexual designs on her make her feel almost...disappointed?

'That's all very well,' she said, ignoring the feeling, 'but I don't trust you.'

He shifted, drawing her attention to his powerful body, making her aware of him in a disturbingly physical way.

'Fair enough. We've only just met after all. Bring your knife with you. And if I try anything romantic feel free to cut me with it.'

'Or you could just decide we don't need to have an interview,' she suggested. 'After all, you've already employed me.'

'It's true—I have. But the process is the process. I can't just let anyone into my house. Security checks need to be done...reference checks, et cetera. It's all very tiresome but absolutely necessary.' He paused, his gaze sharpening on her. 'Especially when said employee hasn't even given me her name.'

Leonie took a silent breath. She should have given it to him last night when he'd asked. What did it matter if he knew? She'd only wanted to retain a little bit of autonomy, but now she'd turned it into a big deal and maybe he thought she was trying to hide something, or that she was on the run from something.

Not the actual truth, which was that she was only a girl who'd been discarded by both parents. A girl nobody wanted.

Her gut tightened. He certainly didn't need to know that. And, anyway, her name was her own and it was hers to give. No one had the right to know it.

Why don't you give him a fake one, then?

She could. But that would be giving in, regardless of whether it was a fake name or not, and something inside her wouldn't let her do that.

What was it about him that had her wanting to fight him all the time? She'd never had such strong reactions to a man before. Admittedly, she hadn't come into contact with a lot of men, since it was better safety-wise to avoid them, but the few she'd had run-ins with hadn't endeared themselves to her. But this man...

He made her want to fight, to stand her ground, kick back. He also made her feel physical things she hadn't felt before in her entire life. A kind of shivery ache. A prickly restlessness. The stupid desire to poke at him just to see what he'd do. What on earth was that?

You know what it is.

But Leonie didn't want to think about it. She couldn't afford to—not when she was seconds away from catastrophe. Who knew how long this job would last? Or when she'd be turned out back on to the streets again?

She'd got herself into this situation, and if she was very lucky it would mean good things for her. So the most logical thing to do now was to be careful with the dangerous panther that lounged on the branch above her head. To keep her head down and perhaps not present herself as so much prey. Keep a low profile and not struggle. If she did that well he might even forget she existed and leave her alone.

So she said nothing, dragging her gaze away from him and looking at the ground instead.

'Ah, so that's how it's to be, hmm?'

Again, he sounded just like that panther—all low and purring and sleek.

'Come to my study when you finish up today. I'll tell Camille that you're expected.'

She nodded silently, and when she finally looked up the doorway was empty.

He'd gone.

CHAPTER FOUR

CRISTIANO FROWNED AT the clock on the mantelpiece, an unexpected impatience gathering inside him. Leonie was late and he suspected it was intentional, since Camille wouldn't have kept her working if she was expected to attend a meeting with him.

And she was definitely expected to attend.

He supposed he could have had the conversation with her in the library earlier that day, rather than make a performance of it over dinner. But trust was a difficult thing. You couldn't compel it and you couldn't buy it—it could only be given.

Which made him a liar in some respects, because he was absolutely planning a seduction. Except sex wasn't the goal. He was planning on seducing her curious mind instead.

He found himself energised by the prospect. It had been a long time since he'd had to exert himself for a woman—for anyone, for that matter—and the idea was more exciting than he'd anticipated. Lately his life of unmitigated pleasure had begun to pall, and it made a nice change to have to put his brain to good use instead of his body.

The thought of de Riero's shock as his daughter was revealed was...

The feeling of satisfaction was vicious, hot, and he had to force it back down—hard. He couldn't let emotion rule him. Not given the mistake he'd made the last time he'd tried to confront de Riero, blundering around in a blind rage, sending his son straight back into the other man's arms.

This time he needed to be casual, detached. Keep his revenge cold.

Mastering himself once more, Cristiano checked the time again, allowing himself some amusement at his own impatience, then crossed over to his desk. Since she was late, he might as well do something. It wouldn't do for her to find him cooling his heels and watching the clock for her arrival; he wasn't a man who waited for anyone, still less looked as if he was.

There were a few business matters he had to attend to, a few calls to make, and he made them, keeping an ear out for the door. And sure enough, ten minutes later, while he was in the middle of a conversation with a business acquaintance, he heard a soft knock.

'Enter,' he said, then turned his chair around so his back was to the room, continuing with his call.

It was petty, but he'd never been above a little pettiness. It would do her good to wait for him—especially since he'd spent the last ten minutes waiting for her.

He carried on with his call in a leisurely fashion, in no hurry to end it since his acquaintance was amusing, and only when the other man had to go did he end the call and turn his chair back around.

Leonie was standing near one of the ornate wooden shelves he kept stocked with his favourite reading material—business texts, philosophy, sociology and a few novels thrown in the mix—staring fixedly at the spines.

She held herself very tense, her shoulders and spine stiff, that waterfall of beautiful hair lying sleek and silky down her back.

He had the sense that she wasn't actually looking at the books at all. She was waiting for him. Good.

'Good evening, *gatita*,' he said lazily, leaning back in his chair. 'You're late.'

Slowly, she turned to him, and his gaze was instantly drawn to the dark circles beneath her eyes. Her pretty face looked pale, her big violet-blue eyes shadowed. One hand was in the pocket of her black trousers—clutching that knife, no doubt.

A feeling he wasn't expecting tightened in his chest. He ignored it, raising a brow at her. 'Well? Any particular reason you're late to your job interview?'

Her determined little chin lifted. 'Because you distracted me in the library I didn't get my work done on time, so I had to make it up at the end of the day.'

He almost laughed. She did like testing him, didn't she? 'I see. Nothing whatsoever to do with the fact that I caught you reading, hmm?'

Colour bloomed across her delicate cheekbones. 'No.'

Which was an outright lie and they both knew it.

Highly amused, he grinned. 'And you took some time to go back to your room for you knife, also, I think?'

Her forearm flexed above where her hand disappeared into her pocket, as if she was squeezing her fingers around the handle of something. But this time she didn't deny it.

'You said I could bring it.'

'It's true. I did.'

He got up from the chair and came around the side of his desk, noting the way she tensed at his approach. She was very wary of him. As wary as she'd been the night before. Understandable, of course, and it was an obvious sign of distrust. In fact, he could probably gauge her progression in trusting him through the way she acted around him physically.

It made him wonder, though, exactly what had happened to her out there on the Parisian streets. How she'd managed to survive. What had happened to Hélène? Why hadn't she gone to her father and told him she was still alive...?

So many questions.

If he wanted answers, he had some work to do.

He moved over to the fireplace against one wall, opposite the bookshelves. He'd had one of his staff light a fire even though it wasn't particularly cold, mainly because it made the room feel more welcoming. The fire crackled pleasantly, casting its orange glow over Leonie's beautiful hair.

She watched him as if he was a dangerous animal she had to be cautious about, yet her gaze kept flicking to the fire as if she wanted to get close to it. As if she was cold.

'You're afraid of me,' he said, and didn't make it a question. 'I can assure you that you have no need to be.'

Her gaze flickered. 'I'm not afraid.'

But the response sounded as if it had been made by rote—as if that was always her answer, whether it was true or not. It made sense, though. When you were small and female you were viewed as prey by certain people, which meant fear wasn't something you could afford. Fear was weakness. Especially when there was no one to protect you.

Had she ever had anyone to protect her? Or had she had to do it herself?

That tight feeling in his chest shifted again. It had been such a long time since he'd felt anything remotely resembling pity or sympathy that he wasn't sure what it was at first. But then he knew. He didn't like the idea of her being on her own. He didn't like the idea of her not being protected. How strange.

'Then come closer.' He thrust his hands in his pockets so he looked less intimidating. 'You want to be near the fire. Don't think I hadn't noticed.'

She didn't like that—he could see the tension ripple through her. Perhaps he was wrong to test her. But if he wanted her trust he had to start somewhere, and having her be less wary around him physically was certainly one way of doing it.

He remained still, not moving, keeping his hands in his pockets, silently daring her. She was brave, not to mention stubborn, and he suspected that if he kept challenging her she'd rise to it.

Sure enough, after a couple of tense moments, she gave a shrug, as if it didn't matter, and then came slowly across the room to stand on the opposite side of the fireplace. Her expression was carefully blank, and when she got closer to the flames she held out her hands to warm them.

Ostensibly she looked as if nothing bothered her and she was perfectly comfortable. But she wasn't. He could feel the tension vibrating in the air around her.

She was like a wild animal, ready to start at the slightest sound or motion.

'There,' he murmured. 'That's not so bad, is it?'

She flicked him an impatient look. 'I'm not afraid of you. I have a knife.'

'Good. Keep that knife about your person at all times.'

He turned slightly, noting how she tensed at his movement. 'So, nameless *gatita*. I suppose my first question to you is why on earth were you spray-painting my limo at two in the morning?'

Her attention was on the flames, but he suspected she was still very aware of him. 'Why shouldn't I be spray-painting your limo at two in the morning?'

'That's not the correct answer,' he reproved mildly. 'Don't you think I'm owed an explanation, considering it was my property you vandalised?'

Irritation crossed her features. 'Fine. The people I was with dared me to. So I did.'

'And if they dared you to jump off the Eiffel Tower you'd do the same?'

'Probably.' She gave him a sidelong glance. 'You can't back down—not even once. Not if you don't want to be a target.'

Ah, so now they were getting to it. 'I see. And these people are your friends?'

He thought not. Not considering how a one-hundred-euro note had been enough to pay for her name.

She shook her head. 'Just some people I was hanging around with.'

'At two in the morning? Didn't you have somewhere else to go?'

Her lashes fell, limned in gold by the firelight. 'It's… safer to be around other people sometimes.'

The tight thing coiled in his chest shifted around yet again, because even though she hadn't said it outright he knew. No, she didn't have anywhere to go, and she didn't want to admit it.

Proud *gatita*.

'I'm not sure those people were very safe,' he murmured. 'Considering how your night ended.'

She gave a shrug. 'Could have been worse.'

'Indeed. You could have spent another night on the streets.'

There was no response to that, though he didn't expect her either to confirm or deny it—not given how reluctant she was to give him any information about herself. Clearly telling her that he knew who she was wouldn't go down well, so he definitely wasn't going to reveal that in a hurry.

A small silence fell, broken only by the crackling of the fire.

'Will you sit down?' he asked after a moment. 'The chair behind you will allow you to stay close to the fire if you're cold.'

She gave him another sidelong glance, then made a show of looking around the room, as if trying to locate the chair. Then, without any hurry, she moved over to it and sat down, leaning back, ostensibly relaxed, though she'd put her hand in her pocket again, holding on to her knife.

There was another armchair opposite hers, so he sat down in that one. A low coffee table was positioned between them, which should present her with a safety barrier if she needed it.

'So what now?' she asked, staring at him, her chin set at a stubborn angle.

'Tell me a little about yourself. If not your name, then at least a few things that will give me an idea about the kind of person I've just employed.'

'Why do you want to know that?'

He smiled. 'This isn't supposed to be a debate—merely a request for information.'

'Why do you need information?'

Persistent, wasn't she? Not to mention challenging. Good. His life had been without any challenges lately, and he could use the excitement.

'Well, since you won't give me your name, I need some indication of whether you're likely to make off with all the silverware.' He paused, considering whether or not to let her know just how much leeway he was allowing her. Why not? If she was testing him, he could test her. 'I do a background check on all employees who are granted access to my house, in other words. For safety reasons, you understand?'

A little crease appeared between her red-gold brows. 'How can you be unsafe? Here?'

Of course she'd find that surprising. Especially if she was living on the streets. She no doubt thought nothing could harm him here, and to a certain extent she was right. Physically, he was safe. But four walls and bodyguards—even if he employed any—didn't equal safety. You could have all the physical protection in the world and still end up broken and bleeding.

Luckily for him, his wounds had healed. And no one could see the scars but him.

'You can be unsafe anywhere,' he said dryly. 'In my experience you can never be too careful.'

'And what is your experience?'

He almost answered her. Almost. Sneaky kitten.

Cristiano smiled. 'It's supposed to be your job interview, *gatita*, not mine. I already have a job.'

'And so do I. You gave it to me, remember?'

'I do. Which means I can take it back whenever I like.'

She sniffed, glancing over to the fire once more. 'I might be more inclined to answer your questions if you answered some of mine.'

Well, this was an interesting tactic…

'That's not how a job interview works,' he said, amused by how she kept on pushing. 'Also, if you'll remember, I gave you my name last night.'

An irritated expression flitted across her face. She shifted in her seat and he didn't miss how her hand had fallen away from the pocket where her knife was kept.

So. Progress.

'I don't know why you keep asking.' Her sweet, husky voice had an edge to it. 'Not when you could just threaten me and be done with it.'

'Threats are effective, it's true. But ultimately they're not very exciting.' He watched her face. 'Not when it's much more fun to convince you to give it to me willingly.'

She flushed. 'You're very sure of yourself.'

'Of course I'm sure of myself. I'm a duke.'

'Duke of what?'

Good question. And because he was enjoying himself, and because it had been a long time since any woman had provided him with this much amusement, he answered it.

'Weren't you listening last night? I'm the Fifteenth Duke of San Lorenzo. It's a small duchy in Andalusia.'

She gave him a measuring look. 'What are you doing in Paris?'

'Business.' He smiled. 'Catching vandals spray-painting rude words on my limo.'

She gave another little sniff at that, but the colour in her cheeks deepened—which was a good thing considering how pale she'd been.

'You didn't sleep well, *gatita*,' he observed quietly.

'But I did tell Camille to let you sleep in a little this morning.'

She blinked and looked away, shifting around in her seat. 'The bed was...uncomfortable. And I'd had a long shower—too long.'

Well, he knew for a fact that the bed wasn't uncomfortable, since he had the same one in his room here. And as for the shower...that may have been the case. But he suspected she hadn't slept well because she wasn't used to having a bed at all.

'What do you care anyway?' she added irritably.

'I care because I like my employees to do a good job. And they can't if they're not well rested.'

'Or well fed,' she muttered.

He thought she probably hadn't meant him to hear that, but unfortunately for her he had excellent hearing. So she was hungry, was she? Again, understandable. If she lived on the streets, decent food must be hard to come by.

How lucky, then, that he'd organised a very good dinner.

Right on cue, there was a knock at the door.

She sat up, tension gathering around her again, instantly on the alert.

'Enter,' he said, watching her response as several staff members came in, bearing trays of the food he'd ordered.

Her eyes went wide as he directed them to put the food on the coffee table between them, including cutlery and plates, not to mention a couple of glasses and a bottle of extremely good red wine from his cellar.

'I told you there would be dinner,' he murmured as his staff arranged the food and then quietly withdrew.

Leonie had sat forward, her gaze fixed on the food on the table. It was a simple meal—a fresh garden salad and excellent steak, along with some warm, crusty bread and salted butter. All her earlier wariness had dissipated, to be replaced by a different kind of tension.

Her hands were clasped tightly in her lap.

She was hungry.

He became aware that her cheeks were slightly hollow, and her figure, now it wasn't swamped by that giant hoodie, was very slender. Probably too slender.

No, she wasn't just hungry—she was starving.

That tightness in his chest grew sharp edges, touching on that dangerous volcanic anger of his. Anger at how this lovely, spirited woman had ended up where she had. On the streets. Left to fend for herself with only a knife.

Left to starve.

Hélène had taken her and disappeared, letting Victor de Riero think she and his daughter were dead, but what had led her to do that? Had de Riero treated them badly? Was there something that had stopped Leonie from seeking him out?

A memory trickled through his consciousness...a small green-eyed boy running into de Riero's arms in fear...

Fear of you.

Red tinged the edges of Cristiano's vision and it took a massive effort to shove the rage back down where it had come from, to ignore the memory in his head. He had to do it. There would be no mistakes, not this time.

But her challenging him so continually was dangerous for them both. It roused his long-dormant emotions and that couldn't happen. Which meant she had to give him the answers he needed. Tonight. Now.

As she reached out towards the food Cristiano shot out a hand and closed his fingers around her narrow wrist.

'Oh, no, *gatita*. I've given you enough leeway. If you want to eat, you must pay me with some answers first.'

Leonie froze, her heart thudding hard in her ears, panic flooding through her. When his fingers had tightened her free hand had gone instantly to her knife, to pull it out and slash him with it.

'No,' he said, very calmly and with so much authority that for some strange reason her panic eased.

Because although his grip was firm, he wasn't pulling at her. He was only holding her. His fingers burned against her skin like a manacle of fire—except that wasn't painful, either. Or rather, it wasn't pain that she felt but a kind of prickling heat that swept up her arm and over the rest of her body.

She felt hypnotised by the sight of his fingers around her wrist. Long, strong and tanned. Competent hands. Not cruel hands.

'You'd stop me eating just to get what you want?' she asked hoarsely, not looking at him, staring instead at that warm, long-fingered hand gripping her wrist.

'No,' he repeated, in that deep, authoritarian voice. 'But I've given you food and a bed. A job that you'll be paid for. I haven't touched you except for twice—once when I grabbed you last night, and once now. I've given you my name and told you a few things about me. I have let you into my home.'

He paused, as if he wanted those words to sink in. And, as much as she didn't want them to, they did.

'I'm not asking for your date of birth or your passport number, or the number of your bank account. I'm not even asking for your surname. All I want is your first name. It's a small thing in return for all that, don't you think? After all, it was you who decided to deface my car, not me.'

Then, much to her shock, he let her go.

Her heart was beating very fast and she could still feel the imprint of his fingertips on her skin. It was as if he'd scorched her, and it made thinking very difficult.

But he was right about one thing. He wasn't asking for much. And he hadn't hurt her or been cruel. He *had* given her a bed and a job, and now there was food. And he hadn't withheld his name from her the way she had withheld hers from him.

She didn't trust him, but giving him this one small thing wouldn't hurt. After all, there were probably plenty of Leonies around. He couldn't know that she was Leonie de Riero, the forgotten daughter of Victor de Riero, the rich Spanish magnate, who'd tossed her and her mother out because he'd wanted a son. Or at least that was what her mother had told her.

'Leonie,' she said quietly, still staring at her wrist, part of her amazed she didn't have scorch marks there from his hand. 'My name is Leonie.'

There was a silence.

She glanced up and found his green gaze on hers, deep and dark as forests and full of dangerous wild things. She couldn't look away.

There was a kind of humming in the air around them, and the prickling heat that had swept over her skin was spreading out. Warming her entire body. Making her feel restless and hot and hungry. But not for food.

'Thank you,' the duke said gravely.

He was not triumphant or smug, nor even showing that lazy amusement she'd come to associate with him. It was as if her name had been an important gift and he was receiving it with all the solemnity that entailed.

'Pleased to met you, Leonie.'

Just for a moment she thought he might reach out and take her hand, shake it. And, strangely, she almost wanted him to, so she could feel his fingers on her skin again. How odd to want to touch someone after so long actively avoiding it.

But he didn't take her hand. Instead he gestured to the food.

'Eat.' His mouth curled. 'Not that I was going to stop you from eating.'

Leonie decided not to say anything to that. She was too hungry anyway.

Not wanting to draw his attention, she didn't load her plate with too much food and she tried to eat slowly. It was all unbelievably delicious, but she wanted to pace herself. It had been a while since she'd eaten rich food and she didn't want to make herself sick. But it tasted so good—especially the fresh vegetables.

The duke poured her a glass of wine and she had a sip—and her toes just about curled in the plain black leather shoes she'd been given. Everything tasted amazing. She wanted to eat and drink all of it.

He didn't eat—merely sat there toying with a glass of wine in a leisurely fashion and studying her. It was disconcerting.

'You're not hungry?' she asked, feeling self-conscious.

Had she been gorging herself? She didn't want to give away how starving she was, wary of him asking more questions that she wasn't prepared to answer.

What does it matter if he knows you're homeless?

Perhaps it didn't matter. Perhaps it was only instinct

that prevented her from revealing more, the long years of being wary and mistrustful settling into a reflex she couldn't ignore. Then again, there were reasons for her mistrust and wariness. She'd seen many young women in the same situation as herself fall victim to unscrupulous men because they'd trusted the wrong person, revealed the wrong thing.

Easier to keep to oneself, not let anyone close and stay alive.

It was a habit her wary, bitter mother had instilled in her long before she was on the streets anyway, and she'd seen no reason to change it.

Then again, although trusting this particular man might be a bridge too far, it was clear he wasn't here to hurt her. He'd had ample opportunity to do so and hadn't, so either he was saving it for a specific time or he wasn't going to do anything to her at all.

Maybe she could relax a little. Perhaps part of her reluctance to tell him anything had more to do with what he'd think of her, a dirty Parisian street kid, than whether he'd harm her. Not that she cared what he thought of her. At all.

'No, not hungry right now.' He leaned back in his chair, his wine glass held between long fingers. 'Did Camille not feed you enough?'

Despite all her justifications, she could feel her cheeks get hot. When she'd been turned out of the dilapidated apartment she'd shared with her mother, after her mother hadn't ever returned home, she'd had to fend for herself. And that hadn't allowed for such luxuries as pride. So why she was blushing now because he'd spotted her hunger, she had no idea.

'Just hungry today,' she muttered, not willing to give

him anything else just yet. Mainly because she'd been doing nothing but resist for so long she couldn't remember how to surrender.

'I think not.' His tone was casual. 'I think you're starving.'

She tensed. Had the way she'd been eating given her away? 'I'm not—'

'Your cheeks are hollow and you're far too thin.' His gaze was very sharp, though his posture was relaxed. 'You're homeless, aren't you?'

Did you really think you could keep it from him?

Damn. Why did he have to be so observant? Why couldn't be like all the other rich people in the world who never saw the people living on the streets? Who were blind to them? Why couldn't he have simply called the police when he'd grabbed her the night before and got her carted away to the cells?

Why do you even care?

She had no answer to that except to wish it wasn't true. Sadly, though, it was true. She did care. She didn't want him to know that she was homeless—that she had no one and nothing. And she especially didn't want him to know that she'd once been the daughter of a very rich man who'd left her to rot on the streets like so much unwanted trash. Her mother had been very clear on that point.

Except, all the wanting in the world wasn't going to change the fact that he'd picked up on a few things she'd hoped he wouldn't see and had drawn his own conclusions. Correct conclusions. So was there any point in denying it now? She could pretend she had a home and a family, but he'd see through that pretty quickly. He was that kind of man.

So, since pretending was out, Leonie decided on belligerence instead. She stared back at him, daring him to pass judgement on her. 'And if I am?'

His gaze roamed over her face, irritatingly making the heat in her cheeks deepen even more. 'And nothing,' he said at last. 'It was merely an observation.'

'Don't you want to know where and why and how it happened? Whether I'm a drug addict or an alcoholic? Why haven't I found somewhere to go or a shelter to stay in?'

'Not particularly.' His green eyes gleamed. 'But if you want to tell me any of those things I'm happy to listen.'

That surprised her. She'd been expecting him to push for more information since he'd been so emphatic about her name before. Yet apparently not.

A strange feeling settled in her gut. Almost as if she'd wanted him to ask so she could tell him and was disappointed that he hadn't.

To cover her surprise, she reached for another piece of bread, spreading it liberally with the delicious butter and eating it in slow, careful bites.

'I'll have Camille make sure you get enough to eat,' he said after a moment. 'I won't have you going hungry here.'

She swallowed the last bit of bread. 'Don't tell her—'

'I won't. Your secret's safe with me.'

She didn't want it to be reassuring, yet it was. Not that she cared about what Camille thought, but still... Questions would be asked and she didn't want questions. She didn't want to have to explain her situation to anyone—including this powerful, yet oddly reassuring duke.

He could protect you.

The thought was a discomforting one. She'd protected

herself well enough for nearly six years, so why would she need him?

You need someone, though.

No, she didn't.

She picked up her wine and took another sip, allowing the rich, dark flavour to settle on her tongue. It made her a little dizzy, but she didn't mind that.

He began to ask her a few more questions, though these were solely about how she'd found the work today and whether she had what she needed to do her job, so she answered them. Then they had a discussion about what other tasks she might like to tackle and how she'd prefer to be paid—cash, since she didn't have a bank account.

The conversation wasn't personal, his questions were not intrusive, and he didn't make any more of those unexpected movements. And after maybe another half an hour had passed his phone went. Since it was apparently urgent, he excused himself to answer it.

Leonie settled back in the chair and finished her wine. It was very warm in the room, and she was very full, and since they were both sensations she had almost never felt she wanted to enjoy them for a little while.

The deep, rich sound of his voice as he talked to whoever he was talking to was lulling her. There was warmth and texture to that voice, and it was comforting in a way she couldn't describe.

Maybe it was that voice. Or maybe it was the wine and food. Maybe it was fire crackling pleasantly in the fireplace. Or maybe it was simply the fact that she'd barely slept a wink the night before, but she found her eyes beginning to close.

It took a lot of effort to keep them open.

Too much effort.

She closed them, all her muscles relaxing, along with her ever-present vigilance.

And then she fell asleep.

At some point she became aware that she was in someone's arms and was being carried somewhere. Normally that would have been enough to have her struggling wildly and waking up. But a familiar warm and spicy scent wound around her, and a comforting heat against her side was easing her instinctive panic.

And instead of struggling she relaxed. Letting the heat and that familiar scent soothe her. Feeling those arms tighten around her.

Where she was being carried, she didn't know, and a minute or so later she didn't care.

She was already asleep again.

CHAPTER FIVE

CRISTIANO MADE AN effort over the next week to keep an eye on Leonie in an unobtrusive way, stopping by wherever she was working to exchange a few words with her. Sometimes it was just that—a few words—and sometimes it was more of a conversation.

And slowly she began to relax around him. She no longer tensed when he appeared, and during the last two visits, she hadn't even scowled.

He counted it a victory.

Of course the real victory had been that night in his study, when she'd finally given him her name.

Reaching out to grab her wrist had been a gamble, but she'd had to learn that he meant business and that he had his limits. He wasn't a man to be toyed with. Besides, he hadn't been asking for much—just her name.

She'd seemed to understand and the gamble had paid off. She hadn't given him anything else, but he hadn't pushed. He knew when to insist and when to back off. She'd eventually give him what he wanted—he was sure of it.

He'd been even more sure when he'd finished his phone call and turned around to find that she'd fallen asleep in her chair. He hadn't wanted to wake her, since the shadows under her eyes had been pronounced, but nor had he wanted to leave her sleeping in an uncomfortable position. So, compelled by an instinct he hadn't felt in years, he'd gathered her into his arms and carried her up to her room.

Another gamble, considering how hyper-vigilant she was. But she hadn't woken. Or at least she hadn't panicked. Her lovely red-gold eyelashes had fluttered and her muscles had tensed, and then, just as quickly, she'd relaxed against him. As if she'd decided she was safe.

A mistake on her part, because he wasn't safe—not in any way—but he'd liked the way she'd felt in his arms. Liked the way she'd relaxed against him as if she didn't need to fear him. Liked it too much, truth be told.

Anna had never nestled sleepily in his arms. She'd never been comfortable with his displays of affection. But he was a deeply physical man and that was how he expressed it. She had also known his darkest secret, known the damage he was capable of, and although she'd never said it outright he knew she'd always judged him for it.

He'd tried to contain himself for her, change himself for her, but it hadn't been enough in the end. Victor de Riero had offered her what Cristiano hadn't been able to, and so she'd left him.

But it was dangerous to think of Anna, so he'd shoved his memories of her away and ignored the way Leonie had felt in his arms.

Leonie hadn't mentioned it the next day when he'd stopped by the room where she was dusting, so he hadn't mentioned it, either, merely giving her a greeting and then going on his way.

Which was what he'd done the next couple of days, too, only stopping for longer on the subsequent days after that. And the day before, not only had he not had a scowl, but he thought he might have had a smile. Or at least the beginnings of one.

It was very definitely a start.

But he needed to do more.

He wasn't normally an impatient man, since he never wanted anything enough to get impatient about it, but the thought of revenge had definitely put him in an impatient mood. He needed to gain her trust and then either get her to tell him who she was or reveal that he already knew in a way that wouldn't frighten her off.

After that, he had to ascertain her feelings about her father and find out whether she'd agree to let him widen her job description, as it were. In return for a sizeable bonus, naturally.

It was a good plan, and one he was sure would work, but it would require a certain delicacy. So far he'd done well, but more needed to be accomplished—and faster.

It was a pity trust wasn't one of those things that could be compelled.

He was reflecting on that as he arrived back home late one night the following week. He'd come from a party that had started out as tedious, only to descend into unpleasant when he'd heard Victor de Riero's name being bandied about in a business discussion.

Normally that wouldn't have caused him any concern. He'd detached himself so completely from what had happened fifteen years ago that he could even have attended the same party as the man and not felt a thing.

Yet tonight even the sound of that name had set his anger burning so fiercely that some disconnected part of him had been amazed at the intensity of his emotions when for so long he'd felt nothing. It had been disturbing, and it had made him even more certain that he must move his revenge plan on faster—because the quicker he dealt with it, the easier it would be to put out the fire of his anger once and for all.

He'd left the party early, full of that intense directionless anger, and was still in a foul temper now, as he arrived home. He'd been intending to sit in the library alone, with a very good Scotch, so his mood was not improved when he found that the library was already occupied by Leonie, kneeling on the floor in front of the bookshelves once again.

She was still in her uniform, and there were cleaning implements next to her, even though it was nearly midnight and she should be in bed, asleep. Something jolted in his chest at the sight of that familiar red-gold skein hanging down on her back.

He remembered carrying her to bed that night—how that hair had brushed against his forearm and then drifted over the backs of his hands as he'd bent over to lay her down on the mattress. It had felt very silky, and the urge to touch it, to sift his fingers through it, had gripped him once again. She'd felt light in his arms, but very soft and warm and feminine, and she'd smelled subtly of the rose-scented soap her bathroom had been stocked with.

He'd been very good at not paying attention to his physical reactions around her. Very good at not thinking about that moment of chemistry in his study that night when he'd put his fingers around her wrist, touched her soft skin. And it had been soft, her pulse frantic beneath his fingertips.

It hadn't been a problem before. He was always in complete control of himself, even when it looked to the rest of the world as if he wasn't. Yet right now, looking at her kneeling there, that control seemed suddenly very tenuous.

There'd been enough beautiful women at the party tonight for him to take his pick if it was sex he wanted. He didn't have to have her. She'd be a virgin, too—he'd bet his dukedom on it—and he wasn't into virgins. They were complicated, and the last thing he needed was more complications.

Yet that didn't put a stop to the hunger that gripped him, and his temper, already on a knife-edge, worsened.

Meirda, what was she doing here? Hadn't she finished her work? There were plenty of chairs around. Why wasn't she sitting on one of them? But, most importantly, why wasn't she safely in bed and out of his reach? And why did he always find her poring over a book?

He prowled up behind her, where she knelt, but she didn't look around, once again absorbed in whatever she was reading.

'You can take that upstairs if you want,' he said, unable to keep the growl out of his voice. 'You don't have to sit on the floor.'

She gave a little start, then sprang to her feet, turning around quickly. Her violet-blue eyes were very wide, and one hand automatically went to her pocket—as if her knife was still there and not where he'd seen it last, on her bedside table.

And then, as she took in his presence, her posture relaxed as quickly as it had tensed. 'Oh...' she breathed. 'It's you.'

He should have been pleased by how quickly she'd calmed, since it indicated more progress towards her trusting him. But tonight he wasn't pleased. Tonight it rubbed against his vile temper like salt in a wound. She was the daughter of his enemy and he was going to use her to get his revenge on that *hijo de puta*. She should be afraid of him. He was dangerous—and most especially when he was angry.

Hadn't Anna always told him that he frightened her? She'd been right to be scared. He was capable of such destruction when he let his emotions get the better of him. This little kitten should be cowering, not relaxing as if she was safe.

'Yes, it is,' he agreed, his temper burning with a sullen heat. 'What are you doing in the library at this time of night?' It came out as an accusation, which wasn't helpful, but he didn't bother to adjust his tone. He wasn't in the mood for adjusting himself for anyone tonight. 'You should go to bed.'

'I was working late.' Her forehead creased, her violet-blue gaze studying him. 'Are you all right?'

A dart of something sharp he couldn't identify shot through him. Was his temper that noticeable? Maybe it was. He hadn't exactly been hiding it after all. Still, he hadn't been asked that question in a very long time. Years, possibly. Not by his staff, not his few close friends, not his lovers. And the fact that this homeless girl should be the first one to have even a fleeting concern for his wellbeing annoyed him all the more.

He smiled without humour. 'Of course. Why would you imagine I'm anything other than all right?'

'Because you're...' She made a gesture at him.

'Because I'm what?' He took a leisurely step towards her. 'Have you been watching me, *gatita*?'

Her cheeks flooded with telltale colour. 'No, I haven't.'

A lie. She *had* been watching him. How interesting.

You should order her upstairs. Away from you. Nothing good comes from your temper—you know this already.

Oh, he knew. He knew all too well. But he was tired of having to do what he always did, which was to shove that temper away. Beat it down so no one would ever know it was there. Tired of having to pretend he didn't feel it, of having to restrain himself all the time.

Dios, she was the one who'd brought all this to the surface again. This was her fault if it was anyone's.

So what are you going to do? Punish her?

He ignored the thought, taking another step towards her. 'I think you have. I think you've been watching me. And why is that?' He let his voice drop to a low purr. 'Do you see something you like?'

Something flickered through her eyes, though he couldn't tell what it was. It wasn't fear, though, and he didn't understand. She was normally wary, and yet she wasn't wary now, which was strange. Had he done his job already? Did she trust him?

Silly *gatita*. Perhaps he should show her what she had to be afraid about.

He closed the distance between them, crowding her very purposefully back against the bookshelves, and this time obvious alarm rippled across her pretty face. He was standing close enough to feel the warmth of her body and inhale the faint, sweet scent of roses. Close enough to see the pulse beating fast beneath the pale skin at the base of her throat.

Fool. Giving in to your temper will undo all the progress you've made, and you swore you wouldn't make any more mistakes this time.

Cold realisation swept through him—of what he was doing and how badly he'd allowed his control to slip. She was supposed to trust him, supposed to feel safe with him—that was the whole point. And he wasn't supposed to make any more mistakes.

'You should leave,' he forced out, trying to handle the fury that coursed through him. 'I'm not fit company right now.'

She gave him another of those wary looks, but didn't move. 'Why not?'

'Too much wine, too many women, and not enough song.' He tried to hold on to his usual lazy, casual demeanour, baring his teeth in what he hoped was a smile, but probably wasn't. 'Leave, Leonie. I'm not in the mood to be kind.'

Yet again she made no move, only studied him as if he was a mystery she wanted to unravel and not a man she should be afraid of. A man whose passions ran too hot for anyone's comfort.

'Why?' she asked again. 'What happened?'

His fury wound tighter. He didn't want to talk about this with her and he didn't know why she was even interested. She shouldn't be wanting to know more; she should be running back upstairs to the safety of her room.

'I commend your interest in my wellbeing, *gatita*. But I think it is a mistake.' He moved closer since she wasn't getting the message. 'I'm telling you to leave for a reason.'

She was still pressed up against the bookshelves behind her but, strangely, her earlier alarm seemed to have vanished. Instead she was frowning slightly, searching his face as if looking for something, her gaze full of what looked like...concern, almost.

You've done nothing to deserve it.

No, he hadn't. Not a single damn thing.

Her scent wrapped around him and he was aware that the black T-shirt of her uniform was very fitted, outlining to perfection the soft curves of her breasts. They were round and full, just the right size for his hands. Would they be sensitive if he touched them? If he put his mouth to them? Kissed them and sucked on her nipples? Some women were very sensitive there, the slightest touch making them moan, while others needed firmer handling...

'What reason is that?' Leonie asked, and her sweet husky voice did nothing to halt the flood of sexual awareness coursing through him.

There was no alarm in the question, and her gaze was direct. Almost as if she was challenging him. Which would be either very brave, or very foolish, especially when he was in this kind of mood.

'You don't want to know,' he said roughly. 'It might frighten you.'

A spark glowed suddenly in the depths of her eyes. 'I'm not scared of you.'

It was fascinating, that spark. It burned bright and hot and he couldn't drag his gaze from it. Yes, this time it was definitely a challenge, and all he could think about was the fact that Anna had never looked at him that way. Anna had never challenged him—not once.

'You should be.' His voice had deepened, become even rougher, and his groin tightened in response to her nearness. 'I've told you before. I'm not a kind man.'

'That's a lie.' She gave him another searching look, apparently oblivious to the danger. 'You've been nothing but kind since I got here.'

Naturally she'd think that. She wasn't to know that he was being kind only because he wanted something from her. That he wasn't doing this out of the goodness of his heart, but to appease his own desire for vengeance.

Tell her, then. Tell her so she knows.

But if he told her she might run, and he couldn't afford for her to do that. Not yet.

She might run from you anyway if you keep on like this.

It was true. Which meant he needed to pull himself together—perhaps call one of those women who'd indicated interest tonight. It had been a while since he'd taken anyone to bed, so maybe it was that getting to him. Sex had always been his go-to when it came to working out his more primitive emotions. That was why he revelled in it.

'My kindness has a threshold,' he said instead. 'And you're approaching it.'

Her head tilted, her gaze still bright. Almost as if she was pushing him.

'Why? What have I done? You're not very good at answering questions, are you?'

He should have moved—should have stepped away. Should definitely not still be standing there, so close to her, now he'd decided he was going to find some alternative female company.

Yet he couldn't bring himself to move. He was caught by the bright spark in her eyes and by her sweet scent. There was colour in her cheeks still and the pulse at the base of her throat was beating even faster. Her mouth was full and red. Such temptation.

He could kiss that mouth. He could stop her questions and her ill-considered challenges simply by covering it with his own. Would she taste sweet? As sweet as she smelled?

'You haven't done anything but be where you shouldn't

be.' He lifted his hand before he could stop himself and gently brushed her bottom lip with his fingertips. 'Which is a mistake, *gatita*.'

Her mouth was as soft as he'd thought it would be, and velvety like rose petals. She stilled, her eyes going wide. But she didn't pull away.

Aren't you going to find yourself another woman?

He was. So why he wasn't—why he was standing here and touching *this* woman he had no idea. It shouldn't matter which woman he touched, and since Anna he'd made sure it didn't. He didn't need someone who was his—not again.

Not when you can't be trusted with them.

The thought should have made him move away. But it didn't. Instead, he put one hand on the bookshelf behind her head, leaning over her while he dragged the tip of his finger across the softness of her skin, tracing the line of her lower lip.

She shivered, taking another audible breath, her gaze never leaving his face. Her body was stiff with tension and yet she didn't move, the spark in her eyes leaping higher.

'Why are you touching me?' Her voice had become even huskier than normal.

'Why do you think?'

Every muscle in his body had tightened; his groin was aching. His anger had dulled. Physical desire was smoothing the sharp edges and making it less acute. Replacing it with another, safer hunger.

'This is the reason you should have left, Leonie.' He dragged his finger gently over her bottom lip once more, pressing against the full softness of it. 'Because you're a lovely woman and I'm a very, *very* bad man.'

* * *

Leonie couldn't move. Or rather, she probably could—it was more that she didn't want to. And she didn't understand why, because what the duke was doing to her should have sent her bolting from the room in search of her knife.

A week ago it would have.

But that had been before she'd spent a whole week in his house, cleaning the rooms she'd been assigned to. A whole week of a comfortable bed and good food, of being clean and dry and warm. A whole week of being safe.

A whole week of him stopping by every day to visit her—sometimes just to say hello, sometimes to chat.

She hadn't realised how much she liked his little visits until the fourth day, when he hadn't stopped by the room she was cleaning and she'd begun to feel annoyed, wondering if she'd missed him. Wondering if she'd been forgotten.

If she'd still been the Leonie of a week ago being forgotten would have been preferable. But she wasn't that Leonie. Not since she'd fallen asleep in his study that night and he'd gathered her up in his arms and put her to bed.

She'd woken the next morning disorientated and restless, panicking slightly when she'd realised what had happened. But when she'd jerked back the quilt she'd found she was still fully clothed. Only her shoes had been removed. She'd been asleep, at her most vulnerable, and all he'd done was tuck her into bed.

Perhaps that was why she felt no fear now, even though he was definitely touching her and threatening her into the bargain. But it wasn't a threat like those she'd experienced before, that promised only violence and pain. No, this was different. This promised something else, and she wasn't at all sure she wouldn't like whatever it was he was promising.

Especially if it was this prickling kind of heat sweeping over her, making her mouth feel full and sensitive. Making something inside her pulse hard and low, with that same hunger she'd felt the night he'd gripped her wrist.

Unfamiliar feelings. Good feelings.

She didn't want to move in case they vanished, as everything good in her life always seemed to do.

She tipped her head back against the bookshelf, staring up him, right into those intense green eyes. There was a flame burning there, giving out more heat than the fire that night in his study, and she wanted more of it. More of the heat of his tall, powerful body so close to hers.

Men had never been anything but threatening to her before, and sex something only offered as a transaction or taken with violence. She knew that there was more to it than that, because she'd watched couples holding hands in the streets. Couples hugging. Couples kissing.

She'd once been interrupted by a well-dressed man and woman slipping into the alley she'd been sleeping in at the time, and had watched unseen from behind a pile of boxes as the man had gently pressed the woman to the brick wall of the alley and lifted her dress. The woman had moaned, but not in protest. Her hands had clutched at the man, pulling him to her, and when she'd cried out it hadn't been in pain.

Leonie had wondered what it would be like to be that woman, but she knew she never would be. Because to be that woman she'd have to be clean and wear a nice dress. To be that woman she'd have to be cared for, and the only person who'd ever cared for her was herself.

So, since physical pleasure was not for people like her, she'd had to settle on invisibility instead. Blending into the background and never calling attention to herself, staying unnoticed and unseen, the way her mother had always taught her.

Except she wasn't unseen now. The duke had seen her, and continued to see her, and with every brush of his finger he made her more and more visible. More and more aware of how she liked that touch, how she wanted it. How cold she'd been before, and also how lonely.

And now he was here, with his hot green eyes and his hard, muscular body, and he was touching her.

He was turning her into that woman in the pretty dress in the alley and she liked it. She didn't want to run away. She wanted to be that woman. The woman who deserved pleasure and who got it.

'I don't think you're bad.' She held his gaze, every nerve-ending she had focused on the touch of his finger on her mouth. 'If you were that bad you wouldn't have told me to leave.'

'I don't think you know bad men, in that case.'

His gaze was all-consuming, a dark forest full of secrets, making her want to journey into it, discover what those secrets were.

'Of course I do.' Her mouth felt achingly sensitive. His touch was so light it was oddly maddening. 'I see them all the time on the streets. And I avoid them whenever I can.'

'So why aren't you running now?'

He shifted, leaning a fraction closer, bracing himself on the bookshelf behind her while his fingers moved on her mouth, his thumb pressing gently on her lip as if testing it.

'Or perhaps it's because you can't see past a warm bed and good food.'

That could be true. He might have lulled her into a false sense of security. She'd been wrong a couple of times before. But she didn't think she was wrong now. He'd had plenty of opportunity to touch her, to take what he wanted, and he hadn't. He had no reason to do so now.

Yes, so why now?

Good point. His obvious sexual interest was rather sudden. Perhaps he didn't want her the way she thought he did. Perhaps he was only trying to frighten her away.

After all, he'd been in a strange mood when he'd come in, with a sharp, raw energy to him, his eyes glittering like shards of green glass. Anger, she was sure, though she wasn't sure why.

Perhaps he'd come into the library hoping for some time to himself and found her there instead, intruding. Ignoring him when he told her to leave. And now he'd had to take more drastic steps to scare her off.

He doesn't want you, idiot. Why would he?

Her stomach dipped, an aching disappointment filling her. There was no reason for him to want her. She was just a homeless person he'd rescued from the streets and for some reason been kind to. And because she hadn't taken the hint and left when he'd asked her to he'd had to be more explicit. All this touching and getting close to her wasn't actually about *her*, and she'd be an idiot to think otherwise.

She tore her gaze away, not wanting him to see her disappointment or the hurt that had lodged inside her. 'Perhaps you're right. Perhaps you're really not all that kind after all.' She tried to sound as level as she could. 'If you want me to go, you'd better move.'

Yet the hard, masculine body crowding her against the bookshelves didn't move. She stared at the fine white cotton of his shirt—he was in evening clothes tonight, so it was obvious he'd been to some fancy party or other—her heartbeat thudding in her ears, a sick feeling in her gut.

Then the finger stroking her mouth dropped, as did the arm near her ear, and the duke straightened up, giving her some room.

The feeling of disappointment deepened.

She pushed herself away from the bookshelf, wanting to get away now, to get some distance from him. But before she could go past him, his fingers closed around her upper arm.

Her bare upper arm.

Leonie froze. His fingers burned against her skin the way they had that night in his study, making her breath catch and that restless heat sweep over her yet again.

She didn't look at him, staring straight ahead, her pulse racing. 'I thought you wanted me to go?'

'I thought I did, too.' His voice was dark, with threads of heat winding through it. 'You're really not scared of me, are you?'

'Does it matter?' She tried not to shiver in response to the sound of his voice, though it was difficult. 'I'm sorry I was here when you came in. I know you wanted to be alone, and I shouldn't—'

His fingers tightened around her arm abruptly and she broke off.

'Why did you think I wanted to be alone?' he demanded.

'You looked angry, and I shouldn't have been in here.'

'You're fine to be in here. Also, yes, it does matter.'

His fingers felt scorching. 'You should let me go.' She

kept her gaze on the wall opposite, trying to ignore his heat and the delicious scent of his aftershave. 'I know you were trying to scare me away—but, for the record, it won't work.'

There was a tense silence, full of the same humming tension that had surrounded them last week in his study.

'It won't, hmm...?'

Unexpectedly, his thumb stroked the underside of her arm in a caress that sent goosebumps scattering all over her skin. 'That's something you shouldn't have told me.'

'Why not?'

'Because it only makes me want try harder to scare you, of course.'

The sound of her heart hammered in her ears. She stared blindly across the room, every sense she possessed concentrated on the man standing beside her, holding her.

Was that another warning? And if it was, why was he still holding her? If he really wanted her to leave he only needed to open his hand and she'd be free.

Yet he hadn't.

She tried to process what that meant, but it was difficult when his thumb was pressing against the sensitive flesh of her under-arm, caressing lightly.

You could pull away. You don't have to stand here.

That was true. She didn't need to stand there being reminded of how empty and cold her life was, of all the good things she was missing out on. She didn't need to be reminded of how unwanted and unneeded she was.

Anyway, she had a warm bed, and food, and a job. Wanting more than that was just being greedy. She should be happy with what she had.

'All this talk of scaring me and being bad—yet you're not doing anything but hold on to me.' She kept her gaze resolutely ahead. 'I know you don't really want me. So why don't you just be done with it and let me go?'

There was a moment of silence and then she was being tugged around to face him, his glittering green gaze clashing with hers.

'What on earth makes you think I don't want you?' he demanded.

'Why would you?' She lifted her chin, prepared for the truth, ignoring the hurt lodged deep inside her. 'I'm just some poor homeless woman you picked up from the streets. No one else has ever wanted me so why should you?'

The hot flame in his eyes leapt, an emotion she couldn't name flickering over his handsome face. *'Gatita...'*

He looked as if he might say something more, but he didn't. Instead he jerked her suddenly towards him.

Not expecting it, she flung up her hands, her palms connecting with the heat and hardness of his broad chest. His fingers had curled around both her upper arms now, keeping her prisoner, and he'd bent his head, so his green eyes were all she could see.

'You are very foolish indeed if you think that,' he said, in a soft, dangerous voice.

Then, before she could say anything more, his mouth covered hers.

She froze in shock. She'd never been kissed before—had never wanted to be. Although sometimes, when the nights were very dark and she was especially cold, she'd remember that man and woman in the alleyway. Remember how the woman had cried out and how the man had kissed her, silencing her. And she'd wonder what it would feel like to have someone's mouth touching hers. Kissing her...

Now she knew. And it became very clear why that woman had clutched at the man kissing her.

The duke's lips were warm, so much softer than she'd expected a man's lips to be, and the subtle pressure and implicit demand were making a river of unfamiliar heat course the length of her spine.

She trembled, curling her fingers into the warm cotton of his shirt, her own mouth opening beneath his almost automatically. And he took advantage, his tongue pushing inside, tasting her, coaxing her, beginning to explore her.

A low, helpless moan escaped her. The delicious flavour of him was filling her senses and making her want more. She clutched at his shirt tighter, pressing herself closer. The heat of his kiss was melting all the frozen places inside her. All the lonely places. Lighting up all the dark corners of her soul.

Her awareness narrowed on the heat of his mouth, the slow exploration of his tongue, the dark, rich flavour that was all him and the iron-hard body she was pressed against.

It was overwhelming.

It was not enough.

It was everything she'd missed out on, all the good things she'd never had, and now she'd had a taste she wanted more.

She wanted them all.

'Cristiano…' she murmured against his mouth. And the name he'd given her, that she'd only used once before now, came out of her as easily as breathing. 'Please…'

CHAPTER SIX

HE SHOULDN'T HAVE kissed her. Yet now her mouth was open beneath his, the sweet taste of her was on his tongue and the slender heat of her body was pressed against him, he couldn't stop.

She was right in thinking he'd been trying to scare her. And he'd expected it to be easy—that a blatantly sexual touch would have her jerking away from him and leaving the room.

But she hadn't run as he'd anticipated. Because it seemed she never did the thing he anticipated.

Instead she'd only stayed where she was and let him touch her. Let his fingers trace her soft mouth, looking up at him, her eyes darkening with what could only be arousal.

He should have let her go. He hadn't needed to keep holding on to her and he wasn't sure why he had. He certainly shouldn't have compounded his mistake by covering her mouth with his—not when he'd already decided that he wasn't going to have her.

But something in his heart had stopped him. Because the way she'd looked so defiantly up at him, telling him that no one had ever wanted her before and why should he… Well, he hadn't been able to stand it.

A kiss to prove her wrong—that was all it was supposed to be. A kiss to ease the hurt she hadn't been able to hide. And maybe, too, a kiss to frighten her away once and for all.

No, you kissed her because you wanted to, because you wanted her.

Whatever the reason, it didn't matter. What did matter was the furnace that had roared to life inside him the minute her mouth was under his. The very second he'd felt her soften and melt against him, a throaty, husky moan escaped her.

And he wasn't sure why, or what it was about her that had got him burning hot and instantly hard. Yet as she arched against him, her fingers tugging on his shirt, the desire that just about strangled him was as if he hadn't had a woman in months. Years, even.

He could taste her desperation, could feel it in the way she pressed against him, in the sound of his name whispered in her husky voice, so erotic it felt as if she'd reached inside his trousers and wrapped her fingers directly around his shaft.

Anna had never done any of those things during sex. She'd never clutched at him, never moaned his name or pressed herself against him. She'd found his brand of earthy, physical sexuality uncomfortable, telling him he was too demanding. He'd tried to be less so, restraining himself to make her comfortable, turning sex from something passionate into something softer, more palatable, and thus more acceptable. Though it still hadn't been enough for her.

Since she'd left, and since his son had been claimed by another, he'd lost his taste for passion. Something easy, fun and pleasurable—that was all he wanted from sex, nothing more. His lovers could touch his body but they touched nothing else, and that was the way he made sure it always was.

But there was something about the way Leonie clutched at his shirt, her mouth open and hungry beneath his, whispering his name against his lips, that reached inside him, unleashing something he'd kept caged for a long time.

Raw, animal passion.

Perhaps it was because she wasn't a random woman he'd met at a party, or some pretty socialite he'd picked up at a bar. A woman who didn't want more from him than one night and a couple of orgasms, and that was all.

Perhaps it was the wrongness of it. Because there were so many reasons why it was a bad idea. She'd been living on the streets. She was homeless. She was a virgin. She was the daughter of his enemy and he was going to use her to get his revenge. He should not be hard for her, let alone kissing her hungrily late at night in his study.

And yet when she whispered, 'Cristiano... Please...' and arched against him, the soft curves of her breasts pressing against his chest, the sound of his name spoken in her husky voice echoing in his ears, all he could think about was giving her exactly what she was begging for.

After all, who was he to deny her? He'd never been a man to refuse anyone when it came to sex, still less one bright and beautiful woman whom he wanted very much.

Besides, perhaps taking her would cement what trust there was between them rather than break it. And when desire was this strong it was always better not to fight it. Always better to take command and sate it so it was easier to control later on.

That all sounds like some excellent justification.

But Cristiano was done listening to his better self.

He dropped his hands from her upper arms to her hips, letting them rest there a second to get her used to his touch. Then he slid them higher, until his palms were gently cupping her breasts.

She gave another of those delicious little moans, shuddering and then arching into his hands like a cat wanting to be stroked. He kept his mouth on hers, making the kiss teasing as he traced her soft curves with his fingertips before brushing his thumbs over the hard outlines of her nipples.

She gasped and he wanted to devour her whole, but he forced himself to lift his mouth from hers instead, to stare down into her face to check if she was still with him. Her cheeks were deeply flushed, her lips full and red from the kiss.

'Why did you stop?' she asked breathlessly. 'Please don't.'

Oh, yes, she was with him.

Satisfaction pulsed through him and he took her mouth again, nipping at her bottom lip at the same time as he pinched her nipples lightly, making her jerk and shudder against him.

His own heartbeat roared in his ears; his groin was aching. He wanted her naked, wanted her skin bare to his touch, wanted her hands on him, clutching at him. He wanted her desperate for him.

He'd given her food and drink. Given her a job. Given her a bed. And now he wanted to give her pleasure, too. He didn't pause to examine why this was important to him—he just wanted to.

Dangerous. You know how you get when you give in to your passions.

Ah, but this was only sex. It wouldn't touch his emotions in any way. He'd make sure of it.

'Gatita,' he murmured roughly against her hungry mouth. 'In ten seconds I'm going to have you naked on the floor, so if that's not what you want you'd better tell me right now.'

'I want it.' There was no hesitation in her voice, no coy dancing around the subject. 'Cristiano, please—I want it.'

Desire soaked through every husky word, and when he lifted his head and looked down into her eyes a part of him was shocked by the nakedness of her desire. Because she made no effort to hide it. Everything she felt was laid bare for him to see, exposing a vulnerability he was sure she hadn't meant to expose.

He could use that against her if he chose—get her to do anything he wanted if he handled it right. Even convince her to be his wife, for example. And if he'd been a more unscrupulous man...

What are you talking about? You are an unscrupulous man.

Oh, he was. But there was something innocent about Leonie, an honesty that he found almost painful. And he could not bring himself to take advantage of it.

Though she should know better than to let herself be so vulnerable—especially with a man like him. He was dangerous and hadn't he told her that? She needed to be more wary, more on her guard.

He bent his head further, moving his mouth to her jaw, kissing down the side of her neck and nipping her again in sensual punishment. But, again, she didn't push him away, only pulled harder on his shirt instead, as if she wanted more.

It was like petrol being poured over an already blazing fire, making his own passion leap high and hot.

Without another word, he lifted her into his arms and carried her over to the soft silk rug in front of the empty fireplace. Then he laid her down on it and took the hem of her T-shirt in his hands, dragging it up and over her head.

She didn't stop him, and a wave of gorgeous pink swept down her throat and over her chest as he uncovered her. The colour turned her eyes a vivid blue and made the plain black bra she wore stand out. But not for long. He undid the catch and stripped that from her, too, leaving her upper body bare.

Instantly her hands went to cover herself, but he caught her wrists, preventing her. 'No,' he said roughly, unable to keep his voice level. 'I want to look at you.'

She swallowed, but there was no resistance in her as he pushed her down onto her back, taking her arms above her head and pinning them to the rug, gripping her crossed wrists in one hand.

Lying there stretched out beneath him, all silky pale skin, her breasts exposed, hard nipples flushed a deep pink, she was the most delectable thing he'd ever seen.

He stared down into her eyes, watching the passion that burned there burn even higher as he stroked his free hand up and down her sides.

'Cristiano...' she said breathlessly, shivering.

'What it is, *gatita*? Do you need more?' He moved his hand to cup one of those perfect breasts, felt her skin hot against his palm. 'This, perhaps?'

'Oh...' she sighed. 'That's so—'

She broke off on a gasp as he rubbed his thumb over one hard nipple before pinching it, watching the pleasure chase itself over her lovely face. Her body arched beneath his hand, her lashes half closing.

'Oh…that's so good. More…'

His little kitten was demanding.

Yours? Already?

Maybe. And why not? No one else had claimed her, so why couldn't he? She was so very responsive, so very rewarding. Making her gasp like that might even become addictive.

He pinched her again, rolling her nipple between his thumb and forefinger, making her writhe. 'You'd best be more respectful,' he murmured, teasing the tip of her breast relentlessly. 'Please and thank you are always welcome.'

'Please…' She moaned softly, arching yet again beneath him. 'Please, more…'

'So obedient.' He eased his hand lower, over the soft skin of her stomach to the fastening of her plain black trousers. 'I like that, though. I like how you beg for me.'

Flicking open the button of her trousers, he grabbed the zip and drew it down. Then he pushed his hand beneath the fabric and over the front of her underwear. She shuddered as his fingers traced her through the damp cotton, pleasure and a certain wonder making her eyes glow. She was looking at him as though he'd shown her something amazing, the most precious thing in all the universe.

'Oh…' Her eyes went very wide as he pressed a finger gently against the most sensitive part of her and then circled around it, making her hips shudder and lift. 'What are you doing?' She didn't sound alarmed, only a little shocked.

'Giving you pleasure.' His voice came out rougher

than he'd intended. 'Does it feel good, Leonie? Does it feel good when I touch you?'

'Yes, oh, yes...' The breath sighed out of her and her gaze fixed to his, more wonder and amazement in her eyes. 'I never thought...it would...feel like this.'

She was so unguarded, so sincere. This woman had been denied a lot of things—warmth and comfort and safety. She'd been denied physical pleasure, too, and that was a crime. Because it was becoming apparent to him that she was a creature of passion, greedy for all the pleasure he could give her. And he had a lot of that to give.

Pleasure wasn't new to him, but for some reason introducing her to it was completely addictive. From the way she shivered under his hand to the flush in her silky skin. From the sounds she made to the wonder of discovery as she looked at him.

It was a discovery for him as well, he realised. It had been a long time since he'd been engaged in bed. He always gave his partners pleasure, but only in so far as it affected his own reputation. It was never about the woman in particular.

But now it was about this woman. He wanted to give her something she'd never had before—wanted to show her something new. He wanted her to look at him exactly the way she was looking at him now, as if she'd never seen anything or anyone so amazing in all her life.

The way no one, not even Anna, had ever looked at him.

You can't give that up.

A dark, ferocious thing stretched out lazily inside him, flexing its claws.

Well, maybe he didn't have to give it up. Why should he? She wanted him—that was obvious—and passion like hers didn't stay sated. This needn't be a one-off thing. He was planning on marrying her anyway, so why not make it a true marriage for a time?

Are you sure that's a good idea? Look what happened last time with Anna.

Yes, but that had only been because those dangerous emotions of his had been involved, and they weren't here. He didn't love Leonie and she didn't love him. He was simply taking advantage of their intense physical chemistry, nothing more.

She might not feel that way when you tell her you've known who she is all along.

Cristiano ignored that thought, slipping his hand beneath the fabric of her underwear, then sliding his fingers over her slick, wet flesh. She gave a little cry, pushing herself into his touch, her eyes darkening as her pupils dilated.

Satisfaction deepened inside him. He could have watched the pleasure rippling over her face for ever. 'You like that, *mi corazón*? Do you like it when I stroke you here?'

He found the small, sensitive bud between her thighs and brushed the tip of his finger over and around it. She gasped, shivering.

'And here?'

He shifted his hand, put his thumb where his finger had been, then slid that finger down through the slick folds of her sex to the entrance of her body, easing gently inside.

'Do you like it when I touch you here?'

Her cheeks were deeply flushed and she moved restlessly, unable to keep still. 'Yes...' Her voice had become even more hoarse. 'Oh, yes... Cristiano... I need...'

He could become addicted to hearing his name spoken like that...husky and soft and desperate. Just as he could become addicted to the silky, slippery feel of her flesh and the hot grip of her body around his finger. To the way she shook and gasped and arched. To the obvious pleasure she was feeling and didn't hide.

His groin was aching, his own desire winding tight, and he wanted to be inside her with a desperation he hadn't thought possible.

But he wanted to watch her come even more. So he eased his fingers in and out of her, adding more pressure and friction with his thumb until her eyes went wide and her mouth opened and her body convulsed.

She cried out in shocked pleasure as her climax hit, and he leaned down and kissed her, tasting that pleasure for himself.

Cristiano's mouth on hers was so hot and so delicious she could hardly bear it. Waves of the most intense pleasure were shaking her, and all she could do was lie there and let them wash over her.

She'd told him the truth when she'd said she'd had no idea it would feel like this. She really hadn't. Had the woman against that wall felt the same pleasure? Was it this that had made her cry out? Because, yes, *now* she understood. Now she got it completely.

When Cristiano had touched her she'd felt as if something was blooming inside her. A flower she'd thought had died, which had turned out to be only dormant, waiting for the sun, and now the sun was shining and she was opening up to it, revelling in it.

She hadn't been afraid. His kiss had been hot but his hands gentle, and when a fit of modesty had overcome her when he'd taken her bra off he'd been very clear that he wanted to look at her. That he liked looking at her.

And so she'd let him. And the longer he'd looked, the more she'd wanted him to. Because she'd seen the effect she'd had on him, the heat burning in his eyes, and it had made her feel...beautiful. She'd never felt that before, nor ever been conscious of her own feminine power. Her ability to make him burn as much as he made her.

Then he'd touched her, and the world around her had turned to fire.

Perhaps she should be ashamed that she'd been so open with her responses. Perhaps she should have been more guarded. But the pleasure had been too intense, and she simply hadn't been able to hide her feelings.

He'd touched her as if she wasn't some dirty forgotten kid that he'd found on the streets of Paris. He'd touched her as if she was precious...as if she was worth something. He'd touched her as if he cared about her, and she realised that she wanted him to.

It didn't make any sense—not when she hadn't known him long—yet every touch had only made her more certain. He'd given her many things she'd been missing in her life and now he was giving her another—something she'd never thought she'd want.

And, despite the fact that he'd seemed so angry when he'd come into the library earlier, he wasn't taking that anger out on her. He wasn't taking from her at all.

He was giving to her. Giving heat and a shivery desperation. A delicious need. Pleasure to chase away the cold and the dark, the fear and the loneliness. So much pleasure...

She wanted more of it.

She tried to pull her hands away from his restraining

hold, but his grip only firmed as his glittering green eyes scanned her from head to foot.

'Are you okay?'

His voice was a soft, roughened caress, whispering over her skin like velvet.

'Did you like that?'

'Yes. Very much.' She didn't sound much better herself. 'But I want you. I want to touch you.'

There was no hiding it so she didn't bother.

He swept his free hand down the length of her body in a long stroke that soothed her at the same time as it excited her.

'There will be time for that. But first, you're wearing far too many clothes.'

With practiced, careful hands he stripped the rest of the clothing from her body, finally baring her.

She'd thought she might feel terribly vulnerable and exposed, being naked in front of a man. Being naked in front of anyone, really. But she didn't feel either of those things. Only strangely powerful as he pulled the fabric away from her and she saw the look on his face became hungrier, sharper, as if the sight of her was something he'd been waiting lifetimes for.

And when she was finally naked, lying back on the rug, he knelt over her, his gaze roaming all over her body, and she felt for the first time in her life as if maybe there was something worthwhile about her after all.

What it was, she didn't know. But it was certainly something that had this powerful duke looking at her as if she was the Holy Grail itself.

He ran his fingertips lightly all over her, inciting her, watching her face as he did so, gauging her every response as if there was nothing more important in the world than discovering which touches made her shiver and which made her moan. Which ones made her pant his name.

She'd long since lost any shyness by the time he pushed apart her legs, brushing his mouth over her trembling stomach before moving further down. And then all she could do was thread her fingers in his hair as he put that clever mouth of his between her thighs.

Pleasure exploded through her as he began to explore, his fingers delicately parting her wet flesh while his tongue licked and caressed, driving her higher and higher. Making her cry out as the most delicious ecstasy threaded through her.

She'd never thought this feeling would be hers. Never thought that sex could be something so intense, so incredible, that it would feel so good. She'd never thought it would make her feel treasured and desired rather than dirty and worthless, but with every flick of his tongue and stroke of his hand that was what he made her feel.

She pulled on his hair, crying his name as he pushed his tongue inside her and she shattered for a second time, her climax so all-consuming that all she could do was lie there with her eyes closed as it washed over her, feeling him stroke her gently as he moved away.

Then there came the rustle of clothing and the sound of a zip being drawn down, the crinkle of foil. And then the brush of hot skin on hers, setting every nerve-ending to aching life once again.

She opened her eyes.

The duke was kneeling between her spread thighs, tall, powerful and extremely naked. And somehow he seemed even more intimidating without his clothes on, because all that lazy amusement, the studied air of ennui, had vanished completely as if it had never been.

It was a smokescreen, she realised. A distraction. A disguise hiding the true nature of the man beneath it.

She'd imagined him as a panther, lazily sunning himself on a branch, and he was that. But a panther was a predator—and that was what she was looking at now, not the lazy cat.

He was all velvet tanned skin drawn over sharply defined muscle, broad and powerful and strong. A work of art. A Greek statue come to life. As hard as the bronze from which he'd been fashioned yet not cold, but hot. Heated metal and oiled silk.

And his beautiful face was drawn tight with hunger and intent. His eyes had narrowed; hot emerald was glittering from between silky black lashes. The panther ready to pounce. The predator ready to feast.

A delicious shiver chased over her body and she allowed herself to look down to where he was hot and hard and ready for her. She'd never thought that could be beautiful as well, but it was. She pushed herself up on one hand and reached to touch him, and he made no move to stop her, letting her fingers brush along the velvet-smooth skin of his shaft.

She looked up at his face as she did it, wanting to see what effect her touch had on him, and was thrilled to see a muscle jump in the side of his impressive jaw.

'No playing, *gatita*,' he murmured, his rich voice dark and thick with heat. 'Like I said, my patience is limited.'

'I want to touch you, though.' She closed her fingers around him, marvelling at how hard he was and yet how soft and smooth his skin felt. 'You're so hard…' She squeezed experimentally.

He hissed, and then suddenly everything was moving very quickly. He pulled her hand away and pushed her down on her back, his long, muscular body settling over hers. She protested, but he shook his head, the smile he gave her sharp and edged.

'You can touch me later. Seems I have limited patience where you are concerned.'

She liked that. Liked the way her touch could incite him the way his could incite her.

She wanted to help him with the protection, too, but he gave a sharp shake of his head, dealing with it himself. And then his hands were sliding beneath her bottom, gripping her tight and lifting her, and he was positioning himself so he was pressing gently at her entrance.

'Are you ready for me?'

His jaw was set and hard, every muscle in his body drawn tight and ready. All that strength and power was held back, and not without effort. But it was definitely held back. For her.

'Answer me. I'm not made of stone.'

What a lie. He *was* made of stone. Not bronze after all, but hard, living rock that she couldn't stop touching. Enduring and powerful. She could shelter beneath him right here and nothing would touch her.

The feeling was so intense she put her hands on his chest and spread out her fingers, stroking up over all that hard muscle to his strong shoulders. Holding on.

'I'm ready,' she whispered.

And he didn't hesitate, his fingers tightening as he pushed into her. She gasped as she felt her flesh part for him, in an intense yet delicious stretch, and tensed, ready for pain, because this was supposed to hurt. Yet apart from a slight pinch there was nothing. Only more of that sensual stretch that had her panting and twisting in his arms as she tried to adjust to the sensation.

'Look at me,' he ordered. 'Look at me, Leonie.'

So she did, staring straight up into his eyes, and suddenly everything clicked into place. She was made for him. Her body was made especially for him—for his hands and his mouth, for the hard, male part of him, and he was where he was supposed to be. He might be holding her, but she was also holding him.

'Cristiano...' She lingered over the sound of it, loving how it felt to say it. Loving, too, the way his eyes flared as she said it. So she said it again, digging her nails into his skin, lifting her hips, because she was ready for him to move. Ready for him to take her on another journey.

'Demanding, *gatita*,' he growled. 'You are perfect.'

Then he covered her mouth in a kiss so hot and blinding she trembled and he began to move, the long, lazy glide of him inside her making more of that intense, delicious pleasure sweep over her.

She tried to press herself harder against him, because it wasn't quite enough and she didn't know how to get more, and then he reached down and hooked one hand behind her knee, drawing her leg up and around his hip, allowing him to sink deeper, and she moaned in delight against his mouth.

He felt so good. The glide of his hips, the silk of his skin, the flex and release of all those powerful muscles as he thrust in and out. The warm spice of his scent was cut through with the musk of his arousal. It was delicious.

She sank her teeth into his lower lip, hardly aware of what she was doing, only knowing she wanted even more of him and this insanely pleasurable movement.

He growled in response—a deep rumble in his chest that sent chills through her.

Yes, she wanted the panther. The raw untamed part of him, not the lazy, civilised man he was on the outside. Not the smokescreen. Did anyone else know he was this way? Was he like this when he made love to other women?

She didn't like that thought—not at all. She wanted him to be like this with her and only her.

She bit him again, scratching him with her nails, thrilled when he grabbed her hands and held them down on either side of her head.

He lifted his mouth from hers and looked into her eyes as he thrust hard and deep. 'You like showing me your claws, don't you?' He sounded breathless. 'What's that all about, hmm…?'

'You're not the only one who's bad.' She put a growl of her own into her voice as she pulled her hands away, running her nails down his back in a long scratch, lifting her hips to meet his thrust. 'You're not the one who's dangerous.'

'Is that so?' He thrust harder, pushing deeper, making her gasp and arch her back, her nails digging in. 'Show me how bad you are, then, *leona*. Show me your teeth.'

Pleasure twisted inside her and she turned her head, bit his shoulder, tasting the salt and musk of his skin, loving how he gave another growl deep in his throat and moved faster.

She clung to him, licking him, biting him, scratching him as pleasure drew so tight that she didn't think she could bear it. She called his name desperately and he answered, shifting one hand down between them and stroking her where she needed it most. And then she had to turn her face against his neck as everything came apart inside her. Tears flooded her eyes and she was sobbing his name as ecstasy annihilated her.

She had a dim sense of him moving faster, harder, and then she heard his own roar of release, felt his arms coming around her and holding her, his big, hot body over her and around her, inside her.

Protecting her.

CHAPTER SEVEN

CRISTIANO PULLED A shirt on, slowly doing up the buttons, then methodically starting on the cuffs. He stood at the window of his bedroom while he did so, his attention on the garden below, though he wasn't looking at the view.

He was too busy thinking about what he was going to say to the woman still asleep in the bed behind him. His little *gatita*. Though she wasn't really a kitten. Not after last night. Last night he'd discovered she was a lioness, and he had the scratches down his back to prove it.

It would have made him smile if he'd been in a smiling mood, but he wasn't.

There were a number of things he wanted to do, and he couldn't do any of them until he'd told her that he'd known who she was from the moment he'd taken her home. And that he intended to marry her to take his revenge on her father.

She probably wasn't going to take either of those things well.

Are you sure it's wise to tell her now?

He frowned at the garden for a moment, then turned around.

Leonie was curled up in the centre of his bed, her hair a scatter of brilliant red-gold across his white pillows.

She was fast sleep, with the sheet falling down off her shoulders a little, revealing pale, milky skin.

Last night she'd felt like pure joy in his hands, passionate and generous and honest. Pleasure had been a discovery and she a fascinated explorer. She'd denied him nothing, taken everything he'd given, and now all he could think about was doing it again. And again and again.

He hadn't had sex like that in years—if ever.

Leonie hadn't found his passion frightening or uncomfortable, the way Anna had. No, she'd demanded it. And then, when he'd given it to her, she'd demanded more.

His groin hardened, and the decision he'd made in the early hours of the morning, when he'd had to get up and have a cold shower so he could sleep, was now a certainty.

He'd take her back to San Lorenzo, his ancestral estate. There he would have her all to himself. He could certainly tell her about his plans here, but perhaps it would be better if she was at home in Spain. Where he could keep an eye on her.

The chances of her running away or not wanting anything to do with him once she found out about his plans were slim—or so he anticipated—but it was better to be safe than sorry.

Plus, marrying her in the ancient Velazquez family chapel would no doubt rub further salt in the wound for Victor de Riero. A further declaration of Cristiano's possession.

And if she refuses to marry you?

He would just ensure that she wouldn't. Everyone had a price, and no doubt so did she.

Finishing with his cuffs, he moved over to the bed and bent, stroking his fingers along one bare shoulder, smiling as she shivered. Her red-gold lashes fluttered and then she let out a small sigh, rolling over onto her back. The sheet fell all the way to her waist, exposing those small, perfect breasts and their little pink nipples.

He was very tempted to taste one of them, to make her gasp the way he had the night before. But that wouldn't get them any closer to San Lorenzo, and now he'd decided to go he saw no reason to linger in Paris.

'Wake up, sleepy *gatita*,' he murmured, unable to stop himself from brushing his fingers over one pert nipple, watching as it hardened, feeling his own hunger tighten along with it.

She sighed and lifted her arms, giving such a sensual stretch he almost changed his plans right there and then in favour of staying a few more hours in bed with her.

Her eyes opened, deep violet this morning, and she smiled. It took his breath away.

'Good morning.' Her gaze dropped down his body before coming to his face again. 'You're dressed. That's unfortunate.'

He smiled, the beast inside him stretching again, purring in pleasure at her blatant stare. 'Hold that thought. I have plans for us today.'

'What plans?' Her eyes widened and she sat up suddenly. 'What's the time? Am I late for work? Where are my—?'

'There will be no work for you today. Or perhaps any other day.'

He saw shock, hurt and anger ripple across her lovely face. 'Why not? I thought I—'

'Relax, *mi corazón*. I have another position in mind for you.' He sat on the side of the bed and reached for her small hand, holding it in his. 'I'm planning to return to my estate in Spain.'

'Oh.' Her expression relaxed. And then she frowned. 'Why?'

Naturally she would have questions. She was nothing if not curious.

'I have some things that need attention and I haven't been back for a while.'

Years, in reality. Fifteen of them, to be exact. But she didn't need to know that.

He turned her hand over in his, stroking her palm with his thumb. 'It would please me very much to take you with me.'

She glanced down at her hand, enclosed in his. 'But what about my job here? Camille wouldn't like it if I suddenly left with no word.' Another troubled expression crossed her face. 'She wouldn't like it if she knew what I…what we…'

'Leave Camille to me.' He stroked her palm reassuringly, noting how she shivered yet again. 'And, like I told you, I have another position in mind for you.'

She looked up at him, her gaze very direct. 'What position? Your lover?'

There was a challenging note in her voice and he couldn't help but like how unafraid she was to confront him. She was strong, that was for certain, and although she might have been an innocent when it came to sex, she wasn't an innocent in anything else. She'd lived for years on the streets. She would have seen all kinds of cruel things, seen the basest of human nature. She knew how the world worked and knew that it was not kind.

If you tell her the truth she'll understand. She, more than anyone, will know what it's like to lose everything.

It was true. And if she didn't—well, there was always the money option. Either way, it wouldn't be an issue.

'Is there a problem with that?' he asked casually. 'You seemed to enjoy it well enough last night.'

She glanced down once again at her hand resting in his, at his thumb stroking gently her palm. 'So will that now be my job?'

The question sounded neutral, but he knew it wasn't.

'To be your whore?' The word was like a stone thrown against glass, jagged and sharp. 'Will you pay me more to be in your bed, Cristiano?'

The question sounded raw in the silence of the room. It wasn't a simple challenge now, because there was something else in her tone. She sounded…vulnerable, and he had the sense that he'd hurt her somehow.

You have hurt her.

Anger twisted sharply inside him and he dropped her hand and pushed himself off the bed, striding restlessly over to the window, trying to get his thoughts in order and his ridiculous emotions safely under control again.

The issue, of course, was that she was right. That was exactly what he'd been planning to do. Pay her to be his wife. And since he was also thinking their marriage would include sex, essentially he was paying her to sleep with him.

'Would that be so very bad?' he asked harshly.

There was a brief silence, and then she said in a small voice, 'So that's all last night was? Just a…a transaction?'

Ah, so that was what this was about. She thought the sex had meant something.

It did.

No—and he couldn't afford it to. His emotions had to remain detached, and already they were more engaged than he wanted them to be. His anger was far too close to the surface and she had an ability to rouse it too easily. He had to make sure he stayed uninvolved—that his feelings for her didn't go beyond physical lust.

'I thought last night was all about mutual pleasure,' he said, keeping his tone neutral. 'Though if there was anything transactional about it I apologise.'

'Oh.' Her voice sounded even smaller. 'I see.'

Cristiano's jaw tightened. He hadn't thought about her feelings and he should have. Because of course the sex for her wouldn't simply have been physical. It had been her first time, and she didn't have the experience to tell the difference between great sex and an emotional connection.

Are you sure you do?

He shoved that thought away—hard. Oh, he knew the difference. He wasn't a boy any more. But he couldn't have her thinking that the sex between them had meant more than it had. He also couldn't have her getting under his skin the way she was currently doing.

Which left him with only one option.

He would have to give her the truth.

It would hurt her, but maybe that would be a good thing. Then she would know exactly what kind of man he was. Which was definitely not the kind of man she could have sex that meant something with.

She might not want to have anything to do with you after that.

His chest tightened with a regret and disappointment he didn't want to feel, so he ignored it, placing his hands on the sill and staring sightlessly at the rooftops of Paris.

'I was married years ago,' he said into the silence. 'Both of us were very young—too young, as it turned out. She found me…difficult. And I *was* difficult. But I didn't know that she was so unhappy.' He paused, the words catching unexpectedly in his throat. 'At least not until she left me for someone else.'

Leonie was silent behind him.

'That someone else was an old enemy of my family's,' he went on. 'Someone who befriended me after my parents died and became a mentor to me. I told him about my marriage difficulties in the hope that he'd give me some advice, and he did. All the while using what I said to seduce my wife away from me.'

His grip on the sill tightened, his nails digging into the paintwork.

'And that's not all. I didn't realise that Anna was pregnant when she left me for him. In fact, I only found out when he came to tell me that not only was the baby mine, but he'd organised it so that legally he was the baby's father. I could never claim him.'

There was a soft, shocked sound from behind him, but he ignored it.

'This enemy was a powerful man,' he said roughly, 'and even though I tried to uncover what he'd done I was unable to. I was young and had no influence, no power and no money.'

He paused yet again, trying to wrestle the burning rage that ate away at him under his control again.

'I felt I had no choice. If I wanted my son I would have to take him by force. And so I planned to do that. I crashed a party they were giving and tried to confront the man who'd taken my child. But I was…angry. So very angry. And I ended up frightening my son. He ran straight into my enemy's arms—'

His voice cracked and he had to fight to keep it level.

'I knew then I had to let him go,' he went on, more levelly this time. 'That I had to let everything go. And so I did.'

Even though it had cut him in half. Even though it had caused his heart to shrivel up and die in his chest.

'I cut my marriage and my son out of my life, out of my memory. I pretended that it never happened, that he never existed. And then...then I found a woman in the streets. A woman who was defacing my car. I found out her name. Leonie de Riero. The long-lost, much-loved daughter of Victor de Riero.'

Cristiano let go of the windowsill and turned around to face the woman in the bed.

'Victor de Riero is the man who first stole my wife and then stole my child from me. And he owes me a debt that I will collect.' He stared at her, let her see the depth of his fury. 'With you.'

Leonie clutched the sheet tight in her hands, unable to process what Cristiano had just told her.

He stood with the window at his back, his hands at his sides, his fingers curled into fists. His beautiful face was set in hard lines, the look in his emerald eyes so sharp it could cut. The smokescreen had dropped away entirely. He looked fierce, dangerous, and the fury rolling off him took her breath away.

What little breath she had, given that apparently all this time he'd known who she was. Known *exactly* who she was.

That's why he picked you up off the streets. That's why he gave you a job. You were never anything to him but a means to an end.

Pain settled inside her, though she ignored it. As she

ignored the cold waves of shock and the sharp tug of pity because there was so much to take in.

He'd been married. He'd had a child. A child that had been taken from him. God, she could still hear his voice cracking as he'd told her what had happened, and that pity tugged harder at her heart.

But she didn't want to feel pity for him.

'You knew,' she said thickly, focusing on that since it was easier than thinking about the rest. 'All this time, you knew.'

His expression was like granite. 'Yes. I went to get my driver and found him playing a dice game with one of your friends. I gave the kids a hundred euros to tell me what your name was.' His mouth quirked in a humourless smile. 'Everyone has their price.'

She felt cold. But it was a cold that came from the inside, something that no amount of blankets or quilts could help. 'But…how could you know who I was from my first name?'

His gaze went to her hair, spilling down her back. 'You were familiar to me and I couldn't put my finger on why. But the colour of your hair gave it away. Anna and I used to go to many events hosted by your father and you attended some of them.'

Her stomach dropped away. Her memories of that time were so dim they were only blurry impressions. A pretty dress. A crowd of adults. Nothing more.

But Cristiano had been there. She must have seen him and clearly he'd remembered her.

She stared at him, her heart pounding. Before, she'd noted that he was older, certainly much older than she was, but she hadn't thought about it again. She hadn't thought about it last night, either—had been too desperate for him.

There had been a vague familiarity to his name when she'd first heard it, but she hadn't remembered anything. She'd been too young.

'Why…?' She stopped, not sure which question to ask first since there were so many.

'Why did I bring you here? Why did I not tell you I knew?' He asked them for her. 'Because you were familiar and I wanted to know why. And when I discovered who you were I didn't tell you because I wanted you to tell me. I wanted you to trust me.'

A sudden foreboding wound through her. 'What do you want from me?'

He smiled again, his predator's smile, and it chilled her. 'What do I want from you? I want you to help me get my revenge, of course.'

Ice spread through her.

Did you think he wanted you for real?

She fought to think, fought her pity for him and for what had happened to him.

'How? I don't understand.'

'I'm going to marry you, Leonie. And I'm going to invite your father to our wedding, to watch as a Velazquez takes a precious de Riero daughter the way he took my son.'

The ferocity on Cristiano's face, gleaming in his eyes, made the ice inside her deepen, yet at the same time it gave her a peculiar and unwanted little thrill.

'You will be mine, Leonie. And there will be nothing he can do to stop it.'

You want to be someone's.

The thought tangled with all the other emotions knotting in her chest, too many to sort out and deal with. So she tried to concentrate only on the thing that made any kind of sense to her.

'It won't work,' she said. 'My father doesn't care. He left me to rot in the streets.'

Something flickered across Cristiano's intense features. 'No, he didn't. He thought you were dead. Didn't you know?'

Her stomach dropped away. Dead? He thought she was dead?

'What?' she whispered, hoarse with shock. 'No, my mother told me he got rid of us. That he'd wanted a son, and she couldn't have any more children. And he...he...' She trailed off, because it couldn't be true. It couldn't.

Maybe it is and your mother lied to you.

This time the expression on Cristiano's face was unmistakable: pity.

'He didn't get rid of you,' he said quietly. 'I know. I was there. Your mother left him, and took you with her, and you both disappeared. A week or so later he got word that you'd both died in a fire in Barcelona.'

'No,' she repeated pointlessly. 'No. We came to Paris. Mamá had to get a job. I wanted to go home, but she told me we couldn't because Papá didn't want us. She couldn't give him the son he'd always wanted so he kicked us out.' Leonie took a shaken breath. 'Why would she say that if it wasn't true?'

Cristiano only shook his head. 'I don't know. Perhaps she didn't want you to find out that he'd been having an affair with my wife.'

Does it matter why? She lied to you.

The shock settled inside her, coating all those tangled emotions inside her, freezing them.

'All this time I thought he didn't look for me because he didn't care,' she said thickly. 'But it wasn't that. He thought...he thought I was dead.'

Cristiano's anger had cooled, and a remote expression settled over his face. 'I wouldn't ascribe any tender emotion to him if I were you. He didn't demand proof of your deaths. He merely took some stranger's word for it.'

A lump rose in Leonie's throat. There was a prickling behind her eyes and she felt like crying. Okay, so not only had her father thought she'd died, and hadn't much cared, but her mother had lied to her. Had lied to her for years.

Does knowing all that really change anything?

No, it didn't. She was still homeless. Still in this man's power. This man who'd known who she was all this time and hadn't told her. Who was planning to use her in some kind of twisted revenge plot.

It made her ache, made her furious, that all the heat and passion and wonder of the night before had been a lie. The joy she'd felt as he'd touched her as if she mattered was tainted.

He'd lied to her the way her mother had lied to her.

Bitterness and hurt threatened to overwhelm her, but she grabbed on to that thread of fury. Because fury was easier than pain every single time.

'So that's why you slept with me?' She fought to keep the pain from her voice. 'To make sure I'd do what I was told?'

Something flickered through his green eyes, though she didn't know what it was.

'No, sleeping with you was never the plan. I was going to make sure you trusted me and then I was going to put it to you as a business proposition. If you'd agree to marry me I would pay you a certain amount, and then in a few years we would divorce.'

'I see.' Carefully she drew the sheet around her, though it didn't help the numbness creeping through her. 'The sex was part of building trust, then?'

A muscle flicked in his jaw. 'That wasn't the intention.'

But it was clear that he wasn't unhappy that it had happened between them.

Of course he wasn't. It was another thing for him to use. And you thought you could trust him...

The cold in the pit of her stomach turned sharp, digging in, a jagged pain. She was a fool. The last person she'd trusted had been her mother and look how that had turned out. She'd thought after that she'd be more careful about who she gave her trust to, but apparently she'd learned nothing.

Though, really, what did it matter? The sex had been amazing, but so what? It was only sex and he wasn't different. He was a liar, like everyone else. And one thing was certain: he would never touch her again.

'Then what was your intention?' She was pleased with how level her voice was.

He stared at her for a long moment, his gaze unreadable. 'You're beautiful, Leonie. And I thought—'

'You thought, *Why not? A girl from the streets could be fun? Something a bit different.*'

Bitterness was creeping in now, which wasn't supposed to happen, so she forced it out.

'It doesn't matter,' she went on dismissively. 'It was a nice way to pass the evening.'

Shifting, she slid out of the bed, keeping the sheet

wrapped around her as she took a couple of steps towards him, then stopped.

'You didn't need to bother, though. If you'd asked me the night you picked me up if I wanted to help you get revenge on my father I would have said yes. Especially if you're going to pay me.'

Cristiano didn't move, but the line of his shoulders was tense, his jaw tight. His gaze was absolutely impenetrable.

'You have no loyalty to him, then?'

'Why should I? I barely remember him. Money is what I need now.'

There was silence as he stared at her and she couldn't tell what he was thinking.

'For what it's worth,' he said quietly, 'I slept with you last night because you're beautiful and I wanted you, Leonie. Because I couldn't stop myself.'

She hated him a little in that moment, and part of her wanted to throw it back in his face. But that would give away the fact that their night had mattered to her, and she didn't want him to know that. She didn't want him to know *anything*.

Last night she'd trusted him, but she certainly wasn't going to make that mistake again. His money, on the other hand, was a different story. She could buy herself a new life with money like that. Buy that little cottage in the country, where she'd live with the only person she trusted in the entire world: herself.

So all she did was lift a shoulder as if she didn't care and it didn't matter. 'Fine—but I want the money, Cristiano.'

His features hardened. 'Name your price.'

She thought of the most outrageous sum she could and said it out loud.

'It's yours,' he replied without hesitation.

'There's a condition,' she added.

His granite expression didn't change. 'Which is?'

'You can never touch me again.'

The muscle in the side of his jaw flicked, and there was a steady green glitter in his eyes. 'And if I don't like that condition?'

'Then I'll refuse to help you.'

He said nothing, and didn't move, but she could sense the fury rolling off him in waves. He didn't like her condition. Didn't like it one bit.

'I could make you change your mind.'

The words were more a growl than anything else, and the fighter in her wanted to respond to that challenge, relished it, even.

'Could you?' She gave him a very direct look. 'Why would you bother? I'm just a girl from the streets. You could get better with a snap of your fingers.'

'It's true, I could.' His gaze clashed with hers. 'But I don't want better. I want you.'

That shouldn't have touched her own anger, shouldn't have made it waver for even a second. But it did. Not that she was going to do anything about it. He was a liar, and even though that nagging pity for him still wound through her anger she ignored it.

'That's too bad.' And then, because she couldn't help herself, 'Feel free to try and change my mind if you can. But you won't be able to.'

The flame in his eyes blazed and he pushed himself away from the window, straightening to his full height.

A wild thrill shot straight down her spine. Oh, yes, challenge accepted.

'You shouldn't say things like that to men like me,' he murmured. 'But, fine, you'll have your money. You'll have to come to San Lorenzo with me if you want it, though. We'll be married in my family chapel.'

Leonie didn't think twice. She wanted the money—what did she care if she had to return to Spain to get it?

Are you sure it's a good idea to be near him?

Why wouldn't it be? She didn't care about him—not now. She didn't care about her father, either. Now all she cared about was the money, and she had no problem with using Cristiano the way he'd used her.

'Fine,' she said, shrugging. 'I don't care.'

'Good.' He moved, striding past her to the door of his bedroom without even a glance. 'Prepare to leave in an hour.'

And then he went out.

CHAPTER EIGHT

CRISTIANO FILLED THE flight to Spain with business. It was the only way to distract himself from the fact that Leonie was right there, sitting casually in one of his jet's luxurious leather seats, leafing through a magazine as if the night before and the morning after had all been just a passing encounter for her.

It was a performance worthy of himself.

It also drove him mad enough that he stayed on the phone even as the car they'd transferred to from the small airport where they'd landed wound its way through the sharp crags of the mountains on the road to San Lorenzo.

He could think of no other way to handle having her in his vicinity and not touching her.

Since she had no other clothes, she wore the black T-shirt and black trousers of his staff uniform, the small bag at her side containing only her old clothes and her useless phone—items she'd insisted on bringing with her for no reason that he could see.

He hadn't argued. She could bring them if she wanted to. He was planning on providing her with a proper wardrobe anyway, once they'd got to his estate, since if she was going to be his duchess he would need her to look the part.

But even that plain black uniform didn't stop memories of the night before rolling through him. Of her silken skin beneath his fingers, of the cries she'd made, of how tightly she'd gripped him as he'd slid inside her, of the look in her eyes as she'd stared up at him.

He'd told himself that the sex didn't matter, that it was physical, nothing more, and yet he couldn't get it out of his head. Couldn't get the memory of her white face as he'd told her the truth that he'd known who she was all this time out of his head, either.

He'd been right. Not only had he shocked her, he'd hurt her, too. She hadn't even known that her father thought she was dead. And what had been worse was the feeling that had swept through him as those big violet eyes had stared back at him in shock and betrayal. The need to go to the bed and sweep her into his arms had been strong. To hold her. Soothe her. Comfort her.

But he hadn't allowed himself to give in to those feelings. Instead he'd watched as his little *gatita* had drawn on some hidden core of strength, her pain and shock vanishing beneath her usual stubborn belligerence and an emotion he was all too familiar with.

Anger.

He'd hoped telling her the truth would make her aware of what kind of man he was and put some distance between them, and it had. He just hadn't expected to feel quite so disappointed about that—or disappointed in her demands. The money wasn't important—it wasn't an outrageous sum—it was the fact that she didn't want him to touch her again that he cared about. Which was especially enraging since he wasn't supposed to care.

Your emotions are involved with her whether you like it or not.

Yes, which meant he had to *un*-involve them.

Difficult when touching her was all he wanted to do.

The car wound through yet another green valley, with vineyards spread out on either side, almost to the foothills of the sharp, jagged mountains rising above them. But Cristiano wasn't watching the homeland he hadn't been to in years unroll before him. He was too busy watching the woman sitting beside him.

She had her head turned away, and was staring at the view outside. The sun was falling over the fine grain of her skin and turning her hair to fire.

Beautiful *gatita*.

He couldn't stop the sound of her voice replaying in his head, even huskier than it normally was, telling him how her mother had told her that her father hadn't wanted her, that he'd wanted a son instead.

Cristiano didn't know what to think about that, because it was certainly something that Victor de Riero had wanted. And maybe it had been true that Hélène couldn't have any more children. Maybe that had been part of the reason for de Riero targeting Anna. He'd wanted a new, more fertile wife for an heir.

'*I thought he didn't look for me because he didn't care...*'

A deep sympathy he didn't want to feel sat in his chest like a boulder, weighing him down. All those years she'd been on the streets, thinking herself unwanted. Where had Hélène been? Gone, it was clear, leaving Leonie to fend for herself. Alone.

He knew that feeling. He knew what it was to be alone. He'd had it all his childhood, as the only child of a man who'd cared more about his duties as duke than being a father, and a woman who'd preferred socialite parties to being a mother.

No wonder you scared Anna away. You were an endless well of need.

Cristiano dragged his gaze from Leonie and tried to concentrate on his phone call instead of the snide voice in his head.

Another reason not to care—as if he needed one. His emotions were destructive, and he had to make sure he stayed detached from them, which meant caring about Leonie wasn't something he should do.

He shouldn't give in to this sexual hunger, either, no matter how badly he wanted to. Letting one little kitten get the better of him just wasn't going to happen.

He leaned back in his seat, shifting slightly, uncomfortable with being so long in the car. Then he noticed that Leonie had tensed. Her gaze was flicking from the window to him, her hand lifting an inch from her thigh before coming down again. Colour crept into her cheeks as she turned towards the window again.

Interesting. So she was physically aware of him, perhaps as painfully as he was aware of her, which made sense. Because she'd loved everything he'd done to her and had answered his passion with her own fierce, untutored desire. A hunger like that, once released, didn't die. It burned for ever. She wouldn't be able to ignore it the way she had on the streets.

Cristiano didn't smile, but he allowed himself a certain satisfaction, filing away her response for future reference. Then he focused completely on his phone call as the car wound its way through another vineyard and then the tiny ancient village that had once been part of his estate. They moved on up into the mountains, and from there down a rocky, twisting driveway that led at last to the *castillo* he'd been born in.

The *castillo* he'd grown up in.

The big, empty *castillo* that had echoed with nothing but silence after his parents had been killed.

And that was your fault, too.

Cristiano tensed as the car cleared the trees and Leonie sat forward as the *castillo* came into view.

'You live here?' she asked, in tones of absolute astonishment. 'In a castle?'

It was literally a castle, built into the hillside. A medieval fortress that his warlord ancestors had held for centuries. Had it really been fifteen years since he'd been back?

After Anna had gone, and he'd lost his son, it had felt too big and too empty. It had reminded him of being seventeen once again, of losing his parents and walking the halls, feeling as if the silence and the guilt was pressing in on him. Crushing him.

After Anna, he hadn't been able to get out of the place fast enough, filling up his life with music and talk and laughter. With the sound of life.

A cold sensation sat in his gut as the car drew up on the gravel area outside the massive front doors. Why had he thought coming back was a good idea? He didn't want to go inside. The whole place had felt like a tomb the last time he'd been here and nothing would have changed.

Something's changed. You have Leonie.

She was already getting out of the car, walking towards the doors, looking up in open amazement at the *castillo* towering above her.

Ah, but he didn't have her, did he? She wasn't his. She'd made that very clear.

Still, if he was going to make her his duchess he

wanted it to happen on Velazquez ground, and he'd already sent messages to his PR company to let them know he'd be bringing his 'fiancée' back to his estate, and that more information would follow. They were naturally thrilled that the duke of San Lorenzo, infamous for his pursuit of pleasure, would be marrying again. The press would be ecstatic.

Gathering himself, Cristiano got out of the car and strolled after Leonie, letting none of his unease show. He'd called his staff here before he'd left Paris, telling them to prepare for his arrival, so everything should be in place.

Sure enough, they were greeted in the huge, vaulted stone entrance hall by one of his family's old retainers. The woman spoke a very old Spanish dialect that no one spoke outside the valley, and the memories it evoked made the cold inside him deepen.

He answered her in the same language, issuing orders while Leonie wandered around, looking up at the bare stone walls and the huge stone staircase that led to the upper levels. Portraits of his ancestors had been hung there. He'd always hated them—dark, gloomy paintings of stone-faced men and women who looked as if they'd never tasted joy in their entire lives and perhaps hadn't.

Leonie had started climbing the stairs to look at them and he walked slowly after her, the familiar cold oppressiveness of the ancient stones wrapping around him, squeezing him tight.

'Are these people your family?' she asked, staring at the portraits.

'Yes. Miserable bunch, aren't they?'

'They don't look that happy, no.' She frowned. 'But... they're so old. How long has your family been here?'

He climbed up a little way, then stopped one step below her, looking at her since that was better than looking at those ghastly portraits. She was all pale skin, bright hair and deep blue-violet eyes. Life and colour. Unlike these dim, dark portraits of people long dead.

'Centuries.' He thrust his hands in his pockets, his fingers itching to touch her. 'Since medieval times, if not before.'

'Wow...' she breathed, following the line of portraits on the walls. 'And what about this one?'

She pointed at the last picture, the most recent—though it didn't look like it, given it had been painted in the same dark, gloomy style. Her earlier anger at him seemed to have faded away, and interest was alight in her face.

Cristiano didn't look at the picture. He knew exactly which one it was. 'That one? Those are my parents. They were killed in a car accident when I was seventeen.'

She flicked him a glance, a crease between her brows. 'Oh. I'm sorry.'

It sounded almost as if she really meant it—not that he needed her sympathy. It had happened so long ago he barely remembered it.

That's why you can never escape the cold of this place. That's why you carry it around with you wherever you go. Because you can't remember how you tried to warm it up...

Cristiano shoved the thoughts away. 'It was a long time ago.'

'Your mother was pretty.' She leaned closer, studying the picture. 'Your father was handsome, too. But he looks a little...stern.'

'If by "stern" you mean aloof and cold, then, yes. He

was. And my mother was far more interested in parties than anything else.' He was conscious that he hadn't quite managed to hide the bitter note in his voice.

Leonie straightened and turned, studying his face. 'They weren't good parents?'

He didn't want to talk about this. 'What happened to Hélène, Leonie?' he asked instead. 'What happened to your mother?'

Her lashes fluttered; her gaze slid away. 'She left. I was sixteen. I came home from school one day and she was just...gone. She left me a note, saying she was leaving and not to look for her. But that was it.'

His fingers had curled into fists in his pockets, and that same tight sensation that Leonie always seemed to prompt was coiling in his chest. 'She just left? Without saying why?'

'Yes.' Leonie was looking down at the stairs now. 'I'll never know why.'

So. She'd effectively been abandoned by the one person in the world who should have looked after her. At sixteen.

'What did you do?' he asked quietly.

She lifted a shoulder. 'Eventually I was evicted from our apartment. No one seemed to notice I was gone.'

He felt as if a fist was closing around his ribs and squeezing, and he wanted to reach out, touch that petal-soft cheek. Tell her that he would have noticed. That he would have looked for her.

But then she glanced up at him again, a fierce expression in her eyes. 'Don't you dare pity me. I survived on my own quite well, thank you very much.'

'Survived, maybe,' he said. 'But life isn't just survival, Leonie.'

'It's better than being dead.'

Proud, stubborn girl.

'You should have had more than that.' This time it was his turn to study her. 'You deserved more than that.'

Colour flooded her pale cheeks, shock flickering in her eyes. 'Yes, well, I didn't get it. And you didn't answer my question.'

'No,' he said. 'Mine were not good parents.'

She blinked, as if she hadn't expected him to capitulate so quickly. 'Oh. Do you have brothers or sisters?'

'No.'

'So it was just you? All alone in this big castle by yourself?' There was a certain knowledge in her eyes, an understanding that he'd never thought he'd find in anyone else.

She knew loneliness—of course she did.

'Yes.' He lifted a shoulder. 'I was alone in this big castle by myself. This mausoleum was my inheritance.'

'Is that what it felt like? A mausoleum?'

'Don't you feel it?' He moved his gaze around the soaring ceilings and bare stone walls. 'All that cold stone and nothing but dead faces everywhere. I never come here if I can help it. In fact, I haven't been here in fifteen years.'

There was silence, but he could feel her looking at him, studying him like an archaeologist studying a dig site, excavating him.

'What happened here, Cristiano?'

That was his *gatita*. Always so curious and always so blunt.

'Do I really have to go into my long and tedious history?' he drawled. 'Don't you want to see where you're going to be sleeping?'

'No. And isn't your tedious history something I should know? Especially if I'm going to be marrying you.'

He looked at her. She was so small; she was on the stair above him but she was still only barely level with him. He didn't want to talk about this any more. He wanted his hands on her instead. He wanted her warmth melting away the relentless cold of this damn tomb.

'What is there to say?'

He kept his gaze on her, hiding nothing. Because she was right. She should know his history. So she knew what to be wary of.

'It was my seventeenth birthday, but my parents had some government party they had to attend. I was lonely. I was angry. And it was the second birthday in a row that they'd missed. So I took a match to my father's library and set it on fire.'

Leonie's gaze widened. 'What?'

'You think that's the worst part? It's not.' He smiled, but it was bitter. 'One of my father's staff called him to let him know the *castillo* was on fire. So he and my mother rushed back from the party. But he drove too fast and there was an accident. They were both killed.'

She hadn't understood until that moment why he so obviously hated this place, with its ancient stones and the deep silence of history. She'd thought it was wonderful—a fortress that no one could get into. A place of security and safety. She'd never been anywhere so fascinating and she wanted to explore it from top to bottom.

But it was clear that Cristiano did not feel the same. It was obvious in every line of him.

This man had used her, hurt her, and no matter that he'd said their night together had been because he'd wanted her, she couldn't forget her anger at him and what he'd done.

Yet that didn't stop the pulse of shock that went through her, or the wave of sympathy that followed hard on its heels.

There was self-loathing in his voice, a bitterness he couldn't hide, and she knew what that meant: he blamed himself for his parents' death.

No wonder he hated this place. No wonder he thought it was a tomb. For him, it was.

'You blame yourself,' she said. 'Don't you?'

He gave another of those bitter laughs. 'Of course I blame myself. Who else is there? No one else started a fire because he couldn't handle his anger.'

Her heart tightened. Although their stations in life were so far removed from each other that the gulf between them might have been the distance from the earth to the sun, they were in fact far closer than she'd realised.

He'd lost people the same as she had.

'For years after Mamá left I blamed myself,' she said. 'I thought that maybe it was something I'd done that had made her leave. Perhaps I'd asked too many questions, disobeyed her too many times. Nagged her for something once too often.' Her throat closed unexpectedly, but she forced herself to go on. 'Or…been a girl instead of a boy.'

The bitter twist to his mouth vanished. 'Leonie—' he began.

But she shook her head. 'No, I haven't finished. What I'm trying to say is that in the end I didn't know why she'd left. I'll never know, probably. And I could have chosen to let myself get all eaten up about what I did or didn't do, or I could accept that it was her choice to leave.' Leonie stared at him. 'She didn't have to leave.

I didn't make her. She choose that. Just like your father chose to return here.'

Cristiano's expression hardened. 'Of course he had to return. His son had just set fire to the—'

'No, he didn't,' she interrupted. 'He could have got a staff member to handle it. He could have decided he wasn't fit to drive and had your mother drive instead. He could have called you. But he didn't do any of those things. He chose to drive himself.'

Cristiano said nothing. He was standing on the step below her but still he was taller than she was, all broad shoulders and hard muscle encased in the dark grey wool of his suit. He wasn't wearing a tie, and the neck of his black shirt was open, exposing the smooth olive skin of his throat and the steady pulse that beat there.

She didn't know why she wanted to help him so badly—not after he'd hurt her the way he had. But she couldn't help it. She knew loneliness and grief, and she knew anger, too, and so much of what had happened to him had also happened to her.

'You are very wise, *gatita*,' he said at last, roughly. 'Where did you learn such wisdom?'

'There's not much to do on the streets but think.'

'In between all the surviving you had to do?' A thread of faint, wry amusement wound through his beautiful voice.

You deserved more than that...

A shiver chased over her skin. He'd said it as if he meant it, as if he truly believed that she had. But why would she trust what he said about anything?

'Yes,' she said blankly, her gaze caught and drawn relentlessly to the pulse at the base of his throat once again. 'In between all that.'

She'd put her mouth over that pulse the night before. She'd tasted his skin and the beat of his heart, had run her hands over all that hard muscle and raw male power.

A throb of hunger went through her.

She'd spent most of the day trying to ignore his physical presence. She'd thought it would be easy enough to do since he'd ignored her, spending all his time on the phone. She'd been fascinated by all the new sights and sounds as they'd left Paris and flown to Spain, so that had made it easier.

But despite that—despite how she should have been concentrating on her return to her long-forgotten homeland—all she'd been conscious of was him. Of his deep, authoritative voice on the plane as he'd talked on his phone. Of his hard-muscled thigh next to hers in the car. Of the spice of his aftershave and the heat in his long, powerful body.

And she'd realised that she might ignore him all she liked, but that didn't change her hunger for him, or her innate female awareness of him as a man. It couldn't be switched off. It pulsed inside her like a giant heartbeat, making her horribly conscious that her declaration of how she wasn't going to let him touch her again had maybe been a little shortsighted.

That was another thing she hadn't understood before, yet did now. Sexual hunger hadn't ever affected her, so she'd imagined that refusing him would be easy. But it wasn't, and she felt it acutely now as he stood there staring at her, his jungle-green eyes holding her captive. As if he knew exactly what she was thinking.

Her heartbeat accelerated, the ache of desire pulsed between her thighs, and she knew her awareness of him was expanding, deepening.

He wasn't just a powerful and physically attractive man. He was also a man who seemed not to care about very much at all on the surface, yet who burned on the inside with a terrible all-consuming rage. And a rage like that only came from deep caring, from a man with a wounded heart who'd suffered a terrible loss.

At least after the deaths of his parents he'd been able to grieve. But how could he grieve a child who wasn't dead? Who was still alive and who had no idea that Cristiano was his father?

He hasn't grieved. Why do you think he's so angry?

'You'd better stop looking at me that way, *gatita*,' he murmured. 'You'll be giving me ideas.'

She ignored that, feeling her own heart suddenly painful in her chest. 'I'm sorry about your parents,' she said. But she wanted him to know that although his son might not be aware of Cristiano, she was. And that she acknowledged what the loss had meant for him. 'And I'm so sorry about your son.'

A raw emerald light flared in the duke's eyes. That wry amusement dropped away, his whole posture tightening. 'Do not speak of it.' His voice vibrated with some intense, suppressed emotion.

She didn't want to cause him pain, yet all of a sudden she wanted him to know that she understood. That she felt for him. And that to a certain extent she shared his loss—because she, too, had lost people she'd once felt something for: her mother and her father.

So she lifted a hand, thinking to reach out and touch him, having nothing else to give him but that.

'No, Leonie,' he ordered.

The word was heavy and final, freezing her in place.

'I have respected your wishes by not touching you, but

don't think for one moment that it doesn't go both ways. Not when all I can think about is having you on these stairs right now, right here.'

Her heart thudded even louder. He had respected her wishes. He hadn't made one move towards her. And she... Well, she'd never thought that even though he'd broken her fledgling trust she'd still want him—and quite desperately.

So have him. It doesn't have to mean anything.

It didn't. And now there were no secrets between them, no trust to break, it could be just sex, nothing more. After all, she'd been denied so many good things—why should she deny herself this?

He'd told her she deserved better and he was certainly better than anything she'd ever had. So why couldn't she have him?

She lifted her hand and, holding his gaze, very deliberately placed her fingertips against the line of his hard jaw, feeling the prickle of hair and the warm silk of his skin.

'Then take me,' she said softly.

He was completely still for long moments, unmoving beneath her hand. But his eyes burned with raw green fire.

'Once you change your mind there will be no coming back from it, do you understand me?' His voice was so deep, so rough. The growl of a beast. 'This is the place of my ancestors, and if I have you here that makes you mine.'

He was always trying to warn her, to frighten her. Letting her see the fire burning in the heart of the man he was beneath the veneer of a bored playboy. But Leonie had never been easily frightened. And the man behind that veneer, with his anger, his passion and his pain, was far more fascinating to her than the playboy ever had been.

She wanted that man. And she wasn't frightened of him. After all, she'd always wanted to be someone's. She might as well be his.

'Then I'll be yours,' she said simply.

Cristiano didn't hesitate. Reaching out, he curled his fingers around the back of her neck and pulled her in close, his mouth taking hers in a kiss that scoured all thought from her head. He kissed her hungrily, feverishly, his tongue pushing deep into her mouth and taking charge of her utterly.

But his wasn't the only hunger.

Desire leapt inside her and she put her hands on his chest, sliding them up and around his neck, threading her fingers in the thick black silk of his hair and holding on tight. She kissed him back the way she had the night before, as hard and demanding as he was, showing him her teeth and her claws by biting him.

He growled deep in his throat. His hands were on her hips, pushing her down onto the cold stone of the stairs so she was sitting on one step while he knelt on the one below her.

He didn't speak, making short work of the fastenings of her trousers and then stripping them off her, taking her underwear with them. The stone was icy under her bare skin, but she didn't care. She was burning up. Everywhere he touched felt as if it was being licked by flame.

His mouth ravaged hers, nipping and biting at her bottom lip before moving down her neck to taste the hollow of her throat. She sighed, her head falling back as he cradled the back of it in his palm. His hand slid between her bare thighs, stroking and teasing, finding her slick and hot for him.

Leonie moaned, desperate for more pressure, more friction. Desperate for more of him.

And it seemed he felt the same, because there were no niceties today, no slow, gentle seduction. He ripped open the front of his trousers, his hands falling away from her as he grabbed for his wallet and dealt with the issue of protection. Then his hot palms were sliding beneath her buttocks, lifting her, positioning her, before he pushed into her in a hard, deep thrust.

The edge of the stair above her was digging into her back. She didn't care, though, was barely conscious of it as she gasped aloud, staring up into his face. Again, he was nothing but a predator, his eyes glittering with desire, his sensual mouth drawn into a snarl as he drew his hips back and thrust again.

All she could see was that hot stare and the possessive fire in it, and it twisted the pleasure tighter, harder. She wanted to be possessed. She wanted to be taken. And she wanted to take in return. Because, as much as he wanted her to be his, she wanted something to call her own.

He could be that for you.

Her heart slammed against her ribs and she curled her legs around his lean waist, holding him tightly to her, forgetting how he'd hurt her, how he'd lied to her in that moment.

'You could be mine, too,' she whispered hoarsely as he thrust into her again, making her gasp in pleasure. 'You could be, Cristiano.'

He didn't reply, but the fire in his eyes climbed higher. His fingers curled into her hair, protecting her head from the hard stone of the stairs, but he gave her no mercy from the brutal thrust of his hips. As if he could impress himself into her. As if he was trying to make her part of the stones of the castle itself.

And beneath the passion she could feel his need, could sense it in some deep part of her heart. The need for touch and warmth and connection. So she gave it to him, wrapping herself around him, and he took it, holding tight to her as he gave her the most intense pleasure in return.

It didn't take long.

He grabbed one her hands and guided her own fingers between her thighs, holding it down over that tight, aching bundle of nerves. And then he thrust again, deeper, harder, as he held her fingers there until the desperation inside her exploded into ecstasy and the entrance hall rang with the sounds of her cries.

She was hardly aware of his own growl as he followed her, murmuring her name roughly against her neck.

For long moments afterwards she didn't want to move, quite happy to sit on the cold stone of the stairs, with Cristiano's heat warming her through. But then he was shifting, withdrawing from her, dealing with the aftermath. Only after that was done did he reach for her, gathering her up into his arms and holding her close against his chest as he climbed the rest of the way up the stairs.

He carried her down a long and echoing stone corridor and into a room with a massive four-poster bed pushed against one wall. There he stripped her naked, put her down on it, and proceeded to make her forget her own name.

CHAPTER NINE

CRISTIANO FINISHED UP the phone call he was on with his PR people then leaned back in the old hand-carved wooden chair that sat behind his father's massive antique desk, reflecting once again on how hideously uncomfortable it was.

His father had liked the chair—his father had liked all the heavy old wooden furniture in the ducal study—but Cristiano had already decided that the chair had to go. Especially if he was going to make his home here—and he was certainly considering it.

The *castillo* was different with Leonie in it. She'd spent the past week investigating every corner of the ancient stones, exclaiming over things like the deep window seat in the library that could be enclosed when the heavy velvet curtains were drawn. Like the big bathroom that had been modernised to a point, but still retained a giant round bath of beaten copper. The cavernous dining room, where he'd had many a silent dinner with his parents, now filled up with Leonie's questions about the history of the estate and the *castillo* itself. Like the tapestries on the walls and the huge kitchen fireplace that was large enough to roast a whole cow in and probably had. The courtyard with the overgrown rose garden, the orchard full of orange trees, and the meadow beyond where he'd used to play as a child, pretending he had brothers and sisters to play with him.

But those memories seemed distant now—especially now he'd created new ones. Memories that were all about her laughter, her husky voice, her bright smile. Her cries of pleasure. Her bright hair tangled in his fingers and her warmth as he took her in yet another of those old, cold rooms.

He'd even taken her in that window seat in the library, and the memories of books flaming and shelves burning as bright as his anger were buried under flames and heat of a different kind.

It was better—much better. And the castle didn't feel so cold any more, or so silent. In fact, it felt as if summer had come to stay in the halls, making the place seem warmer and so much brighter than he remembered.

He was even considering staying on here with her after the wedding—and why not? She would be his wife, after all, and now they were spending every night, not to mention quite a few days, exploring the chemistry between them, it seemed only logical to indulge in a honeymoon, as it were. Maybe even beyond that.

He'd thought about the possibility of having an heir with her and tainting that precious de Riero bloodline even before they'd left Paris, and the idea certainly still held its appeal. He could create a home here with her. Create a family the way Victor de Riero had created a family.

You really want to have another child?

Something jolted inside him, a kind of electric shock, and he had to push himself out of his chair and take a couple of steps as restlessness coiled tight through his muscles.

Another child...

Intellectually, the idea was a sound one, and it would certainly make his revenge all the sweeter—so why did the thought make him feel as if ice was gathering in the pit of his stomach?

'I'm so sorry about your son...'

The memory of Leonie's voice on the stairs drifted back to him, the sound husky with emotion, her eyes full of a terrible sympathy, bringing with it another hard, electric jolt.

It had felt as if she was cutting him open that day, and he'd told her not to speak of it before he'd been able to stop himself. Before he'd been able to pretend that the thought of his child no longer had the power to hurt him.

So much for detachment.

His hands dropped into fists at his sides and he took a slow breath.

Yes, he could recognise that the thought of having another child was difficult for him, but he also had to recognise that this situation was different. Any child he had with Leonie would be born in pursuit of his revenge, nothing more. It would not be for him. Which meant it was perfectly possible for him to remain detached.

He would simply choose not to involve himself with any such child, and that would be better for the child, too. Certainly he wouldn't love it—not when love led to nothing but pain and destruction. The cost of love had been too high the first time; he wouldn't pay it again.

At that moment the heavy wooden door of the study burst open and he turned to find Leonie sweeping in, a blur of shimmering white silk and silvery lace, her hair in a loose, bright cascade down her back. She came to a stop in front of him, her cornflower-blue eyes alight with excitement, and put her hands on her hips.

'Well?' she asked. 'What do you think of this?'

He stared, all thoughts of children vanishing, his chest gone tight.

She was wearing a wedding gown. It was strapless, the gleaming white silk bodice embroidered with silver and cupping her breasts deliciously. Then it narrowed down to her small waist before sweeping outwards in a white froth of silky skirts and silver lace.

She looked beautiful—a princess from a fairy-tale or a queen about to be crowned.

'You forgot, didn't you?' she said as he stared at her in stunned silence. 'The designer's here with a few of the dresses we picked last week.'

He *had* forgotten. He and Leonie had sat down the previous week to choose a gown for her—not that he'd been overly interested in the details of the wedding, since it was the revenge that mattered. But Leonie had been excited, and had enjoyed choosing a gown for herself, and he'd surprised himself by enjoying helping her, too.

'So I see.' He tried to calm his racing heartbeat, unable to take his eyes off her. 'I'm not supposed to see the final gown before the wedding, am I?'

'Well, it's your revenge. I thought you might want to make sure the dress is…' she did a small twirl, the gown flaring out around her '…revengey enough.'

Her excitement and pleasure were a joy, and yet they only added to that tight sensation in his chest—the one he hadn't asked for and didn't want, and yet had been there since the night he'd picked her up off the street.

He fought it, tried to ignore it. 'You like it, don't you?'

She smiled, her expression radiant, her hands smoothing lovingly over the silk. 'I love it. I've never had anything so pretty or that's felt so lovely.'

She'd been like this over the past couple of weeks as he'd bought clothes and other personal items to add to her meagre stock of belongings, greeting each new thing with a thrilled delight that was immensely gratifying. And it didn't matter whether it was expensive or not—the fact that she had something of her own seemed to be the most important thing.

It made sense. She'd literally had nothing when he'd found her that night on the streets of Paris except for a very old cellphone and some dirty clothes. Now she had a wardrobe full of items she'd chosen with great care herself and a new phone, not to mention shoes and underwear and perfume and lots of other pretty girly things.

But he hadn't felt like this when he'd given her those things and she'd smiled at him. Not like he did now, with her so radiantly lovely in a wedding gown, full of excitement and joy. He hadn't felt as if he couldn't breathe... as if the world was tilting on its axis and he was going to slide right off.

All he could think about was the day they'd arrived here and how he'd told her that once he took her here, in the place of his ancestors, she'd be his. And how she'd surrendered to him as if she'd never wanted to be anyone else's, all the while whispering to him that he was hers, too.

You want to be hers.

No, he didn't. He couldn't be anyone's—just as he couldn't have anything that was his. Not any more. Not when he couldn't trust himself and his destructive emotions. And this tight feeling in his chest, the way he couldn't breathe…

You're falling for her.

Absolutely not. He had to stay detached and uninvolved. Keep it all about revenge. Because that, in the end, was the whole point of this charade: a cold and emotionless revenge against the man who'd taken his wife and son from him.

Which meant he had to keep his emotions out of it.

Yet still he couldn't stop himself from touching her, reaching out to brush his fingers over the lace of her bodice, watching as her eyes darkened with the passion that always burned so near the surface. She was always ready for him. She never denied him.

'You are beautiful, *gatita*,' he murmured. 'You are perfect in every way.'

She flushed adorably, giving him a little smile. 'Thank you.' Then that smile faded, a look of concern crossing her face. 'Are you all right?'

How she'd picked up on his unease he had no idea, because he was sure he'd hidden it. Then again, she was incredibly perceptive. Too perceptive in many ways.

'What? I can't give my fiancée a compliment without my health being questioned?' he asked, keeping his voice casual. 'Whatever is the world coming to?'

She didn't smile. 'Cristiano…'

The tight thing in his chest tightened even further, like a fist. 'You know this will be a proper marriage, don't you?' They hadn't had this conversation and they needed to. It might as well be now. 'You'll be my wife in every way?'

'Yes,' she replied without hesitation. 'You made that clear.'

'I will want children, too.'

This time her gaze flickered. 'Oh.'

'It makes my revenge even more perfect, *gatita*. Don't you see? He took my son and I will have another with his daughter.'

An expression he couldn't catch rippled over her face, then abruptly her lashes lowered, veiling her gaze. 'I do see, yes.' Her tone was utterly neutral.

He stared down at the smooth, silky curve of her cheek and the brilliant colour of her lashes resting against her pale skin. She seemed a little less bright now, her excitement dimming, disappearing.

'You don't like the idea of children?' he asked.

'No. I just…just hadn't thought of them before.'

He couldn't blame her. She was young, and probably hadn't considered a future with a family. But still, he didn't think it was surprise she was trying to hide from him—and she was definitely hiding something.

Reaching out, he took her chin between his thumb and forefinger and tilted her face up so he could look into her eyes. 'This bothers you. Why?'

She made no attempt to pull away, her violet gaze meeting his. 'You'd really want another child? After what happened with your son?'

Ah, she never shied away from the difficult questions, did she?

'It will be different this time.' He stroked her chin gently with his thumb, unable to resist the feel of her satiny skin. 'Because the child won't be for me. The child will be for the pleasure of seeing Victor de Riero's face when I tell him he will have a Velazquez grandchild.'

That way he could retain his distance. He'd never have to feel what he'd felt for his son for another child again. Never have to experience the pain of another loss. Anger was the only emotion he could allow himself to have.

Some expression he couldn't name shifted in her eyes. 'That's a terrible reason to have a child, Cristiano.'

The flat note of accusation in her voice burrowed like a knife between his ribs, making him realise how cold and callous he'd sounded.

He let go of her chin, felt the warmth of her skin lingering against his fingertips. 'Too bad. That's the only reason I'll ever have another.'

Cold and callous it would have to be. He couldn't afford anything else.

'Revenge…' The word echoed strangely off the stone walls of the room, her gaze never leaving his. 'Don't you want more than that?'

Something inside him dropped away, while something else seemed to claw its way up. Longing. The same kind of longing that had gripped him the day he'd taken her on the staircase of this *castillo*. The need for her touch, for the feel of her skin and the taste of her mouth. The heat of her body burning out the cold.

The need for *her*.

He couldn't allow that. Need had caused him more pain than anything else ever had, so he'd cut it out of his life. Successfully. He had no desire to let it back in again.

'No.' He kept his voice cold. 'I don't.'

But she only looked at him in that direct, sharp way. Seeing beneath the armour of the playboy duke that he wore, seeing the man beneath it. The desperate, lonely man…

'Yes, you do,' she said quietly. 'Would it really be so bad? To let yourself have more?'

Ah, his *gatita*. She couldn't leave well enough alone, could she? She should really learn when to stop pushing.

'I had more once,' he said. 'And I lost it. I do not want it again.'

Those big violet eyes searched his. 'Because of your son? Because of Anna?'

He should have laughed. Should have lifted a shoulder and made a joke. Should have closed the distance between them and put his hands on her, distracted her the way he knew so well how to do.

But he didn't do any of those things. He turned away from her instead and moved around his desk. 'I told you before—do not speak of them. They have nothing to do with our wedding.'

He sat down in his father's uncomfortable chair, ignoring the way his heart was beating, ignoring the pain that had settled in his heart for absolutely no reason that he could see.

'Now, if there's nothing else, I have some work to do.'

Except Leonie didn't move. She just stood there in the lovely gown, looking at him. Sympathy in her eyes. 'It wasn't your fault, Cristiano. What happened with my father and Anna…with your son.'

The knife between his ribs sank deeper, pain rippling outwards, and he found he was gripping the arms of the chair so hard his knuckles were white. 'I told you. Do not—'

'You were young and you didn't know.' Leonie was suddenly standing right in front of his desk, that terrible piercing gaze of hers on him. 'You were used. You were betrayed by someone you thought you could trust.' There was blue flame burning in her eyes, conviction in her voice. 'And you had every right—*every right*—to be angry.'

'No,' he heard himself say hoarsely, and then he was on his feet, his hands in fists, fury flooding through him. 'Maybe I did have every right, but I should have controlled it. Controlled myself. I barged into that party, shouting like a monster, and I scared my son, Leonie. I *terrified* him. And he ran straight to Victor as if I was the devil himself.'

His jaw ached, his every muscle stiff with tension, and he wanted to stop talking but the words kept on coming.

'I would have taken him, too. I would have ripped him from Victor's arms if Anna hadn't stopped me. If she hadn't thrown herself in front of Victor and told me that this was why she'd left me. Because I terrified her.'

Leonie was coming, moving around the side of the desk towards him, and he shoved the chair back, wanting to put some distance between them. But she was there before he could move, reaching out to cup his face between her small hands.

'You're *not* to blame,' she insisted, her voice vibrating with fierce emotion. 'That man—my *father*—' she spat the word as if it were poison '—took your son from you. He seduced your wife from you. He had no right. And it was *not* your fault. Just like the deaths of your parents weren't your fault.'

The fire in her eyes was all-consuming, mesmerising.

'Just like it wasn't my fault my mother left and my father just accepted I was dead and never once looked for confirmation.'

Her grip held him still, her conviction almost a physical force.

'You were angry because you cared about him, Cristiano. And, yes, caring hurts—but wouldn't you rather have had the pain than feel nothing for him? Than for all of that to have meant nothing at all?'

He couldn't move. He was held in place by her hands on him. By the passion and fierce anger that burned in her lovely face. Passion that burned for *him*.

His world tilted again and he was falling right off the face of it. And there was no one to hold on to but her.

Cristiano reached for her, hauled her close. And crushed her mouth beneath his.

Leonie was shaking as Cristiano kissed her, sliding her hands down the wall of his rock-hard chest, curling her fingers into his shirt, holding on to him.

She hadn't meant to confront him. Hadn't meant to hurt him. But she knew she *had* hurt him. She'd seen the flare of agony in his green eyes as she'd mentioned his son, had heard the harsh rasp of it in his beautiful voice as he'd told her that he'd lost what he'd had. And so, no, he didn't want more.

But he'd lied. Of course he wanted more. She felt his longing every time he touched her, every time he pushed inside her. It was there in the demanding way he kissed her, in the brutal rhythm of his hips as he claimed her, stamping his possession on her. In the way he said her name when he came, and in the way he held her so tightly afterwards, as if he didn't want her to get away.

That was fine with her; she loved the way he wanted her. But she hadn't understood why he kept denying that was what he wanted until now. Until he'd tried to end the conversation.

It had all become clear to her then.

Of course he didn't want more. Because he blamed

himself for the loss of his wife and child and he thought he didn't deserve more.

She'd told him that day on the stairs that he wasn't responsible for his parents' death, but it was clear that he hadn't taken that on board. That the guilt he was carrying around extended to the loss of his son.

And she didn't know why, but his pain had felt like a knife in her own heart.

She hadn't been able to stop the fierce anger that had risen inside her on his behalf, the fierce need to make him understand that he didn't have to take responsibility for what had happened because it wasn't his fault. None of it was.

He might act as if he was frightening, as if he was bad, but he wasn't. There was nothing about him that was cruel or mean or petty. That was violent or bullying. He was simply a man whose emotions ran fathoms deep and so very strong. A man who'd lost so very much.

She couldn't bear to see him hurt.

He gripped her tight, lifting her, then turning to put her on the desk, ravaging her mouth as he did so. She spread her legs, dropping her hands to his lean hips to pull him closer, the fall of her skirts getting in the way.

'Leonie,' he said hoarsely against her mouth. 'Not like this, *gatita*. Not again.'

'But I—'

He laid a finger across her mouth and she was stunned to feel it tremble lightly against her lips. His eyes had darkened, the green almost black.

'I want to savour you, *mi corazón*. I don't want to be a beast today.'

'I like the beast,' she murmured.

But that was all he gave her a chance to say, because

then his mouth was on hers again, his hands moving down the bodice of the beautiful wedding gown, his fingers shaping her through the fabric, cupping her breasts gently in his palms.

She shivered, because there was something reverent in his touch that hadn't been there before. As if she was a work of art that he had to be careful in handling.

You're not a work of art. You're dirt from the streets—don't forget.

No, she didn't believe it. And she didn't feel it, either—not as his kiss turned gentle, teasing.

The passion between them that normally flared hot and intense had become more focused, more deliberate, settling on delicacy and tenderness rather than mastery.

He tasted her mouth, exploring it lightly before brushing his lips over her jaw and down the side of her neck in a trail of kisses and gentle nips that had her shuddering in his hands. He didn't speak but he didn't need to; the reverent way he touched her made it clear. He'd said he wanted to savour her and that was exactly what he was doing.

He unzipped the gown and slid it down her body, lifting her up so he could get it off her, then laying it carefully over the desk. He turned back to her and pushed her down over the polished wood, so she was lying across the desk next to her gown.

Slowly, carefully, he stripped her underwear from her, his fingers running lightly over every curve, and with each touch she felt something inside her shift and change. She had become something else...something more. Not the dirty, unwanted girl from the streets but someone treasured. Someone precious.

His hands swept down her body, stroking, caressing,

as if she was beautiful, wanted, worth taking time over. And, perhaps for the first time in her life, Leonie actually felt that. Tears prickled behind her lids, her throat was tight, but she didn't fight the sensations or the emotions that came along with them, letting them wash through her as he touched her, as if his hands were sweeping them away for good.

He kissed his way down her body, teasing her nipples with his tongue, then drawing them inside the heat of his mouth, making her arch and gasp. His hands stroked her sides and then moved further down, along her thighs. With each caress the dirt of the streets fell away, and with it the cold loneliness and the isolation.

She would have let him touch her for ever if she could, but soon her entire body was trembling and she wanted more from him than gentle touches. She sat up, pushed her hands beneath his shirt, stroking the hard, chiselled muscles of his stomach, glorying in the heat of his skin. Glorying too in the rough curse he gave as she dropped one hand to the fastenings of his trousers and undid them, slipping her hand inside, curling her fingers around his shaft.

'Ah, *gatita*...' he murmured roughly, letting her stroke him. 'You should let me finish proving my point.'

'Which is...?' She looked up into his green eyes, losing herself in the heat that burned there. 'That you're not a beast? I know that already.'

'No. My point is that you're worth savouring.'

'Well, so are you.' She ran her fingers lightly along the length of him, loving how he shuddered under her touch. 'You're not the only one worth taking time over.'

His gaze darkened. *'Mi corazón...'*

He didn't believe her, did he?

'Here,' she said thickly. 'Let me show you.'

And she pushed at him so he shifted back, then slid off his desk to stand before him, going up on her tiptoes to kiss the strong column of his neck and then further down, tasting the powerful beat of the pulse at his throat. Then she undid the buttons of his shirt, running her fingers down his sculpted torso, tracing all those hard-cut muscles before dropping to her knees in front of him.

Her hands moved to part the fabric of his trousers, to grasp him and take out the long, hard length of him. And then she closed her mouth around him.

His hands slid into her hair and he gave a rough groan, flexing his hips. He tasted so good, a little salty and musky, and she loved the way she could make his breath catch and his body shake. But she also loved giving him pleasure—because if she deserved to feel wanted and treasured, then he did, too.

So she showed him, worshipping him with her mouth until he finally pulled her head away, picking her up in his arms and taking her over to the butter-soft leather couch under the window. He laid her down on it, dealt with protection, then spread her thighs, positioning himself. And when he pushed inside her it felt like a homecoming, a welcome rather than something desperate and hungry.

He didn't move at first, and she lost herself in the green of his eyes and the feel of him inside her, filling her. There was a rightness to this. A sense of wholeness. As if she'd been waiting for this moment, for him, her entire life.

You're in love with him.

Something shifted in her chest, a heavy weight, and it made her go hot and cold both at the same time. Made her dizzy and hungry, bursting with happiness and aching with despair all at once.

Was what she felt love? How would she know? No one had ever given her love. She'd never even contemplated it before.

Yet the hot, powerful thing inside her, pushing at her, was insistent, and she had no other name for it. And it was all centred on him. On his beautiful face and the heat in his eyes. On his smile and the dark, sexy sound of his laughter. On the way he touched her, the way he made her feel. As if she wasn't broken or dirty, but beautiful and full of light. A treasure, precious and wanted.

He began to move inside her and she couldn't look away. The feeling suffusing her entire body was making her ache. She'd never known till that moment that pain could have a sweet edge.

Words stuck in her throat. Part of her wanted to tell him. Yet something held her back.

'I had more. And I lost it.'

And she was simply a replacement for what he'd lost, wasn't she? A handy vehicle for his revenge. He pitied her and wanted her, that was clear, but that was all she was to him.

Why don't you just ask him?

But she didn't want to ask him. She would lose this moment, and the moment was all she'd ever had. The moment was all there was.

So she ignored the heavy feeling in her heart, in her soul, and pulled his mouth down on hers. Losing herself to his heat and his kiss and the pleasure he could give her and letting the future take care of itself.

CHAPTER TEN

CRISTIANO WAITED IN a small side room in the ancient chapel that had once been part of the Velazquez estate. Many of his ancestors had been christened and married in this same place, before making their final journey from there to the small cemetery at the back.

He'd waited for a bride here before, his heart beating fast with happiness and excitement as he'd watched through the window for her arrival.

Today, although he was waiting for another bride, it wasn't her he was watching for, and he felt neither excitement nor happiness. He felt cold, and a bone-deep anger was the only thing warming him as he watched for de Riero.

Initially there had been some doubt as to whether the man would accept the invitation, but curiosity and perhaps a chance to gloat had clearly won out, because he'd passed on his acceptance to one of Cristiano's staff.

Guests were already streaming in, and journalists were gathering as per his instructions to his PR people. He wanted as many news media people there as possible to record the moment when he would lift Leonie's veil and reveal her for the first time. To record Victor's face when he realised that it was his daughter standing at the altar.

The daughter who was supposed to be dead.

The daughter who was now his hated enemy's bride.

The daughter who doesn't deserve this pettiness.

Cristiano gritted his teeth, shifting restlessly as he watched the guests enter the chapel.

It wasn't pettiness. It was necessary. How else was he to deal with losing everything that had ever meant something to him?

Doesn't she also mean something to you?

The memory of Leonie's touch wound through him. Not her mouth on him, but her hands cupping his face. That fierce, passionate gaze staring up into his, telling him that none of it was his fault. As if it was vitally important to her that he understand that. As if *he* was important to her.

His hands closed into fists as he gazed sightlessly through the window.

No, he couldn't think about this—about her. It was vital his emotions stay out of it. The important thing was that he was very close to finally getting the satisfaction he craved from de Riero—payback for the agony he had caused him—and nothing was going to stop him from getting it.

And after that?

Cristiano ignored the thought, focusing instead on the long black car that now drew up in the gravel parking area outside the chapel and the tall man that got out of it.

De Riero.

Cristiano began to smile.

And then de Riero turned as another person got out of the car. A tall, gangly teenager with a shock of black hair. De Riero said something and the boy straightened up, looking sullen. Then he reached to adjust the boy's tie, and he must have said something else because the boy lost his sullen look, grinning reluctantly.

An arrow of pure agony pierced Cristian's heart.

His son.

He couldn't move, couldn't tear his gaze away. He purposely hadn't looked at any pictures of the boy, or read any news stories about him. He'd simply pretended that the child had never existed.

But he did exist. And now he was here. And he was tall, handsome. He'd grow into those shoulders one day, just as he'd grow into his confidence, and then the world would be his oyster. He'd be a credit to his parents…

But Cristiano would not be one of those parents.

Pain spread outwards inside him, a grief he wasn't prepared for. Why had de Riero brought the boy? To gloat? To rub salt in the wound? As a shield? Why?

And then another person got out of the car—a woman with dark hair in a dark blue dress. Anna.

She came to stand by her son, smiling up at him, saying something to both him and de Riero that made them laugh. De Riero put a hand at the small of her back and leaned in to kiss her cheek while Anna's hand rested on her son's shoulder.

Something else hit Cristiano with all the force of a quarrel shot from a crossbow.

They were happy.

His son was happy.

You will destroy that. Publicly.

Realisation washed over him like a bucket of ice water and he found himself turning from the window and striding into the middle of the room, his hands in fists.

Anger was a torch blazing inside him. Of course de Riero had brought the boy. Yes, he *was* here as a shield—

to protect de Riero against anything Cristiano might do. The coward. Well, he was mistaken. This wedding would go ahead, and Cristiano would parade his daughter in front of him, and...

In front of your son.

Cristiano took a breath, then another, adrenaline pumping through him, anger and bitterness gathering in his throat, choking him.

He couldn't stop thinking about it—about what would happen when Leonie was revealed. What de Riero would do and, more importantly, what his son would do. Did he know he had a stepsister? If he did, how would he react to the knowledge that she wasn't dead, but alive? And if he didn't what would he think about the fact that his so-called father hadn't told him?

That happiness you saw outside... You will destroy it. In front of the world.

The breath caught in his throat, an arrow reaching his heart.

He couldn't do it.

He couldn't destroy his son's happiness.

He'd already done it once before, when the boy had been small, frightening him and sending straight into de Riero's arms. He couldn't do it again.

And all the revenge in the world wouldn't give him back what he'd lost. That was gone. For ever.

Love. That was the problem. That had *always* been the problem.

He'd loved his parents and, no matter what Leonie said, that love had destroyed them. He'd loved Anna once, and had nearly destroyed her. And this love he had for his son—well, now he was on the brink of nearly destroying him, too.

This revenge wasn't cold. It burned like the sun and that was unacceptable.

Love. He was done with it.

And Leonie? What about her?

Yes, she was another casualty of his caring. He'd drawn her into his orbit and kept her there—a tool he could use, a weapon he could wield against Victor de Riero.

Lovely, generous, passionate Leonie, who didn't deserve the use he'd put her to.

Who deserved so much more than being tied to man who only saw her only as something he could use.

He was selfish and he'd hurt her. And he would keep on hurting her. Because that was all he knew how to do.

Hurting people was all he ever did.

Certainty settled down inside him, along with a bone-deep pain and regret. He should never have picked her up off the street and taken her home. Or at least he should have found her a place to live and a job far away from him, where she would have been able to create the kind of life she wanted, not be dragged into his own self-centred plans.

Anna was right to be afraid of you.

His hand was shaking as he grabbed his phone from his pocket and called one of his assistants to get Leonie's location. Luckily she was still a few minutes away, so he ordered the assistant to get the driver to bring the car around to the back of the chapel instead of the front. He'd get another member of staff to intercept her and bring her here, where he could talk to her, tell her what he intended to do.

He paced around for ten minutes, conscious that the moment when they were supposed to exchange vows was getting closer and closer, and that the sooner he made an announcement the better. But he needed to tell her first. She deserved that from him at least.

Finally the door opened and Leonie was ushered in.

His heart shuddered to a complete halt inside his chest.

She was in that gorgeous wedding dress, a princess out of a fairy-tale. The veil that covered her face was white lace, densely embroidered with silver thread, and all that could be seen was the faint gleam of her red-gold hair. In one hand was a spray of simple wildflowers, gathered from the meadow near the castle, while the other held her skirts out of the way so she could walk.

His beautiful *gatita*.

She will never be yours.

He hadn't thought that particular truth would hurt, but it did, like a sword running through him. He ignored the pain. He wouldn't be the cause of any more hurt for her. She'd had enough of that in her life already.

'What's happening?' Leonie pushed back her veil, revealing her lovely face, her cornflower-blue eyes wide and filling with concern as they saw his face. 'What's going on, Cristiano? Are you okay? You look like you've seen a ghost.'

The deep violet-blue of her eyes was the colour that he only ever saw on the most perfect days here in the valley. The warmth of her body was like the hot, dry summers that were his only escape from the silence and the cold. Her rich, heady scent was like the rose garden hidden in the courtyard, where he'd used to play as a child.

She was everything good. Everything he'd been searching for and never known he'd wanted.

Everything he could never have—not when he'd only end up destroying it.

He stood very still, shutting out the anger and the pain, the deep ache of regret that settled inside him. Shutting out every one of those terrible, raw, destructive emotions.

'I'm sorry, *gatita*,' he said. 'But I'm going to have to cancel the wedding.'

Leonie stared at the man she'd thought she'd be marrying today, shock rippling through her. She'd been nervous that morning as a couple of Cristiano's staff had helped her prepare for the ceremony, doing her hair and make-up, preparing her bouquet and finally helping her into the gown.

But she wasn't nervous about finally seeing her father after all these years. In fact, she'd barely thought about him, and even when she had it had only been with a savage kind of anger. Not for herself and what he'd done to her, but for what he'd done to Cristiano.

No, it was marrying Cristiano that she was nervous about. And she was nervous because she was hopelessly in love with him and had no idea what that was going to mean. Especially when she was certain he didn't feel the same about her.

She'd had a battle with herself about whether or not to tell him about her feelings and had decided in the end not to. What would telling him achieve? Who knew how he'd take it? Perhaps things would change, and she didn't want that.

Anyway, she knew that he did feel something for her, because he showed her every night in the big four-poster bed in his bedroom. It was enough. She didn't need him to love her. She'd survived for years without love, after all, and she'd no doubt survive the rest of her life without it, too.

Of course there had been a few nagging doubts here and there. Such as how he'd mentioned having children, but said they wouldn't be for him. They'd only be in service to his grand revenge plan. That had seemed especially bleak to her, but then she couldn't force him to care if he didn't want to. She would just love any children they had twice as much, to make up for his lack.

What was important was that now she had her little cottage in the countryside—although the cottage had turned out to be a castle and she had a genuine duke at her side. She had more than enough.

More than the homeless and bedraggled Leonie of the streets had ever dreamed of.

Except now, as she stood there in her wedding gown, staring at the man she'd been going to marry, whose green eyes were bleak, she suddenly realised that perhaps all of those things hadn't been enough after all.

'What do you mean, cancel the wedding?' Her voice sounded far too small and far too fragile in the little stone room. 'I thought you were going to—?'

'I thought so, too,' he interrupted coolly. 'And then I changed my mind.'

She swallowed, trying to get her thoughts together, trying not to feel as if the ground had suddenly dropped away beneath her feet. 'Cristiano—' she began.

'De Riero has arrived,' he went on, before she could finish. 'And he has brought my son and my ex-wife with him.'

Leonie stared at him. 'You...weren't expecting them?'

'I didn't even think about them.' He was standing so still, as if he'd been turned to stone. 'Until I saw them get out of the car. And then there he was—my son. And Anna. De Riero's *family*.'

He said the word as if it hurt him, and maybe it did, because it was definitely pain turning his green eyes into shards of cut glass.

'They are happy, Leonie. My son is happy. And going through with this will hurt him. Publicly. I have no issue with doing that to de Riero, but I cannot do that to my child.' He paused a moment, staring at her. 'And I cannot do that to you, either.'

She blinked. 'What? You're not hurting me. And as for my father—'

'It won't bring my son back,' Cristiano cut her off, and the thread of pain running through his voice was like a vein of rust in a strong steel column. 'It won't make up for all the years I've missed with him. And I've already hurt him once before, years ago. Revenge won't make me his father, but…' A muscle ticked in his strong jaw, his eyes glittering. 'Protecting him is what a father would do.'

Something twisted in her gut—sympathy, pain.

How could she argue with him? How could she put herself and what she wanted before his need to do what was right for his son?

Because that was the problem. She wanted to marry him. She wanted to be his.

'I see,' she said a little thickly. 'So what will happen? After you cancel the wedding?'

He lifted a shoulder, as if the future didn't matter. 'Everyone will go home and life will resume as normal, I expect.'

'I mean what about us, Cristiano? What will happen with us?'

But she knew as soon as the words left her mouth what the answer was. Because he'd turned away, moving over to the window, watching as the last of the guests entered the chapel.

'I think it's best if you return to Paris, Leonie,' he said quietly, confirming it. 'It's no life for you here.'

Why so surprised? He was only ever using you and you knew that.

No, she shouldn't be surprised. And it shouldn't feel as if he was cutting her heart into tiny pieces. She'd known right from the beginning what he wanted from her, and now he wasn't going to go through with his revenge plan he had no more use for her.

He'd told her she was his. But he'd lied.

Her throat closed up painfully, tears prickling in her eyes. 'No life for me? A castle in Spain isn't as good as being homeless on the streets of Paris? Is that what you're trying to say?'

He glanced at her, his gaze sharp and green and cold. 'You really think I'd turn you back out onto the streets? No, that will not happen. I'll organise a house for you, and a job, set up a weekly allowance for you to live on. You won't be destitute. You can have a new life.'

She found she was clutching her bouquet tightly. Too tightly. 'I don't want that,' she said, a sudden burst of intense fury going through her. 'I don't want *any* of those things. I'd rather sleep on the streets of Paris for ever than take whatever pathetic scraps you choose to give me!'

He looked tired all of a sudden, like a soldier who'd been fighting for days and was on his last legs. 'Then what do you want?'

She knew. She'd known for the past few weeks and hadn't said anything. Had been too afraid to ask for what she wanted in case things might change. Too afraid to reach for more in case she lost what she had.

But now he was taking that away from her she had nothing left to lose.

Leonie took a step forward, propelled by fury and a sudden, desperate longing. 'You,' she said fiercely. 'I want you.'

His face blanked. 'Me?'

And perhaps she should have stopped, should have reconsidered. Perhaps she should have stayed quiet, taken what he'd chosen to give her and created a new life for herself out of it. Because that was more than enough. More than she'd ever dreamed of.

But that had been before Cristiano had touched her, had held her, had made her feel as if she was worth something. Before he'd told her she deserved more than a dirty alleyway and a future with no hope.

Before he'd told her that she was perfect in every way there was.

'Yes, you.' She lifted her chin, held his gaze, gathering every ounce of courage she possessed. 'I love you, Cristiano. I've loved for you for weeks. And the kind of life I want is a life with you in it.'

For a second the flame in his eyes burned bright and hot, and she thought that perhaps he felt the same way she did after all. But then, just as quickly, the flame died, leaving his gaze nothing but cold green glass.

'That settles it, then,' he said, with no discernible emotion. 'You have to leave.'

She went hot, then cold, an endless well of disappointment and pain opening up inside her.

You always knew he didn't want you. Come on—why would he?

She ignored the thought, staring at him. 'Why?' she demanded.

His eyes got even colder. 'Because I don't love you and I never will. And I have nothing else but money to give you.'

The lump in her throat felt like a boulder, the ache in her heart never-ending. She should have known. When he'd told her that any children they had wouldn't be for him, it had been a warning sign. If he had no room in his heart for children, why would he have room for her?

'So everything you said about me deserving better?' she said huskily. 'That was a lie?'

An expression she couldn't interpret flickered over his face.

'You do deserve better. You deserve better than me, Leonie.'

'But I don't want better.' Her voice was cracking and she couldn't stop it. 'And what makes you think you're not better anyway?'

'What do you think?' His face was set and hard. 'I hurt the people I care about. I destroyed my parents, I nearly destroyed Anna, and I almost destroyed my son.' There was nothing but determination in his gaze. 'I won't destroy you.'

Her heart shredded itself inside her chest, raw pain filling her along with a fury that burned hot. She took a couple of steps towards him, one hand crushing the stems of her bouquet, the other curled in a fist.

'Oh, don't make this about protecting me,' she said, her voice vibrating with anger. 'Or your son. Or Anna. Or even your parents.' She took another step, holding his gaze. 'This is about you, Cristiano. You're not protecting us. You're protecting yourself.'

Something flickered in the depths of his eyes. A sudden spark of his own answering anger. 'And shouldn't I protect myself?' he demanded suddenly, tension in every line of him. 'Shouldn't I decide that love is no longer something I want anything to do with? Losing my son just about destroyed me. I won't put myself through that hell ever again.'

Her throat closed up, her heart aching. She had no answer to that, no logical or reasonable argument to make. Because she could understand it. He had been hurt, and hurt deeply, and that kind of wound didn't heal. Certainly she couldn't heal it.

You will never be enough for him.

Her anger had vanished now, as quickly as it had come, leaving her with nothing but a heavy ache in her chest and tears in her eyes. But still she tried, reaching out to him, trying to reach him in some way.

He caught her by the wrist, holding it gently. 'No, *gatita.*'

His touch and that name. It hurt. It hurt so much.

Her heart filled slowly with agony as tears slid down her cheeks, but she refused to wipe them away. Instead she tugged her hand from his grip and stepped away.

She wouldn't beg. She had her pride. He might not want her, but that didn't change what she felt for him, and she wouldn't pretend, either.

Leonie drew herself up, because to the core of her aching heart she was a fighter and she never gave up. 'I love you, Cristiano Velazquez, Duke of San Lorenzo. I know I can't change the past for you. I can't ever replace what you lost. And I can't heal those wounds in your soul. And I know you don't love me back. But…' She lifted her chin, looked him in the eye. 'None of that matters. You made me see that I was worth something. You made me want something more and you made me think that I deserved to have it. I think we both do.'

A raw expression crossed his face and she couldn't help it. She reached up and touched one cheek lightly, and this time he didn't stop her.

'I just wish… I just wish you believed that, too.'

But it was clear that he didn't.

She dropped her hand and stepped away.

Her poor heart had burned to ash in her chest and there were tears on her cheeks, but her spine was straight as she turned away.

And when she walked out she didn't falter.

CHAPTER ELEVEN

CRISTIANO DIDN'T ARRIVE back at the castle till late that night. Stopping a wedding certainly took less time than planning one, but still it had taken hours of explaining and arranging things until everyone's curiosity had been satisfied.

It would be a scandal, but he didn't care.

He'd told everyone that his bride had taken ill unexpectedly and that the wedding would have to be postponed.

He would naturally cancel everything once the fuss had died down.

The first thing he'd done on arriving back was to see where Leonie was. He'd given orders that she was to be granted anything she wanted, and he'd expected that she'd probably have holed herself up in one of the *castillo*'s other guest rooms.

But what he hadn't expected was to find that she had gone and no one knew where she was. She'd come back from the chapel, disappeared into the bedroom to change and then had apparently vanished into thin air.

When he found out he stormed upstairs to the bedroom, to see if she'd taken anything with her, and was disturbed to find that she hadn't. Not even the new handbag and purse he'd bought her, with all the new bank cards he'd had set up for her.

In fact, she hadn't taken anything at all.

She'd simply...gone.

He got his staff to check every inch of the castle, and then the grounds, and then, when it was clear she wasn't anywhere on the estate, he called his staff to start searching the entire damn country.

He wanted her found and he wouldn't rest until she was.

Why? She's gone and that's how you wanted it. You threw her heart back in her face. Did you really expect her to stick around?

Something tore in his chest, a jagged pain filling him.

He could still feel the imprint of her skin on his fingertips as he'd taken her wrist in his, still see the pain in her eyes and the tears on her cheeks. See her courage as she'd lifted her chin and told him that it didn't matter if he didn't love her. That she loved him anyway.

Dios, she was brave. It wasn't her fault he didn't deserve that love and never would. That he never wanted anything to do with love and the pain it brought, the destruction it wreaked, not ever again.

It's not her fault you're a coward and ended up hurting her anyway.

The tearing pain deepened, widened, winding around his soul.

He shoved himself out of his uncomfortable chair and paced the length of his study, his fingers curled tight around his phone, ready to answer it the second someone called, telling him they'd found her.

He didn't want to think about what she'd said. He only wanted to think about whether or not she was safe.

And she would be, surely? She could look after herself. After all, she had for years before he'd taken her from the streets, so why wouldn't she be safe now?

Yet he couldn't relax. Couldn't sit still. Couldn't escape the pain inside him or the cold feeling sitting in his gut.

It's too late. Too late not to love her.

He stopped in the middle of his study, staring out at the darkness beyond the window as the cold reached into his heart.

Because he knew this feeling. It was familiar. He'd felt it once for Anna and for his son. Fear and pain, and longing. An all-consuming rage. An endless well of need that no one could ever fill.

She can. She did.

Cristiano froze, unable to breathe.

Leonie, her face alight with passion as she took his face between her small hands...

Leonie, touching him gently, as if he was precious to her...

Leonie, filling his *castillo* with sunshine and warmth, with her smile and her laughter.

Leonie, whose love wasn't destructive or bitter, despite the long years she'd spent on the streets. Whose love was open and generous and honest, with nothing held back or hidden.

Leonie, who loved him.

She's what you need. What you've always needed.

Everything hurt. It was as if every nerve he had had been unsheathed, sensitive even to the movement of air on his skin.

Love was destructive, but hers wasn't. Why was that?

You know.

Cristiano closed his eyes, facing a truth he'd never wanted to see.

It wasn't love that was destructive, because there had been nothing destructive about the way Leonie had looked at him. Nothing cruel in the way she'd touched him gently as he'd thrown her love back in her face. Nothing angry.

Because it was anger that destroyed. Anger that frightened. Anger that made him bitter and twisted and empty inside.

Anger that made him a coward.

Anger that had hurt her.

He took a shuddering breath.

His proud, beautiful *gatita*. He'd hurt her and she'd simply touched his cheek. Told him that she wished he could see what she saw when she looked at him.

His brave Leonie. Walking away from him with a straight back, unbowed. A fighter in every sense of the word. But alone. Always alone.

Not again.

It was the only thought that made sense. He'd made mistakes in his life—so many mistakes—but the one mistake he'd made, that he kept making over and over again, had been to let his anger win. And he couldn't let it.

Once…just this once…he would let love win.

And he loved her.

Perhaps he had loved her the moment he'd picked her up from the street, seen her staring at him with wide blue eyes, her hair a tangled skein down her back.

He'd tried to deny the emotion, tried to ignore it. Tried to squash it down and contain it because his love had always been such a destructive thing. But he couldn't stop it from pouring through him now, intense and deep. A vast, powerful force.

He remembered this feeling—this helpless, vulnerable feeling. And how he'd fought it, tried to manage it, to grab control where he could. The anguish of wanting something from his parents that they were never going to give, and their instinctive withdrawal from him and his neediness. The pain of it as he'd tried to hold on to Anna. As his son had slipped through his fingers.

The vulnerability that he'd turned into anger, because that was easier and he'd thought it more powerful.

But it wasn't. This feeling was the most powerful. It was everything and he let it pulse through him, overwhelm him, making everything suddenly very, *very* clear.

He had to find her. She thought that they both deserved more. He wasn't sure that was true for him. But she definitely did. And though he had nothing to give her but his own broken, imperfect heart, it was all he had.

He just had to trust it was enough.

Cristiano turned and strode out of the study, his heart on fire, his phone still clutched in his hand.

Leonie waited outside in the garden of the tiny hotel in San Lorenzo, hiding in the darkness. She'd gotten good at it in Paris, and it seemed she still had the gift since no one had spotted her.

It was a long wait. But she had nowhere to go, and nowhere to be, so she stood there until at last the door to the wide terrace opened and a man came out to stand there, gazing out over the garden.

De Riero.

She really didn't know why she was here, or what she intended to do by coming—maybe just see him. Her memories of him were very dim, and they were still dim now. She didn't recognise his face. He was a stranger.

After she'd left the castle, walking to the village in the dark, she'd thought she'd probably have to hitchhike or stow away in a truck or something in order to leave San Lorenzo. The thought hadn't worried her. She just wanted to get as far away from Cristiano and his cold green eyes as she could.

But then, outside the small village hotel, she'd spotted a tall boy with vaguely familiar features and vivid green eyes and she'd known who it was. And who the tall man beside him must be, too.

And she hadn't been able to go any further.

She hadn't wanted to go into the hotel, so she'd slunk into the gardens and skulked in the shadows, watching the hotel terrace.

Waiting for what, she didn't know, but she hadn't been able to leave all the same.

De Riero reached into his jacket and took out a cigarette, lit it, leaning on the stone parapet of the terrace.

She could step out of the shadows now, reveal herself. Show him that she was still alive—though at the moment 'alive' was relative. Especially when she felt so hollow and empty inside.

What do you want from him?

She didn't know that, either. An apology? An acknowledgement? To be welcomed into his family with open arms?

Her father leaned his elbows on the parapet, his cigarette glowing.

Would he be disappointed if he found out she wasn't dead after all? Would he be angry with her for disrupting his family? Or would he be grateful? Happy?

Does it matter?

Her throat closed and her chest ached. And she knew the truth. It wouldn't change a thing. Because her heart was broken and it had nothing to do with her father. Nothing to do with his acknowledgement of her or otherwise. She felt nothing for him. Nothing at all.

Because her heart wasn't with him. It was with another man. A man who didn't want it and yet held it in his strong, capable hands anyway.

Whether her father wanted her or not, it wouldn't change that feeling. Wouldn't alter it. Which meant it wasn't this man's acceptance that would make her whole.

Only Cristiano could.

The boy came out onto the terrace, tall and already broad, joining the man. Cristiano's son.

The sounds of their voices carried over the garden, and then their laughter. There was happiness in their voices, an easy affection, and Leonie knew she wasn't going to reveal herself. That she would stay out of it.

That wasn't her family. Not any more.

It felt right to melt away into the shadows and leave them behind.

Her future wasn't with them.

A certain calmness settled inside her, along with determination.

She would find her own family and her own future. She would carve it with her bare hands if she had to, but find it she would. Her future wasn't as a de Riero and it wasn't as a Velazquez, but she would find something else.

She wasn't lost. She'd found herself.

Slowly she walked down the tiny street of San Lorenzo, alone in the dark. And then a car came to a screeching halt beside her and a man leapt out of it.

'Leonie!' a dark, familiar voice said desperately. 'Stop!'

She stilled, staring as Cristiano came towards her, his hair standing up on end, his wedding suit rumpled, the look on his face as raw and naked as she'd ever seen it.

He stopped right in front of her, staring at her, breathing hard. 'Don't leave,' he said hoarsely before she could speak. 'Please don't leave me.'

Shocked tears pricked her eyes, her heart aching and burning. What was he doing here? He'd been very clear on what he'd wanted and it wasn't her, no matter what he was saying now.

Resisting the urge to fling herself into his arms, she drew herself up instead, lifting her chin. 'What are you doing here, Cristiano?' Her voice was hoarse, but she was pleased with how calm she sounded.

'What you said in the chapel…' The look in his eyes burned. 'About deserving more.'

'What?'

'You told me that we both deserved more and that you wished I could believe it, too.' He stared at her. 'I want to know why.'

She blinked her tears back furiously. 'Does it matter?'

He moved then, taking her face between his big, warm palms, his whole body shaking with the force of some deep, powerful emotion. 'Yes,' he said fiercely. 'It matters. It matters more than anything in this entire world.'

His touch was so good. The warmth of it soothed all the broken edges of her soul, making her want to lean into his hands. Give him everything she had.

But he didn't love her, did he? And he never would. And that wasn't enough for her any more. It just wasn't.

'Why?' She forced away the tears. 'Why does it matter to you?'

The street lights glossed his black hair, made his eyes glitter strangely. 'Because you matter, *gatita*. You matter to me.'

Her breath caught—everything caught. 'What?' The question came out in a hoarse whisper.

'I came back and you were gone, and no one knew where you were.'

There was something bright and fierce in his expression.

'I couldn't rest and I couldn't sit still. I was afraid for you. And I knew it was too late. I've been trying not to love you, my little *gatita*. I've been trying not to care, trying to protect myself. But you're so easy to love, and I fell for you without even realising that I'd fallen.'

His thumbs moved gently over her cheekbones, wiping away tears she hadn't known were there.

'I resisted so hard. Love is so destructive, and I've hurt so many people. But it was you who showed me another way. You made me see that it wasn't love that destroyed things, it was anger. My anger.'

He loved her? He really loved her?

Everything took on a strange, slightly unreal quality, and she had to put her hands up and close her fingers around his strong wrists to make sure he was real.

'How?' she asked hoarsely. 'I didn't do—'

'You've spent years on the streets. Years fighting for your survival. Years with nothing and no one. And, yes, you're angry—but you haven't let it define you. You haven't let it make you bitter. No, it's your love that defines you. Your joy and your passion. And that's what

I want, *mi corazón*. I want you to teach me how to love like that...teach me how to love *you* like that.'

She was trembling, and she didn't want to look away from him in case this wasn't real. In case he disappeared, as all the good things in her life seemed to do.

'You don't need me to teach you,' she whispered in a scratchy voice. 'You already know how to love, Cristiano. You just have to let go of your anger.'

He said nothing for a long moment, staring down into her face, holding her as if he was afraid of exactly the same thing she was: that this thing they were both within touching distance of would vanish and never come back.

'Is that what you see?' he asked roughly. 'When you look at me? How do I deserve anything if anger is all there is?'

His face blurred as more tears filled her vision and she had to blink them away fiercely. 'That's not all there is. You're a good man, a kind man. A man who feels things deeply and intensely. A protective man desperate for something to protect.'

She slid her hands up his wrists, covering the backs of his where they cupped her face.

'A man who wants someone to be his—and you deserve that, Cristiano. More, I think you need it.'

'I don't know that I did to deserve it. But I'm willing to spend my life trying.' His eyes burned with an intense green fire. 'Will you be mine, Leonie?'

'You don't have to try,' she said thickly. 'And I'm already yours. I've never been anyone else's.'

'Then please come back to me, *gatita*.' He searched her face as if he couldn't quite believe her. 'Please come home.'

But she didn't need him to plead. She'd already decided.

She went up on her toes and pressed her mouth to his, and when his arms came around her and held her tight she became whole.

With him she would never be homeless.

Because he was her home.

EPILOGUE

CRISTIANO PAID THE bill and pushed back his chair, standing up. The restaurant was very crowded and no one was looking at them, too involved with their own conversations to pay attention to the tall man with green eyes and the other, much younger man opposite him, who also stood, and who also had the same green eyes.

The lunch had gone surprisingly well, but it was too soon for an embrace so Cristiano only held out his hand, looking his son in the eye. 'It was good to meet you, Alexander.'

His son frowned, looked down at his extended hand, and then, after a moment, reached out and took it, shaking it firmly. 'I can't call you Papá—you know that, right?'

'Of course not,' Cristiano said easily. 'You already have one of those.'

De Riero—which wasn't what Cristiano had either wanted or chosen, but he couldn't change what had happened twenty years ago. All he could do was let go of his anger and accept it.

It hadn't been easy, but he'd done it. With a little help from Leonie, naturally enough.

In fact, that he'd made contact with his son at all had been all down to her. After a few years—after their lives had settled down and his son had become an adult in his own right—she'd encouraged Cristiano and supported him to reach out.

De Riero hadn't liked it, but something must have mellowed him over the years, because when Alexander had asked him about his parentage he apparently hadn't denied that Cristiano was his father.

He'd even tried to make contact with Leonie, when word had got out about the identity of Cristiano's wife. She hadn't wanted to take that step yet, but Cristiano knew she would one day. When she was ready.

As for Alexander... Cristiano didn't know what de Riero had told the boy about him, but clearly nothing too bad, since he had eventually agreed to meet him.

It had been tense initially, but Alexander had eventually relaxed. As had Cristiano.

'I'd like to meet with you again,' Cristiano said after they'd shaken hands. 'Lunch? Once a month, say?'

The young man nodded, looking serious. 'I think I'd like that.' He paused, giving Cristiano another measuring look. 'You're not what I expected,' he said at last.

Cristiano raised a brow. 'What did you expect?'

'I don't know. You're just...' Alexander lifted a shoulder. 'Easier to talk to than I thought you'd be.'

Something in Cristiano's heart—a wound that hadn't ever fully healed—felt suddenly a little less painful.

He smiled. 'I'll take that.'

Ten minutes later, after Alexander had left, he stepped out of the restaurant and onto the footpath—and was nearly bowled over by two small figures.

'Papá!' the little boy yelled, flinging himself at his father, closely followed by his red-haired sister.

The pain in Cristiano's heart suddenly dissolved as if

it had never been. He opened his arms, scooping both children up. They squealed, his daughter gripping onto his hair while his son grabbed his shirt.

It was soon apparent that both of them had been eating ice cream and had got it all over their hands.

'They're too big for that,' Leonie said, coming up behind them, her face alight with amusement. 'And look what Carlos has done to your shirt.'

Cristiano only laughed. 'That's what washing machines are for.'

She rolled her eyes. She'd lost nothing of her fire and spark over the past five years, coming into her own as his duchess. Not only had she proved adept at helping him manage the San Lorenzo estate, as well as becoming the driving force behind various charities aimed at helping children on the streets, she'd also proved herself to be a talented artist. Luckily she used oils and canvas these days, rather than spray cans and cars.

She was looking at him now in that way he loved. Sharp and direct. Seeing through him and into his heart. 'How did it go?' she asked.

He grinned. 'It went well. Very well indeed.'

Her eyes glinted and he realised they were full of tears. 'I'm so glad.'

His beautiful, beautiful *gatita*. She had worried for him.

Cristiano put down the twins and ignored their complaints, gathering his wife in his arms. 'He wants to meet again. Lunch, once a month.'

'Oh, Cristiano.' Leonie put her arms around his neck and buried her face in his shirt.

He put his hands in her hair, stroking gently, his heart full as he soothed his wife while two of his children tugged at his jacket, oblivious, and the third…

The third he'd find out more about soon.

It was enough. It was more than he'd ever thought he'd have.

After winter there was summer.

And after rain there was sunshine.

After anger and grief and loss there was love.

Always and for ever love.

Cristiano kissed his wife. 'Come, Leonie Velazquez. Let's go home.'

* * * * *

COMING SOON!

We really hope you enjoyed reading this book.
If you're looking for more romance
be sure to head to the shops when
new books are available on

Thursday 28th August

To see which titles are coming soon, please visit
millsandboon.co.uk/nextmonth

MILLS & BOON

FOUR BRAND NEW BOOKS FROM
MILLS & BOON MODERN

The same great stories you love, a stylish new look!

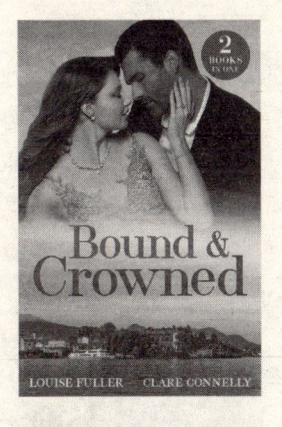

WED IN A HURRY
KIM LAWRENCE — LORRAINE HALL

Bound & Crowned
LOUISE FULLER — CLARE CONNELLY

Love to HATE HIM
JULIA JAMES — MILLIE ADAMS

RECLAIM ME
CATHY WILLIAMS — DANI COLLINS

OUT NOW

Eight Modern stories published every month, find them all at:

millsandboon.co.uk

afterglow BOOKS

Afterglow Books is a trend-led, trope-filled list of books with diverse, authentic and relatable characters, a wide array of voices and representations, plus real world trials and tribulations. Featuring all the tropes you could possibly want (think small-town settings, fake relationships, grumpy vs sunshine, enemies to lovers) and all with a generous dose of spice in every story.

@millsandboonuk
@millsandboonuk
afterglowbooks.co.uk

#AfterglowBooks

For all the latest book news, exclusive content and giveaways scan the QR code below to sign up to the Afterglow newsletter:

SCAN ME

afterglow BOOKS

THE CODE FOR LOVE
Her perfect plan has a gorgeous glitch...

NEW YORK TIMES BESTSELLING AUTHOR
ANNE MARSH

✈ International

⛅ Grumpy/sunshine

🏙 Fake dating

OUT NOW

To discover more visit:
Afterglowbooks.co.uk

OUT NOW!

THE TYCOON'S AFFAIR COLLECTION

TEMPTED BY DESIRE

USA TODAY BESTSELLING AUTHOR
ABBY GREEN

Available at
millsandboon.co.uk

MILLS & BOON

MILLS & BOON

THE HEART OF ROMANCE

A ROMANCE FOR EVERY READER

MODERN — Prepare to be swept off your feet by sophisticated, sexy and seductive heroes, in some of the world's most glamourous and romantic locations, where power and passion collide.

HISTORICAL — Escape with historical heroes from time gone by. Whether your passion is for wicked Regency Rakes, muscled Vikings or rugged Highlanders, awaken the romance of the past.

MEDICAL — Set your pulse racing with dedicated, delectable doctors in the high-pressure world of medicine, where emotions run high and passion, comfort and love are the best medicine.

True Love — Celebrate true love with tender stories of heartfelt romance, from the rush of falling in love to the joy a new baby can bring, and a focus on the emotional heart of a relationship.

HEROES — The excitement of a gripping thriller, with intense romance at its heart. Resourceful, true-to-life women and strong, fearless men face danger and desire - a killer combination!

afterglow BOOKS — From showing up to glowing up, these characters are on the path to leading their best lives and finding romance along the way – with plenty of sizzling spice!

To see which titles are coming soon, please visit

millsandboon.co.uk/nextmonth

LET'S TALK
Romance

For exclusive extracts, competitions and special offers, find us online:

- MillsandBoon
- @MillsandBoon
- @MillsandBoonUK
- @MillsandBoonUK

Get in touch on 01413 063 232

For all the latest titles coming soon, visit
millsandboon.co.uk/nextmonth